LIFE ON THE PRESERVATION
JACK SKILLINGSTEAD

First published 2013 by Solaris
an imprint of Rebellion Publishing Ltd,
Riverside House, Osney Mead,
Oxford, OX2 0ES, UK

www.solarisbooks.com

ISBN: 978 1 78108 117 4

A CIP catalogue record for this book is available
from the British Library.

Designed & typeset by Rebellion Publishing

Printed in the US

LIFE ON THE PRESERVATION

PRESERVATION

JACK SKILLINGSTEAD

SOLARIS

For Daniel Skillingstead
Nothing says love like a paranoid science fiction
novel.

"Our identities have no bodies..."

JOHN PERRY BARLOW

"Nothing is going on
and nobody knows what it is."

THE EXEGESIS OF PHILIP K. DICK

SEATTLE, OCTOBER 5, 2012

AT TEN PM on a Saturday he was hanging his ass in the wind. It was like he *wanted* a police cruiser to light him up. Ian's canvas was the parking-lot wall of Dick's Drive-In on Broadway. Tweaks, drunks and college kids wolfed cheeseburgers and watched him paint. He triggered the spray can, swept his arm in familiar flourishes, then stood back, scowling at: WHO CARES. Street lamps desaturated the green paint, flattened the letters. WHO was what Ian used to be but wasn't anymore, an identity tag on a hundred post-midnight walls. WHO CARES – it was no good. His trademark style ran out of gas and definition a mile before the S curves. His audience applauded, but Ian's shoulders sagged. He'd put up everything he had left. Empty, he dropped the Sabotaz 80 can. It clunked heavy and rolled on the pavement as he walked away, hood up and head down; it wasn't the can that was empty.

PART ONE

CHAPTER ONE

A YEAR AFTER the world ended, Kylie sat on the floor at her boyfriend's house, picking through stacks of DVDs. The living room was small and over-crowded with deep bookcases, bulky leather chairs and a matching sofa big as a Buick. The carpet held dust like a dry sponge. It hadn't been vacuumed since Judgment Day. Once a week a power strip drew electricity for the TV setup plus one pole lamp. A thick extension cord snaked out of the living room and through the kitchen window to a noisy generator on the back porch. Most of the time Kylie was used to the lack of animating electricity. But when movie night ended and Billy switched the gennie off, the house always felt dead to her again. She wouldn't give up the movies, though. Not for anything.

Kylie was eighteen and hungry for things she couldn't have. "This one?" she said, holding up a movie.

Billy slumped in a corner of the sofa with a warm can of Mountain Dew in his lap. He looked up. His shaggy beard and patchy hair made him look older than he really was – though he was already pretty old for Kylie. At thirty-five Billy was played out, overweight, and impotent. Well, all the men in Oakdale were impotent, not just Billy; the poison rain saw to that. It also accounted for the patchy hair. At least Billy hadn't scabbed up yet. His eyes were mostly clear, his finger and toe nails hadn't fallen off, his breath was mostly okay. It was all coming, though; everybody got it bad, eventually. Everybody except Kylie.

Usually Billy drank beer or wine, especially on movie night. The Mountain Dew didn't make him as happy. Not that he was *ever* exactly 'happy'. But when he was drunk, at least, he tended to be less gloomy. Billy wasn't drunk now. His shirt was untucked and missing a couple of buttons. Billy's navel squinted in a wiry tangle of black hair. He nodded at Kylie's movie choice. "Again? Sure, yeah."

The cover of the DVD case depicted a man and a woman: John Cusack and Ione Skye – Lloyd and Diane in the movie; two people no doubt annihilated by The Judgment (as Father Jim called it) but miraculously existent in Kylie's hand, their endlessly repeating lives waiting to be unlocked by laser light. Kylie pried the case open. She tilted the silver disk under the lamp, watching colors bend over its surface. Then she fed it into the machine and sat next to Billy on the sofa. He slung his arm around her, pointed the clicker and pushed PLAY. The empty blue screen filled with images of a lost world and the things Kylie couldn't have.

Two hours later she said, "They were meant for each other."

"Movie people," Billy said.

She snuggled against his body. He was big and warm. Well, he was bound to be big, with all the crap he ate. Kylie rested her head on his chest, which rose and subsided heavily with each breath. Her nose twitched at the sour smell of his sweat. But she didn't mind that. He took care of her, protected her. She thought: *I love him.* Like telling herself something and hoping she believed it. *I love Billy.* But maybe not like Diane loved Lloyd.

Billy came from outside the town. This was almost unheard of. Wanderers did occasionally straggle into Oakdale but they tended to straggle right back out again. Unless they were skin-and-bone people, SABs, in which case townies *drove* them back out. Billy had grown up in Oakdale, but had been gone almost as long as Kylie had been alive, and so his arrival in the aftermath of disaster was simply a return home.

"Do you want to watch a sex one now?" she asked. Kylie didn't really get the sex movies, the pornos. But sometimes watching a little of one got Billy in the mood, even if his poisoned body could no longer perform the way men in those movies did. Kylie was more turned on by *love* scenes. In a love scene you saw people who cared about each other kissing and caressing. Maybe once in a while there was a bare breast or exposed behind, but it was the love that mattered. Kylie was the youngest survivor in town and the only one not sick. That's probably why she still cared about love scenes.

"I don't think so," Billy said.

"Are you sure?"

He patted her shoulder. "I don't really like them anymore," he said. "They're depressing."

"Oh. What about one of your gangster movies or Westerns?"

"They're depressing, too."

"It's okay, Billy. Don't be sad again."

"I'm not sad."

"Do you want a beer?"

"I don't think so."

They were quiet a while.

"Let's go to bed," Kylie said.

Billy grunted. He turned off the TV and the DVD player then got up to kill the generator. He carried his extra weight awkwardly. Billy ate a *lot* of crap food. He hoarded it in the spare bedroom, cases of Doritos, potato chips, candy bars and soda pop. "Might as well eat what I want," he liked to say. "All bets are off."

Kylie lit a candle that smelled like strawberries. A minute later the generator cut out. In the absence of its muted racket the profound silence of the world returned. It was God listening to the souls of the survivors. That's what Father Jim said, and the hundred or so dying, rag-tail remnant souls of Oakdale believed in Father Jim. Kylie used to believe in him, too. In fact, she used to be hooked up with him – *definitely* not like Diane and Lloyd; but all that was before.

To Kylie the silence was like a bottomless well into which everything she knew had been discarded – every comfort and familiar joy and expectation, every hope. Even Kylie's father was in the well, she supposed, though he had been gone anyway for many years. Her mother, who said her rosary every day, maintained her own silence on the subject of Kylie's father. He was dead by now, anyway. The Judgment had killed almost everybody outright. Those few who survived were dying by slow inches.

Except for Kylie.

In the bedroom she stripped down to a t-shirt and panties. The t-shirt was gray with black letters that spelled: PROPERTY OF U DUB, one of Billy's old shirts. Kylie liked candlelight, enjoyed the way it fell on the pages of the books she found in Billy's house. She looked through a collection of poems by Yeats, hoping Billy would come in soon. Mostly she didn't understand the poems (Robert Frost was easier and Charles Bukowski the *best*) but she liked how the words sounded together in her mind and the way the lines of black type assembled in orderly ladders on the thick white paper. She read silently, moving her lips. Her father used to read to her when she was very little. Kylie remembered that much about him.

Lying on her back, reading, Kylie had a strange feeling she wasn't alone. She looked up. The blinds were open and the window was a black mirror capturing a girl, a book, and a candle. Then Billy appeared in the doorway and she let the feeling go. He didn't come in but only stood there, the candle making shadows on his face, hiding his eyes.

"What's wrong?" she said.

"Nothing. Maybe I'll stay up for a while."

She put her book on the bedside table. "Billy?"

"Yeah?"

"I really don't want to be alone."

He didn't say anything.

She patted the bed beside her. "Come on."

He scratched his cheek, stalling.

"Don't you want to be with me?"

For a moment it seemed he really *didn't*, and Kylie's heart sank.

"'Course I do," he said, not very convincingly. He lay beside her, the mattress springs groaning. Like he's

17

doing her this big favor. Kylie stifled her irritation, tried to relax back into the right mood. After a while she said, "Touch me," and he began to caress her breasts. His hand knew what it was doing, even if the rest of him was checked out. Kylie closed her eyes and let her mind hover around certain images from the movies, and then she slid her hand between her thighs. After a long while, her breathing changed. She made a sound in her throat. Some of it was acting, like people in the movies, but not all of it. She slipped her hand inside her panties. Things became mixed up in her mind, Billy and Lloyd and John Cusack and the good feeling of her body, and the way her dreadful loneliness retreated. Time began to unwind in sensation, and then the acting part was over, and the heat built and spread through her thighs and belly until it became bigger and bigger and was through all her body and she was almost *outside* of herself with the intensity of it. She arched her hips and cried out: "I love you, I love you, I love you," like that had to be part of it, then fell back, panting, while the glow subsided.

She wanted to cuddle now. Touching herself could banish loneliness for a few moments, but sometimes when Billy held her it was as though loneliness could be extinguished forever. Not this time, though. She slung her arm and leg over him, and he held her but was distant, staring at the ceiling.

"Tell me what's wrong," she said.

"Nothing. I'm thinking."

"What about?"

"I'll tell you later."

He patted her raggedy hair. Kind of patronizing. Kylie made a face. Her mother cut Kylie's hair short, using the big kitchen shears, and it was uneven and choppy. Kylie *hated* her hair.

"I wish you would get undressed one of these times," Kylie said.

"What would be the point?" Suddenly he crushed her hard against his body. He was trembling, and she could hardly breathe, he held her so tight. Then he let go and stood up, wiped his eyes and put his glasses back on. He turned away and said, "I'm going to stay up for a while."

She started to get up.

"Kylie, I want to sit by myself and think."

She chewed her lip, said, "I love you," throwing it out there like a ball he was supposed to swat back to her. She didn't even believe herself. She was scared was all. Why couldn't it be simple and real?

"Love you too," he said.

"I doubt it."

He looked back at her. "I really do, Kylie."

"How about a beer?" she said. There was plenty of beer in town, since Father Jim told everyone God didn't want them to drink 'spirits'. Billy never quit, though. Billy didn't give a shit what Father Jim said. And Billy was *so* much better with the beer.

"Naw," he said, "I'm sick of warm beer."

There was plenty of beer but the fire-extinguishers had run out ages ago. Billy had used the fire-extinguishers to cool off six-packs. He didn't want to waste generator fuel running a refrigerator. Because Father Jim had told everybody God wanted them to live simply, without electricity ("God's a real killjoy in this town," Billy liked to say), Billy was the only one using a generator; but sooner or later the gas would be gone, and that would be the end of movie night.

"Anyway," he said.

He pulled the door shut behind him. She felt like everything was ruined from the inside out. Kylie stared at the door like she was staring at some pain inside her secret heart, which she was.

ALONE IN BED, she listened to the deep-well silence and fought off tears. Crying didn't do any good. The town dentist, Dr. Lee, had cried himself crazy after The Judgment left him standing but killed his wife and kids. Eventually his crazy tears got *him* killed, too, which Kylie guessed was all right with Dr. Lee.

She thought about getting up and closing the blinds. Instead she rolled onto her side, yawning, drawing her knees up, exhausted. Random pictures drifted through her mind, like clouds in a foreign sky, and she passed into sleep.

Some time later the sound of the generator entered her awareness and putt-putted her awake. She opened her eyes, not fully conscious. The candle, bed and girl floated in the black glass, and something else. Kylie blinked slowly, not really taking anything in, her mind mostly asleep. But she had to pee, and she got up and padded out of the room.

Billy was watching the TV. She could hear it while she was in the bathroom, squatting over a bucket. Her pee rang against the galvanized tin. She struggled to remember something on the edge of her mind. Had she dreamed of the normal days again? Somehow remembering those days didn't hurt but dreaming about them left her feeling disoriented – almost as if her dreams were real and her reality a bad dream.

She finished peeing, covered the bucket with a towel, pulled on a pair of tight black Levi's, and went down the hall. Billy lay on the sofa, facing away from the set, the light shifting on the broad back of his wrinkly shirt. Seven or eight bottles of the beer he was so sick of stood empty, guarding a tower of DVDs. Billy's favorite Western was playing. *Tombstone*. The volume was low, but she heard Val Kilmer say, "I'm your huckleberry," followed by a gunshot. Kylie touched Billy's shoulder.

"Are you awake?" she said

"Yeah." He rolled over and faced her, his eyes bleary. He reached for a bottle, like a reflex.

"Are you still sad?" Kylie asked.

"More like drunk. But don't worry – I'm turning over a new leaf as of right now. Anyway, I am as soon as the beer wears off."

She sat on the edge of the sofa. "What new leaf?"

"Kylie, if that crazy priest knew what we were up to he'd probably chop my head off. You know how he's always blathering about 'purity' and all that shit. Besides, I think he'd like to chop my head off just on general principles, since I'm the only one around here besides you not falling into lock-step."

Father Jim delivered weekly sermons standing in the bed of a burned out F-350 in the middle of Main Street. He really worked on those sermons – and the sermons really worked on *him*. Like everybody else in town, except Billy, Kylie showed up to listen. There was pressure to do so, an un-stated threat if you didn't. Nevertheless, she would have quit going except that Billy told her that was a bad idea, told her it would draw attention to her. Father Jim's early sermons had been almost incoherent, filled with emotion and desperation. But over the last few months the priest seemed to be *building* something. To Kylie it sounded like he was building the world from the inside of his head. The Judgment had come sheeting out of the sky like a vast white lightning, killing billions in an instant, transforming most of the world into blasted destruction and leaving the survivors to fade into a slower, more cruel death. In his sermons Father Jim was practically writing a new book for the Bible. The Word According To Jim made sense out of what didn't make sense.

"I wonder," Billy said, "how that idiot felt about purity *before* God took the steel out of his dick. "

"He felt guilty, I think."

Billy grunted. Father Jim had been a pilot in the Marines, and he still retained a private license. The way he started with Kylie was by giving her flying lessons in his Cessna. Eventually that's what they called it when they were going to meet for the other things: flying lessons.

"That was just him grooming you," Billy told her. "Like he did practically your whole life. The bastard."

She had told Billy about Father Jim. The priest had always been around, but the grown up part, the really bad part, began when she was sixteen and ended, abruptly, a year later when the world did the same.

What she hadn't told Billy was how *crazy* Jim had sometimes acted. Once, they had sex on the day bed in her mother's basement. Her mother, a nurse, had been at work. Father Jim pulled out of Kylie before he finished, disappeared into the bathroom, and stayed there a long time. Kylie got up to see what was wrong. (Of course at this point, deep down, she knew *everything* was wrong). The door was open a little, so she said his name and pushed it open wider. Jim stood there naked, his half-erect cock bloody from multiple nicks. He held a Gillette blade between his thumb and forefinger, the tab of blue steel shining in the fluorescent light. He had taken it out of the pink safety razor her mother used to shave her legs. She always shaved in the downstairs bathroom because the light was better. The empty razor now sat on the edge of the sink behind Jim. He stared at Kylie with guilt-stricken eyes and said, "What we do isn't *right*. I have to mortify my appetites." Shocked, Kylie couldn't look away. That was probably a mistake. Jim seemed to get something out of her looking at him. In moments the superficial little cuts ceased to effectively mortify his 'appetites'. He pushed her back to the bed and took her, grunting with pain and animal excitement. No, it hadn't been anything like Lloyd and Diane.

"Mom says The Judgment unbalanced him," Kylie said to Billy.

"Yeah. Unbalanced like Charlie Manson. Don't forget the dentist."

Instead of Dr. Lee she pictured a sign that used to hang in the dentist's waiting room: *A smile is your first hello!* Near the end, the man used to stand on the roof of the Ace Hardware store yelling at God. Father Jim hadn't appreciated that blasphemy. He hadn't actually chopped Dr. Lee's head off, but he *had* whacked it pretty hard with a baseball bat.

"I doubt that idiot appreciates you living with me."

"Who cares what he appreciates," Kylie said.

Billy picked up a DVD case. *The Dong of Man.* There were two naked 'cave women' on the cover, also a guy with a thick black mustache wearing a bear pelt, or

23

maybe it was just his own chest. Billy had found the pornos on top of a bookshelf. The two bedroom ranch house had belonged to Billy's father, a retired history professor and Oakdale's only resident atheist. Growing up in Oakdale, Billy liked to say, was like growing up a leper in Mayberry. Billy had one of his gloomy quiet days when he found *The Dong of Man* and the other pornos. He didn't talk about it, but Kylie guessed the videos made him think of his history prof dad in a way he didn't like to think of him.

"It used to be everybody got off once in a while," Billy said, waving the DVD. "Now it's only you."

"Have another beer," Kylie said, hoping that yet *more* alcohol would cheer him up.

"No. Listen, we have to talk seriously."

"What about?" Something was nagging at the back of her mind and had been since she woke to the sound of the generator. Something she had seen. It seemed to her she must have seen it in a dream, this scary thing that she couldn't quite recall, couldn't quite bring into focus.

"Leaving Oakdale," Billy said.

She stared at him. "But it's too dangerous outside of town."

"It's getting too dangerous *inside* of town. I've been planning this since everybody started paying too much attention to that lunatic priest. You said yourself he's even started mentioning me in his sermons-on-the-Ford."

"But where would you go?"

"Back to the Big Boat." The Big Boat was what Billy called the *USS Carl Vinson,* an aircraft carrier stranded in sudden shallows after The Judgment. A small number of survivors lived on the carrier, most of them Navy personnel, though there were also some stragglers like

Billy. Billy had been living in Seattle but was visiting a friend in Bremerton, a port town south of Oakdale, when the world ended. "Kylie, I thought you might–"

"But why would you go there? You said everybody was dying and some of them were crazy. Just like here."

"Take it easy–"

"I don't want you to *go*."

"Come with me. There's more to the world even now than this stupid hick town. Don't you want to see the Dome? It's pretty close to the Big Boat. At night you can see the glow."

Billy had talked about the giant Dome before, how it stood over the place where Seattle had been, but it was so fantastic and Billy was usually so drunk, that she hardly believed him.

"Come on, Billy. That can't be real."

"It's real." Billy looked at her seriously. "It covers the whole city, and you can see through it a little bit. Like you can see the buildings and water, but everything is all wavy and dim, like looking through thick green glass." He held his empty beer bottle, bottom-up, to Kylie's eye. "Kind of like this. Kylie, there's a reason I want you to come with me."

"Because you love me so much?"

"Yeah, sure. But–"

She pushed the bottle aside. "I couldn't leave my mom, Billy. She'd be all alone."

"She's as frightened as everybody else." Billy swung his feet to the floor, fumbled for the clicker and turned *Tombstone* off. "But Kylie, I *have* to go – and soon. We both do, before Jim gets your neighbors whipped into a real mob. And everybody being afraid of the world outside Oakdale can work in our favor."

"They aren't a *mob*," Kylie said, deeply distracted now, looking around the room to make sure the blinds were all closed; the thing she had seen without registering was coming closer. She could almost remember.

"They aren't yet," Billy said. "But it's only a matter of time before– What's wrong?"

Kylie stood up. The thing had finally come forward. In the bedroom's black glass mirror window: a bed, a candle, herself... and behind the reflections a face swam into view, and Kylie caught her breath.

"I think Father Jim is outside."

THE NOBLE CORPSE

TO BECOME HIMSELF, Travis Dugan had to leave himself. At age twenty-three he started by leaving his name, then his family (who after all had already left him, his mother weeping and his father stone-faced in the cyclone wind of Travis's coming out politically and sexually), and finally Chewelah, Washington.

He shed 'Travis Dugan' like a dun-colored humpback carapace he'd been forced to wear his whole life, a name that defined him in the schoolyard pecking order and the expectations of small-town gossips. His new name was Charles Noble, who had been a minor character in a minor French novel. A Spokane County superior court judge signed the necessary document, the clerk stamped the paperwork, and Charles Noble was re-born in the real world.

But Travis was not reborn out of his isolation. Twelve years later, modestly prosperous but alone, Charles remained a minor character in his own life, the carapace invisible but intact, shielding his truest identity from the world – and most especially from one Curtis Sarmir, proprietor of the bookshop next door. At 10:30 in the morning of October fifth, 2012 on a shabby by-street of Seattle's Pioneer Square neighborhood, in the small apartment in the back of the art gallery he owned, Charles removed his clothes and hanged himself.

It wasn't the first time.

But it was the first time the act proved fatal. Charles Noble's corpse swayed forward on its knees, the noose buried in its fleshy neck, the rope stretched taut behind it, knotted to a three-foot bar of doweling in the open closet. The corpse's tongue, swollen and purple, protruded like a fig from its pale lips.

LATER THE CORPSE opened its eyes and sat back on folded legs, making the rope go slack between the noose and the closet doweling. The noose glowed briefly, blackened, unraveled in wisps of smoke, became a ring of ashes and flaked away. Noble's strangled airway swelled open, drawing air into collapsed lungs. The body heaved, chest expanding, tendons cracking, then fell heavily forward, a fading red circlet around its neck. Neurons sparked through the brain, chemical transmitters re-activated, and dead matter became enlivened. The heart muscle labored, then discovered its accustomed rhythm. Arterial circulation resumed. Livid bruises caused by pooled blood faded, were gone.

What had been Charles Noble stood up and got dressed.

CHAPTER TWO

REPEAT. THEN GRAB a cup of Joe.

IAN PALMER CAME to himself at the kitchen counter of his studio apartment in Seattle's Capitol Hill neighborhood. Wearing only boxer shorts, he was pouring steaming hot water into a single-cup Melitta coffee filter – like watching himself perform a familiar task, not quite there yet. His senses assembled themselves haltingly. The aroma of the coffee, Colombian roast fresh ground from Espresso Vivace, drew him forth. He lifted away the filter in its little plastic holder, still dripping, and set it atop a crusty pile of dishes in the sink. Almost fully present now, he added a dollop of heavy cream to his coffee, slopping some onto the counter. He set the carton down, his hand trembling. Staring at the hand, he clenched it into a tight, shaking fist, then flexed the fingers a couple of times. It seemed all right now, the tremor gone. Ian picked up his coffee mug and carried it into the other room.

The hardwood floor was cold under his bare feet. He stopped abruptly. Three pill bottles stood on the bedside table with their caps removed. Ian closed his eyes, trying to remember, then opened them again. If he had taken the pills he wouldn't be standing here. Yet he seemed to remember taking them, or was it the intention he remembered? He couldn't distinguish.

Ian's heart began to beat rapidly. His breath shortened. He put his mug down and capped the bottles, deliberately not acknowledging the depleted quantities, moving fast, like a kid hiding his pornography before the door opened. He returned the bottles to the bathroom, catching a glimpse, when he slammed the mirrored cabinet, of his sweat-shiny face.

Standing at the window with his coffee, he racked the blinds up, his breathing and heartbeat under control again. In the alley twenty feet below, his restored 1947 Indian Chief leaned on its kick-stand, front wheel with its distinctive wide-flaring fender cocked over. Not really *his* bike. His Dad had given him two parting gifts. He didn't want either one but kept them both. That was three years ago. The other 'gift' was kind of a family heirloom: .38 Police Special. Fucking *Dragnet* gun. It had belonged to Ian's grandfather, originally. Ian wrapped it in a towel, stuffed it in a shoebox and put it way back on the closet shelf. Out of easy reach and temptation. He knew it was there, though. Like the prescription bottles in the medicine cabinet.

The sun, low-angled and rising, lit up the Chief's brake cover and winked on dull, spotted chrome. The "magnificent machine" as his father used to refer to it, was looking tired; Ian rode the Chief but didn't take care of it beyond the rare oil change. He knew approaching a vintage bike in this manner was tantamount to slow murder, but so what? For Ian, the Chief was basic transportation, and maybe a grudge on wheels.

"Stupid," he said, not meaning the bike.

He thumbed Sarah's speed-dial number on his cell. This was the thing he had dreaded. Sarah thought he was coming to see her, but that wasn't going to happen. With any luck at all she would be asleep and he could leave a message, delay the inevitable break-up conversation. The phone began to ring in her dorm room at WSU, two hundred and eighty-five miles east, in Pullman, Washington. Except Ian suddenly had the eerie feeling it *wasn't* ringing in Pullman. He had the even more eerie feeling Pullman didn't even *exist*.

While the phone rang through, Ian let the tension in his mind go slack – a meditative technique a therapist had taught him back in high school. It was the only useful thing he retained from six months of sessions. That guy had been waiting the whole time for Ian to break down, but Ian never did. And at night he was WHO and nobody could touch him or ever would.

For a suspended moment between rings, raindrops appeared on the Chief's red paint job, cracked leather seat, and chrome. Ian's eyes widened and he threw his attention forward again. The slack disappeared, and so did the raindrops. It was a brilliantly sunny morning in Seattle. October fifth, 2012, *I'm losing it,* he thought.

Sarah picked up. "Hello?"

"It's me."

Sleepy sounds. Then: "Ian? What *time* is it?"

Like an echo with variations: *What time* is *it?* Or: *Baby, what time is it?*

Deja Voodoo.

"It's early. Seven-ish."

"Is something wrong?"

Or: *What's wrong?* or *What's the matter, Ian?*

Like he'd had this conversation already, more than once, perhaps dozens of times. Or was *about* to have it only a few seconds ahead of the present moment, and the dialogue was still fluid. The words felt both remote and too close, almost as if he were talking to himself – or with some kind of souped-up Eliza program. Listening to Sarah's responses, he wondered if a really sophisticated program might trick him into believing he was conversing with a human being.

"Ian? Are you there?"

Am I? he thought.

The super-Eliza idea was beyond paranoid. Other echoes traveled up from a buried place: his mother raving; bloody Pollock art on the kitchen walls. And later: a lifeless manikin in the tub. He hadn't actually *seen* her body, only heard his father, drunk, describe it. What was real? Ian was used to restraining these echoes and phantoms, and he did so now, bringing the force of his will down like a wall of steel.

Empty air on the phone line. He could feel Sarah, or the program, waiting to speak echoes.

Ian killed the connection.

The real Sarah Darbro would call him back. But his cell didn't ring. So she wasn't real. Or it could mean that she knew he had been wanting to break up with her and had decided that this was his idiot method of doing it. What she couldn't know, what he found impossible to explain, was that he was as desperate *not* to break up with her as he was *to* break up with her. Distance and intimacy was the irreconcilable equation of his life.

He sipped his coffee, gazed out the window, and experimented with his elastic concentration. Wet Indian, dry Indian. Sun flared across the dirty window pane. Shadows occupied the room then instantly retreated. Ian began to lose himself.

The phone rang. It wasn't Sarah *or* Super Eliza.

Ten minutes later Ian shambled into Espresso Vivace. The familiar aromas, the voices of a dozen overlapping conversations, the expected baristas (Cyndi of the Peter Pan hair and plaid shirt waved at him) – the world ordered itself around him. He bought a double cappuccino. All the tables – Formica-topped 'kitchen' tables and bent chrome chairs with vinyl seats – were occupied, so he sat at the wrap-around counter. Other people at the counter stared at their phones, thumb-stabbing virtual keyboards like they were trying to crack the secret code and release their souls from the little boxes. Ian watched Cyndi and the other baristas work and didn't let his mind wander or, God forbid, go *slack*.

After a while his best friend Zach came in and sat on the stool next to him "Man oh man," Zach said.

"Hey."

Zach was lanky and round-shouldered, with a shaved head that really didn't improve his looks much, and a pair of square, black plastic-framed geek glasses that he was always punching back up the bridge of his nose. On any other day Ian would have been surprised or even amazed to see his friend at this hour of the morning. But this wasn't any other day. Zach had called him.

"Thanks for meeting me," Zach said.

"What's happening?"

"You're not going to fucking believe me."

"I might."

"Seriously, you won't."

"I won't unless you *tell* me."

Zach looked around the room at the other customers, swiveling on his stool to make sure he didn't miss anyone. Then he leaned into Ian.

"Okay," he said. "It's like – '*they're here*'."

"Who's here?"

"I don't know."

"*Zach*."

"Okay, okay. There's this guy. I call him the Boogeyman. He's like stalking me or something. And he doesn't belong here. I mean I don't even think he's human. Except in some other way he *does* belong here, and *we're* the ones who don't belong."

"Thanks for including me. It's a game idea, right?"

At twenty-two, Zach was a staff writer for a Bellevue-based game company called Mindwerks, and he was very good. His most popular creation was a 'future noir Western' called *Peacemaker*, a game that ratcheted the violence into the M zone and beyond. Ian had known Zach since grade school. At Mindwerks Zach pulled down 90k; Ian grilled things at Charlie's and didn't declare his tips.

"Come *on*," Zach said.

"Okay, okay. Tell me about the Boogeyman. And trust me, I've got something even weirder to tell you."

Zach pushed his glasses up with his index finger. "Yeah?"

Ian picked up his empty cup, put it down, studied his hand for tremors. "Yeah, but you go first."

"Okay, look. I wake up today and I'm majorly weirded out. For one thing, what the fuck am I doing awake at seven A.M.? It's unnatural. But I have this feeling that I've got to get *moving*. There's shit to do, only I don't know what it is, right? The other thing, it's not like I usually wake up, especially on a freaking Saturday. It's like all of a sudden I'm *there*, wide-awake. Practically before I know it I'm up eating a bear claw. I mean there's no wake-up transition. I'm on my feet and the day is rockin'."

Something uncoiled in Ian's stomach. *Repeat. Then grab a cup of joe.*

"I'm all anxious and nervous," Zach said. "So I call you. It's like I'm *supposed* to call you. I've got this energy and I've got to do something with it. On the way here I pass a guy sitting on that bench across from my building. And I *recognize* him. Not like, Hey, it's good old Bob. I mean I don't know how I recognize him. But this is what I think. I think I recognize him the same way a rabbit recognizes a fox, even though it's never seen one. It's like *genetic* memory. You always recognize the predators. I walk by him, and the predator feeling is all over me."

"What did he do?" Ian said.

"Nothing. Sat there with this dopy look on his face. I keep walking. And all this shit rises up in my head. The whole Boogeyman thing. Like I've known about that guy forever. Now get this." He gripped Ian's arm, digging his fingers in.

"*What?*" Ian said.

Zach glanced at Cyndi, who was kind of watching them while she slung espresso, then whispered. "I think we – I mean you and me, bro – are the only rabbits in town."

Ian stared at him.

"Tell me yours," Zach said.

He told Zach about the phone conversation with Sarah that was full of echoes and déjà vu's. For now he kept the slack mind trick to himself.

"I started getting the idea that I was talking to *myself*," Ian finished. "Or to some kind of super Eliza program."

"What's an Eliza program?"

"Back in the sixties this guy Weizenbaum wrote a program that imitated a basic psychiatric interview by rephrasing people's statements. It fooled everybody."

"That's cool," Zach said.

"Yeah, but this *isn't* cool. This is scary." Ian rubbed his forehead. "Don't you get it? What if there isn't any real Sarah out there? Do me a favor."

"What?"

"Call somebody. I mean somebody who doesn't live in the city. Call your brother."

"Why?"

"I want to know if your conversation echoes like mine did."

"It won't." Zach didn't sound too sure.

"Call."

Zach thumbed in a text. "I never actually call him."

A moment later Zach's phone chimed.

"What's he say?" Ian asked.

"Sent a fucking smiley face."

"Is that normal? Hey, what's wrong?"

"The Boogeyman. Shit, he's coming in."

The Boogeyman walked into Espresso Vivace. Ian watched him closely. Zach fidgeted with his glasses.

"That's him?" Ian asked.

"Yeah."

"He looks harmless."

Zach's Boogeyman was maybe twenty pounds overweight. He wore tan Dockers, an REI Gore-Tex parka and a Mariners baseball cap. Standing in line on the other side of the wrap-around counter, he glanced at Ian and Zach but his gaze didn't linger. He ordered something and paid for it. Presently the cashier handed him a to-go cup and a scone, and he left.

"See?" Zach said.

"See what?"

"He acted so fucking normal."

"He *was* normal. Though not for this neighborhood."

"Didn't you get the vibe?"

"No."

"Come on."

"I'm sorry. I didn't notice anything weird about him."

"No, I mean: come *on*. Let's follow him." Zach stood up.

Ian remained on his stool. "Following people is crazy."

"So what?"

Ian gestured to Cyndi. She came over. "What's up with you two?" she said.

"Did you see that guy with the Mariners cap a minute ago?"

"Sure."

"What'd you think of him?"

"A harmless dork. He bought a lemon scone."

"See?" Ian said to Zach.

Zach was on his feet. "Can we please go before we lose him?"

"Okay, okay."

They followed the Boogeyman to Broadway, hanging back a discreet distance. Ian, nocturnal as a bat, found the early morning ambience disorienting. Capitol Hill, and Broadway in particular, was ground zero for the city's GLBT sub-culture. In this neighborhood of gay couples, severe haircuts, aggressive piercings and chains, leather, transgender experiments, fashionable and unfashionable tats, runaway kids and junkies, the Boogeyman's yuppie-lite presentation should have stood out like a crust of Wonder Bread in a bowl of jambalaya. Instead, he almost fit in with the crazy early-bird types on their way to work – Zach's Boogeyman with his scone and coffee and bland, touristy gawking.

"What the fuck is *that*?" Zach said, pointing at WHO CARES spray-painted on the side of Dick's Drive-In. "I thought you quit."

Ian stared at the graffiti, as surprised by it as was Zach. He groped at a vague memory of Saturday night, dropping his can and walking away. But Saturday night hadn't even happened yet. "I don't know. Maybe some toy trying to rip off my old style."

"Are you bullshitting me?"

Ian didn't want to discuss it. His half-assed memory of creating this half-assed piece was almost as disturbing as the Eliza conversation and the slack mind thing.

"It's not mine," Ian said.

The Boogeyman boarded a city bus. "Come on," Zach said, "my car's only a couple of blocks from here."

Zach's ride was a new VW Beetle, bottle fly green. Ian's feet disappeared in a swamp of game boxes, Taco Bell wrappers, empty pop cans, notebooks, gaming manuals, and comics. They caught up with the bus as it turned down the hill toward midtown.

"Do you think he jumped off while we were going for my car?"

"How should I know?" Ian slumped against the passenger door and wished he hadn't gotten out of bed. And all at once he realized he couldn't *remember* getting out of bed. He concentrated, but it was dead space, the time right before he found himself making coffee.

"I think I see him," Zach said. "Is that him, about halfway back on the right side of the bus?"

Ian just shook his head. "I repeat: following people is crazy."

"So's thinking your girlfriend is a computer program named Eliza."

"I think I changed my mind about that."

Zach looked at him then back at the bus, which was lumbering steadily from block to block on its way down Pine Street.

"Explain."

"It's simple. The Sarah situation has been stressing me out for a long time. And then today was like the *culmination* of all that stress. Besides, I always get crap sleep. That's probably why the hallucinations came on. Like your brain can totally hallucinate reality. I mean every drug imaginable is produced naturally in the thalamus or somewhere. Shit, my sister thought she could talk to the dead. And my mom, you know. I probably inherited the crazy gene."

"That's tortured, man. Besides, you don't even know what a thalamus is."

Tortured, yeah – and a flat-out lie, of the sort Ian was accustomed to spinning. Sometimes his mouth just ran, and it all seemed to hang together. The truth was he *didn't* want to break up with Sarah. He just couldn't tolerate the intimacy so he *had* to break up with her. Had to and couldn't. If he were saying this out loud,

Ian wondered, would it be the truth? Or was the truth something that lurked outside of his thinking mind altogether?

"What hallucinations are you talking about, anyway?" Zach said.

Ian hesitated then explained about the rain on his Indian and the rest of it, the trick of the taut and slack mind. It seemed to make sense while he was saying it.

"Shut up," Zach said. "Are you fucking serious?"

The bus turned on Third Avenue and made a stop. Several people got off, including the Boogeyman. They paced him in the VW until Zach cut into a parking spot, even though it was yellow-striped for thirty minute load-unload. The Boogeyman continued on his way down the hill to Second Avenue, seemingly oblivious of them, as they continued the pursuit on foot.

"This is ridiculous," Ian said. "Let's grab breakfast."

"After we see where our boy is headed. *Holy shit!*"

A giant had appeared on the sidewalk right in front of the Boogeyman. The giant must have been over eight feet tall. He wore a long tan raincoat-looking thing. He was bald, his eyes deep-set under ridges of bone. The Boogeyman halted, made a very fast sideways movement – and the sidewalk, impossibly, was empty.

"What the fuck," Ian said.

"There," Zach said, pointing. The giant was a block away. Passersby stopped and stared openly at him until he turned down an alley and disappeared.

"What happened?" Ian said.

"You tell me."

"I asked you first."

"This is messed up. Like somebody just edited thirty seconds out of the fucking world."

Ian noticed the Boogeyman. He was standing in front of a pawn shop window. Had he been there a second ago? "There's your guy."

The Boogeyman started walking, as if he'd been waiting for them to notice him. They followed him several blocks. The neighborhood drifted into seediness. Finally the Boogeyman stopped at a vacant structure. The unlit Vegas-style sign said: XXX GIRLZ. Graffiti tags claimed the walls, aggressive tangles of black paint – gang stuff. An empty wine bottle and some paper trash littered the sidewalk. The Boogeyman touched the door and it opened. Ian didn't see him use a key or even turn a handle. In fact, it almost seemed as though the door *dissolved* into a black rectangle. The Boogeyman entered and the door was there again. A breeze hustled a Burger King bag into the recessed doorway and back out.

"You see *that?*" Zach said. "What's up with the door?"

"I don't know. It's just shadows, or something."

"Right. I don't think so. And there is no normal reason for anybody to go into that shit pile strip joint."

"How do you know there isn't a reason? Maybe he owns it."

They stood across the street. The block was a kind of no-man's land between two tourist focal points, the International District and Pioneer Square. But *this* street was deserted, not even a wino. Despite the sun, the breeze was cold. "Come on," Ian said. "Let's get the hell out of here."

"I want to see what's in that building."

"Just forget it, okay?" Ian looked around the deserted street. He shoved his hands in his pockets and hunched his shoulders. But it was more than the cold that made him uncomfortable. He felt an unpleasant tingling, almost like a mild electric charge passing under his skin.

"Do you feel something?" Zach said.

"No."

"Are you lying? You're lying."

"Look," Ian said. "I don't want to go near that place, okay?"

"Me neither. But the question is: *Why* don't we want to? Other than the general creep factor."

"General creep factor is good enough for me." Ian pictured the giant. What was he, a basketball player? There had been something otherworldly about him, and not Dennis Rodman otherworldly.

"Something's going on," Zach said. "There's some serious shit going on, and we both know it. We can't pretend it's not happening."

"Can't pretend *what's* not happening?"

"Ian. Do that slack mind thing you were telling me about."

"Why?"

"Don't you feel it? It's like we've been here before – *right here*. I feel totally buzzed, but not in a good way."

"Oh shit."

"You feel the buzz!"

"Maybe."

"You *do*, you fucker."

"Whatever. That just tells me we should get out of here."

"My skin's *crawling*. Like the invisible fence for dogs? You ever hear those dumbass radio ads? We're not *supposed* to get any closer. But we got to ignore it."

"No we don't."

"You're in denial."

Ian turned away from him and looked directly at the strip joint. It appeared abandoned, condemned, even though they'd just seen the Boogeyman go inside. Zach was right. They had been here before. *Right here on this street corner.* Ian felt the buzz, all right. It was like being in a dream and more or less knowing it, and not being able to wake up. The intense anxiety of that. The dream looked and felt like the usual reality, but under the surface things were cosmically warped. The XXX GIRLZ sign shifted slightly in Ian's vision as he released his conscious intent and allowed his presence of mind to go slack.

Suddenly the quality of light altered. The sun was a few degrees higher in the sky. The breeze ceased. Ian projected forward, like one of those dizzy Hitchcock shots in *Vertigo*. Without moving he was suddenly much closer to the building, or seemed to be, right in the doorway, and a man screamed, but Ian couldn't move. The buzz that had been repelling him now rooted him to the spot. The scream cut off. The door started to dissolve. He had been here before, he had been here before...

Ian jerked free of his trance, or whatever it was. Zach was shaking him. "Dude, snap out of it."

Ian worked his mouth, which had gone dry as old shoe leather. He tried to swallow and almost couldn't. "We are not going anywhere near that door," he said.

"But–"

"Zach, we're *not*."

Zach grinned. "You did the thing. The slack thing. Tell me what happened."

"I'll tell you at breakfast. Far away from here."

Zach looked back at XXX GIRLZ. Ian didn't like the obsessed light in his friend's eyes. "I think we have to do something today," Zach said. "If we don't we're going to piss our chance away. Maybe our last chance. Don't even ask me what I'm talking about. All I know is, we have to do something, man. We *have* to."

Ian grabbed his arm and pulled him around. "Listen to me. We cannot go any closer to that building. I mean it."

Slowly Zach began to nod. "Yeah, well, we can't stand here all day, either. Let's re-group."

A yellow parking ticket fluttered under the VW's wiper blade, like a trapped bird. Zach grabbed the ticket in his fist and absently crammed it into his back pocket. They re-parked the car closer to the Pike Place Market. A tourist Mecca, the Market was bustling. Cars crawled down the brick street that divided vendor stalls and pocket restaurants. Ian and Zach stepped between the cars, passed under the giant red clock, past the carcasses of salmon, gooey ducks, sole and crabs laid out odoriferously on beds of white ice, and proceeded downstairs to the Sound View Café. Beyond the wall of windows, Elliott Bay gleamed like hammered tin in the morning sun, and the Olympic Mountains sketched themselves out of the western haze.

Ian took slight notice. The buzz was gone. He felt drained and listless. He didn't talk about what happened when he let his mind go slack across the street from XXX GIRLZ, and Zach didn't ask again. Ian picked at his scrambled eggs and barely finished half a cup of coffee. Sleep dragged at him like an irresistible tide. Zach nodded over his plate. "What a fucked up day," he said.

"Yeah." Exhausted, a sense of alien exclusion overcame Ian. The café was crowded and noisy but he felt alone in the midst of it, as if it were a room full of barking dogs instead of human beings.

"Let's go," Zach said.

They pulled up to the curb in front of Ian's building, the Gregory. Ian climbed out of the Bug and paused, hanging on the open door, feeling some muted urgency struggle to assert itself. The Gregory, which was slated to be bulldozed along with everything else on the block to make way for the new light rail station, loomed over them, its brick face soot-blackened by decades of neglect. Some local toy had slashed a tag on the glass of the entry door, total amateur bullshit. Ian looked back into the car. "Don't do anything," he said. "Don't go back there without me."

Zach looked at him like he didn't know what Ian was talking about. "Sure, whatever."

"Promise."

"Cross my fucking heart."

IAN COLLAPSED ON his unmade bed. Sleep ran through him in a sluggish current. He thrashed in the current but could not drown. Sunlight slipped over the ceiling, gleamed briefly on the Nihiljizum band poster thumbtacked next to his bed. Smells came and went: cooking scents, brewed coffee. His palate enjoyed a fleeting smorgasbord of flavors. He heard traffic, no traffic, traffic. Once, he opened his gummy eyelids, face mashed into one of his notebooks, and the apartment was dark except for a light in the bathroom. The faucet was running, and then it shut off. Ian's eyes started to close. Before he could fall back into the current he twisted himself off the edge of the bed. Morning light moved across the floor. Dust kittens drifted like tumbleweeds. He grabbed the broken barrel of a pencil, crawled to the nearest wall and squatted there – Paleolithic cave tagger, or Goya doing his Black pieces on the walls of his own house, trying to paint out his insanity.

Ian pressed the pencil tip to the wall and made the letter W, focusing minutely, then made another letter, becoming absorbed. WHO tracks expanded in a spiral out of the pencil and Ian's fevered brain, creating a mandala. The shadow and light show slowed down. Time began to behave. Ian became aware of the cramps in his legs. He tipped away from the wall, rolled onto his back, finger bones crabbed around the pencil stub.

The WHO mandala was big as a pizza pan. Other WHOs flung off it in every style Ian knew, varying in size from insect feet iterations to fully shaded dynamic blocks a foot high. Staring at the wall, Ian could breathe.

But he was tired. His head lolled over. The cheap digital clock on the bedside table read: 11:32 AM / Saturday / October 5.

Less than an hour had elapsed. Which was impossible; it felt like days since Zach dropped him off.

Sleep dragged at Ian but he drove his body to its feet and racked up the window blinds. The sun stood a few degrees off midday. Okay, got it. He grabbed his phone. Zach's number went straight to voicemail. After a moment he killed the connection, thumbed out a text message. Waited. Nothing. He put the phone down. The apartment was safe – or at least safer than it had been. He could further improve on that, break out his markers, pull a full-scale Goya, make his apartment insane-proof.

Or he could go find Zach.

*　　*　　*

STRADDLING THE CHIEF, Ian reached under the tank and turned on the petcocks. He closed the choke, cracked the throttle, stood on the kicker. Nada. He adjusted the choke, stood on the kicker some more. Cold starting the Chief was like throwing the prop of a World War One biplane on an icy winter morning. What was he forgetting *this* time? Oh, yeah. Retard the spark. Now he stood on the kicker and the engine lit up. It was a *big* sound, a window-rattling sound. Good morning, friends and neighbors.

Wind stung his eyes. The off-timing blat and throb of the Chief rattled his brains. The mirror vibrated so badly it turned the rear-view into a disturbed puddle of colors. After Ian's mother killed herself his dad had found his own way to check out of Ian's life. The old man spent two years restoring the basket case Chief and ignoring him. At least, that's how it felt. After Ian graduated from high school, his dad moved to Phoenix with a twenty-five-year-old redhead. On his way out he bestowed upon his son the antique motorcycle. Like *Ian* wanted the damn thing. Maybe he did, since he was still riding it four years later. When he could get it to start.

ZACH'S VW ANGLED into the curb across from XXX GIRLZ. In the middle of the street Ian straddled the Indian. He studied the sloppy turf-claiming gang tags. It wasn't his shit to know, but he should have at least recognized one or two. All he could think was: You dumbshit. Meaning Zach, for coming back here alone.

CHAPTER THREE

OAKDALE, WA., 2013

FOR A MOMENT Billy's face went blank. Then what Kylie had said about Father Jim being outside sank in. Billy lurched to his feet, knocking over a few beer bottles.

"What do you mean, he's outside?"

"I saw him at the bedroom window, when I woke up a few minutes ago. Only I wasn't really awake yet. I think he was there before, too. I had a feeling about it."

"He was *watching?* Jesus Christ. Was he alone?"

"I don't know. I think so."

Billy crossed the room and pulled out the middle drawer of his father's roll top desk. He reached in and came up with a revolver, a big one, with a long barrel. He hefted the weapon, seemed to reconsider, then put it back and took out a much smaller gun, an automatic.

"What's that for?" Kylie said.

Somebody knocked on the front door.

They looked at the door then at each other. Billy dropped the magazine out of the automatic's grip, glanced at the little bullets, slapped it back in. The weapon was so small it was almost like a toy.

Kylie said, "Father Jim didn't mean to hurt Dr. Lee."

"No?"

"I think Jim was drunk when he hit him. He stopped drinking after that and made everybody else stop, too. Remember? Billy, you get drunk, too. One time when you were drunk you smashed that Pepsi machine with a hammer."

"That was different. The Pepsi machine deserved it. The dentist didn't. Why are you defending him, anyway?"

"I'm *not* defending him." But she knew she was and didn't even understand it herself.

"He groomed you and then he raped you. It's rape whether you let him do it or not, because you were only like sixteen. You have to not romanticize it."

Heat rose in Kylie's cheeks. Billy was right, she knew that, but a piece of her fought against accepting the truth. She had told herself that what she had with Jim was a *relationship* – a forbidden one, but a relationship, anyway. Romeo and Juliet were forbidden, too. Society was always forbidding relationships that didn't look normal from the outside. Kylie didn't have to give up anything for this interpretation of what had gone on between her and Father Jim. How sick to think of herself as a kid raped by a pedophile. Sick, but there it was.

Somebody knocked on the door again. Louder

"Don't shoot him," Kylie said. Now she was mad at *Billy* for saying the truth so meanly when before they had always talked around the edges of it.

"I don't plan to." Billy lifted his shirt and tucked the automatic under the waist of his jeans. He pulled his shirt back over it, but the handle stuck out of the gap where the buttons were missing. Adjusting the gun didn't help. Even when the grip didn't stick out in the open, his stomach was too big and the gun bulged obviously under the stretched shirt. He ended up switching it to his back pocket.

Kylie bit her lip, watching Billy anxiously. Despite it all, she wanted to believe everybody, including Father Jim, had a good 'core'. (Kylie's mother was always talking about people's 'cores'.) One of the few things she remembered from her childhood was the priest reading his Bible to her in her own living room, like she was somebody special. She knew he didn't go to the other girl's houses. He read to her like she pretended her father used to read to her. Probably that was just more of Jim's sick grooming. But the man on the front porch wasn't the pervert Billy talked about. He wasn't even the forbidden lover, who could touch her face so tenderly one time and another be pounding into her with his engorged, razor-nicked cock, his face all knotted up with pain and the filthy things he was saying. The man on the porch was a trigger, and if the trigger got pulled the last good feelings in Kylie's world would blow up and be gone forever.

"I'm going to open the door," Billy said. "Talk to him. You wait in the kitchen and listen. If he gets too nutty go out the back door and run to your mother's house, okay?"

"Define 'too nutty'."

"Kylie, will you *please* do what I tell you, just this one time?"

"What are *you* going to do if he gets 'too nutty', shoot him with your gun?"

"I won't have to. He isn't completely out of his mind. Guys get really sane when a gun is pointed at them. Trust me."

It was like a line someone would say in the cowboy movies Billy watched, not something Billy himself would say. He delivered the line without much conviction, Kylie thought.

"Why don't we both go out the back door right now," she said. She could feel the big-ass God finger trembling on the trigger. Kylie wasn't mad at Billy anymore; but with all her heart she didn't want him to open that door. "If nobody's home," she said, "maybe he'll go away."

"I'm not sneaking out the back door of my own damn house."

"Why not?"

Somebody *pounded* on the front door. "Kylie, for Christ's sake."

So Kylie stood in the kitchen. She heard Billy unlocking the front door, and she peered around the corner to see what happened next. Billy opened the door. Jim stood there, a big man framed in a doorway that seemed almost too small to admit him. He wore his usual overcoat and that floppy black hat. Like Billy, Father Jim suffered only the very early stages of the sickness.

There was no talking. Father Jim made a sudden movement. Actually it had started as soon as Billy opened the door. The movement concluded with a downward swing, and Billy collapsed, never having reached for the toy automatic. Guns evidently only made guys sane if guys actually *saw* them.

Ice water flooded Kylie's bloodstream.

She staggered out of the kitchen and pointed. "Leave him alone!" Her voice shook.

"Girl," Father Jim said. "You are not right."

He stepped over Billy's body, grasping the Louisville slugger midway up in his big left hand. Kylie turned to run. He covered the distance between them in a few strides and caught her by the hair, hauling her back. She screamed, wrenched away from him, hair ripping from her scalp. Bright needles of pain lit her up. She bolted through the kitchen, hit the back door, struggled with the lock, got it open and threw herself outside.

Kylie was eighteen years old. In junior high school she had run the 440. She could *haul ass*. If she wanted to get away from Father Jim she could certainly do it by sprinting across town to her mother's house. But Kylie wasn't interested in running away; she was interested in knocking Father Jim's head off with a shovel. The trigger was pulled. Fuck his core. She kept seeing Billy crumple and Jim standing over him with his stupid bat, and she was furious. *Furious*.

She ran to the garden shed and grabbed at wooden handles, discarding rakes, hoes, an edger, until she found the shovel. It had a handle almost as tall as she was and a square steel blade.

She spun around with it, but the priest wasn't there. She stepped into the yard. The night sky was starless and black, the air damp with an expectation of rain. High up, a faint glitter occurred in the atmosphere, as if the stars had been crushed to microscopic powder and sown by a miserly hand. Kylie let it distract her a moment, and Father Jim got her, his arm an iron bar locked across her throat. She dropped the shovel and clawed at him. She thrashed and kicked. Kylie was five foot one and weighed one hundred and five pounds. Father Jim was built to Biblical proportions. He increased the pressure on her throat. Her vision throbbed and she went limp.

When she came to, Jim had her slung over his shoulder, her head hanging straight down, the taste of vomit in the back of her mouth. Kylie's head pounded. She swallowed and it hurt because of the crushing pressure Jim had applied to her throat. Though it felt like she'd been unconscious a long time it couldn't have been more than a minute. He carried her through Billy's house, crossing the open dining area toward the hallway to the bathroom and bedrooms. Billy lay sprawled by the open front door, where Father Jim had left him. Only not quite. He was in a different position, having stretched out his right hand, reaching forward, dragging himself, his face down. Kylie saw this very briefly, and then they passed into the hallway.

Jim dumped her on the bed. The candle still glowed calmly next to the Yeats book. Now captured in the black window glass were a bed, a girl, a candle and a tall man with straggly gray hair; he had lost his hat. Kylie tried to sit up. Sickening pain swooned through her head. The priest pushed her firmly back down and held her there.

"Don't move," he said, his hand hard against her chest.

"I'll tell my mother," Kylie said.

"You have to get right. I finally realized that was the problem. Even your mother realizes it and accepts it. Maggie isn't stupid."

"I don't know what you're *talking* about."

"Lie still now."

He removed a ball of twine from his overcoat pocket. Kylie stared at it. He grabbed her right wrist and pulled her arm over her head and began tying her to the bed post. Kylie tried to pull free, and he squeezed her wrist so hard she thought it would snap.

"Lie *still*."

"Don't do that, please don't."

He quickly finished with the left wrist. When he reached for her right she swung her fist into his neck with all the strength she could summon, which wasn't much. But it was enough to make him gag and back away from her. It didn't matter, though. Before she could even try to untie her left wrist, Father Jim struck her an open-handed blow across the face, his callused hand like an oak plank. The blow left her mostly insensible while he finished tying her. After a while she regained some presence of mind. Her wrists were secured to the headboard posts and her ankles were tied to the footboard posts, her legs spread wide apart. He had removed her pants.

At first she didn't see him. Then his voice came out of the darkness in the corner of the room, where the candlelight barely reached his eyes. He was sitting in a chair, holding something in his lap, contemplating it. Kylie couldn't see what the thing was.

"When God's Judgment befell the Earth," he said, "I thought He had forsaken us, and I despaired. I imbibed and became cruel to my brothers." Father Jim spoke in a measured, practiced tone, as if delivering one of his pickup truck sermons, as if he had rehearsed the words.

"My faith broke utterly," he continued. "Broke upon the rock of my despair. In my mind there *was* no God. But in time I came to realize that of course the Creator was indeed in perpetual residence, and that He had a plan. He always has a plan."

Kylie pulled at her restraints. The twine dug into her skin.

"'Be as little children,'" Father Jim said. "This was the Lord's admonishment. And after God smote the world those who remained did became as children, and the filthiness of men and women was eradicated and we were cleansed by the purifying rain. *I* was made right, and I perceived the wickedness of my former life, and my days of fornication ended. So The Judgment was in fact a Great Cleansing. For me, for everyone. Everyone except you. Do you see?"

"Jim?"

"Yes?"

"Can you please untie me?"

"In good time."

"It hurts, and I can't feel my fingers anymore." The second part wasn't true, but Kylie wanted Father Jim to feel sorry for her. She remembered him touching her cheek tenderly when they were lovers, touching the same cheek that now stung after his slap.

"I've been praying for a solution to our dilemma," he said.

"What dilemma?"

"Remember. Be as little children. You are the only one among us who is not."

"That isn't *my* fault."

"No, it's mine. I defiled us both with my lust. Now I will undo that which I defiled and put you right. Before the purifying Judgment, Kylie, many Middle Eastern and African nations – Somalia, for example – practiced a ritual of female genital alteration. Did you know that?"

"What?" Kylie tasted her gorge and struggled to hold it down.

"One advantage of the procedure, especially Type 2," Jim went on, now in a kind of lecturing voice, as if he were reading directly from a text book, "was that it inhibited females from experiencing sexual stimulation. It's all right there in the *National Geographic.*"

Kylie's heart began to beat faster.

"Type 2," Father Jim said, "is Excision." She strained to see what he was handling in his lap. Finally it caught a gleam of candlelight, a gleam that slid along its blade.

CHAPTER FOUR

ACROSS THE STREET from XXX GIRLZ Ian tweaked the throttle, which, contrary to anything that made sense, was on the *left* side. His dad could just as easily have switched it to the right handlebar, but that would have been 'inauthentic'. The Chief's engine rattled and coughed (authentically), flirted with dying, soldiered on. In Ian's mind somebody screamed and a door opened to take him in and maybe never let him out again. Ian closed his eyes tight. Pain throbbed at his temples. He anchored himself to the throttle and followed the pain down. He began to feel distant and borne up, yet still anchored to the Indian's shuddering throttle; Zen And The Art Of Mindfucking.

Ian opened his eyes, looked at his watch. High noon, October fifth.

Am I even here? Yes. The question was: how many times before? Ian clenched his jaw, made tight, shaking fists, concentrating. Something like a subcutaneous electric current prickled under his skin. His memory dimmed, brightened, dimmed again. He *had* been here, many times. That's how it felt. The breeze was winter cold on his face. (Later the day would warm toward a ghost of summer, and people would crowd the streets, a perfect day until the rain arrived late in the night; he knew this day so well).

The breeze hustled a Burger King bag out of the recessed doorway of XXX GIRLZ and sailed it into the air.

The door dissolved in shadow.

Ian cranked the throttle and popped the clutch, swung tight onto Mission Street, accelerated, aiming for the ramp to the 90. He had to get out of the city. Get away right now. Out of the bubble. Every instinct begged him to turn back *and* go forward. His usual dilemma. Then the I-90 tunnel enclosed him and he had no choice. He was going to Pullman, to Sarah – if Pullman and Sarah even existed anymore.

Ian shot into the sodium-lit sleeve of concrete and presently emerged into brilliant afternoon sun. Ahead of him moderate traffic traversed the floating bridge across Lake Washington. He eased up on the throttle. Somebody honked. Cars swung around him into the passing lane and proceeded unmolested to the end of the bridge and beyond, or so it appeared. Ian experienced the solid conviction that he would not be so lucky. It hadn't been a dream of crashing. It had been much weirder than that. The details were gone but a residue of fear remained.

Ian slowed to a crawl and edged the Chief into the breakdown lane to let traffic pass. The engine popped and farted, threatening extinction. When he was a kid

Ian had loved the look of the Chief as it finally began to emerge out of the random collection of parts strewn around the garage. The long flare of the fenders and low-slung retro impression appealed to him. But Ian had also resented the bike. His father lovingly, obsessively assembling the thing around a skeletal frame, while Ian sat ignored in a corner with a sketchpad or a book; his Dad, always with an open can of beer within reach, telling him, "...a bike like this is like a flesh and blood person," and other such bullshit, not even really talking to Ian but meditating to the sound of his own voice...

The wind off the lake was bitter cold. Cars and trucks blasted by him. *They aren't going anywhere*, Ian thought without even knowing what he meant. A moving van roared past, staggering him in its slipstream.

He had been here before.

He was *always* here, stuck between two commitments. Seattle was home, but it was no longer a safe place. It had gone all *wrong*. But crossing the bridge would take him into an unknown, vulnerable sphere that terrified him.

He idled in the breakdown lane, shuddered as traffic blasted by.

Fuck this.

He throttled up and swayed back into the traffic flow. As he approached the mid-span his stomach muscles clenched. A big Dodge Ram filled the lane about fifty feet ahead of him, guy with a Kenny Chesney cowboy hat behind the wheel.

Something in the sky caught Ian's attention. High over the lake half a dozen green blisters appeared. They bulged, as if something was trying to poke through a membrane. The blisters popped, and flashing silver pinwheels scattered across the sky. At the same moment the truck crossed the mid-span, and Ian's Chief did the same.

The Indian wobbled between his legs. So familiar. Like hitting a slick patch and momentarily losing control. *Like* that but not the same.

The Indian wobbled.

The Indian wobbled.

Then everything changed. Silence enclosed him, and the space was saturated in yellow and emerald light.

Ian hung in the void, able to move his limbs but without effect, like a stranded astronaut. The Dodge was still in front of him but now appeared to be the size of his thumb. Distance and dimension became meaningless. As his eyes adjusted he perceived that his green-yellow universe swarmed with the detritus of a vanished world. Cars, planes, boats, people and animals – all of them propelled outward as if in a very slow and controlled explosion.

The Dodge was like a matchbox car drifting inches from his nose, its tiny driver the most delicately detailed doll imaginable. Ian could have flicked the truck around with a touch of his finger, or so it seemed. He elected not to test appearances. Looking down the length of his body, he saw that he drifted above a vast pebbled plane. Because of the insane perspective, it was a while before he realized the pebbled plane was actually the Chief's brake light cover, stretched to football field proportions. Ian closed his eyes. His heart lugged in muffled panic. He wanted to scream but could not utter a sound as he slow-tumbled outward.

When he opened his eyes he found himself looking at a side view of a jet airliner. It was of normal proportions. Faces peered out of the passenger windows. A woman in the first window forward of the wing stared directly at him. Many of the faces were terrified, but not this woman's. Ian looked into her eyes and discovered some kind of serenity there. She smiled at him, as though they had both been through this time and again and wasn't it funny that they were here yet again. He wondered what it must be like for her inside the cabin. In the slow course of things the wing tilted up, and as it did so the jet's physical dimensions warped out of proportion and it became tiny, a jeweler's delicacy, position lights winking in the yellow-green gloom.

Gradually the gloom brightened, and Ian realized he was coming to the outer limit of the bubble. He couldn't see what lay beyond. As objects and people arrived at the outermost lightness they simply vanished.

Ian drifted inexorably toward that outer lightness, the skin of the bubble. He thrashed his limbs with a baby's feeble protest.

...IAN STOOD IN his kitchen pouring steaming hot water through a Melitta coffee filter. He yawned, so tired he could not even remember crawling out of bed. He had promised Sarah he'd arrive in Pullman in time to take her to dinner, and he felt bound to keep that promise. Pullman was almost three hundred miles away. Something close to panic agitated him at the prospect.

He lifted the filter away from the coffee mug and set it in the sink then leaned over and inhaled the fresh ground scent of Vivace's Italian roast. He added a dollop of heavy cream and took his first sip, hoping it would spike his brain. It didn't.

Stepping out of the narrow kitchenette, he noticed pill bottles arrayed on the bedside table. He froze, recalling a dreadful sense of being sucked away down a dark funnel, of yearning back toward life...

He put his coffee down and picked up one of the pill bottles, the Halcion. There were only a couple of pills left in it. He stilled himself, listened to his body. Had he done it? Had he finally, really done it? No. He felt tired but not like he would had he ingested a dozen or so Halcion, not to mention the contents of the other, equally depleted bottles.

Something was going on.

He turned to the window. His restored but neglected '47 Indian Chief stood wheel-cocked, the morning light shining on its red paint and dull, spotted chrome. The fringe around the leather seat looked limp and sad. His father would have hated to see how Ian had failed to maintain 'a relationship' with the bike. Well, not all relationships were *good*. At least he had permission from the building management to park in the alley. Persistent anxiety enveloped him. It was Sarah. He missed her but he was also relieved that she had returned for her second year at WSU. He almost preferred her as a text message attached to a memory. It was safer that way. Not so close.

"What the fuck is wrong with me?" Ian said out loud.

His cell rang. Immediately he hoped it was Sarah calling to cancel the weekend. With that thought, fresh anxiety trickled through him. What if she *did* cancel? He wanted it both ways.

But it wasn't Sarah.

"Ian?" Zach said.

"What'd you do," Ian said, "stay up all night?"

"I don't know."

"How can you not know?"

"Listen, I don't feel so great."

"What's the matter?"

"It's like there's ants under my skin or something. You know what? It's like a panic attack. Ian, there's something going on, man."

Ian frowned. "What do you mean?"

"You'll think I'm crazy."

"I already think that."

"I'm not kidding."

"Just tell me. I'm listening."

"Okay this is how bad it is," Zach said. "I wanted to come over there but I couldn't force myself to leave the fucking building. I mean I couldn't go out the door. I feel like Howard Hughes."

Ian sighed inwardly. "Are you high?"

"No, I'm not *high*. Jesus Christ."

"Then what is it? Do you want me to come over?"

"No, don't do that."

"Why not?"

"This is one of the crazy parts," Zach said. "If you come over, they might see you."

"Who might see me? Who's 'they'?"

"I don't know."

Zach always got paranoid when he smoked too much grass.

"I know what you're thinking," Zach said.

"Really? What am I thinking?"

"You're thinking I'm acting all paranoid because I smoked too much weed."

"I might be thinking that. It's not as if there's no precedent."

There was a long pause, then Zach said, "Never mind," and broke the connection. Ian picked up his coffee, wandered into the kitchen, drank a little and poured the remainder over the dirty dishes in the sink then added the empty cup to the pile. He peeled a banana and ate it. Then he called Zach's number. It rang three times and went to voicemail. Whatever. Suddenly the prospect of riding to Pullman appeared slightly more inviting. He knew Zach would eventually call him back, and he knew that his whole Saturday would be co-opted by a babysitting mission. On the other hand, that would be a good excuse *not* to go to Pullman. On the *other* other hand he suddenly wanted to get out of the apartment, out and away from the sleeping pill bottles that were begging questions from him that he didn't want to ask.

Beautiful day for a ride, even if the wind was sharp. He intended to head straight to the 90, but instead found himself detoured, riding by Zach's 14th Street condo. Behind these ivied walls dwell today's dope heads and game geeks. One of them, at least.

He rang the intercom. Zach didn't answer.

"Fine," Ian mumbled.

He got back on his bike.

Ten minutes later he roared out of the I-90 tunnel. Bright morning sun struck him full in the face. He throttled up – then immediately backed off. Cars were stopped all over the floating bridge. Ian swerved to avoid running into a yellow Lexus. The driver stood next to his open door, looking at the sky, as were many other people. Ian continued to make forward progress, weaving slowly between the stopped vehicles and gawking pedestrians. He kept glancing up. Finally, craning his head back toward the city, he saw them: like silver pinwheel lights hovering in formation. Only

Seattle's tallest building, the Columbia Tower, was visible above First Hill. One of the pinwheel lights stopped spinning and descended toward it. The skin prickled over Ian's back, and he knew he was witnessing something otherworldly. Then the Chief crept past the bridge's mid-span.

The Indian wobbled....

DEFINITION OF FUNCTION

WHAT HAD BEEN Charles Noble stood in the middle of the Noble Gallery and lifted his hand, as if bidding an orchestra take up their instruments. There was no orchestra – only an empty oak floor. The image existed in Noble's mind and naturally came forward with the gesture. The new Charles examined the connective association and found it appropriate. Then he closed his eyes and became a Lens, focusing energy, reconfiguring local space. He opened his eyes. A small wine bar had risen out of the floor, a fluted vase and red rose in one corner. It was something the other Charles had often thought about doing but could never afford.

THE NOBLE GALLERY'S door opened, and Charles looked up from the crystal stem glass he was polishing. Charles wore a white linen jacket, a red tie, and a fedora.

He owned a number of hats and generally felt better when he was wearing one. This was partly vanity. His prematurely thinning hair made him self-conscious. But also he simply liked hats; they made him feel more like himself. The Curator, who was the new Charles, noted the irrationality of this but mentally shrugged and surrendered to it. Curator defined his usual function but now things were different. So very different.

"Hello," said the man who had just entered the gallery. His skin was olive and his eyes almond brown. "I'm Curtis, that's my bookstore next to you. We haven't met, so I thought—"

"Biblio," Charles said. "'Books New And Rare'."

"Yes."

Charles knew all about Biblio. He knew about Curtis Sarmir, too. The old Charles had thought very often of Curtis, had devised elaborate scenarios in which they became acquainted – scenarios that the old Charles often dismissed later as stupid 'meet cute guy' fantasies. The Curator now allowed Charles to invite the acquaintance he had previously been too afraid to pursue.

"I'm Charles Noble."

They shook hands.

"Hence 'The Noble Gallery'," Curtis said.

"Exactly. Would you care for a glass of wine?"

Curtis Sarmir grinned, his mouth coming open slightly in mock surprise. "Actually, I would."

"White or red?"

"If it's before noon it simply must be white."

The Curator poured two glasses of Riesling and handed one to Curtis, who wandered around the small gallery, sipping. Paintings and photographs of dancers, classical ballet and modern interpretive, occupied the white walls, illuminated by cunning little lights. On a pedestal in the center of the room stood a blue marble sculpture of a swan copulating with a ballerina.

"A theme emerges," Curtis observed.

"I suppose, yes. The exhibit is changing soon, though."

"To what?"

"I haven't yet decided."

Curtis handed Charles his glass. "I have to get back to my shop. No one's watching the register."

A minor current of panic rippled through Charles and he blurted: "Maybe we could... brainstorm?"

Curtis raised his eyebrows.

"About the next exhibit," Charles said. "I really can't quite decide."

"Brainstorm over dinner?"

"I think I'd like that."

When the door closed behind Curtis, the Curator noted the panic current had become electric anticipation. He tried to withdraw from it, but already he was as much Charles Noble as he was Curator, and withdrawal was not a simple option.

He did not understand his new function.

CHAPTER FIVE

KYLIE PULLED AT her restraints. The twine cut into her wrists and ankles. She sucked air between clenched teeth. The blood was slippery. The twine was not cinched as tightly around her right wrist. She kept twisting her arm, deliberately using the rough twine to saw at her flesh, slicking it up with blood so she might squeeze free.

"Child, be still," Father Jim said.

"Don't *touch* me."

He stood and moved into the candlelight. Father Jim seemed too big for the room. He looked crazy with his messed up comb-over and little knife. No, not a knife – a *scalpel*.

He was going to cut her.

He put the scalpel down and withdrew a small glass bottle from his pocket.

"This will numb you. That pagan dentist had it in his office. If it works on gums it will work down there, too."

He unscrewed the cap and upended the bottle, saturating a cotton swab. He capped the bottle and replaced it in his pocket.

"You must lie still, Kylie."

He put his hand on her knee and pushed it down. His hand was cold and dry. "Don't be afraid. The blade is very sharp. At first I was going to use a razor, but then I found the scalpel, while I was looking for Novocain. The dentist provides. There was a reason, a plan, for what I did to him. There's always a plan, Kylie. It's a mistake to believe otherwise. If the path diverges, you follow the obvious signs. This is how God wants you made right, Kylie. He spoke to me by making me remember that *National Geographic* story about the Africans."

Kylie wasn't merely afraid – she was riding the flashing edge of hysterical panic. Using that panic, she pulled with almost superhuman strength, and her right hand, incredibly, came free. Father Jim immediately seized hold of it. She twisted and thrashed but his grip was unbreakable.

"Let her go," Billy said.

Kylie stopped struggling. Father Jim did not let go but looked over his shoulder. Billy leaned against the door jamb. The blood seeping from the split lump on his forehead looked black as oil in the candlelight. For a moment no one moved. Then Father Jim released Kylie, grabbed up the scalpel, and turned on Billy.

"Drop it," Billy said, raising the toy-looking gun, like Doc Holliday in one of Billy's movies. Like Val Kilmer. The priest hesitated, then lunged. Billy fired. Father Jim threw himself to the left, his head snapping in the opposite direction. Kylie couldn't tell if the bullet had struck him or not. Jim crashed his face into the door frame and went down, hitting the floor hard. The candle holder jumped on the bedside table, and the flame guttered. The acrid smell of gun smoke hung in the air.

"Guess he's my huckleberry," Billy said. The automatic slipped from his hand. He swayed dangerously and did a slow, graceful drop back into the hall.

"Billy?"

He didn't respond. Kylie leaned as far forward as she could, which wasn't very far at all. She could see Billy's legs. The rest of him was out of sight. The lamp in the living room made a dull gleam on the hardwood floor between Billy's feet and Father Jim. The priest, lying face down, was still alive, and breathing in a peculiar way, making wet huffing noises at irregular intervals.

Kylie went to work on the knot that bound her left wrist to the bedpost. This one was tighter than the right one had been, a pea-sized gnarl. She picked at it with her fingernail and thumb. She tried to get her teeth on it, but, maddeningly, couldn't stretch her neck that far. Nor could she pick at it long without resting. Reaching up and across with her free arm put a strain on her back and shoulder. Beyond that, her abraded wrists and ankles stung like mad. Now with every movement the rough twine sawed into her bleeding skin. In her initial terror she had been oblivious to the pain. But not any more.

After half an hour of picking at the knot her back cramped and she had to stop. Frustrated, she began crying. She couldn't help it. She lay back and let it all out, deep sobbing hopeless despair. When she was cried out she lay quiet and began to push the despair aside.

There was no point in despair, in giving up. The strained muscle in her back gradually relaxed. Kylie sat up and resumed working on the knot. On the porch the generator halted, probably out of fuel. The lamp in the living room winked out, taking the hardwood gleam with it.

Father Jim's breaths were long and clotted-sounding. At times he seemed to *stop* breathing.

Kylie forced herself to remain calm. She concentrated on the knot, *staring* at it in the dim candlelight, prying with her fingernail. Patient, shutting out Father Jim, shutting out her fear about Billy. Gradually the knot began to yield to her efforts. She kept at it until it was loose enough to squeeze her left hand free. The skin was torn in a circlet around her wrist.

She sobbed with relief and immediately sat forward to work on the ankle restraints. In this position she could see more of the floor beyond the foot of the bed. Father Jim was still gripping the scalpel in his right hand. Kylie wanted it.

She clambered over the footboard and dropped, hands-first, to the floor, her ankles straining at the twine. Kylie held her breath and reached for the scalpel. Suddenly the priest clutched down on it, big veins standing out on the back of his hand.

Kylie snapped *her* hand away as if she'd stuck it into a flame. But Father Jim didn't seem to be conscious. Again she reached out. Boldly, she pulled his fingers open and worked the scalpel free.

The surgical steel cut effortlessly through her ankle restraints. She dropped the blade, yanked on a pair of pants and jammed her feet into sneakers. With the candle she stepped into the hall, certain that Billy was dead. She set the candle on the floor and knelt beside him. The bump on his forehead was like a cracked egg, oozing fluid. *I loved Billy,* she thought. She touched his hair, petting him tenderly, kind of watching herself do it. After a while Billy's eyes opened.

"Kylie," he said.

She stopped petting him, startled. "Your poor head," she said.

"Aspirin."

"What?"

"In the bathroom. Aspirin – for my poor head."

Kylie jumped up, found the aspirin and a bottle of water. The town had run out of real bottled water ages ago. This was rain water collected from catch basins. At first people feared drinking water that fell out of the poisoned sky. They blamed it for the their loss of sexual function and for the wasting illness that was slowly finishing off the stragglers left behind after The Judgment. But Father Jim had taken to blessing the town's catch basins after every rainfall, transforming poison into safe Holy Water. Of course, everybody was still dying.

She helped Billy sit up. He dropped the first two aspirins she gave him. She placed the next ones directly on his tongue and helped him with the water bottle. Some of it dribbled into his beard but he managed to swallow the pills. To Kylie, those little white tablets seemed frighteningly inadequate.

"Can you stand?" she asked Billy.

"If you help me."

She tried but she was a small person and Billy was not. He leaned heavily on her, and they staggered into the living room, colliding with furniture, kicking empty beer bottles over. It reminded her of other clumsy waltzes they'd performed when Billy was blind staggering drunk. She helped him make a semi-controlled crash onto the sofa. He groaned loudly and held his hand up to his forehead without actually touching it. "Jesus Christ," he said.

"What can I do?"

"Nothing. Unless you can pull a doctor out of your butt."

"I don't think I can."

She covered him with a blanket. "Spinning," Billy mumbled and then was quiet.

Father Jim was finally quiet, too. Billy had shot him in the head, so he *should* be quiet. Kylie took what remained of her candle and hunkered in the short hallway where Billy had fallen. She held the candle out and above her eye level, moving it side to side, searching for the dropped pistol. The priest resumed his clotted, wet snoring. Kylie tried to ignore it. Candlelight revealed the little automatic where it lay next to the priest. She reached for it. Even in *Kylie's* hand it was small.

Before The Judgment, it had seemed to her Father Jim could do anything, overcome anything. He often told the story of his 'wayward' teenage years and how joining the Marines had saved him, matured him. He was scary-intelligent when he wanted to be, and he had gotten into officer's training and eventually became a pilot. Later, he heard the Lord calling him to serve a higher organization, and he left the Marines. He could still fly airplanes, though. He could still give flying lessons. Jim owned a little red and white Cessna 150. It had only two seats and was so small Kylie laughed the first time she saw him fold his body into the cabin.

It was in that little airplane that Father Jim finally took advantage of all his years of grooming Kylie. She was thrilled the first time he took her flying. She hadn't been in the least bit frightened. "It's no harder than learning to drive a car," he said. "I'll teach you." And that's all it was for several lessons. She was good and hooked and wouldn't have given up those lessons for anything, the first time Jim put his hand on her thigh. He had been touching her for a while, of course, though never in front of other people and never *there*. But it seemed he was always rubbing her back or taking her hand, or playing with her hair.

But that first time, in the airplane flying over the Kitsap Peninsula, that he settled his hand on her thigh – that was the true start. It was August and hot even at two thousand feet. Father Jim's hand was firm. Kylie tried to keep her thighs tight together but she couldn't really do that and work the rudder pedals. Jim kept giving her instructions about what to do with the airplane. "Make a left turn, Kylie. Watch your horizon. Pull back on the yoke a little to keep your nose up. And keep the little ball centered on that instrument. There you go." His hand worked around to her inner thigh, where it remained for the rest of the lesson – just that far. A week later he made love to her on a cot in the airport office. No, 'made love' is what she told herself. The truth was, he *raped* her. And from then on whenever he called her his 'little co-pilot' that former term of endearment meant he *owned* her.

And now he was about to be dead with a bullet in his head.

It was too dark in the house. Kylie decided to re-start the generator, even if it *was* a waste of fuel. Billy stored the spare gas in five-gallon cans next to the side of the house. Using both hands, Kylie picked one up

75

and lugged it to the porch. She poured a gallon of gas into the generator, spilling quite a bit in the process. Then she thumbed the START button and the generator kicked on immediately. It was lucky for her and Billy that Father Jim had convinced everybody that God wanted them to live without machines or booze, otherwise the town would have run out of both a long time ago.

She returned to the kitchen and closed the door behind her. In the dark she waited a minute, listening.

Something was different.

Kylie stepped out of the kitchen. The lamp was on, and Father Jim wasn't dead. He was standing in front of the fireplace, looking at himself in the mirror above the mantel, carefully combing his stringy iron-gray hair with his fingers. He turned when Kylie came in. His nose was bent and his upper lip was crusted with blood. He must have broken the nose when he ran into the door frame. But worse than that, there was a black hole in his forehead about the diameter of a pencil, an inch or so above his left eye. A crooked line of blood ran from the hole to Jim's eyebrow. The eye below the brow was so bloodshot it had no visible pupil. Either the bullet or the door frame had knocked him cold. "Have you seen my hat?" he said.

Kylie stared at him.

"Have you seen my *hat*?"

She noticed it on the floor under the roll top desk but didn't say anything. She raised the baby automatic and pointed it at Jim.

"I thought I dropped my hat around here."

"You better go away now," Kylie said.

"I will if it's not raining."

"It's not," Kylie said.

He looked confused, his jaw hanging loose. Kylie said, "The door's over there, behind you."

Father Jim turned and shuffled to the door. Leaving the door open he walked out onto the dead lawn and halted, staring at the sky, at the dull glitter that was not stars. Father Jim called this phenomenon the Apocalypse Sky. Billy just said it was 'some alien shit'.

"Go on!" Kylie said, but Father Jim didn't move. She retrieved his hat and sailed it out to him like a saucer. It hit the back of his leg. He picked it up and placed it carefully on his head, covering the bullet hole.

"You're not right yet," he said.

Kylie slammed the door.

CHAPTER SIX

IAN STOOD BARE-chested in the kitchen, pouring hot water through a Melitta filter. He leaned over the rising steam and inhaled deeply. The aroma was wonderful. But that didn't mean it was worth getting up at seven o'clock in the morning. He lifted the filter away and set it in the sink, added a splash of heavy cream to the cup.

He stepped into the living room – and stopped.

His stash of pill bottles stood arrayed on the bedside table, caps off. Sudden fear drew at him like a black tide.

Ian put his cup down, gathered the bottles in trembling hands, replaced the caps and put the bottles back in the bathroom medicine chest.

In the living room, he racked up the window blinds and gazed down at the Chief. If only he didn't have to ride the damn thing to Pullman. It probably wouldn't make it the whole distance, anyway.

So he should skip it.

Sarah would almost certainly be asleep at this hour. He composed a bullshit text message about his bike crapping out on him again, hit SEND. Totally plausible. It wasn't even really a lie, just a truth that hadn't happened today but could have. Okay, cowardly. Cowardly but *foolproof*.

The phone rang and he answered it before he could stop himself.

"Hello? Ian?"

Sarah. *Fuck*.

"Yeah," he said. "Good morning."

"Is something wrong, baby?" (echo: Babe, what's wrong?)

"No, no. I didn't think you'd be awake. I mean I was going to leave you a good morning message, kind of, before I left."

"That's *so* sweet," Sarah said. (echo: How *sweet!*)

It was as if he'd had this conversation before and the other words were still running on a loop somewhere. "Yeah, isn't it?" he said. Ian's phone beeped with an incoming call. He held the phone away from his face, saw it was Zach, and frowned.

"You're not supposed to *agree* that you're sweet," Sarah said. "Oh, I can't wait till you get here."

"Me neither."

The incoming call quit beeping.

"Do you love me oodles and oodles?"

"With extra oodles," Ian said. He hated when she lapsed into baby talk. "Anyhow, I better get moving."

"You better, sweetie. Love you."

"Love you, too," Ian said.

Sarah hung up. "Fuck!" Ian looked at the missed call. If Zach was calling at seven in the morning it meant he'd been up all night and was still drunk or, worse, high, and wanted to talk about some mad inspiration for a new game. Ian turned his cell off and finished dressing.

Ten minutes later he was on the road, wind in his face, feeling more alive than dead but not much more.

The closer he got to the I-90 ramp the more his nerves jumped and popped. Deciding it was guilt, he pulled into the curb and dug his cell phone out. The engine idled roughly then died. Ian thumbed Zach's number and it rang through to voicemail. He tried again with the same result. Probably Zach had passed out asleep (drunk) or gone for breakfast (high).

Ian looked at his watch. It was coming up on eight. He wasn't sure whether it was intuition or simply his mind hunting excuses to forego the Pullman trip, but he adjusted the choke, kick-started the Chief, then swung around and headed back to Capitol Hill to check on his friend.

He parked in front of the brick and ivy condo on 14th Street, called Zach's number and got no answer. He rang Zach's buzzer in the alcove outside the front door of the eight-unit building. Again: no answer. He buzzed again. Still nothing. Enough? Ian stood listening, as if somebody was going to tell him. And somebody did, sort of. His intuition or whatever.

Not enough.

Ian walked around to the back of the building. Zach's new Beetle was snug as, well, a bug in the garage. So he was up there not answering his phone or intercom buzzer. Or he could have walked to he Deluxe, or Charlie's, or the Grill for breakfast.

Ian had keys. Zach had given them to him months ago so Ian could feed his fish when he was out of town. Not that Ian wanted to use the keys now. It was perfectly possible his friend had a girl up there. Okay, not all that possible; Zach was almost morbidly self-conscious around girls. But even if he was alone he was entitled to his privacy.

Ian let himself in the front door and mounted the carpeted steps. Outside Zach's door he hesitated, then knocked. Waited. Knocked again. So he was out. Or something.

Ian slotted the second key and opened Zach's door. He leaned into the entry, feet still planted in the hallway.

"Zach, it's me."

The tropical fish tank bubbled away in the front room.

"Zach?"

Suddenly Ian didn't want to go any further. He felt strongly compelled to withdraw, pull the door shut, and get back on the road. Instead he stepped inside, closed the door partway but not enough for the latch to engage. There was a framed Billy The Kid Wanted poster on the wall of the entry. It was real, preserved and sealed under glass. Zach had a thing for Old West outlaws. He even had a brace of Colt revolvers, Peacemakers from the 1870's. Ian had accompanied him to the shooting range once, but didn't get it.

"Zach?"

He followed the bubbling sound of the fish tank to the front room. Zach was sitting at the Danish desk that faced the bay window. On the desk his iBook was running a text document. But Zach, slouched in his office chair, was swiveled toward Ian, watching him through his black-framed geek glasses. Ian caught his breath, surprised. Zach took his glasses off and said, "Hi."

"Jesus Christ," Ian said. "What the hell are you doing?"

"Waiting for you, I guess."

"Waiting for me."

"Yeah. I mean I didn't know I was but I was."

"Why didn't you say something when I came in?"

"I don't know. I feel weird. Aren't you supposed to be on your way to Pullman?"

"Yeah. Why'd you call me an hour ago?"

Zach put his glasses back on and swiveled around to face the iBook again.

"Zach?"

"I was afraid."

"Of what?"

"That I was going to do something. Then I decided to do it anyway. I was writing it all out for you. I was going to call you back, in case you skipped Pullman. You do skip it, about half the time."

"What are you talking about? Writing what all out?"

"Stuff. Never mind, it doesn't matter now."

Ian crossed the room but before he could read any of the words, Zach closed the document. A black lacquered box sat on the floor next to Zach's chair, the world COLT engraved on a brass plate affixed to the hinged lid.

"Man," Zach said, "I'm a gutless wonder. Seriously."

"You're acting weirder than usual, you know." Ian glanced at the gun box

"I know."

"You been up all night?"

Zach chuckled.

"What?"

"Yeah. I've been up all night. Whatever you want to call it."

"Come on, I'll buy you breakfast."

Zach tapped a pencil on the edge of his desk. It was a

black pencil with gold lettering stamped on the side that said, MINDWERKS.

"The Grill," Ian said to the back of Zach's head. "I guess you didn't hear me when I said I was buying?"

"That place is so gay."

"You'd be doing me a favor. Give me an excuse to skip Pullman."

"Oh, you aren't going to Pullman."

"Why do you say it like that?"

Zach swiveled around to face him again. His eyes were red behind his glasses.

"You're buying? That's an event. Let's go."

Outside, Zach kept looking at the sky. He did it so often Ian finally asked, "What are you looking for?"

"I don't think they come every day, but I don't really *know*."

"You don't think *who* comes every day?"

"Never mind."

At the Broadway Grill Zach sat listlessly in the corner of the booth under a picture of James Dean. The Grill was crazy busy, as usual, mostly with twenty-somethings looking at least as hip and gay as the movie stars pictured on practically every wall. The waiter brought Zach's Monte Cristo sandwich. Zach looked at it then asked for a beer. It wasn't quite nine in the morning. "And a shot of Jameson's," he said.

"What's that," Ian said, "the breakfast of champions?"

Zach managed a weak grin. In a few minutes the waiter brought his drinks. He downed the whiskey in a gulp and followed it with a deep draught of Fat Tire.

"When you're done with those eggs," Zach said, "would you mind doing me a favor?"

"What favor?"

"Drive me someplace. I've been drinking and I don't think I should be behind the wheel." Zach giggled.

Ian looked at him closely. "Drive you where?"

"It doesn't matter. North?"

As they were leaving the Grill, two young women came in. Zach stopped dead in his tracks, staring at one of them, a waifish blond with a military buzz cut and a platinum stud in her left nostril. She scowled at him, and her companion, a mannish Amazon with jet black hair and a spiderweb tattoo on her neck, said, "You got a problem?"

Zach's face had gone white.

Ian pulled him out the door. "What's wrong with you? Did you know that girl?"

"No, but I saw her die once."

"What–"

"Come on, come on. Let's get going."

Ian drove the VW. Zach rode shotgun with a bottle of Red Hook retrieved from a case in the trunk. They came to a stop sign.

"Well?" Ian said.

"Go thataway," Zach said, pointing with the hand holding the bottle.

"What'd you take?" Ian asked, reaching over to push the bottle down, in case there was a cop around.

"Take?"

"Peyote, mescaline, what?"

Zach shook his head, drank his ale. "North, my good man."

By now they had migrated off Capitol Hill. Ian accelerated onto Aurora Avenue North.

"I think it's the shock," Zach said. "That's why I remember better this time. It's the shock."

"What?"

Zach twisted around in his seat to look out the back window. "God," he said. "Oh, God."

"What's wrong?" Ian stared at the rearview mirror. A Toyota and a couple of guys on motorcycles occupied the lanes behind them, the motorcycles a little further back than the car. Suddenly the Toyota swerved into the breakdown lane, skidding to a halt, leaving its rear end sticking into the highway. A man jumped out of the passenger side and pointed at the sky. The motorcycle riders, who had slowed and swerved to avoid the Toyota, looked back over their shoulders.

"Step on it," Zach said, his voice high and cracking with fear.

In the wing mirror, which was adjusted too high for Ian, half a dozen brilliant pinwheel lights hovered over the skyline. Then the city passed out of sight behind the east slope of Queen Anne Hill. Moments later the VW sped onto the Aurora Bridge. The bridge was huge, a cantilever and truss design almost three thousand feet long and a hundred seventy feet above the water. Ian knew *all about* the Aurora Bridge. He had walked across it numerous times. Research. It was the number two suicide bridge in the United States, only beaten out by the Golden Gate. But this time he never made it to the other side. A hundred feet shy, the car began to shudder. At that moment, he remembered, and he let go of the wheel and looked at Zach. The light shifted, and they were tumbling in a yellow-green void...

THE HUNTERS

ENERGY BEAMS CRISS-CROSSED out of the sky, reducing buildings to smoldering slag. Fire devoured the city. Bloody and broken limbs twisted out of rubble. Sirens wailed in desperate alarm. The stink of death rose up. The Curator stepped forth as Charles Noble, concealed within a Shadow that rendered him invisible to the Hunters who sought him. Charles shook his head. Hunter methods were primitive, brutal and ineffective. Laying waste to a Preservation city (even this anomaly of a Preservation city) was no more effective than disrupting a holographic projection. The city merely resumed its steady state upon the next Advent.

The Hunters would never find him. But would they ever give up? Was he condemned to an infinite lifetime of hiding?

Hunter ships, like brilliant pinwheel lights, finally ceased their attack and darted away. Pillars of thick black smoke rolled in their wake.

A woman stood with slack arms and jaw, weeping before a minivan flattened under a tumbled brick façade. "My baby, my baby..." A haze of dust hung in the air. Charles caused his Shadow to dissolve and approached the woman. She raised her lightless eyes to him. "My baby," she sobbed. He touched her shoulder. Compassion resonated through his body. It hurt. The compassion belonged to the old Charles. The Curator shrank from it, likening it to the irrational current of panic he'd endured when Curtis Sarmir was about to leave the gallery. But now the woman grabbed his arm, clinging with ferocious strength. She went to her knees, weeping, dragging on him. Charles instructed himself to endure it; this was his future.

CHAPTER SEVEN

MORNING. IAN POURED hot water through the Melitta filter, his movements mechanical as a windup toy's. He seemed to hover over his own head, attached by invisible threads, a balloon person. The rich coffee aroma began to assert itself, and he found himself inhaling fragrant steam, present in his body but slightly disoriented. Then his phone rang. He wandered out of the kitchen. The phone was on the table beside his futon. So were three uncapped prescription bottles. The bed cover still held an impression of Ian's body.

My body, he thought, and a ripple of pure atavistic dread surged through him. The phone stopped ringing. The little window showed a missed call from Zach. Ian really wasn't up for it. The phone blooped a text message: *Know you're there. Call now. Emergency.*

Ian sighed, hit speed dial. "Zach?"

"Man, come over here, okay?"

"Right now?"

"Yeah."

"I'm supposed to meet Sarah in Pullman."

"I know but come over anyway. It's important."

"What's going on?"

"It's life and death. I'm serious. Hey, bring your keys. I can't get the door."

"Why not?"

"Just hurry, okay?"

"Okay, okay."

"Ian?"

"*What?*"

"I'm sorry."

Zach broke the connection. Ian stared at his phone a moment then closed it and got dressed. He was only six blocks from Zach's condo. It would have taken as long to cold-start the Chief, so he walked. It was a beautiful morning, a little chilly. He started off walking but by the time he reached Zach's building he was running flat out, alarms bonging away in his head. He didn't bother buzzing. He got through the lobby door, took the stairs three at a time, and let himself into the unit. The fish tank bubbled, tetras and rainbows serenely finning back and forth. There was a funny smell. A *bad* smell.

"Zach?"

Ian came around the corner. Zach lay sprawled on the floor with one of his antique revolvers in his mouth. There was a big hole in the top of his head and a gruesome spray of ejecta on the hardwood floor. Taped to his chest was a big manila envelope. On the envelope in block letters were the words: IAN READ THIS RIGHT NOW.

CHAPTER EIGHT

OAKDALE, WA., 2013

KYLIE RODE HER bicycle down a residential street in Oakdale. The daytime sky was pearlescent, glaring. The air felt dense. The whole town was only a dozen square blocks. Many of the houses and commercial structures had been blown over or severely damaged. Being snug against the foothills of the Olympic Mountains probably spared the town from total annihilation. Mount Constance loomed, as it had Kylie's whole life. Only now it looked like the whole mountainside had been clear-cut. The coniferous forest of spruce, cedar, hemlock and Douglas fir hadn't been cut, though; a massive shockwave had flattened it. A year ago, at midnight, the sky had flashed white. Those who looked up were instantly struck blind. Kylie and her mother, both night owls, were arguing in the basement at the moment of the apocalyptic detonation – Maggie calmly folding laundry while Kylie lost her temper over some curfew issue. Kylie halted in mid-yell when the little window over the dryer blazed up, like a thousand camera flashes popping off in the garden at once. Shadows of Maggie's nodding tulips imprinted on Kylie's corneas. Moments later the shockwave rocked her and Maggie off their feet as it swept half the town away – swept most of the *world* away. Not their house, though. All it did was rip off part of the roof and take down the attached car-port. But life as Kylie had known it was over forever. Judgment Day had arrived, according to Father Jim and the handful of Oakdale survivors. Only Billy, returning from outside the town, believed differently. Only Billy maintained the Earth had been attacked by an alien force. The tulip shadows were an hour fading from Kylie's corneas.

In the basket attached to the bike's handlebars five of Kylie's favorite DVDs plus a couple of books bounced with every bump in the road. She had gathered them from Billy's house and was bringing them to her mother's. Billy was there, recovering – or trying to. This wasn't her first trip. A couple of days ago Billy had sent her back to retrieve the other gun, the big revolver. The Magnum. When she brought that one home she made sure her mother didn't see it.

As she coasted by a row of mailboxes a rock flew by Kylie's face. It struck one of the mailboxes and the little door dropped open. Kylie swerved, stubbed her front tire into the curb. DVDs and books bounced out of the basket.

Ray Preston, whose major accomplishment since The Judgment was burning down what remained of the high school he had previously dropped out of, regarded her from across the street. A faded pink plastic flamingo on a spike tilted in the dead lawn behind him. Ray had another rock in his hand.

"Why'd you do that!" Kylie shouted at him.

"Because you ain't right, that's why. You're holding us back."

"Back from what, you idiot?"

Preston was so skinny he looked like a starving man. His clothes hung in rags. He never cut what was left of his hair. Scabs crusted the bald patches of his scalp. His scraggly gray and black beard grew down his neck like diseased moss. He had been the last person in town to quit drinking 'spirits', and Kylie doubted he had quit for real. Father Jim had worked on him a long time but people had been working on Ray Preston his entire worthless life. Kylie wasn't afraid of him. Ray looked like one of the skin-and-bone people who occasionally lurched into town. The SABs didn't act human, most of them. They were kind of like movie zombies, except they didn't eat people. When skin-and-bone people appeared they were always run right back out of town. Ray Preston was terrified of the SABs, even though he looked like one himself. Father Jim said the SABs were people whose souls had been stolen by the Devil.

"Holding us back from the *Lord*," Preston said.

"You better not throw that rock in your hand."

"Why not?"

Kylie withdrew Billy's baby automatic from the zippered pocket of her leather jacket and pointed it at Preston. Billy had the big revolver, but he had told her to keep the small gun for protection. It had belonged to his mother. He said it was a good gun for a girl. Kylie let that pass. "That's why not," she said to Preston, leveling the good-for-a-girl gun.

After a moment Ray casually tossed the rock behind him. "I wasn't going to throw it anyway." The rock landed next to the flamingo. Ray wiped his hands on his filthy Levi's. He picked at a scab on his nose. "That the gun you shoot Father Jim with?"

"I didn't shoot him, but it's the gun." Kylie tucked the automatic back in her jacket. She picked up her bike and leaned it against the mailboxes. Ray watched her but stayed where he was. She gathered the spilled DVDs and books and replaced them in the basket. The dust jacket was torn on one of the poetry books, a vertical tear right through Robert Frost's head.

"He's a prophet," Ray said, referring to Father Jim. "Everybody says so. A Prophet of the fuckin' Apocalypse."

"Who's everybody, you and all the other idiots in this town?"

"Why don't you shut up, you little cunt."

"Watch your mouth," Kylie said, "or you might get shot in the head yourself."

"Day's coming when getting shot in the head won't mean nothing," Ray said, looking like he wanted to ask *himself* what that meant. He pointed at Kylie. "That's a warning."

Kylie pulled out the .22 and fired into the air.

"So's that!" she said, but Ray Preston was already halfway down the block.

HER MOTHER LOOKED at her suspiciously when Kylie shouldered through the front door with her arms full of the stuff she'd retrieved from Billy's house.

"What's all that?" Maggie said.

"Some books."

"I mean those other things."

"Movies."

"What for? You can't play them here."

"I don't *know*, Mom, I just wanted them. They're not going to hurt anything, don't worry."

"Did I say I was worried?"

"Whatever." *You don't have to say it,* Kylie thought. Her mom worried constantly and always had, even before The Judgment. She followed Kylie to the top of the basement stairs and said, "Wait just a minute, please."

Billy had been living in the basement for three days. It was almost a week ago that Father Jim had hit him in the head with a baseball bat. Kylie had stayed with him at his house for two days, and Billy never once got off the sofa or ate anything. Every time he tried to sit up dizziness overcame him, and with no food in his stomach he couldn't afford to do any more retching. Frightened, Kylie had gone to her mother and told her what happened. Maggie had been a nurse in the days before The Judgment. She came, looked at him, and pronounced him, "Seriously concussed, maybe dead serious." Kylie refused to leave him alone, and Maggie wouldn't allow Kylie to stay in the house with him, now that he was incapacitated. The two of them moved him across town, rolling him in big wheelbarrow. People came out to watch. Some of them looked like they had wanted to throw rocks, just like Ray Preston. It was better at Kylie's mother's house. Maggie had superior pain pills for Billy. She had OxyContin.

Maggie said, "I heard a shot."

Kylie didn't say anything.

"What happened?" Maggie said. Yellow discharge had accumulated in the corners of her eyes, a progressive sign of the illness. It hurt Kylie to look at her mother. "You might as well tell me," Maggie said. "I can smell that little gun in your pocket, so I know you fired it."

Kylie shrugged. "Ray Preston threw a rock at me, so I scared him off is all."

"Dear God," Maggie said.

"He's stupid."

"Kylie."

"Well, he is."

"He has a good core, I'm sure. I remember before the–"

"His core's not *good*. He tried to hit me with a *rock*. Father Jim put him up to it. Father Jim's going around telling everybody he's some kind of prophet, just because he got shot in the head and didn't die."

Maggie pressed her lips together and blew air out her nose, a trick she used when she didn't want to speak in anger.

"He's *not* a prophet, Mom."

"No, he's just lucky," Maggie said. "But Kylie, God does favor the lucky. Gunshot wounds are tricky. A boy came into the ER one time, his friend had shot him in the back of the head. An accident. God knows how you accidentally shoot your friend in the head. Doctor couldn't remove the bullet. It was lodged deep in the brain. Didn't know that at the time, of course. Just this boy acting perfectly normal except guess what? He's got a hole in the back of his head, and all of a sudden he's left handed when all his life he had been right handed. Plus he said he could see light around people, like auras? That might have been a miracle wound or dumb luck, who knows? I'd guess dumb luck. Now Father Jim, that little bullet never penetrated his skull. It's either stuck in the bone or under the skin someplace, guaranteed. Most people who survive headshots, that's the case. That little hole in his forehead should have healed over by now. My guess is he gouges at it with something to keep it looking fresh. Starting to look *infected*, you ask me. None of that matters to the people in this town, though. It's a miracle of God, and that's that. Because they need it to be one."

"I have to see Billy now," Kylie said.

He was lying on the day bed in the basement room Maggie had formerly used for entertaining. It was the same bed where Father Jim had thrown her after he razor-nicked his cock. Kylie's mother, of course, knew nothing of *that* incident.

"I'm back," Kylie said to Billy. "Are you awake?"

"Yeah."

"Will light hurt your eyes?"

"No, it's okay."

She quickly lit a few homemade candles, and the room became cozy, almost, except the floor was cold linoleum.

"I brought some books."

"Okay."

"Want me to read one to you?"

"Sure." Billy tented his fingers delicately over his eyes.

"It sucks God made you all dizzy and blurry so you can't even read, while He lets Father Jim limp all over town with a *bullet* in his head."

"Yeah, God's a jerk. Anyway, I can see okay now, most of the time."

"Mom says God favors the lucky."

"Right."

Kylie flipped through the pages. "It's poems. I want to read the one about the wall."

"Kylie, we have to talk first. Go shut that door. You know how Maggie always listens."

Kylie closed the book and the door then returned to the bed.

Keeping his voice low, Billy said, "I heard what you said to your mother."

"That rock wasn't anything."

"Shhh."

"It wasn't anything," Kylie repeated, in a softer voice.

"It'll get worse."

Kylie zipped her thumbnail down the pages of the book.

"A *lot* worse," Billy said.

"Mom won't let them hurt me. And I won't let anybody hurt you, Billy."

"Kylie–"

"I want to read the one about the wall."

Billy was quiet a minute, then quoted, "'Something there is that doesn't love a wall.' That's totally you, Kylie."

"I guess," Kylie said.

"There are walls, then there are walls."

"I like the part about the apple trees not sneaking into the neighbor's field," she said.

"Yeah, it's funny."

"Okay, okay, Billy, go ahead."

"What?"

"Go ahead and tell me how it's going to get worse. I know you're dying to."

"First let's talk about something good," Billy said.

"Okay."

"You remember what I was saying before the priest came to the door?"

"About running away?"

"That and the Seattle Dome."

"What about it," Kylie said.

"I know what's inside it."

"How could you know?"

Billy sat up a little. "The skin-and-bone people come from the Dome. They were inside, all of them."

Kylie stared at him. "I don't believe it," she said, not knowing whether she believed it or not. She was thinking about the city under the Dome. Seattle. It was the *Say Anything* city, the *Sleepless* city. Kylie had been to Seattle in real life, but the movies she watched were more vivid than her memories.

"If they were really in there," Kylie said, "how did they escape?"

"They didn't escape. They got thrown out."

"Why?"

"That part I'm not sure about. When I lived on the Big Boat we saw a lot of SABs. Most of them were like what you're used to seeing, barely human. But some were fresh. The fresh ones looked more normal and they could talk. They were in shock, most of them, and confused. They talked about being in Seattle, living their lives and then slowly becoming aware that something was wrong. From what they said we started to piece it together, Kylie. We think the Dome is some kind of zoo or living museum. Like one of those natural history museums where you can see what life was like in prehistoric times? Only this one's for humans and it's way more sophisticated than a natural history museum. It's a whole functioning world and nobody knows

98

they're in it. They think it's just regular Seattle. Except sometimes they *do* know they're in it. At that point they get thrown out."

"You know, I'm probably not as dumb as I look, right?"

"You're not dumb at all. And everything I'm telling you is true. Listen, we have to make a plan and get moving before things really go to hell around here. I want to take you to the Big Boat. It's relatively safe there, at least it was when I left. Probably a lot of people have died since then, but there will be plenty left, too. They aren't ignorant hicks, Kylie. They aren't scared of Father Jim's stupid Judgment Day. They're hard-headed people, some of them, engineers and scientists. They've studied the Seattle Dome. They have a plan. And they'll welcome you with open arms, Kylie, because you can do something none of them has ever done."

"What can I do that guys like that don't know how to do?"

"Fly an airplane."

Kylie laughed. "They want me to fly a Cessna?"

"Not a Cessna. They were modifying a fighter jet they called the *Penetrator*. Some of them thought it might be able to penetrate the Dome, reach Seattle."

"I can't fly a jet. Jesus, Billy! I never even got my license to fly little prop airplanes."

"You won't have to, trust me. The *Penetrator* is just something to give the boat people hope. Not hope for survival. They're all sick. The *Penetrator* gives them hope that they can strike back, at least once. A lot of them were military."

"Strike back at what?"

Billy subsided into the pillows and closed his eyes. He looked drawn and exhausted. It wasn't just the concussion. Billy was getting sick. "Strike back at the zoo-keepers, I guess."

Kylie opened her mouth. Excitement, fear, anxiety, confusion – they all passed through her. She closed her mouth, then opened it again and said, "Billy, does your head hurt much?"

"Like murder."

"I'm going to read to you now, okay?"

"Okay."

She opened the book and squinted at the contents page until she found *Mending Wall*, but didn't turn to the page. "Billy, are the SABs real people?"

Billy moved his shoulders in a tiny shrug. "Did I ever tell you that you ask a lot of questions?"

"Why do you always say that?"

"Never mind. Go ahead and read, okay. I don't want to talk anymore. I feel wore out."

"'Something there is that doesn't love a wall,'" Kylie began, but her mind wasn't on the poem, not even the non-trespassing apple trees, which were her favorite. She wasn't thinking about the Big Boat, or the jet airplane she would probably get killed in if she tried to fly it. She was thinking about Seattle.

CHAPTER NINE

IAN SAT ON a bench in the park behind his apartment building, holding Zach's crazy suicide note. Shock, the anonymous call to the police, and then the call to Zach's brother (thinking, *Am I really talking to anyone?*) had hollowed him out, but he was here where his friend had told him to be in the note:

Ian, you aren't going to believe this but you're fucked if you don't. Have you felt weird lately, like déjà vu all the time? Never mind, I know you have. This is the reason: You have been here before. I mean right here on October 5, 2012. That's because the day has been here before, over and over again. But you woke up, man. I don't know how, but you did. And then you woke me up and I stayed awake, but you went back to sleep, and I've been trying to snap you out of it but you don't want to believe me and you keep doing the same kinds of dumbass things. Over and over. Here's the basics. The Day starts at 7AM and stops, I think, at midnight. During The Day you have free will and all that, but it doesn't matter. You can't leave the city. As soon as you try you wind up in some kind of limbo until it starts again. And there's this guy I call the 'Boogeyman'. He isn't even human, I don't think. Anyway, he runs the show. What a fucking game. Except there's no way to score points and jump levels. By the way, I said I stayed awake? That's not completely true. Some 'Days' I'm wide awake, totally sharp. But usually I'm only partly here. I remember some stuff, but not all of it. Mostly I feel anxious and weirded out and I don't know why. But today I'm in the fucking ZONE, I know what's happening. That's why I'm going to kill myself. It's the only way I can control my destiny. Okay that sounds crazy. I know. But here's the thing. I'm going to kill myself and leave this letter for you so you'll take me seriously, so it'll jolt you out of your trance or whatever it is. This is going to traumatize you, man. That's the point. Sorry to do it to you, but I'm desperate. It's hell being the only one who knows. So if this works, then you'll be awake again. Killing myself probably won't make any difference to me because when The Day starts over I'll probably start over too. There's no escaping The Day. Even dead people come back. Remember that chick at the Grill? We're all Zombies, man. So here's some proof for you: A few times I hung out in that park across from your building, hoping you'd come back. And I noticed at the exact time every day – 4:06PM – there's this cool sunbeam that lights up the top of the third tree from the southwest corner of the park, and right when it lights up, this black crow, that you can't even see until then, jumps into the air and flies away north. It happens every time. It's like people have free will and can change their actions inside The Day, but nature is totally predictable. The weather, for instance. October 5 starts out cold and clear in the morning then warms up like spring all afternoon. At sunset the clouds move in, and at about 11:00 it starts to rain. That's nothing but a weather report, man. But the tree and bird, that's not predictable. Okay, I'm getting sick of writing. But... there's one more thing I have to tell you. I wasn't going to, but I guess it's the main reason I'm doing this. Something happened a couple of Day cycles ago. Something horrible. I can't remember all of it, but the parts I DO remember I wish I could forget. Aliens. Their ships appeared in the sky over the city. Everybody was staring at them. Then the ships started cutting the city to pieces with some kind of energy weapon. Everything was burning. And I remember giants in the streets. I don't want to think about them. I saw one of them kill that girl from the Grill. They were killing a lot of people, cutting them up, burning... Anyway, I'm going to do it now. I think it was the shock of that invasion that makes me remember so much this time. So now I'm going to shock you. I have to. And I don't want to lose my nerve. So I'll talk to you the next time around. And you know what? If I don't come back from the dead, that's cool with me. Because I can't take it anymore. I can't.

Ian consulted his watch. Almost four o'clock. 4:06 was the magic moment. It had to be a natural event, Zach had written. The actions of people were variable, but the weather never changed. Cold in the morning, sunny afternoon, clouds at dusk, rain starting in the night around eleven. Generalities you could get on the morning news. But from the vantage of this particular park bench at the particular approaching minute, something specific was supposed to occur. It wouldn't, though. Of course it wouldn't; Zach had been suicidally out of his mind. Just like Ian's mother.

Tony, the guy who lived down the hall from Ian, came striding up the sidewalk with a pair of drumsticks in his fist. Tony 'the tiger' he called himself – totally, simplistically, a drummer. Ian privately mocked his flaming red mohawk and weight-lifter's pointless physique (just how heavy were a couple of sticks?) but simultaneously envied him his apparent sense of unwavering identity. Tony jogged up the steps and disappeared into the building.

At 4:06, low in the western sky, a crack opened in a pink billow of cloud. A sunbeam lit the upper branches of the third tree from the southwest corner of the park, and from the new-lit place a crow jumped into the air and flew off.

"No fucking way," Ian said. A panhandler shambling by in a grimy duffel coat stared at him then moved on. Ian scanned the suicide note, looked at the tree again. *Coincidence*. Except the sunbeam/bird acted as a memory toggle. Ghosts appeared on his conscious horizon, like images from a forgotten dream. *(XXX GIRLZ.)* He couldn't quite see them, and when he tried harder they vanished.

The clouds moved, shutting off the sunset. All afternoon had seen a resurgence of summer. Now autumn was back. As twilight came on, the park emptied. Ian folded his arms, hands tucked under his armpits, the sheet of printer paper crackling in his fist. A profound loneliness overcame him.

Suicide.

His mother lifeless in cold bath water twelve years ago. Zach's blood and brains sprayed across the hardwood floor of his condo as the stupid fish tank bubbled placidly. Ian hadn't actually seen his mother dead. She had taken pills that time. His father, months later, reported the detail of the cold bath water, and it had stuck with Ian like something he'd witnessed first hand. But even though he hadn't seen his mother dead Ian *had* been in the house when his father discovered the body. His father came out of the bathroom, his face ashen, and said, "She's dead." Ian had run out of the house, into the night, and didn't come back for almost two days. In some ways, he had never come back.

This is going to traumatize you, man. That's the point...

Fuck you, Zach.

IAN'S SISTER VANESSA practiced hypno-therapy in an office on Second Avenue in the Bell Town neighborhood of Seattle, just a couple of blocks north of the Pike Place Market. It was a tiny space, the glossy red door and brass shingle tucked between the Lava Lounge and the Suite 100 Gallery. Ian was not at all sure he wanted to talk to Ness. But she was the only person who might understand. As he pulled into the curb Vanessa was letting an old man out the door. The man wore a blue seersucker sport coat, gray slacks, and one of those foxy-old-man caps, like what Sean Connery would wear. Vanessa, fifteen years older than Ian, wore a knee-length red skirt and pearl gray blouse. She looked good. Ian hadn't seen her in well over a year. He killed the engine, removed his helmet, and shook his hair out. The seersucker guy said something to Vanessa.

"It's my brother," she said. "Hello there, Icky. Where have you been hiding?"

The seersucker guy nodded to him and walked away.

"All the usual places," Ian said. "Mostly under rocks. Can we talk? I'll buy you a drink."

"You're lucky you caught me," she said. "Let me lock up."

At The Pink Door, a funky Italian restaurant and bar in the Market, Vanessa ordered a green apple Martini. Ian had a bottle of Moretti, no glass. The bar was not too crowded yet. A waiter went around lighting candles in red glass cups on each of the tables.

"So how's everything going?" Ian said.

"Splendidly. Icky, what's wrong? I haven't heard from you in forever. You don't look well."

"Zach's dead."

"Your friend, the game guy? I'm so sorry."

"He killed himself this morning."

"Oh my God, Ian."

She reached across the table and touched his hand. He had to resist the urge to pull away from her. Generally, Ian didn't like to be touched, and it was especially true today.

"There's more," he said.

Vanessa withdrew her hand and sat back.

"Tell me."

Ian sighed, looked away, then said, "Nothing's what we think it is."

After a while, Vanessa said, "And...?"

He looked at her, cleared his throat, and plunged in. "This day is the same day, over and over again. It repeats. Endlessly. There's a bubble over the city. If you go outside the bubble you get trapped in some kind of limbo until the day starts over. That's what Zach believed. He wrote it all down in his suicide note."

Vanessa sipped her drink, never taking her eyes off Ian. She set her glass down. "Well. He must have been very disturbed."

"Maybe."

"What else could it be?"

"I don't know."

"Icky."

Ian slid his beer bottle around on the table top. "Some stuff has happened to me, some strange stuff."

Vanessa nodded slightly, her expression neutral.

"The thing is," he said, "I don't feel completely rational."

"What did your friend's note say?"

"I have it here." He took it out of his coat pocket and handed it to her.

"I'm surprised the police didn't want to keep this," Vanessa said.

"I took it with me before I called them."

"Icky, I doubt that's legal."

"I doubt it, too. But if the note's true, it doesn't matter. If the note's true, *nothing* matters. Anyway, the original is probably on Zach's hard drive."

Vanessa smoothed the crumpled paper out on the table top, put on her glasses and read it carefully. She removed her glasses and said:

"You believe this might be *true?*"

"Not in my mind I don't."

"Where else do you believe things?"

"Gut? I don't know. That sunbeam really did touch the third tree at exactly the minute the note said it would, and the crow jumped off and flew north. I'm just saying."

Vanessa sipped her green Martini.

"Look, I *don't* believe it," Ian said. "I think Zach must have been out of his mind. But after the crow flew I sat on that bench and sort of remembered things. Vaguely. I'm not even sure I saw what I saw. I don't know. Did the tree light up at that exact minute? You see what I mean? My mind feels slippery. But it always does. For instance, I know Mom overdosed. I know that. But I saw this movie once where a woman used a razor on her wrists. Since then I keep thinking of Mom that way. I even dreamed it. Like the real thing is mixed up in my head with fantasy. Then when Dad described her–" Ian choked up, paused, went on. "–described her in the cold bath, it's like I saw her myself. It's like a memory of seeing her."

Ian's hands were cold. He worked them together nervously, not meeting Vanessa's eyes.

"Ian," Vanessa said. "I think I understand."

"You do?"

"Yes."

She seemed a little cool all of a sudden. Ian felt confused.

"Anyway, I had this idea that maybe you could hypnotize me."

"Why would I do that?"

"I don't know, to find out something? Find out if I'm nuts, I guess."

"I see."

"What?"

"You're in Crazyland," Vanessa said. "So naturally you come to me. The expert. Otherwise you keep your distance. Like I'm a plague sister. It's all right, I do understand."

"Come on."

"Mom freaked you out, I had a breakdown, then Dad left as soon as you graduated high school. You didn't want to catch 'it' so you stayed away. Now you think you've caught 'it' anyway."

Ian blushed. "Something like that, I guess."

"Icky, I'm sorry. I don't want to be mean. But I could have used you around when they had me in that hospital. I felt like I didn't have anybody in the world. Dad visited but I could tell he was forcing himself. It was hard for him to accept that I was even in there."

"I'm a jerk."

"No, you aren't. You're a sweet man who went through something dreadful before you were mature enough to deal with it. At least I was an adult when Mom... died. And besides, I'm the jerk for complaining about you not visiting. You were just a kid. Dad probably wouldn't let you."

"He would have let me, I think. I was afraid to come. Maybe I should go back under my rock."

"You better not." Vanessa tossed down the last of her Martini and stood up, pulling her coat around her. "Come along, let's go have a look inside that head of yours, shall we?"

"We don't have to do this," Ian said.

"Poor Icky. Don't be afraid."

"I'm not afraid."

"Yes you are. But never mind."

Outside, Vanessa fished her car keys out and jingled them. "You follow me. I doubt you remember where I live."

"Can't we go to your office, Ness?"

"Of course. But you haven't been to my place in a long time. Afterwards I could make some dinner. And I have something I've been holding onto for when you turned up again."

"I think we better stay in the city."

"But– oh, yes. I forgot. If we leave the city we'll get stuck or disappear or something until tomorrow. I mean until the day starts again. Right?"

He nodded, embarrassed. It sounded ridiculous the way she stated it. It sounded ridiculous what*ever* way it was stated.

"Let's forget the whole thing," he said.

"No. You've got me curious."

Vanessa's office wasn't much bigger than a walk-in closet. A print of Van Gogh's *Starry Night* failed to transcend its mass-produced-image status. On another wall there hung a framed license or certificate. Ian slumped in the tan loveseat, far from relaxed. He tried to ignore the disagreeable scent of drugstore potpourri.

Vanessa dialed down the lights then pulled her chair close and sat facing him. Music from the Lava Lounge next door thumped through the wall.

"Have you ever been hypnotized?" she asked.

"Nope."

"Not everybody *can* be," she said. "But we'll see. Are you ready?"

"I guess so. I don't like losing control."

"You don't have to lose control, Icky. Take a few deep breaths, hold them here in your diaphragm."

She placed her hand flat on her own diaphragm to demonstrate.

"Good. Release slowly, and breathe again. As you're breathing I want you to imagine yourself in a safe place, a safe and peaceful place. It doesn't have to be a real place. It could be a garden of your imagination, or a quiet room. But in your mind fill the space with peace and light. And keep breathing and concentrating on your safe place, Ian. Make it as real as you can. Now begin to relax your body, start with your toes and work your way up until you are completely, blissfully, relaxed..."

Vanessa's voice soothed him past his initial resistance. Concentrating on it, he was able to shut out the Lava Lounge. After a while even her voice seemed to fade. He thought: *is this what it's like?* He felt that if he wanted to he could stand up at any time and it would be over, the spell broken. But he didn't want to; he wanted to stay in the room he'd made, the peaceful place of rose colored walls, rounded smooth, no sharp corners, a fire in the deep hearth, and round hobbit windows looking out on blue sky. Was he describing this to Ness? Now he didn't seem to be hearing any words at all. He was in the rose colored room gazing at a fire, watching the flames, listening to their soft crackle as they consumed a log. There was a door behind him. He couldn't see it yet, but he knew it was there. In a moment he would stand up and turn around and open it. The moment arrived. He stood, turned, and approached the door. Above the lintel was a gold plate engraved with the word: TOMORROW. Ian opened the door. White emptiness lay beyond. Suddenly his peaceful feeling evaporated. Light dimmed and the room became cold. The crackle of the fire ceased. Ian was afraid to turn around. The great white emptiness yawned before him on the other side of the TOMORROW door. He could neither go forward nor turn back. Then the world began to dissolve around him.

IAN FOUND HIMSELF walking down the hallway outside his apartment, his mind blank. Seconds passed. He didn't feel fully connected. It was like riding inside an automaton, watching as it withdrew a ring of keys from its pocket and slotted one into the apartment door. When it turned the key over, Ian entered fully into himself and felt the key between his thumb and finger. He crossed the threshold then fell back against the door, panting, slamming the door shut behind him. He had no memory of anything happening after his safe place dissolved. "Jesus Christ," he said, almost sobbing.

The apartment was dark. He fumbled for the wall switch, and the furnishings leapt out of the dark, dead things briefly animated by sudden illumination. Ian touched his forehead, which was damp with cold sweat. He got his cell phone out and searched for Vanessa's number, found it and called her. She picked up after a couple of rings. "Hello?"

"It's me."

"Icky, are you all right?"

"I don't know."

"I was worried when you left."

"Ness, I don't remember *anything*, except you hypnotized me. What happened?"

"That's very strange," she said. "We talked for quite a while after I brought you out of the trance. You seemed distracted, but you *must* remember. Hold on a minute, I have to switch lanes."

"You're driving?"

"Yes, just hitting the Aurora Bridge."

Ian could hear the car, Vanessa's radio turned to a jazz station, KPLU probably. A low surge of static occurred on the phone connection, so brief he almost didn't notice it. Ian flashed on the time he and Zach crossed the bridge in the VW, panic-accelerating to get away from the city, how right before they reached the far side the car had begun to shudder. The end of the bridge must be at the outer boundary of the bubble. And Vanessa had just crossed it.

"Okay, Icky, go ahead."

Ian turned the phone off. It wasn't her anymore.

DRIFTER

BENEATH THE CITY the Curator reverted to his deep space soma and oozed through a complex network of tunnels. Bioelectrical impulses shimmered over his body. He projected outward to the Cloud, but encountered only void. He tried again, increasing his intention, straining.

And failed.

The Preservation appeared to function as others had. His Lensing ability was intact. He could effect whatever changes in the city he desired, he could manufacture Shadow camouflage in which to hide from the Hunters. But he was no longer himself, a light in the Cloudmind. He felt more akin to Charles Noble than he did to either his old star-dwelling soma or the Cloud.

The Curator expelled himself into Elliott Bay to drift in the salty cold water and contemplate the situation. Jellyfish floated around like immature versions of himself.

He regarded them. Natural evolution suggested greater complexity, not simplification toward a rudimentary state. Had he naturally evolved into this expression, this perfect body for extended life in deep space, prior to his final transphysical evolution and joining with the Cloud? Or had he been made this way deliberately?

What was he before?

It had never occurred to him to ask such a question of himself. Perhaps because he had never before been so abandoned.

But having asked it, he must answer it: No. The Cloud had discovered his race, recognized the evolutionary potential, and so began the long... adjustments. Just as the Cloud had begun the long adjustments on the human race.

Before the Hunters intervened.

CHAPTER TEN

THEY CAME IN the night while Billy was sleeping in the basement.

Kylie sat upstairs with her mother. The house dated from the 1950s. In a time before Kylie's memories jelled, her father had put a lot of effort into eradicating the 50s feel. He had torn out the funky stone fireplace, for instance, and replaced it with marble facing and a heat-efficient glass front. He took down all the old light fixtures and installed modern, if cheap, replacements from Home Depot. All that was before the marriage disintegrated. It wasn't so easy to renovate a wife, Kylie supposed. Maggie kept the house spotless, even now. Every week she laboriously vacuumed the wall-to-wall carpeting, using a non-electric carpet sweeper. She was getting sicker, though; she wouldn't be able to keep that up.

Maggie was showing Kylie the album of old

photographs. The room pulsed with the light of homemade candles.

"See," Maggie said, tapping a picture with her finger. "Your grandparents."

"Uh huh."

Kylie had seen the pictures many times. This one showed a sixty-something couple standing in front of a yellow frame house. The man was wearing a bulky white sweater, the woman's sweater was red cable knit. They looked happy. There was a pattern of sunlight and shade on the side of the house. Flame colored leaves lay scattered over the lawn.

"That's their house," Maggie said. Maggie was only forty-five but looked old, her hair gray and stringy, pouches under her eyes and the eyes seeping with the telltale discharge; she was sick and getting sicker. The people in the picture looked younger, more alive.

"I know," Kylie said.

"In Seattle," Maggie said.

"I–"

Maggie closed the album. Kylie had told her mother what Billy said.

"I pray to God what he told you isn't true," Maggie said. "The thought of your grandparents being kept like zoo animals, it's sickening."

"It might not be real people under the Dome," Kylie said.

"Well, pray they're not."

"Mom, have you ever seen the Dome?"

"No."

"Do you ever think about... leaving Oakdale?"

"Leaving? I guess I'd have to be out of my mind to do something like that."

117

"Don't you ever wonder what it's like?"

"I already know what it's like. It's like nothing good. It's death and more death, and chaos."

"But that doesn't–"

Maggie touched her knee and said: "We're as safe as we can be, right here in Oakdale. There's *structure* here, and a leader."

"Father Jim? He tried to kill Billy and wants to *cut* me."

Maggie looked down, her hand still on Kylie's knee. After a moment she looked up again, and there was flinty determination in her eyes. Kylie had seen that look before, right after The Judgment, when even Oakdale was full of death and chaos instead of just death. *We're going to live*, Maggie had said. *You* believe *that, baby*.

Now Maggie took her daughter's hand and squeezed it hard. "Things aren't always easy, honey. You know that. It wasn't easy when your father left us. It wasn't easy after The Judgment. But we overcame what we had to overcome. You always trusted me to make the right choices, didn't you?"

Confused, Kylie nodded, "Yeah, I guess so. But what–"

"Shush now, baby. Something unpleasant is going to happen, but it's necessary."

"What? What's going to happen?"

"Everybody knows about you, Kylie. They know you're different. Do you understand how dangerous that is? There are people in this town who would kill you for it."

"I won't let them."

"Honey, if enough of them try, you won't be able to stop them and neither will I or even your Billy. They will come for you because they're superstitious and they believe in the Judgment and they believe in Father Jim."

"They won't get me if I go away with Billy, like he said."

"Put that idea out of your mind."

"But–"

"Put it out. You couldn't survive."

"Then what am I supposed to *do?*"

"There is something we can do. Father Jim is right. He might be right for the wrong reasons, but he's right. What everyone has to have is a ritual, like the Church used to provide. A sacrament. The wafer, the wine, the confessional, absolution to take away your sins."

"I haven't sinned," Kylie said.

"Rituals to put in order what's out of order."

"You want to let him *cut* me?"

"All I want is for you to live."

The door to one of the bedrooms opened and someone walked down the hall, stepping heavily. Kylie thought it must be Billy, except that didn't make sense, since Billy was in the basement and never came upstairs. When Father Jim appeared, Kylie jumped up. Her mother, still holding onto her, stood also.

"There's my little co-pilot," Father Jim said.

"Some more time," Maggie said.

Father Jim was carrying a small black bag, like a doctor's bag. His right eye was clouded red. It looked like the eye of a bear. His big shoulders sagged. He said, "My lambs are lost," which made no obvious sense to Kylie.

"Mommy," she said.

"I'm sorry, honey, it has to be."

Kylie twisted and pulled on her hand to get free, but Maggie's bony grip was like steel.

"Show her the children," Father Jim said. "They're outside now."

"Billy!"

"The children are gathered in the street," Father Jim said. "Show her, Maggie."

"I... I've changed my mind," Maggie said.

"It's too late for that," Father Jim said.

Kylie wrenched loose and ran to the big window and pushed the curtain aside. A silent mob filled the street in front of the house, a number of its members holding burning torches. It was the entire remaining population of Oakdale, under a hundred people. At the sight of Kylie they surged forward.

Father Jim lurched to the front door and threw it open. He stood before them on the porch. They stopped. He removed his hat.

"Hear me! The Lord hath given me a third eye through which to receive his visions. I require two children to help me complete the ritual of purification." He pointed. "You and you."

Ray Preston and another, beefier, man came up the steps and into the house, preceded by Father Jim. The bullet hole in the priest's head was leaking, the flesh around it proud. Kylie tried to break for the back door but the heavier man ran ahead of Ray Preston and caught her from behind and held her arms pinned against her body, his hands locked in a wrestler's hold around her waist.

"Let me go! Billy!"

"Don't hurt her," Maggie said.

"They're going to *cut* me," Kylie said.

"Please don't hurt her," Maggie said. "I've changed my mind. She's a good girl, a good girl."

Father Jim pushed Maggie aside and stood before Kylie. He spoke to Preston without taking his eyes off

Kylie. "Raymond, go to the basement. Billy's there. See that he doesn't interrupt us."

Preston headed for the stairs.

Father Jim produced a rag and a glass bottle from his doctor's bag. Watery, mustard colored fluid seeped from the hole in his forehead. It *did* look infected. Did he use his scalpel to keep it open? Kylie struggled harder to get free. Father Jim touched his finger to the fluid.

"God weeps at your impurity," he said. He uncapped the bottle. Kylie and the man holding her reacted to the smell, coughing, turning their faces away.

"*My* impurity, what about your impurity what about when–"

Jim slapped her so hard she saw stars.

"When God expelled Adam and Eve from Paradise," he said, "Eve began to bleed. And so the world was stained."

Kylie lifted her chin and glared at him.

"This will make you sleep," Father Jim said.

"Don't," Kylie said. "No."

She struggled helplessly. Maggie grabbed at the priest's arm. "I've changed my *mind*," she said.

The man holding Kylie said, "We're gonna make her right."

"Mommy!"

Father Jim saturated the rag and pushed it into Kylie's face. She held her breath and jerked her head violently side to side. But the fumes pried into her brain and the world began to soften and blur around the edges. She saw Billy, then, but was he real or just a desperate picture in her mind? He was holding a gun, the big revolver, and Ray Preston was walking ahead of him. Billy spoke in a loud voice that made Father Jim turn around. The man holding Kylie released her.

Kylie discovered that her legs were now made of rubber. They would not support her, and she folded down to the floor and sat there, the chemical stink infiltrating her. Billy was talking, but the words didn't seem to connect to any meaning.

"–over here," he said, maybe.

She crawled to him, her head pounding. Up close, she noticed the toes of his boots were scuffed. He touched her head. He kept asking her questions and arguing with the three men. Kylie concentrated until the words came together in proper order.

"Can you stand?" he said.

"Uh huh."

She got one foot under her, pitched forward, tried again. After a while she was upright. It felt like she was very high off the ground, swaying on stilts, her fuzzy head wobbling on top of her neck.

Billy waved the gun at the men. "You three sit on the sofa."

They sat shoulder-to-shoulder, Father Jim in the middle, and stared at Billy.

"Okay, Jim, hold that rag over his face." With the barrel of the gun Billy indicated the wrestler. Father Jim did as instructed, and the man slumped, unconscious. "Now Ray," Billy said, pointing the gun at Preston, who appeared scared and ready to try something.

"Come on," Ray said, "we can jump him."

Father Jim shook his head. "Don't be afraid."

"If you let us have guns this wouldn't even happen," Ray said, and then Father Jim pressed the chemical-soaked rag to face. Ray held his breath. Jim stroked his head with his free hand. "It's all right, Raymond." After a moment, Ray sighed and slumped over.

"Your turn," Billy said.

Father Jim set the bottle and rag on the coffee table and stared at him. Billy rubbed his temple, pressing his fingertips in hard. Kylie thought he looked on the verge of fainting. "Maggie," he said, "soak that rag again and hand it to me."

"Oh, I couldn't," Maggie said.

"If you don't, I might have to shoot Jim, and *this* gun makes bigger holes than the other one."

Maggie hesitated, then stepped forward, quickly grabbed the stinky rag, upended the bottle into it, then handed the rag to Billy.

Father Jim looked at her and said, "Eve became a vile thing, and Man was lost."

"Shut up," Billy said. He slipped behind the sofa and moved in close, pressing the barrel of the revolver to the side of Father Jim's head. "Don't move." With his other hand he held the rag tight over the priest's mouth and nose. Father Jim stiffened, and for a moment Billy thought it wasn't going to work, that somehow Father Jim could resist the fumes. Billy's finger tensed on the trigger, but Jim finally went limp, and when Billy removed the rag, the priest slumped against Ray Preston and began to snore.

Billy used his shirt sleeve to blot the sweat from his face. "We have to go now."

"Okay," Kylie said.

"Maggie?" Billy said.

She shook her head. "I can't."

"You have no idea what that lunatic will do when he wakes up. You better come with us."

Maggie looked at the snoring Father Jim. "What if he's right?"

"Right about *what?*"

"Everything. The Judgment. God. How do we *know* he's not?"

"Come with us, Mom." Kylie was crying. "Please come with us."

Maggie was crying, too. "You go. You have to now," Maggie said. "I can give you time. If they come to the door, I can tell them it isn't over yet and Jim wants them to wait."

"You're better off coming with us," Billy said.

Maggie shook her head.

Kylie felt sick and dizzy. It was the fumes, but it was also her mother. Billy started to say something, but Kylie interrupted him. "Wait," she said and stumbled to the coffee table. She opened the photo album, flipped over the big clear plastic pages, stopped at one, and took a single photograph from its sleeve. Maggie watched her, tears shining in her eyes. "My baby girl."

Kylie hugged her fiercely, felt her mother's sobs shuddering through the older woman's body. Finally, Billy pulled Kylie away.

They left by the back door and made their way through yards, vacant lots, and the rubble of destruction. Billy could only go a short way before he had to stop and rest. After a couple of minutes they continued. The night sky threatened rain.

"They'll get us," Kylie said. "Won't they."

Billy shook his head. "Nobody will follow us out of town – at least, I doubt they'll follow us very far. For one thing, they'll be on foot, but we won't. And they're afraid."

They arrived at Billy's house. "Help me open the garage," he said. "Hurry."

The night air had cleared her head a little. She helped him shove the garage door up on its tracks, springs squealing. A big Honda motorcycle – a Goldwing – stood on its kickstand in the middle of the floor. The bike had storage compartments and tandem seats. It even had a rifle in a scabbard attached to the side, as if it were a *horse*. "Get on," Billy said. She swung her leg over the rear saddle. Billy got on in front of her.

"I didn't even know this was here," Kylie said.

"I've kept it packed and ready," Billy said over his shoulder. "I knew I'd have to get us out of here eventually. I was stupid to wait so long."

He turned the key and the bike rumbled to life.

They rolled down the driveway and into the street, where he paused, letting the engine idle. "Okay, here we go," he said.

She circled her arms around his big waist. He worked the throttle, took the bike out to Main Street.

The street was filled with people, many of them holding burning torches, axes, knives – and Father Jim's signature corrective action tool: baseball bats. No guns, though. Jim had outlawed them.

A brilliant white flash crossed the sky, followed by a deep rumble.

Billy drew up short, facing the mob. A man in overalls, with a Jim-style Louisville slugger in his fist, pointed the bat at them. There they are!"

"Hold on," Billy said.

Kylie pressed against Billy's leather clad back and held on with all her strength. The heavy bike lurched forward.

CHAPTER ELEVEN

IAN THUMBED HIS sister's number again, but before it could start ringing he turned the phone off and tossed it on the chair. He felt with absolute certainty that if the call was answered at all it wouldn't be by Vanessa. The thing answering might *sound* like her, might reply in roughly the way he would expect Ness to reply. But it wouldn't be her.

"I'd be talking to myself," he said to the empty apartment. "Which is crazy."

Ian switched on every light, the docked iPod, the television, filled the apartment with light and sound. He didn't want to be alone, but there was no one to call. Zach had been his only close friend. And how weird was that, to be twenty-two years old and not have even one close friend other than the guy who just killed himself?

For that matter, did he *really* believe his sister wasn't his sister, or was he just afraid of the connection?

He sat at his desk and pulled Zach's crumpled suicide letter out of his pocket. Ian had been messing around with a Dell Notebook he bought for twenty bucks at Value Village. He could figure out any mechanism, taking devices apart and putting them back together again in working order. Half the time he didn't even know what he was doing. It was some kind of intuitive genius, Zach had told him, and asked, "Why the fuck are you working in a kitchen, man?"

Ian shoved the Notebook aside and spread the suicide letter flat. He could decipher any mechanism, but he couldn't decipher the meaning of this death, or of himself, or even figure out what this day meant to him, minute by minute.

He read the letter again. "You crazy asshole." Ian wiped his eyes roughly. "*Why?*" Unable to stand himself, Ian grabbed his phone off the chair, turned it on, and called Vanessa one more time. It went to voicemail, which didn't mean anything. He left a message to call him back, texted the same thing, and closed the phone. A weird idea lurched drunkenly in front of him, grabbed him by the shoulders and shook him:

What if Zach wasn't dead?

"He's dead, all right," Ian said.

Audioslave tore out of the iPod, TV people barked at each other.

But really. What if Zach wasn't dead? What if Ian hadn't seen his body at all? The whole day had felt surreal. And Ian hadn't been right in a long time. He had drifted further and further into estrangement, to the point where even going to his crappy restaurant job was an effort. What if this whole day was some kind of *Twilight Zone* dream or hallucination? There was obvious precedent. It wasn't that long ago that Vanessa had been lost in her own delusions. It required some powerful meds to balance out the chemical equation in her head. And his mother had been delusional when she killed herself. She must have been. Maybe the nut *didn't* fall far from the nut tree. It's what he'd always feared.

Ian turned the sound off on the TV, dialed the music low but left it on, and waited for his sister to call back. If she didn't call back that would be significant. Or it wouldn't be. After a while he got up for a beer. There wasn't any. He thought about going down the street to buy some but couldn't bring himself to do it. Saturday night on Capitol Hill, all those people out there. On bad days (and what day was badder than this one?) the world seemed populated with automatons. A society from which he felt mortally separated. Or maybe *he* was the robot. Like the way he felt out in the hall after Ness hypnotized him. On bad days, on *particularly* bad days, the world fractured into puzzle pieces that he couldn't rationally arrange into a picture that made sense. He thought of Zach holed up in his condo with paranoid suicidal delusions. Was he, Ian, going the same route?

He stood abruptly and started pacing; he needed to get *out* of himself.

In the kitchen he ransacked the cupboards until he found the bottle of white Zinfandel he'd bought months ago to share with Sarah. They had never opened it. Now Ian held the bottle in his hands like a dead baby. Tears seeped from his eyes. He put the bottle down hard on the counter. He needed to be out of himself, but he didn't really want to be drunk.

His black canvas backpack slumped in a corner of the closet. He grabbed it by a strap, spray cans clunking together, slung the pack over his shoulder and bombed out of the apartment.

On the sidewalk he ran. Saturday night and there were too many people. Ian ran as if he could leave the fearful part of himself behind.

They were going to tear down the old Greek Orthodox church on 17th. There was still some white space begging for WHO. But standing before the wall he encountered another Wall. He was standing still but he was still running. Maybe it had always been that way. But before, it hadn't mattered. Before he hadn't known it was running – running from the body in the tub, from his old man in the garage with his beer and tools and distance. From *himself*.

So do the wall or don't do the fucking wall.

Ian hunkered over his backpack and unzipped it. His mind wouldn't stop talking to him; he couldn't see what he was supposed to paint. Slowly, he drew the zipper closed again. Graffiti was just sex misspelled. If you couldn't do it without thinking, then you couldn't do it.

ZINFANDEL SLOPPED OVER the top of a water glass. He slurped down enough to make it safe to carry. On the bed, back propped against the wall, he watched TV and didn't think. He drank, though – the entire bottle. It took that much to blur the picture in his head of Zach's head-blown body. And even then it wasn't blurred enough.

He stumbled to the closet, rummaged a handful of markers from his backpack and began writing on the wall beside his bed. It was crap. He killed the TV and continued making crap on the wall. Rain blew against the window. Ian lay on his side, writing, shaping his paranoia, and the rain entered into his mind...

HOT WATER POURED into a Melitta filter, raising steam. Ian watched himself set the kettle down on the stove. His movements were mechanical, halting. Ian *pushed* and he came forward, and the floating part became like a dream fragment.

The coffee smelled good, but Ian felt deeply depressed and didn't even know how he'd managed to crawl out of bed. In fact, he couldn't remember doing it. He dumped the used filter into the trash, added cream to his coffee, and took it into the living space.

He stopped when he saw the pill bottles arrayed on the bedside table.

Seconal, Halcion, Xanax. What the *hell* were they doing out? He tried to remember but could not. A throbbing ache started behind his right eye. He reached to pick up the bottles then left them.

At his desk he sat heavily. Riding three hundred miles to Pullman seemed like an impossible effort to make – physically and mentally. He looked back at his unmade bed – and for a moment, a single beat, he thought he saw *himself* sprawled half off the mattress, his skin death-gray.

He stood up, his body clenching with fear. Willing himself to calm down, he grabbed the phone, held it in his fist a few moments, then put it down again. God, he was tired. He felt drugged. The sleeping pill bottles stood on the bedside table. *Had* he taken the pills? If he had he wouldn't be standing here wondering about it; he'd be dead asleep – or just dead.

Last night, though, knowing he *must* sleep if he was going to be rested enough to drive all the way across the state at such an early hour, he had intended to take two Xanax. Just two. The prescriptions were his 'escape kit', kind of a joke, but not a funny one. He had been collecting the contents of his escape kit over the last year, mostly buying the prescriptions online, where it seemed possible to buy *anything*, legal or not. Nembutal, Seconal, Halcion, Xanax. These were the brands his mother had tried, and a combination of which had killed her. After her death Ian's father had flushed the remaining pills and thrown the empty prescription containers in the trash. Ian had retrieved them. He kept the empty containers for years, setting them on his bookshelf or window sill, like plastic bad luck icons.

Just two Xanax. Intention is everything, though; he brought three full prescription bottles to his bedside.

Ian stood up and went to the window. His dad's Indian Chief sat wheel-cocked in the alley. Maybe if he got on the damn thing it would revive him. There's no way he could skip Pullman, especially without calling. It would be like telling Sarah *outright* that he couldn't keep seeing her. He thought of the inevitable confrontation after his no-show. It might take place on the phone or in person, probably both. It filled him with anxiety. He didn't want to let Sarah go, but he knew he couldn't go forward with the relationship. He had never gone forward.

He sat on the edge of the bed, his mind in shutdown mode. Fucking sleeping pills. Despite the well-provisioned 'escape kit', Ian had never taken even one pill, not even the over-the-counter variety. He had always been afraid to. But last night... last night...

His cell phone started shrilling. Ian reached for it then stopped.

It rang seven times and ceased. A minute later it started ringing again. Ian looked at the caller ID and saw it was Zach. Which made zero sense at seven o'clock on a Saturday morning. Text messages started blooping in. Ian ignored them, switched the phone to silent mode and went back to bed. At some point the intercom buzzed repeatedly, a wasp stitching through his twilight consciousness.

He woke up, or came to, or whatever, and his mouth was dry as shoe leather. Shadows occupied the room. Blocky furniture squatted silently. Pictures too dim to be seen, dead lamps. His only window faced south, and after the sun traveled past two o'clock his apartment was stranded.

Ian made a face at the clock. Almost five pm. He had slept all day. Suddenly he wanted to get outside. Irrationally, he thought if he didn't go out now he might *never* go out again. He rinsed his mouth in the bathroom sink, splashed cold water on his face, threw on a sweatshirt and leather jacket and left every light in his apartment burning so it wouldn't be dark when he returned.

As he stepped out the front door of the building he looked at the sky, searching for something he couldn't remember. He slid his phone out, turned it on. There were like ten text messages from Zach. Instead of reading them he thumbed RETURN CALL on one of the missed incoming. It started to ring – and across the street the tinny theme from *Bonanza* began to play. Zach answered.

"Hello?" Ian said.

"Hello yourself. I see you."

"What?"

"I'm over here, in the park."

Across the street a figure on a bench stood up and started waving.

CHAPTER TWELVE

BILLY RAN THE big Honda Goldwing at the mob. They completely blocked the street and the dead lawns on either side. Those with torches held them high. Kylie, her arms tight around Billy's waist, watched over his shoulder. The mob *had* to give way.

But they didn't.

In fact, they did the opposite. The man who had pointed at them with the baseball bat yelled and charged *towards* the oncoming motorcycle. It was Ralph DeVris. He used to own the town's only movie theater, the Olympic Regal Cinema, a place in which Kylie had spent many hours. It was only open Friday and Saturday nights. Kylie had known Mr. DeVris her whole life. His wife died of breast cancer two years before The Judgment. He had soldiered on, for the sake of his nine-year-old daughter, Sandy. At the Olympic Regal Ralph DeVris had always been a one man band:

ticket-seller, popcorn and Coke slinger, projectionist. You had to buy your snacks before the movie, since the concession closed five minutes prior to show time, so Mr. DeVris could run up the stairs in his trademark hillbilly overalls and start the projector. After his wife's death he started bringing Sandy to the theater. She became the ticket-taker and kept the concession open an extra half hour, just in case, before joining her dad in the projection booth. After the first year of his wife's death, he seemed to finally come back to life a little.

Then the Judgment's shockwave rocked the Olympic Regal off its foundation, crushing Sandy DeVris under a collapsed roof.

And now Ralph DeVris was pounding down the middle of Main Street with a baseball bat in both hands, yelling, "Get them!"

And the mob of dying towns' people surged after him.

Billy turned the bike at the last moment, leaning and accelerating at the same time. DeVris swung his bat and caught the Goldwing's taillight, smashing it off the bike's rear fender. Kylie screamed, craned her head around to see. At the same moment Billy cranked the throttle and the sudden acceleration nearly unsaddled her. She adjusted her hold on Billy's waist and watched the angry mob recede.

Billy took them around the block. His headlamp burned a path down the deserted street. He slowed the bike, yelled to Kylie over his shoulder, above the roar of the powerful engine. "I'm going to try an end run, get behind them, then straight out to the state highway, or whatever's left of it."

"What's an end run?"

"Fuck, I don't know. It's a football thing. Kylie, listen. There will be the usual guards at the end of Main Street.

We're going through them, no matter what. Even if I have to shoot."

Another sheet of lightning ripped across the sky. Revealed in the stark flash, a dozen townspeople poured between the ruins of a couple of tract houses, making for the street to head them off.

Billy goosed the throttle.

One young man, gaunt with post-apocalyptic flu or whatever it was, angled straight for them, ahead of the others, his eyes wild and mouth opened wide, screaming something. He was going to reach them. All that in the instant of the lightning flash before they were plunged back into darkness and the narrow fan cast by the Goldwing's headlamp.

Thunder rolled over them like an iron drum. The bike accelerated and Kylie held on. The man was right there, grabbing the handlebar. The bike veered violently and went down. Kylie rolled into the street. She immediately got up – and someone grabbed her arms from behind.

"Got you, you horny little cunt," a man said right next to her ear, his breath like rancid eggs.

"*Get off me,*" Kylie said, trying to twist free.

The Goldwing's engine was still running and Billy's leg was pinned under the heavy bike. The rest of the mob approached, bringing their torchlight. Ralph DeVris, baseball bat loose in his left fist, walked up to the bike. Billy was trying to get the rifle out of its scabbard. DeVris bent over and slapped his hand back. "None of that," he said, then turned the ignition key back and killed the engine. "Come on, boys, help me move this thing offen him."

Two more men stepped forward and together with DeVris they lifted the Goldwing off Billy, waited for him to scoot out, then dropped it. Even though the engine was off, the headlamp continued to burn. DeVris swung his bat casually into it. "No machines," he said

"Do you even know how stupid that is?" Billy said.

One of the young men slugged him and Billy doubled over. "Do you even know how stupid *you* are," the man said. He wasn't that much older than Kylie. His name was Derrek Goetzinger. She remembered him being a senior when she was a sophomore at Oakdale High. It seemed like a million years ago. Suddenly furious, Kylie drove the heel of her shoe into her captor's shin, wrenched loose and ran to Billy. "You asshole! I know you, Derrek Goetzinger."

"You don't know shit."

DeVris stepped between them. "Back off," he said to Goetzinger. "We're not hoodlums. Leave their junk here and bring them along. We're locking them up, just like we said, until Father Jim comes around."

THEY LOCKED KYLIE and Billy in the basement furnace room of the Presbyterian church and posted Derrek Goetzinger outside as guard – a job Derrek was less than thrilled about. "What am I supposed to do if it rains?" When the Judgment struck, the steeple had fallen, taking out the roof and part of the floor, exposing the basement. But the furnace room was intact and made a secure holding cell. DeVris handed him an umbrella. "Stay dry." He gave Billy and Kylie one homemade candle and a couple of matches, then pushed the heavy fire-resistant door shut, sealing them in. The air tasted rusty and dry. Kylie immediately wanted a drink of water. She scratched one of the stick matches on the cement floor and put the flame to the candle wick then sat on a bench next to Billy, their backs to the wall.

"How long before Father Jim wakes up, do you think?" she asked.

"A while. I don't know."

"Does your head hurt a lot?"

"Like murder. I'm sorry, Kylie. I really blew it."

"No you didn't either."

"Yeah, I did."

"Maybe a little."

He looked up, smiling in a pained way. "You aren't supposed to *agree* with me. Geeze."

They were quiet a minute, then Kylie said, "I won't let him cut me."

"When they open the door I'll rush them, maybe you can make a break for it."

"That won't work. You're not even very good at walking yet."

"I might feel better by the time they come."

"Don't worry, Billy. I'm not going to let him cut me." Kylie reached down and pulled something out of her boot.

The toy-sized automatic.

"You had that the whole time, even at your mother's?"

"You *told* me to keep it with me. But I was afraid when I saw Jim, and then I never had a chance to get it out. Then you rescued me."

"Some rescue."

"It's okay, Billy." She leaned against him and closed her eyes. His breathing was rough. The heat of fever radiated from him. The sound of rain began rattling on the ceiling. After what seemed like a long time there was a heavy, metallic clunk as someone lifted the fire-door's latch. Kylie stood up, holding the automatic behind her back. The door swung out heavily on creaking hinges. Goetzinger stood in the rain gripping a Coleman lantern in one hand and the open umbrella in the other. The ragged umbrella was purple with a pattern of dancing Disney-esque elephants. A broken rib poked out like a bone from a torn wing.

Kylie pointed the gun at him. "We're leaving," she said.

Goetzinger spat. "I know that."

He stepped into the furnace room, and Maggie moved into view holding a butcher knife pointed at his back.

"Mom!"

She was dripping wet, hair plastered to her head.

Kylie ran to her mother and hugged her. "What are you doing here?"

"Like I said to Jim: I changed my mind. You two better get out of here now, before the others come back. Unless you're planning to shoot everybody with your pop gun."

"What you all are doing is getting yourselves in a world of hurt," Goetzinger said.

"You shut up," Billy said.

"Yeah, shut up." Kylie poked the gun at him. "Get over there against that wall."

Goetzinger did as he was told. Billy relieved him of the lantern Goetzinger leaned against the wall and twirled his broken umbrella. Kylie and Maggie shoved the door shut and dropped the latch.

"Did they hurt you, Mom?"

"Of course they didn't. Who would hurt me?"

"Your friends and neighbors," Billy said.

"You're coming with us this time, right?" Kylie said.

"On your motorcycle? I don't think so. Where would I sit? Your boyfriend knew all along I wasn't coming."

Kylie looked at Billy. "That isn't true! You said you wanted her to come. You said it. Why couldn't we drive a car instead?"

"The road's messed up pretty bad," Billy said. "Remember, I walked here. Car wouldn't make it two miles. Even the Goldwing might not make it all the way to Bremerton."

"But–"

Kylie's mom took her hand. "Honey, I'm real sick. Even if we had a car, it wouldn't do me any good to go with you. I don't *want* to go. I don't have the stamina for it. I have a plan for when it gets too much to bear. In the meantime, I just want to be home. Now come on, while it's still raining."

They walked back to the street where Goetzinger had forced Billy to dump the bike. The motorcycle was still there, key in the ignition. "Thank God for godless machines," Billy said. The three of them pushed it up on its wheels. Billy got on. Kylie hugged her mother as hard as she could, and Maggie held her and patted the back of her head.

"Mom, I'm so scared they'll do something to you for helping us." Kylie was crying again.

"They won't, honey. It's just what your boyfriend said, only not the way he said it. They *are* my friends and neighbors – what's left of them. I guess the last of us will die together right here in Oakdale, where we spent our lives. You go now, baby. Go."

Billy keyed the ignition and after a worrisome hesitation the big Honda rumbled into life. Kylie reluctantly let go of her mother and straddled the rear saddle.

"I love you," Maggie said.

"I love you, Mom."

Billy cranked the throttle and the bike accelerated down the street. Kylie looked back as her mother receded, a lone figure with a lantern in dark, steady rain, waiting for her friends and neighbors.

CHAPTER THIRTEEN

SEATTLE, OCTOBER 5, 2012

IAN CLOSED HIS cell, crossed into the park and stood in front of Zach, who had resumed his seat on the bench. He looked shrunken in his olive drab duffel coat. Suddenly Ian felt on the brink of tears.

"I knew you were in there," Zach said. "I can always tell, because the times you don't try to go out of town your bike is parked in the alley. You keep saying how you hate the thing, but you always ride it."

Ian cleared his throat. "I was supposed to visit Sarah, but I couldn't go. I felt sick this morning. I felt really sick."

"What kind of sick?"

"I don't know." Ian sat next to Zach and balled his hands in his pockets. The sunset was failing.

"You missed the bird," Zach said.

"What bird?"

"You know what I'm talking about. Come on, man."

"You're acting weirder than usual."

"What the hell are you grinning about?" Zach said.

"I don't know. I'm–" Emotion rose up in his chest and Ian had to wait a moment. When he could do it without his voice cracking he said, "I'm really glad to see you. I mean I'm glad you're all right."

"Why wouldn't I be all right?" Zach leaned toward him. "Tell me why you think I wouldn't be all right."

"I don't know."

"Think."

"About *what?*"

Zach slumped. "You don't remember. You don't remember what I did, you don't even remember the fucking bird."

In Ian's mind, the top of a tree lit up as if by a stage light and a crow jumped into the air.

The bird.

"What?" Zach said.

"I remember the bird. I think."

"All *right.*" Zach slapped his shoulder. "You're the man."

"But I don't–"

"Never mind the bird. Keep going with the other thing. I can see you're all emotional. Why do you think that is?"

"I don't *know.* I'm depressed or something. All day I've felt exhausted. You seem to know what's going on; why don't you just tell me?"

"I could do that, but you wouldn't believe me. Not if I just *tell* you. But if I do it like a Socratic thing, ask you questions until you remember that you already know what I know you know, that might work."

Ian rolled his eyes. "First of all, you don't know shit about Socrates."

"You're too stubborn, is the problem."

"Let me ask you a question," Ian said.

"Go ahead."

Inside Ian's head the crow kept jumping from the lit-up tree branch. A brief film loop imprinted on his memory.

"How do you make the fucking bird *stop*?"

"By remembering something else."

"Like–?"

Zach pursed his lips, thinking. "The Boogeyman?"

Ian looked blankly at him.

"Fuck's sake," Zach said. "I killed myself practically right in front of you, don't you remember *that*? How can you remember the bird but not me killing myself?"

"That isn't funny."

"I'm not trying to be funny. I'm telling you I killed myself and now I'm back having this idiotic conversation with you. And you know what, man? I'm starting to think this is Hell." His voice cracked on the word and tears spilled down Zach's cheeks, startling Ian. At the same time Zach started laughing.

"What's funny?

"We are. We are both so fucked, and you don't even know it, and I probably won't either next time we come back. I mean, *God damn*."

Zach stood up and started dancing around in a circle, waving his hands over his head like a crazy person. A homeless guy wrapped in a filthy sleeping bag on a nearby bench stared at him.

"Around and around and around," Zach sang.

"Around and around!" the homeless guy yelled.

"What's wrong with you?" Ian said. "Knock it off."

Zach stopped. He was out of breath but not from

dancing. "Even killing yourself doesn't set you free. Even *killing yourself*."

"Za–"

The top of Zach's head blew open like a New Years Eve popper, skull fragments spinning in bloody mist.

Repeat.

Ian shut his eyes and tried to shut his mind, too. But the head-popper replayed until the image refined and resolved into a real memory of Zach laid out on the floor of his condo with an 1870's Colt revolver in his mouth and an envelope taped to his chest. IAN READ THIS RIGHT NOW.

Ian opened his eyes.

"I found you dead," he said. "I did." The rational world tilted. Involuntarily, Ian pressed his feet down hard on the ground and clenched his jaw. He started searching his pockets for Zach's suicide letter but found nothing beyond his wallet, keys and a half-empty tin of Altoids. Where is it, he thought, where the fuck is it? Memories surged over the rim of his conscious mind.

"It's okay," Zach said. "I'm back now, and so are you, man."

Suddenly Ian jumped up and ran for his apartment building. Zach ran after him. "Hey, where you going?"

A minute later Ian slammed into his studio and started hunting frantically for the suicide letter. He dumped desk drawers, looked under the bed, in the closet.

Standing in the open doorway, Zach said, "What the hell are you doing?"

"Looking for your damn suicide letter."

"It's not here."

"It *has* to be here. I left it right on my desk, I know I did."

"That was in the last cycle. The letter doesn't exist in *this* cycle. You're confused. Get used to it."

"Don't say that shit."

Zach shut the door. "Ian, I know it's nuts. Believe me I know. But it's true, all of it. Do you remember what was in the letter?"

"Yes."

Zach hugged him. "Thank God, thank God."

Ian pushed him away. "What are we going to do?"

"Do?"

"Yeah, do. About the Boogeyman, what's going on, all of it."

"I doubt we can do anything about it."

"What?"

"I've tried. Trust me. I can't even remember all the things I've tried. But I know this: we're locked in. There's never enough time to figure out a plan. By the time you get the pieces sorted out – and you never get *all* the pieces sorted out, you always lose something in the daily translation – it's too fucking late to take any action. And the Boogeyman knows about me. He probably knows about you, too. He's messed with my head to make me forget. I keep remembering anyway. At least some of it, every time around."

"What's the point, then? If we can't do anything, why'd you bother with the suicide bullshit?"

"I had to traumatize you to get your attention," Zach said. "You woke me up originally, and I finally found a way to wake *you* up. Psychic trauma, like–"

"Hold on. What do you mean, I woke you up originally?"

"What I said. You still don't remember that part, do you? You were a mess, man. Sincerely. You came over at the crack of fucking dawn and let yourself in. You started talking about how *you* killed yourself with sleeping pills, and how instead of just dying like a normal person you wound up here in Repeat World. I thought you'd lost your mind. I'd never seen you like that before, like you'd had this breakdown or something? You were crying and really, really mad. Said all this shit about how I was your only friend and I just *had* to snap out of it, like you'd been trying to snap me out of it every time the day started over. You said you'd been repeating the same day like a thousand times. It scared me bad. But I didn't believe you. Then you stopped, all of a sudden went all calm and sort of defeated-looking, and said never mind. You went back to your apartment and wouldn't answer the phone or the buzzer. I got even more scared and called the cops on you, told them you were suicidal. They got the manager to let us in, and you were sitting there naked, all catatonic like, and they took you to the psych ward. This shit really knocked me back. You said something. You said, 'Everything's a dream and it doesn't matter.' The next morning, which was the same morning, I started to remember stuff."

Ian remembered the pill bottles on his bedside table. "I wouldn't do that," he said without much conviction. "I wouldn't kill myself. And if we're helpless, like you say, then what difference does it make whether or not we know this is happening?" He looked straight into his only friend's eyes. "Zach, why did you wake me up?"

Zach looked away. "I'm lonely."

"You're lonely."

Zach shrugged.

"So I'm awake in 'Hell' to keep you company?"

"Isn't that what friends are for? Besides, you were the first one to wake up, don't forget that."

"I *have* forgotten it. Totally."

Zach gave him a sideways look. "Anyway, that isn't the *only* reason. I mean, what do you take me for? Listen: my memory varies every day cycle. Sometimes it's all gone and I just feel this vague paranoia. But other times, like in this cycle, I've recovered almost everything, I'm sure of it. But it's always too late by then to do anything. If there's two of us there's more chance one of us will remember something important and remind the other guy. Maybe eventually we could figure out what's really going on. Then we can, I don't know, *fix* stuff. Save the world. You're good at fixing stuff, right?"

"Yeah, right."

"Come on, we'll go someplace and brainstorm. I'm so buying. Cheer up, man. Probably we're both crazy."

On the way to the Deluxe Bar & Grill they stopped and appraised WHO CARES spray-painted across the side of Dick's Drive-In. "That's mine," Ian said, shaking his head.

"You said it wasn't."

"Now I'm saying it is."

"You're lucky you didn't get your ass arrested. Not that it matters in Repeat World. Anyway, I thought you quit."

"More like it quit me." Ian clearly remembered doing the wall; he remembered the empty feeling. For years graffiti seemed to be the answer to a question too painful to ask. Now he was out of answers – but the pain was still there. The only thing about WHO CARES that didn't make sense was the timeframe. He did the wall on the day he failed to meet Sarah in Pullman – a desperation move, something to make life *mean* something to him. That feeling was so sharp and clear in his mind. But the day he failed to meet Sara was *today*. Repeat Day. Did that mean something new could survive from one repeat to the next? He couldn't get his head around any of it.

At the Deluxe they ordered two pints of Fat Tire. When the beer arrived Zach immediately picked his up and drank it down by a third, but Ian only traced the rim of his glass with his fingertip.

"Cheer up," Zach said.

"How'd I look in the psych ward?"

"Like you were home at last."

"Fuck you."

"I'll drink to that."

They both drank to it.

Ian said, "It can't be true."

"I know how you feel."

"It *can't* be," Ian said. "Look at all these people. None of them know what's going on? *None* of them? What makes us so special?"

"Hell, maybe it *isn't* true," Zach said.

"Yeah, maybe not."

Ian picked up his beer. A few hours later he was still picking up his beer, only it was a different one. Like number six or so. Zach, equally loaded, approached a couple of girls shooting pool and asked if they wanted some competition. At a later point, Ian noticed it had begun to rain. He stepped over to the window with a pool cue in his fist. The rain fell in silky curtains through cones of street light. Zach tapped him on the shoulder. "Your shot."

"It's true, isn't it," Ian said.

"Yeah."

"What time is it?"

Zach looked at his watch. "Quarter after eleven."

"Less than an hour."

"There's nothing we can do about it," Zach said. "I've racked my brains all day, trying to remember something useful. Come on, let's finish the game. Maybe on the next cycle we can get on top of it, or at least these girls."

"You haven't been racking your brain," Ian said. "You've been preserving it in alcohol." Ian kept staring at the rain.

"Come on." Zach tugged gently on his arm. They returned to the table.

"I think you're afraid to take your shot," the green-haired college girl said to Ian. She had been saying stuff like that, flirting. Needling him but in a cute way. He forced a grin.

"We'll see about that," he said.

There was a TV mounted in a corner of the ceiling overlooking the pool tables. The eleven o' clock news was on with no sound. Ian took his shot and missed. He stepped aside for the girl. Zach was staring at the TV monitor, mesmerized. KOMO was running footage of a gaudy strip club on First Avenue. The façade of the club featured a big sign surrounded by blinking bulbs. The reporter held his microphone in a low up-angled shot, GIRLS GIRLS GIRLS!!! flashing above and behind him. Suddenly, Ian thought of another sign, similar, but unlit, dead:

XXX GIRLZ.

For a moment Ian wasn't leaning on his cue in the Deluxe. He was straddling the Chief across from a derelict strip club watching the wind hustle a Burger King wrapper in and out of the doorway. He almost didn't notice Zach right in front of him in the bar waving a hand in his face.

"Triple X GIRLZ," Zach said.

"Yeah."

"God *damn*. I told you I don't always remember important stuff."

"Let's go."

"There's no time left."

"We have to try."

Zach threw money on the table.

They ran to Zach's place and piled into the VW, adrenalin pumping illusions of sobriety. Backing out of the garage, Zach ran up on the curb and struck a parking sign, shattering the bug's left taillight. "Damn it."

They jolted off the curb and into the street. The windshield became blurry with rain.

"Turn your lights on," Ian said.

They were racing down the hill in the rain with no wipers or lights. Zach fumbled the lights on just in time to illuminate a tree swinging in front of them. Ian started to yell. They smashed head-on into the tree. Ian found himself lying on his back in the wet street. Blood filled his mouth. Searing pain burned in his thigh. He coughed and choked. Something loose moved under his heart. He tried to sit up and a broken rib pierced the loose thing. Ian screamed and fell back.

He turned his head and saw the VW almost cut in half by the tree. The passenger door hung open like a broken wing. Zach wasn't visible. Ian closed his eyes. He became all the broken, leaking, aching things of his body. A great weight settled upon his chest.

Footsteps approached. The footsteps came close and stopped. Ian opened his eyes. A chubby man stood over him with his hands in the pockets of his long tan overcoat. He wore a hat with a brim, which in combination with the overcoat made him look like a character out of a Bogart movie. Water ran off the down-tilted brim. The man's face was in shadow. He said, "We're going to have to do something about you."

Now there were voices approaching, people running, a siren. As the crowd pressed around Ian, the man in the overcoat faded back.

Ian closed his eyes again and floated in his pain. Later, while the EMTs were trying to stabilize him, Ian died.

CHAPTER FOURTEEN

ON THE ROAD, 2013

THEY RODE OUT of Oakdale with no functioning headlight, Ralph DeVris having smashed it with his bat. Amber running lights produced a fuzzy glow around the bike. The Honda jolted along at slow speed, encountering buckled paving and sudden gaps. Kylie shivered. The rain continued without let-up. Billy said something, turning his head. Kylie couldn't hear him. She pulled herself up by his shoulders, getting her face close to his. "What?" she said.

"I said this is bad. We're going to have to stop before I run into or off of something."

"We're not very far from town yet."

"I know."

He eased the bike off the road, traveled a very short, blind distance, then stopped and killed the engine but left the key on ALT to maintain the running lights, which weren't much but something. Kylie swung off the saddle and immediately caught her shoe on a root. She tried to pull her foot back, slipped in the mud and went down to her knees. "*Fuck.*"

"Are you all right?"

"I can't *see* anything." Kylie was so frustrated and worried about her mother that she wanted to cry again but wouldn't let herself.

"Stay where you are. I've got some chemsticks in the storage compartment."

She could see him, a bearish figure in the amber, rain-blown aura of the Goldwing's running lights. He opened one of the storage compartments, rummaged around in it, then turned to her with something in his hand, a stick about twelve inches long. He twisted it then shook it hard and it lit up green, much brighter than the running lights. "Here." He tossed it to her. Kylie caught it – and saw what had tripped her up: not a root but a human ribcage, half buried. "Oh, *shit.*" She threw herself back, lost the chemstick. It bounced down the hillside, revealing a bas-relief of partially exposed human bones. Then Billy was at her side, helping her stand.

"God," Kylie said.

Billy held her. "There's a lot of crap like this outside of Oakdale."

"Thanks a ton for warning me."

The chemstick had come to rest at the bottom of the hillside. There was a clear, mostly flat space down there.

Billy said, "Come on. We're going to put the tent up and get out of this fucking rain."

The two-man tent was a small blue nylon Dome. Erecting the supporting structure out of flexible rods proved, in the rain and dark, frustratingly difficult. When it was finally up, they crawled inside with their chemstick and Billy pulled the flap closed. They had brought the rifle to get it out of the rain but forgot the food. Neither of them wanted to go back out to retrieve it. Rain crackled on the nylon shell. The tent shuddered in a fresh gust of wind.

"I need my medicine," Billy said, toeing off his shoes. He shoved his stiff, wet jeans down, kicked them off, and pulled the sleeping bag around him. "My head feels like somebody brained me with a baseball bat."

"Somebody did." Kylie dug his Oxy out of her pocket. She passed him a couple of pills and he swallowed them dry then fell back on a pillow he'd made from rolling up his jacket. "Lights out," he muttered. "You can probably see this tent from a mile away." He barely got the words out before passing into sleep.

Kylie observed his face in the green chemstick light. Billy's jaw hung slack, his breath was sour. Fillings gleamed in the back of his mouth. *I love Billy,* Kylie told herself, but didn't think it was *true* love. It was closer to what she used to feel for her best friend, before the Judgment, or even for her mother. She tried, *I like Billy,* but it sounded stupid and lame, even in her mind.

Kylie removed her leather coat and rolled it up like Billy had done, dry side out. She didn't know how to turn the glowing stick-thing off, or even if you *could* turn it off, so she stuck it under her sleeping bag. In the dark, she removed her boots, pants and shirt. Kylie's body was damp and clammy from the drenching she'd taken. Were exotic toxins even now seeping into her bloodstream? Jim said God poisoned the sky as a trial for those who remained after the initial scouring of the Earth. Billy said the high altitude glitter was some kind of alien weapon designed to filter down and kill the survivors. Either way, Kylie tried not to worry about it. But despite her seeming immunity, she couldn't help it. She snuggled down in the bag, shivering, hands clamped between her thighs. After a while, she became warm.

The rain subsided. It popped randomly on the tent. Kylie began to feel drifty. She entered a fragile zone between waking and sleeping, a place where she became unaware of the hard ground upon which she lay. Were those bones poking into her back? It began to not matter.

Then she was immediately wide awake. She sat up, listening, not sure *what* she had heard, only that it had been... something. She sensed Billy sleeping beside her, his breaths labored and deep. She wanted to wake him but decided to wait, in case it was nothing.

She strained to hear. Were those voices up on the road, or just the wind playing tricks with her imagination?

She waited, barely breathing.

Nothing. Wind, rain blowing against the tent.

After a while, she lay back down. But she couldn't sleep. Her body was tense, anticipating. She put her hand on Billy's shoulder, resting it there, not shaking him awake. The contact made her feel better.

After a while the tenseness retreated and she began to drift again, to the random pop of rain on the tent. She was almost gone when she heard, very distinctly, a man's voice.

CHAPTER FIFTEEN

IAN STOOD IN the tiny kitchen of his studio apartment. On the stove top the kettle began to issue wisps of steam. He stood in the kitchen, but he also drifted somewhere as if he himself were a little wisp of steam that might evaporate and be gone. Then the kettle whistled, and Ian came forward. He lifted the kettle off the burner and poured boiling water through a Melitta coffee filter, listening to it trickle into the cup. He was bare-chested and barefoot and bone tired. The wispy feeling was over but he was not yet fully present. He seemed to observe his body performing the routine task of making coffee. When the body brought the cup to its mouth and sipped, *Ian* tasted the coffee and came fully into himself, yawning, his mind more or less tabula rasa. Immediately some secret cache began to fill up the tabula with assorted details and the name: *Sarah*.

He stumbled into the living room, saw the open sleeping pill bottles, and looked away.

The Indian stood wheel-cocked in the alley. Here was the point of ultimate disconnect. He had to go see Sarah today but he couldn't go see Sarah today. Yet, he couldn't *not* go see Sarah today. Ian, as gloomy as he ever got, stared down at his bike.

Then the phone rang.

He slid it open and said, "Hello?"

"Triple Ex Girlz, buddy. Triple Ex fucking *Girlz*."

Ian held the phone out and looked at it. Then he brought it back to his face and said, "Zach?"

The voice on the other end of the line went silent. Then: "Yes. It's me, Zach. Blah blah fucking blah."

The connection broke. Suddenly Ian tasted blood. He brought his fingertips to his mouth, touched his lips, the tip of his tongue. His fingers came away stained. He frowned. Then his mouth *flooded* with blood. He gagged, dropping the phone and his coffee cup. His leg twisted under him, pain flaming up his thigh. He collapsed, more blood erupting into his mouth. Something stabbed at his insides, just under his heart. Ian writhed on the floor. Then, just as suddenly, he was back to normal. No pain. No blood. Spilled coffee but no blood. "What the *fuck?*"

He stood slowly, afraid to trust his body. But there was no pain, no searing agony in his chest, his thigh. But gravity dragged at him and he wanted to go back to bed. He *yearned* to go back to bed.

Instead he picked up the phone and hit return call. "Zach?"

"Did you remember?"

"I don't know what I'm supposed to remember."

Zach sighed. Ian sensed he was about to hang up again. But Zach said, "Meet me at Vivace's. I'll be there in ten minutes."

"All right."

Ian bought a double tall latte from Cyndi, the barista with the Peter Pan hairdo.

"Do you have any idea what time it is?" she asked him. Normally Ian saw her at the end of her shift around one in the afternoon – which was the time he usually tumbled out of bed. "I mean, you look *catatonic*."

"Yeah." He took his latte and sat at a table with a yellow Formica top and warmed his hands around the cup. Zach walked through the door on time, and he looked wide awake. In fact, he looked *extra* wide awake. Like hot-wire-up-the-ass awake. He dropped into the chair opposite Ian and said:

"You ever read *Slaughterhouse-Five?*"

"Vonnegut. Sure."

"I'm like that guy."

"You're like Yossarian?"

"No, numbnuts, that's *Catch* -22. I'm like Billy Pilgrim. I've come unstuck in time. But it's not normal time. It's a time loop. You're unstuck, too, by the way."

"What's this, a game idea you're working on?"

"You always ask me that in your snide little way. For the millionth time: no. It's not a game idea; it's a nightmare idea. Something to keep me on my toes until I go completely insane."

"It's too late," Ian said.

"You can joke."

"Tell me what's going on."

"Like I keep telling you: it's a fucking time loop."

Ian sipped his coffee.

Zach took a deep breath and said, "The day starts over and over again. It stops at midnight, then starts up again early in the morning."

"You mean, the same day?"

"Yeah. Otherwise, it wouldn't be a time loop, would it?"

"I guess not. You're the sci-fi guy. So that's it?"

"No, there's more." Zach told him all of it, but with flagging energy in the face of Ian's incredulity. Ian couldn't help it. He could see his friend wasn't screwing around. But what he was saying was insane. When he got to the part about killing himself, Ian winced and almost interrupted. After a while, Zach trailed off, losing focus, his voice going kind of dead. He was no longer even looking at Ian, almost talking to himself. "That's all of it, all I remember."

"Right. So how did the last one end?" Ian wanted to draw him back. He'd never seen Zach this way. It couldn't be that he was stoned. Dope made him *happy*. And despite the ridiculous premise of the story, it discovered a resonate vibe in some non-rational part of Ian's mind.

"I'm not sure how it ended," Zach said, "but I think I crashed the car and killed us both. Myself, anyway. Not on purpose. I wouldn't do *that* again."

"I got hurt bad," Ian said, the words out of his mouth before he knew he was going to say them.

Zach sat up straight, suddenly focused again. "You remember?"

"No. But right after you hung up on me I had some kind of hallucination. It felt real. I was banged up pretty bad, even fell down in my apartment when the hallucination hit me. But I didn't associate it with a car wreck until you mentioned one just now."

"Try to remember the car wreck."

Ian closed his eyes and concentrated. His imagination offered various accident scenes but none possessed any heat or felt particularly real.

"Well?" Zach said.

"Nothing."

Zach slapped his hand down on the table hard enough to make the sugar spoon jump. A girl dressed all in black reading a book at the next table looked over.

"Take it easy," Ian said.

"I can't. I keep *telling* you. But you don't believe me. Eventually you will, but you don't right now. It goes on and on. Maybe I won't believe it myself next time. Maybe you'll be the one who remembers. You started the whole fucking thing, you know."

"Take it *easy.*"

"Yeah, yeah. I'm taking it easy."

Ian reached across the table and touched his friend's arm. It required an effort of will to do so, make that contact. "Hey, I know you're not bullshitting."

"But you don't believe me, either."

"Well–"

Zach wiped his eyes with the heel of his hand and stood up. "I'm going to surrender to the Boogeyman."

Ian regarded him warily. "Yeah?"

"I think it's a fucking excellent idea. Except I don't think I'll surrender; I think I'll punch his lights out. See you around."

"How are you even going to find this guy?"

"Are you kidding? He's right outside. He's always fucking hanging around us."

Ian followed Zach outside. "Hey, let's get some breakfast," he said.

"There," Zach said, pointing. "I told you."

A chubby man wearing an Indiana Jones fedora stood in front of Dick's Drive-In, picking French fries out of a little paper bag and pushing them into his mouth, a thoughtful, almost analytical expression on his face. Where he got the fries was a mystery, since the place was closed at that hour of the morning. Really there was only one place he *could* have gotten them.

"That guy eating out of the God damn trash is your Boogeyman?"

"Yeah."

Zach walked up to the garbage-eating Boogeyman and threw his arms out, hands open, palms up, like he was going to belt out a song. "I surrender."

The man looked at him impassively.

"Take me to your leader," Zach said.

Ian stepped up and pulled on his friend's sleeve. "Come on, knock it off."

"No. This fuck is going to tell me what's going on."

The man looked down at his French fry bag. Water sluiced off the brim of his hat and pattered on the ground. Ian stared but the water was gone between blinks, the hat dry again. *Dry Indian, wet Indian?* "Hey, did you see that?"

"See what?" Zach said.

Indiana Jones looked at Ian and said, "I like hats."

"Uh, good," Ian said.

"Hats," Zach said. "Jesus Christ."

Still addressing Ian, the man said, "You're the one."

"The one what?"

Zach pushed between them and got in the man's face. "Why don't you tell us what you're up to. Why are you torturing us?"

The man loaded another cold French fry into his mouth then dropped the bag. "Quite the reverse. It's you who are troubling me," he said to Zach. Then, looking past him to Ian, "And you're the source." He started to turn away.

Zach pushed forward. "Hey, I'm *talking* to you!"

Ian held onto Zach's arm. "Let him go."

"Yeah, whatever. You heard him, though. He said you were 'the one'. So what's that supposed to mean? How come I'm not the one? I always remember more than you do."

"I have no idea," Ian said, "but I'll tell you this. He was at the accident. If there was an accident."

Zach had been watching the hat man. Now he turned his attention back to Ian. "You remember the accident?"

"I remember lying in the street at night with rain falling on my face and blood in my mouth, and I remember that guy standing over me. The rain was running off the brim of his hat."

"God *damn*. I told you, man, I told you."

Ian rubbed his forehead. "I don't feel so good."

"Let's get the car and check out Triple Ex Girlz"

"I'll pass on that."

"No, you can't. It's the place, some kind of focal point. We've been there before. It's at the center of it all, I *know* it is. You don't understand because your memory is fucked up. But if we don't do something we might both of us forget by the next cycle. You know what I think? I think they've been screwing with us, trying to disable our ability to remember. Eventually we'll go back to being zombies like everybody else. What I'm saying, *today* might be our last chance."

"I think I want to talk to my sister."

Zach squinted. "For Christ's sake, what for?"

"Come with me," Ian said. "Okay?"

"I'll come with you, but you gotta promise to come with *me* after that. Deal?"

"Deal."

"Wait, where's your sister? We can't leave the city."

"Why not?"

"Ian!"

"Oh. The bubble, or whatever, right?"

"Right. Listen, you've just got to trust me."

"I trust you," Ian said. "I don't totally believe you, but I trust you."

"Thanks. I think."

Ian dragged out his cell and hunted up Vanessa's number. It went to voicemail.

CHAPTER SIXTEEN

ON THE ROAD, 2013

"IT'S BONES," THE man's voice said, words carried on the wind. The voice hadn't been that close, maybe on the hillside, somebody coming down from the road. It was pitch dark. Kylie was afraid to wake Billy, because what if he woke up loud? But she was terrified of *not* waking him. Terror won, and she shook him, her face close to his. The heat of fever radiated from him. He started to mumble, and she *shushed* right in his ear then whispered, "There's somebody out there."

Billy went still, then very quietly said, "Okay."

Okay what? Kylie wanted to know. What were they going to *do?* Billy moved around, doing something she couldn't see. She waited. There were no more voices. Kylie began to doubt there ever had been. After all, she'd been falling asleep. Maybe the man saying "It's bones" had been part of a dream starting. Maybe.

After a long while Kylie noticed she could see. Pre-dawn light had just barely come up. That meant she was wrong and she had been fully asleep, maybe for hours, and then the voice or the dream of the voice woke her.

Billy was a dim figure visible against the pale screen of tent fabric. He was holding the Magnum. "I'm going out," he said, keeping his voice low. "Anybody could see this tent pretty soon. Take this." He handed her the rifle, which she had no idea how to use, then he unzipped the tent flap, slowly, as if that would make less noise. He threw the flap aside and crawled out fast, gun first.

Kylie bit her lip, waiting for shots, or yelling, or *something*. But after a few moments there was just Billy saying, in a normal tone of voice, "It's all right, Kylie."

She pulled on her pants and boots and crawled out into the raw morning. Billy stood in his boxers and black wool socks facing the hillside, the big revolver pointed at the ground. The Goldwing was plainly visible against the overcast sky. "Aren't you freezing?"

"Yeah. Are you sure you heard somebody?"

"I don't know."

"I doubt anybody from town would leave shelter during a rain storm. Maybe it was a SAB from the Dome. They wander up this way, sometimes. But they don't generally talk much after they've been out a while, and it would have taken it days to get here."

"I'm just saying what I thought I heard," Kylie said.

In the burgeoning daylight clouds obscured the Olympic Mountains. It was probably Oakdale's proximity to the mountains that spared it from the more devastating effects of the shockwave. The bones imbedded in this hillside suggested what they had missed.

Billy dressed and hiked up to the bike and came back with a knapsack. He looked ashen. The bandaged lump on his forehead was seeping, the bandage soaked dark.

"You don't look so good," Kylie said, trying to keep the fear out of her voice.

"I'm not a morning person. Here's food." He handed her the knapsack.

They ate in the tent, out of the biting wind. In less than a week the weather had turned to autumn. The knapsack was full of junk food, some of it well past its expiration date. "Doesn't matter with this crap," Billy said. For breakfast he ate two Snickers bars and half a bag of ranch style Doritos. Kylie had a couple handfuls of corn chips. The salt made her thirsty. She washed the chips down with a bottle of Father Jim's holy water.

After eating, Billy just lay there with his eyes closed. Kylie waited a while then said, "Are you sleeping?"

"No."

After another ten minutes, she said, "Billy, I don't know what to do by myself." She was scared but didn't want to come right out and say so.

Billy opened his eyes, which were full of headache. A crust had formed in the corners. First there was fever then discharge from the eyes, and your body ached all the time and then it stopped aching because you were *dead*. "You're not alone," Billy said. "Come on. We have to get moving."

IN LESS THAN a mile they came to a large metal sign in the middle of the road. It had stood on a pair of thirty-foot poles but now lay flat. The sign said: EATS GAS BAIT. Fuel pumps stood in front of the low-slung building, a combination café, gas-station and bait shop. The shockwave had taken the roof off, leaving a few jagged remnants and most of the lower part of the structure. Kylie remembered stopping at EATS GAS BAIT on car trips; they weren't that far from Dyes Inlet and Kitsap Lake. She remembered the cheerful blue checkered table cloths in the café. She patted Billy's shoulder. "Can we stop?"

Billy rolled the Goldwing off the road and killed the engine. "What's wrong?" Billy's words slurred like slippery things trying to grip the edge of the well before falling in.

"I don't know. I used to come here. I just want to look."

"Thing could fall on your head."

"I'll be careful." She nimbly dismounted. Billy stayed on the bike. When she saw his face she felt bad for making him stop. He looked awful, his face drawn down in pain and exhaustion, eyes red and crusty and unfocused.

"You *really* don't look good," Kylie said.

"I wish you'd quit saying that."

"What about another pill?"

"I've had too many already."

"Maybe we should just keep moving?"

"A break's good."

"Okay."

"But I wouldn't go inside that place. Seriously."

"I won't, Billy."

All the windows were blown out. She stood on the porch and looked into the café. It was full of debris, the ceiling having dropped after the shockwave had ripped the roof away. In the midst of it all a table, its blue-checked oilcloth still draped over it, lay on its side. Kylie had once sat at that table, or one just like it, with a boy named Kevin Hathaway. She had been fifteen and he had been seventeen. They weren't exactly dating, but they liked each other and had held hands and all that. It had been *normal*, unlike what she later had with Father Jim. One time Kevin drove them to Seattle to see a Shins concert – an adventure mostly out of favor with Kylie's mother, but allowed. The concert had been great. Seattle had been great. On the way there, Kevin stopped at EATS GAS BAIT and bought her a grilled cheese sandwich. Kevin had been what passed for a rebel in Oakdale. He skipped school a lot but couldn't actually bring himself to drop out; he wasn't a total dipshit like Ray Preston. While Kylie ate her grilled cheese sandwich he had folded back the table cloth and used his pen knife to carve, K + K = Cheese. The waitress caught him at it and made them leave; Kylie dropped half the sandwich in her purse, and they laughed for ten miles. She liked the bad boy aspect.

Kylie wondered if that *was* the same table. She glanced at Billy. His head was down, not looking in her direction. She quickly stepped through the window frame. Glass crunched under her shoes. She moved carefully over the debris, pulled the blue-checked oilcloth off the table, and Ray Preston grabbed her from behind. He locked his arm around her waist and his hand over her mouth. He must have walked all night. Was that him she had heard, the voice that woke her? She screamed into his smothering palm. When she reached back to rake his eyes with her fingernails, he jerked her head over so hard pain spiked at the base of her skull, and for an instant she thought he had broken her neck.

"Just don't you try it," he said, his breath thick with whiskey. He pinched her nose closed with thumb and knuckle and clamped down harder over her mouth. Kylie stopped struggling. She couldn't breathe. "I should cut you right now. But we'll wait for Father Jim."

Kylie made her eyes big. She whimpered, not because she was afraid of Jim (though she was), but because she couldn't *breathe*.

A figure lurched out of the kitchen. It was a skin-and-bone person. This was the worst one Kylie had ever seen. Its tattered clothes hung from its body like a peeling layer of old skin. Its eyes swiveled in deep sockets, as if they lived independently and were nesting in the skull.

"*Fuck*," Preston said. He shoved Kylie at the thing and ran.

CHAPTER SEVENTEEN

"*Icky!*"

Vanessa stopped in the middle of the sidewalk and gaped at him as though he had risen from the dead. If you believed Zach, that was approximately correct. She had been digging keys out of her handbag.

"Hi, Ness."

"*Your* hi Ness," she said, completing an ancient family joke. "What are you doing here?"

He hadn't seen or even talked to her in over a year. Or had he?

"I don't know," he said. "I tried to call but you weren't answering."

"I never turned it on today. Sometimes it's more peaceful that way. Of course I had no idea you might want to talk. It's not exactly the expected thing, is it?"

"I guess not. Ness, I feel bad."

Vanessa hesitated, then hugged him awkwardly,

patting his back with the hand holding her keys. They jangled with every pat. Ian swallowed his emotions. He didn't like being touched, even by his sister, perhaps *especially* by his sister; it seemed to require a conditioned response, which he was uncomfortable providing. In most cases he *couldn't* provide it. And in this case, merely seeing Ness had upset him.

"Tell me what's wrong," she said, standing back but keeping one hand on his arm. "You look dreadful."

"Thanks."

"I'm serious, Ian."

"I *feel* dreadful," he said, "and I don't know why. Zach wants me to go somewhere with him, but I think it's kind of crazy. I told him I wanted to talk to you first. He's at the Market, waiting for me. I've been hanging out here, hoping you'd show up."

"For how long?"

"I don't know, quite a while."

"Good grief. Do you want to go find your friend? I'm meeting a client in a half hour, by the way."

"Oh–"

Vanessa appeared to evaluate him, then said, "One minute."

She rummaged her cell out of the handbag, turned it on and pressed a memory dial. She told whoever answered that she was in the middle of a family emergency and that she would call back to reschedule and she was *so* very sorry.

"You didn't have to do that," Ian said. "This isn't an emergency. I don't know *what* it is."

"I always follow my intuition, Icky. It keeps me on the path, you know?" She looked at her watch. "The Pink Door is open. Let's have a bite and talk. I'm famished."

As soon as they sat down in the bar a distracted air came over Vanessa. She tilted her head, as if listening.

"What?" Ian said.

"The strangest déjà vu."

Ian's stomach muscles tightened. "What's strange about it?"

"It's not passing. Usually you get that feeling for a moment, then it's gone, and you're not even sure it was real. This one is lingering. Oh, my. I could swear we've been right here at this table talking about your friend, Zach." She leaned forward. "Icky, is he all right, your friend? Did anything happen to him?"

"*No.* I told you, he's hanging out. I'll call him."

"Do."

Ian punched up Zach's number. After a couple of seconds, a phone in the bar began playing the theme from *Bonanza*. Ian turned in his chair. The bartender held up Zach's phone.

"You calling this number?"

"Yeah." Ian closed his phone.

"Customer left it here about an hour ago. Tall guy with a shaved head?"

"Right."

A pen stuck out of the bartender's shirt pocket. A black stain about the size of a dime bled through the white cotton. Ian couldn't take his eyes off the stain.

The bartender said, "He was sitting over there by himself, drank a couple of beers, and left."

The ink stain appeared to hang in front of the shirt, an optical illusion. Vanessa was saying something. Ian heard the words distantly and in a way disconnected from meaning. A wave of dizziness overwhelmed him. He swayed, and closed his eyes on throbbing darkness.

173

Instantly he was floating above himself, looking down on the room, everything in sharply defined focus. He could have counted the individual hairs on his own head. In his absence his body continued to perform as if he were still home. It turned back around and spoke to Vanessa. Meanwhile, the bartender was wondering whether he should let Ian take the guy's cell phone. Not that Ian had asked for it, but if he did the bartender (whose name was Robert) would have to decide what to do. Better to keep the phone rather than risk–

Ian pulled himself out of the bartender's head, frightened of his consciousness diffusing into the mind of a stranger. He became heavy, then, and plunged through the top of his own head and found himself in the middle of a sentence, looking out of unfocused eyes at his sister.

"–acting weird, but it's probably…"

"Probably what, Icky?"

He breathed slowly and let the strangeness fall away. In a moment he felt as though he'd just awakened from a vague, confusing dream that he could barely recall.

"I don't know," he said. "I don't remember what I was saying."

Vanessa looked at him closely. "You were saying your friend was behaving oddly."

"It's more than that."

"Icky, are you all right?"

"I don't know."

"You're worried about Zach, but I'm worried about *you*."

"You don't have to be."

"Of course I don't *have* to be. Icky, I know I wasn't much help after Mom died. But I'm here for you now, and have been for years."

"You were okay," Ian said. "That was a long time ago."

"Not so long. My own life was coming apart back then, you know. But I was older than you and I should have helped you, especially when I saw that dad wasn't going to be able to handle it."

"He handled it all right. What was he supposed to do? I don't really want to talk about this stuff, Ness." A knot kept bobbing up in his throat. He struggled to keep it down.

"We've *never* talked about it," Vanessa said. "Don't you think *that's* odd?"

"I'd rather forget what happened."

"But you never forget these things. I work with people all the time whose lives are wrecks because they never processed their trauma."

"Hypno-therapy. I'm not putting it down, but it's not like real therapy, is it? I mean traditional therapy, like with a psychiatrist or psychologist, somebody who's spent eight years or whatever going to school and then passing a licensing board."

Vanessa smiled. "I'm licensed, Icky, and what I do is real. Not everybody benefits from ten years on the couch – or at university, for that matter. I'm not qualified to conduct what you call 'real' therapy. But sometimes that isn't what's needed. Sometimes it's better to expose the nasty core and be done with it."

"I guess." Ian stood up. Vanessa watched him. "I better find Zach."

"Do you know where to look?"

"I think so."

"I'll come with you."

"No, that's okay. I better talk to him myself. I mean, I appreciate it, and I'm sorry about lunch and your client and everything. I don't even know why I wanted to bother you."

"I don't care about lunch, Icky. I care about *you*."

Ian thought she was about to stand up and hug him again. He forestalled her by leaning over and awkwardly patting her shoulder. She looked at his hand. "Well, Icky. Go find your friend. And *call* me, please."

"Sure."

"I mean it."

"I'll call, I promise. And thanks for talking to me. I was feeling pretty whacked out."

"I know."

Outside in Post Alley Ian mumbled, "I'm whacked, all right."

A couple entering The Pink Door glanced at him, and Ian hurried away. Zach's bottle fly green VW was gone from the parking lot where they'd left it a couple of hours ago. On the way down from Capitol Hill Zach had tried to explain where Triple X Girlz was located. Ian was mostly unfamiliar with that part of the city, the no-man's land between the International District and Pioneer Square. But if he wandered around he might find the place.

He wandered for almost an hour, without luck. Then on a dingy trash-blown corner, he spotted the car. He walked up to it and looked in the window. The door was unlocked, and the passenger footwell was a garbage dump. Zach's car, all right. He glanced up and down the street. At the end of the block a derelict building presented a dead Vegas-style sign.

XXX GIRLZ.

Reluctantly, he walked toward the building. If this was Ground Zero, it was pretty God damn low-rent.

He tried to decipher the angry tangle of graffiti tags but recognized none of them. The closer he approached the more ill at ease he felt. The uneasiness increased with every step, a repelling force emanating from the building itself.

The invisible dog fence.

Ian remembered. He stopped walking. Images overlapped in his mind's eye. He and Zach had been here before. On at least one occasion, Zach had disappeared into the building. There had been a scream.

The wind hustled a Burger King bag out of the recessed doorway. For a moment Ian wasn't sure whether he was seeing the bag or remembering it. He felt nauseated, wanted to back away. Instead, he began moving forward against the repelling force and his instinct. His legs were leaden, his steps halting. He had the idea that he must *do* something to prevent the scream from occurring. He pushed against palpable waves of anxiety. Then, when he was half a dozen yards away, the waves ceased, and Ian stumbled off-balance.

He leaned against the building, shaky. Something in the sky captured his attention. Multiple green blisters appeared and a moment later half a dozen pinwheels of light burst through and scattered over the city. They took up hovering positions. Ian stepped away from the building, craning his neck, staring. The decks began spinning faster, transforming into blinding pinwheels. One descended toward the Columbia Tower, the tallest building in Seattle. An energy beam stuttered downward – and the top of the building exploded. Debris rained into the streets.

"Fuck!" Ian pressed back against the wall. The other pinwheels descended and began randomly destroying buildings. Screams and sirens rose up. On the next block a burning man ran across the street, waving his arms frantically.

Ian turned, looking for shelter. The door to XXX GIRLZ dissolved in a shadow. Ian fled into the building. The door resumed and he was entombed in silence. Then there was a sound of running water, and he turned in that direction. An old claw-foot bathtub stood on a green tile floor. The gooseneck faucet ran at a trickle. Cloudy water slopped over the edge of the tub. His mother's waxen face seemed to float on the surface, black hair fanning around it, dead eyes staring.

Ian screamed. At that moment he realized he had been remembering his own scream, not Zach's.

But that was a rational thought and unrelated to the primitive urge toward panic. He turned. A man stood between him and the door. A man in a deerstalker cap. It was the "…I like hats…" guy. The Boogeyman.

CHAPTER EIGHTEEN

KYLIE GRABBED A broken chair and held it up like a lion tamer, but the skin-and-bone woman shuffled past her as if she didn't exist. Billy appeared at the empty window with his revolver drawn. Kylie dropped the chair and ran to him, jumping over debris. She clambered out the window and into his arms, almost knocking him over.

"It's okay. She won't hurt you." Billy was breathing hard, as if he'd run two miles instead of crossing fifty yards or so from the Goldwing. There was a sick, yellow smell about him.

"How do you *know*?" Kylie said. She bent over, reaching into her boot, and came up with her good-for-a-girl gun.

"I've seen a lot of them," Billy said. "They're harmless. This one's stuck in the diner. Probably been in here a long time, like a windup toy, bumping into walls and furniture and crap." It was kind of pathetic, really. A roof beam had fallen, probably after the SAB entered the diner, and blocked the open door. Even a kid would know to move the beam, or duck under it – or climb out the window, as Kylie had just done. But not the skin-and-bone woman.

Kylie looked seriously at Billy and said, "Ray was here."

"What?"

"He grabbed me then let go when the SAB came out of the kitchen. He's even more chickenshit about SABs than I am."

"Where'd he go?"

"I don't know. He ran away."

"Shit. Stay here."

Billy made his way around the side of the building. Kylie followed him. He glanced back at her, his face pale as curds, beaded with sweat, looking like he was about to fall over. "I guess you're not staying there."

"I guess not." Kylie could see no reason why she should. She had her little gun, and it didn't seem like a half bad idea to put a bullet in Ray Preston's ass.

"There he goes," Billy said, pointing with the Magnum. Preston was halfway up a bare hillside behind the diner. "Can't believe that fucker came after us. At least he was alone."

"He said Jim was coming."

"On foot they'll never keep up with us." Billy holstered his gun and wiped his eyes. The bandage on his head was sodden. "Let's get the hell out of here."

"Wait." Kylie put her gun away in her boot, stepped back into the cafe and got her arms around the roof beam blocking the SAB. "I want to let it out."

Billy nodded. The beam was heavy. Together they pulled it rather than lifted it. The upper end came free of whatever had snagged it and crashed down. The SAB turned toward them, hesitated, and stumbled out into the light. Its ragged clothes were some kind of uniform, like a waitress would wear. There was even a grimy name plate pinned to the pink blouse, LINDA, just barely discernible.

"You're welcome, Linda," Kylie said.

LINDA started down the middle of the road, heading south.

"Where's *she* going?" Kylie asked.

"Same place we are, probably. Lot of SABs go back and hang around the Dome." Billy spoke slowly, as if hunting for the words. The uttering of them seemed a huge effort.

Kylie put her hand on his shoulder. "Billy–?"

"Let's get moving, huh?" Billy took a step toward the bike, paused, swaying. Kylie reached for him too late as he pitched forward and rolled onto his side, legs drawn up.

"Billy!"

Kylie dropped beside him but didn't know what to do. His eyes were closed, his breathing raspy, labored. Sweat beaded his face and neck. "God, Billy, don't die."

Billy opened his eyes. "I'm not dead... just felt like resting."

"You *fell down*."

"What's that got to do with it?" He smiled wanly. "Help me up, will you?"

On his feet, Billy wasn't so funny. He leaned heavily on Kylie. "God I'm dizzy," he said.

"I'm sorry."

"My head's fucking killing me."

"I'm *really* sorry, Billy."

"Never mind. But listen. I think you're going to have to drive."

"I don't know how."

"It's easy."

She steadied him while he mounted the Goldwing's passenger saddle. Once he was settled she climbed on in front of him. "Take it slow," he said, "and you'll be okay."

"I'll try."

The Goldwing was too big. She had never ridden anything but a bicycle. Billy handed her the key. She slotted it and turned it over. The powerful engine rumbled up between her legs.

"Throttle on the right grip," he said. "Brake under your right foot. Move out slow, experiment a little. Get the hang of it."

Kylie sat still, not experimenting.

"Let's not waste gas," Billy said.

She moved the clutch and nudged the throttle. The bike jerked forward. She braked hard, and Billy thumped against her. "Fuck," he said, sounding weak and pained. "What are you stopping for?"

"I don't know."

"Jesus Christ, Kylie."

She timidly rotated the throttle. The Honda rolled onto the broken highway.

"That's good, that's good." Billy slurred his words. Kylie wished they were back in the Oakdale house watching *Tombstone* or *Say Anything*. She wished it more than anything, but wishing wasn't going to restore what was gone. She cranked the throttle a little more. With the added speed they caught up to Linda and passed her. Kylie glanced back at the SAB. When she looked forward she saw a section of her lane missing, cracked off and sunk several feet. She swerved, over reacting, crossed the road toward the ditch, swerved back the other way, cutting it too sharply and accidentally applying more throttle. The bike surged and rocked. Billy slumped against her back, a dead weight, and started slipping off the saddle. Kylie twisted around, trying to hold him up, but he was too heavy. She lost control of the bike and dumped them on the road.

CHAPTER NINETEEN

"IT'S TIME TO address your situation," the Boogeyman in the deerstalker hat said. "*Our* situation."

Ian backed away from him. "Who are you?"

"Nominally, the curator of this place."

"Curator of a *strip club?*"

"The Seattle Preservation. In truth, though, I'm curator of nothing. You really don't know what you're doing, do you?"

"What *I'm* doing. I'm not doing anything."

"Wholly unconscious of your role. Astonishing."

Water slopped onto tiles behind Ian. He flinched and resisted a morbid urge to turn around.

"Ignore that," the Curator said.

"Where's my friend, where's Zach?"

"You have no friends here."

Water slopped and splashed on the tiles.

"I'm leaving," Ian said.

184

"I'm afraid not. Hunters are on the Preservation now. Of necessity it is impossible to either leave or enter this structure until they depart. We are bound in camouflage. During previous Advents, Hunters have leveled the city, but it did them no good. Hunter technology is brutishly linear. You will remain with me for a time."

"Advents are days? *The* day, the one that repeats?"

The Curator nodded. "It's a temporal illusion, drawn mostly from the original inhabitants while they sleep."

"Original... I don't get it."

"Outside this structure the Preservation is populated by regenerating androids, shadow people if you will, their memory matrices derived from the city's original population. The Preservation creates a space-time rift and draws on their sleeping minds to recreate conscious-seeming simulacrums. Even the city is merely a recurring representation of the original inhabitants' perceptions of their city. Amazing that you've brought all this into existence, even drew me out of the Cloud to fulfill the meaningless function of Curator. And yet you are completely unaware."

Ian wasn't listening. He stared at the door behind the Curator. "I really want to get out of here now."

"As I've mentioned, that isn't yet possible."

Ian stepped around the Curator, who did not attempt to stop him. The door was so solidly immovable the knob might have been cemented to a wall only painted to *look* like a door. Ian put his shoulder against it and shoved. Surprisingly, the door cracked away from the jamb and Ian stumbled forward. But not onto the sidewalk. Instead he was in another room. This one was glaringly white and lacked defining dimensions. He turned – and the Curator was there, sitting in a bathtub filled with murky water, naked except for a porkpie hat. His saggy female breasts floated in the bathwater. The room without walls was steamy and, paradoxically, claustrophobic.

"I would be delighted if you left–" the Curator said.

Ian's mouth had gone dry.

"–but not in the sense you are thinking. I wish you to relinquish the Ian Palmer android. Once that is accomplished, this ersatz Preservation can end and I can rejoin the Cloud. Perhaps."

"I don't know what you're *talking* about."

The Curator sighed. "Never mind. This event is too deeply imprinted. We will seek something related."

The Curator stood up in the tub. Ian looked away.

"Don't be squeamish."

Ian's heart pounded. "*What* are you?"

"Good question. It's one I've been asking myself lately. Now be still. I am attempting to solve our present dilemma. Come to me."

The light changed, became less glaring. Ian turned slowly. A giant jellyfish swayed before him. It was wearing a Tyrolean hat with a red feather. Ian recoiled, gasping, and tripped over his own feet. What he fell into was something like warm Karo syrup embedded with star dust. "Wrong way," the jellyfish said. "I've been probing you. Now – behold."

A pseudopod snaked out of the Curator's body. Ian flinched, threw his arm up. The room altered drastically, transforming between one moment and the next. Now it was Sarah's apartment, the one she had left when she moved to Pullman to resume college. The Curator, reverted to his human-looking self, wearing a Mariners baseball cap and standing at the foot of Sarah's bed, frowned.

On the bed someone was fucking Sarah. The someone's body was extremely tense, even the cheeks of his pumping ass. His pale body was shiny with sweat. There was a blue cross tattooed behind his left shoulder, throwing off blue ink light. Ian stood paralyzed, watching. He knew the man was tense because he was concentrating on *not* concentrating, on for once losing himself in unconscious immersion and trust. Sarah's eyes were closed and she held the man with her arms and legs. Suddenly the man cried out – and then continued crying. Sobbing as if grief-stricken. The man was Ian himself. Sarah held him while he cried. It had been the first time he arrived at real surrender, and it had frightened him.

"A crucial element," the Curator said. "This memory is not so deeply imprinted, though. Here we can perhaps successfully perform a manipulation."

Ian, observing all this, was crying along with his past-self.

The Curator removed his cap, then put it back on and tugged it down snug by the bill. "There, there," he said. "Let's make it all better."

Once again his past-self was stroking away into past-Sarah. It went on and on until it didn't go on any more, and past-Ian rolled off, unsatisfied but safe – his standard conclusion. Past-Sarah asked what was wrong. *Nothing's wrong. I'm tired, I don't know.* Then the scene shifted and past-Sarah was gone, and past-Ian, alone on a different bed, his own bed, came in his hand and did not cry.

"There's more," the Curator said, and Ian turned. The Curator stood at the end of a short hall, facing the open door of the bathroom. Ian joined him; he didn't have any choice. Yet *another* past-self stood before the medicine cabinet. This one was wearing boxer shorts. His shoulders slumped. Dark bruising discolored the skin under his exhausted eyes. In his left hand were two prescription bottles. That day he didn't go to see Sarah, didn't call her, pretended she didn't exist, and then tried to find escape from himself in a can of spray paint and failed – all of it failed, his whole life. The prescriptions were phony, obtained over the internet through illegal transactions. Duplicates of his mother's suicide pills. The past-self examined a third prescription bottle, studying the label for long moments, before putting it back on the shelf, and the other two as well, shaking his head. In this version the dilemma never occurred, because Ian had never fully surrendered to Sarah – he had maintained critical distance. Safe detachment.

The present Ian moved his lips. *But that's not what happened.*

"No, but it will do." The Curator took Ian's arm and led him away. They walked right through a solid wall to enter a room thumping with disco music. A girl in a bright pink wig wearing nothing but a thong was grinding her crotch up and down a pole. A spot light bathed her in a dusty cone.

"XXX GIRLZ in a less tranquil manifestation," the Curator said. Now he wore an outrageous pimp hat, purple with white fur trim. He waved his hand and the music ceased – not only the music but every sound in the room that wasn't made by Ian and the Curator. "Sit down and relax for a while, why don't you?" The Curator pulled a chair out, the chair legs scraping loud on the hardwood floor. He placed a hand on Ian's shoulder and pushed him gently down. Ian did not resist. He felt stunned. The silent stripper humped the pole and licked her lips in a sensuality as phony as Ian's Xanax prescription.

"I don't believe any of this."

"Of course you do."

"What... what were we looking at back there, that other me–?"

"Externalized memories. It was necessary to make changes, where changes could be made. Your traumas haunt you, so now you're haunting them."

Ian looked away from the girl and straight at the Curator. "I don't know what you're talking about. But if that other stuff about androids is true, then what am *I* doing here?"

"Excellent question. Before, you asked what I am. What *you* are, is more to the point."

"I'm just *me*."

"True but incomplete. Presently you are a non-physical entity inhabiting a recurring android, interweaving with its memory matrix, which is being generated by your own mind across a space-time rift manufactured by the Preservation Dome. A Dome that wouldn't exist if you hadn't Lensed it into existence to begin with."

Ian rubbed his forehead. In high school he had compulsively ingested, inhaled or injected every drug he could get his hands on. Acid had produced the wildest disconnect from consensus reality.

Until now.

Ian *longed* for a consensus reality he could stand in. He glanced at the silent pole-humping stripper. Was any of this really happening? *Had* he taken the pills in his medicine cabinet, and were they straining his mind through some kind of psychedelic filter? Sleeping pills didn't do that. Even super powerful sleeping pills. But when you died, didn't your brain flood with neurochemicals that created hallucinations? He'd read that somewhere. On the other hand, he didn't feel dead.

"Hey," he said, "do you think it's possible to mix sleeping pills, beer and spray paint and come up with lysergic acid?"

"This Preservation came into existence because of *you*. Because of your Lensing ability."

"I don't even get what that means."

"It means," the Curator said, "you are much more than you know you are. Preservation templates exist eternally in the Cloud. Once they were intended as museums – interactive dioramas of civilizations destroyed by Hunter cleansing missions. Civilizations the Cloud had selected and secretly guided. Eventually the Cloud lost interest in Preservation museums, though. Eventually it lost interest in everything but its own expansion."

"Even if believed that – and I don't – what I'm saying, none of that has anything to do with *me*."

"It has everything to do with you. This Preservation came into existence because you Lensed it into existence."

At the edge of the stage, which was only a couple of feet from Ian, the pink-wigged stripper bent over, shoved her ass out and wiggled it. The thong strap vanished between firmly rounded cheeks. Ian scooted his chair around so her ass wasn't right in his face.

The Curator leaned across the table. "I have begun to forget things. I am becoming what I appear to be: a human android. But I used to be one of the billions comprising the Cloud. I was one with them. The

Cloud directed numerous races towards transphysical evolution. It created Preservations for the benefit of material-based civilizations. Educational pointers, you might say. But this Preservation, the one *you* Lensed it into existence, is functionally isolated. The Cloud doesn't even know it exists."

"What you're saying, it couldn't happen. I keep telling you, I'm nobody, I'm *me*. I don't 'Lens' things. I'm a fuckup, end of story."

The Curator shook his head emphatically. "No. You are an extremely rare anomaly. I know, because I am one myself. Out of billions, one may evolve Lensing abilities. Even with that given, you are hundreds of years ahead of where you should be, based on what the Cloud had so far accomplished with your race.

"When you terminated your physical body, your consciousness persisted. It wanted the world back, which at the same moment was undergoing annihilation by the Hunters. Without knowing what you did, you Lensed the Preservation matrix out of the Cloud, complete with a regenerating android of yourself – an ideal receptacle. It received you, and has gone on receiving you, Advent after Advent."

Ian looked at the stripper. She was making love to the pole again.

"It will require one Advent outside this structure for your new memories to fully weave into your android's matrix. Upon the following Advent, your mind will be scoured of Sarah. Once this secondary conflict has vanished you perhaps will vanish as well, no longer compelled to worry after the unfortunate manner of your death, which in turn may release your android to exist on its own terms. At that point the Preservation may cease – along with your obsession. And I, too, will be released."

"Okay, cool." Ian stood up. His legs were weak and he almost sat down again. "I have to go."

"You may. The Hunters have given up, for now; the current Advent is routine."

Ian turned. "What do these Hunters have such a hard-on about, anyway? What did we ever do to them?"

"Nothing. The Hunters consider Cloud interference a menace, one that grows more powerful with each absorption. Hunters eradicate any civilization the Cloud has prepared for transphysical evolution. It's not personal. Goodbye."

Ian closed his eyes, head pounding. Without knowing how he got there, he discovered himself stumping past a bus-stop on Second Avenue, headed uptown, moving fast, hands stuffed in his pockets. The streets were deserted, filled with cold blue shadows of early morning. He slowed his pace then stopped in the middle of the sidewalk, grasping at something important.

Zach?

He looked back the way he'd come. Something was going terribly wrong in his mind. Some kind of dissociative break. His memory felt breezy with holes – holes that were slowly widening.

Ian concentrated. Was it possible he was still asleep, dreaming? His mother's suicide, Vanessa's mental collapse. Certainly they had hallucinated, heard voices, spoken to the dead. Why not Ian, too? He recalled a chubby man with female breasts and a porkpie hat standing up in a bathtub. And a thing like a giant jellyfish swaying before him.

Jesus.

Ian walked all the way back to the Pike Place Market. Vendors were busily arranging their wares but it was still too early for many people to be around. A stake truck idled on the bricks, white clouds chugging from its tailpipe. Ian's own breath condensed in the cold air. The day had just begun.

The Advent.

That word had nearly slipped into a memory hole, but now he had hold of it. The Curator called them "Advents", these days that were all one day endlessly repeating in the Seattle Preservation.

"That's fucking impossible," Ian said out loud, and the Curator in his various manifestations (and *hats*) began to pull apart, lose the coherency of genuine memory. It all might have been something he dreamed or imagined.

He walked past The Pink Door. Post Alley was cold and mostly deserted, the bars and shops locked up. Purple irises trembled in flower boxes. On the next block a Seattle's Best was already open and a couple of people came out holding disposable cups of coffee. Ian took out his cell phone and punched Zach's number. It went straight to voicemail. Everything had seemed so urgent, bordering on desperate. Now Ian felt loose and unfocused. He needed someone to ground him, make him real. The only person other than Zach that he could think of was his sister. But of course she was outside... outside... *the Preservation*. Which meant she wasn't anywhere at all. At least until it was time for her to drive into the city again, an android generated to fulfill that action at the same time of day the real Vanessa drove across the Aurora Bridge on the real October fifth.

"Jesus Christ, it's all true, it's true—" Ian stared at the ground, concentrating, trying to hold it together, the whole fantastic idea. But inexorably it began to pull apart again and slip away down memory-hole drains. What a moment ago was so *present* and real suddenly became a name he couldn't quite remember.

His mind drifted back to Vanessa, a steady state. Recalling their conversation in the Pink Door, he cringed inwardly. *Two crazies sit down in a bar...*

No. Not crazy. *Not* crazy.

He grasped at Ness like a drowning man to a life preserver. Preserve. Preservation.

That was the trick. Locate someone meaningful, someone part of the strangeness (hypnotized and sent ticking away like a windup toy) but separate from it, too. His sister. That continuity of relationship. Cling to her solid presence, and let the other memories build around her naturally.

Caffeine. If he ever needed coffee he needed it *now*.

He jogged up the alley to the Seattle's Best. At the counter he stared at his cup and again *concentrated*. But already the memories had come apart, like oil separating on the surface of water. It was hopeless.

CHAPTER TWENTY

THE BIG BOAT

BILLY LAY WHERE he'd fallen in the road, mouth open, arms flung out, skin paled almost white. Kylie shut off the dumped Goldwing's engine and ran to him. The bandage on Billy's head hung away by one edge, like a big flap of infected skin. The revealed lump looked red and tender.

Billy wasn't breathing.

She knelt beside him, tears blurring her vision. Shuffling footsteps approached then stopped. Kylie turned her head. The SAB, the LINDA-thing, stood over her. Kylie wiped her eyes. The breeze moved the SAB's matted hair. Her eyes had ceased their wild swiveling and they stared half out of their orbits, big and popping-blue.

"He's dead," Kylie said. "I don't know what to *do*."

LINDA stared. Her skeletal hand, bones and veins sliding under parchment skin, moved toward Kylie in stiff little jerks and touched her shoulder. "Gown," the skin-and-bone woman said, then resumed her shuffling progress down the broken highway. It was a while before Kylie realized she had said; *Go on*. Kylie would do that. But first she had to bury poor Billy.

KYLIE STOOD BESIDE a rough cairn she had erected over Billy's body. It was a half-assed job at best. His booted feet remained exposed. It would have to do. Her fingers were bruised and scraped raw from lugging all the stones. "Goodbye, Billy."

She hunkered next to the Goldwing. Using her knees and back, she pushed it upright. In the saddle she keyed the ignition. The bike rumbled. She wiped her eyes one last time then tweaked the throttle and rolled forward, cautious at first, getting the hang of it, weaving around the broken places, then gradually throttling up, building speed and distance. She passed Linda and never looked back. She was on her way to Bremerton – to the Big Boat.

Speed and distance felt good.

KYLIE RODE SLOWLY down the middle of Kitsap Way, in Bremerton. The breeze out of the south carried salt air off the Sinclair Inlet – the deep-water Navy port. Billy's Big Boat was very near. Alone without Billy, she wasn't even sure she wanted to see it.

Few structures remained intact on this commercial street. One of them was rhe Red White and Blue Diner. It stood nearly pristine, compared to the buildings around it. Kitsap Way was almost impassable with debris. Kylie weaved the Goldwing around overturned

cars with skeleton passengers, downed power line poles
– even a roof section that included an intact dormer
window with a Bush-Cheney sticker in the corner. Kylie
kept stealing glances at the diner. It looked so *normal*.
She could almost imagine going inside and finding it
bustling with waitresses and the lunch crowd.

Then she looked ahead and saw *them*.

Skin-and-bone people, at least a dozen of them. They
shuffled and lurched and otherwise somnambulated out
of the ravaged buildings and shadowed places, drawn
by the sound of the Goldwing.

Kylie stopped. Once in the street, the SABs appeared
at a loss. Most of them looked as bad as Linda – or
worse. Starved *things* with eternal clock springs,
bumping around the ruins.

An ear-piercing sound ripped across the sky. Kylie
looked up. Three brilliant pinwheel lights accelerated
bullet-fast and vanished to the east. When she looked
down again a man – a normal man – was walking
toward her through the milling SABs. He was dressed
in a tan Navy uniform and black baseball cap with USS
CARL VINSON stitched in gold letters on the front.
Kylie let the bike idle in place. It was almost as if the
restored world were walking toward her. The SABs, the
destruction, The Judgment – all of it about to be banished
by this perfectly mundane-appearing representative of
The Way Things Used to Be. Only when he got closer
did Kylie see his uniform was ill-fitting, dirty and worn
through at the knees, and the man himself looked as
sick as anyone Kylie had seen in Oakdale. Sicker than
her mother by far. A patchy two-day beard shadowed
his face. His eyes looked a million years old, red and
rheumy. A couple of his fingernails were missing, the

exposed skin pulpy – a later stage indicator of the sickness that killed everyone, eventually. Everyone but her. She guessed the man was about thirty-five.

"You don't look so bad," he said. "My name's Wolcott."

"I'm Kylie. I'm a pilot." That was what Billy had wanted her to tell the Big Boat people, so they would let her stay. She turned the Goldwing's engine off.

Wolcott removed his cap and blotted his fever-damp forehead with his shirt sleeve. His hair was patchy, the bald places red and scabrous. "Is that so," he said. He grinned, revealing teeth yellow as banana skin – another sign of advanced-stage poisoning. Kylie had the feeling he hadn't grinned in a long time.

"I used to be an engineer, before the world ended," he said. "Not much left to engineer, lately. Except the *Penetrator*."

"I know what that is. Billy told me."

"Do tell."

"It's a jet."

"F-18 to be precise. And you think you're gonna fly it. That's why you told me you're a pilot, right?"

"My friend told me to say that, but it's true. I've flown little airplanes."

"Little ones, huh?" He flashed his banana teeth again.

"Back *off*," Kylie said to a skin-and-bone man who was crowding her. He was wearing a long-sleeved shirt, filthy and ragged, the cuffs hanging in tatters around his wrists. A pair of wire-framed glasses sat crooked on his nose, like somebody had tried to slap them off his face and he'd just left them that way. The SAB didn't seem to hear Kylie, but when she pushed at him he shuffled off.

"You don't have to worry about these things," Wolcott said. "They're harmless. They aren't even real people, we don't think. More like malfunctioning biological robots."

"Whatever. That doesn't mean I want them all over me."

"Where's this friend you mentioned?"

"He died."

Wolcott nodded. "Figures."

"What were those lights that flew over us a minute ago?"

"Alien ships, we think. You notice they sped up all of a sudden?"

"Yeah."

"They do that when they go through the Seattle Dome. They're hitting Mach one or better. The idea is maybe we can do the same. Which is the whole point of the *Penetrator*. Not much chance of it, though. There's only a few of us left on the *Vinson*. Six months ago we had a pilot, but he died. Before that, he was of the opinion that anybody trying to fly a jet off the deck of the *Carl Vinson* was committing the next best thing to outright suicide. The carrier's heeled over like six degrees. It'll take some real skill to get airborne. You got that kind of skill, Kylie?"

"No."

In the distance a siren wound up. Wolcott replaced his hat. "That's the P.O. He's probably worried I'll get caught in the rain. Anyway, you *have* flown before, right?"

"Yeah."

"So you might be our last chance, anyway. Me and the P.O. and Vina, we want to launch pretty bad. Our pilot's name was Crenshaw. Nice guy. When he said that stuff about suicide? He was smiling. It's the whole idea of initiating a counter-strike, even if it's hopeless. They – whatever 'they' are – kicked our asses, and we never fired a shot. The *Penetrator* comes equipped with two Hellfire missiles. *Something* generates that Dome. We'd like to knock it out. Too bad Crenshaw croaked before the plane was ready. We're *all* going to be dead soon. Be nice to kick back at least once. Don't you think so?"

"I guess."

"I like your enthusiasm, kid." Wolcott grinned. "Come on. Let's get you prepped for the mission."

The way he said it, it was like a joke Kylie was supposed to get but didn't.

THEY STOOD BEFORE a wall of gray steel twelve stories high. The USS *Carl Vinson* heeled over in the black shallows that had been a deep-water port. A cargo net hung from a large opening into the hangar deck of the crippled carrier. "We have to go up there," Wolcott said. Kylie looked at him doubtfully.

"Are you sure you can climb that?" she said.

He sniffed. "Are you sure you're a pilot?"

"I've flown airplanes."

"Little ones, you said. Piper Cubs and stuff like that, right?"

"Cessna."

"What's up there is not a Cessna."

"I didn't think it was."

Two people appeared at the opening to the hangar deck, a man and a woman. The woman, in Levi's and olive drab tank top, shouted down: "What have you got there, Barry?"

Wolcott cupped hands around his mouth and shouted back: "Cessna pilot."

"Aren't we lucky."

The woman pushed a winch arm forward. A seat hung from it at the end of a chain. A squeaky metal-rolling sound started and the chair began to slowly come down.

"Bosun's chair," Wolcott said to Kylie. "So, no, I can't climb the net. I'm too fucking sick. And I doubt you can fly the *Penetrator* but you're all we got."

THE 'AREN'T WE lucky' woman was a townie, a survivor. Her cheekbones were high and sharp under brown skin. Kylie guessed she was from south-of-the-border, like Argentina or someplace. Her name was Vina. After the shockwave mostly flattened Bremerton she'd made her way to the *Carl Vinson*. It was big and it was still floating and it provided shelter, not to mention food and potable water and a change of clothes. The man who had operated the winch was the only regular Navy among the local survivors. He had been a Petty Officer first class, not on the *Carl Vinson* but on the frigate *Montana*, which had been part of the escort supporting the *Vinson*. The *Montana* was now tits up on the bottom of the bay, the P.O. said. Everybody else was dead or dying. The crew deck of the *Carl Vinson* was rapidly turning into a morgue.

"Nobody comes up anymore," the P.O. said. "We're it."

The four of them stood on the flight deck, which leaned a few degrees to port and was surfaced with skidless rubber.

"We can't let this kid try and fly the *Penetrator*," Vina said. "She'll just crash it." Vina's face was hollow with sickness but her voice was strong, with a bitter edge of fury. She had large breasts, all but nakedly visible under the thin cotton tank top. Neither of the men seemed interested, though; they were just like the men in Oakdale. The poison rain or radiation or whatever it was had gotten their balls.

"Check that," the P.O. said, regarding Vina's observation. "No offence, kid."

The *Penetrator* was an F-18. It stood on the canted deck, its nose wheel hooked to the catapult shuttle. Steam vented around it. Steam powered the huge catapult pistons under the deck. The ship's nuclear reactor provided the steam. Kylie got all this from Wolcott on the walk from Bremerton. Someone had painted 'Penetrator' on the side of the jet.

"At least she's flown a plane," Wolcott said, "even if it was a Cessna."

"Jesus fucking Christ," the P.O. said, without much emotion, as if he were remarking on the weather.

"If she crashes the *Penetrator* we lose our one chance to *strike back*," Vina said.

Wolcott, who had been swaying a little, sat down on the deck. He looked sicker just from the walk back from what was left of Bremerton. He had been an engineer before the world ended, he told Kylie. He had been living on the *Carl Vinson* ever since. All that was about to end, though, especially the living part.

"If we're all dead," Wolcott said, "nobody strikes back."

"Jesus fucking Christ," the P.O. said again. He had the look of a beefy man who had lost his beef all at once. His skin *sagged* on his bones. His hound dog face

Jack Skillingstead

suggested doom wasn't far off. "How much do you know how to fly, kid?"

Kylie shrugged. She knew she didn't have a chance of piloting the military jet safely off the deck of the *Carl Vinson*. She had only told Wolcott she was a pilot so he would let her come to the Big Boat, which Billy seemed to think was a safe place. Now that she was here it didn't seem any safer than Oakdale. In fact, it seemed less safe. And they expected her to fly in the morning? What bullshit. Besides that, they would have let her stay, whether she was a pilot or not. Everybody was dying. The people would run out long before the food and water.

"Did you solo, at least?" Wolcott asked.

"Yeah. I had like twenty-five hours."

Vina spat and shook her head.

"That's twenty-five hours more than *you*," Wolcott said. "Kylie flies. One of us goes with her."

"Which one?" Vina said.

"Whichever one is still alive in the morning, I guess."

After sunset the eastern sky turned green. Kylie stood on the deck, arms folded, looking at it.

"It's the Seattle Dome," Wolcott said. He held a Navy duffel bag in his arms. He looked weak. "Brought you some blankets and a pillow. You should come below decks, though. It might rain."

"I want to sleep in the open," Kylie said. Everything below decks smelled like death and rot. "I don't care about the rain. I'm immune."

"Nobody's immune. You're just young. It's epigenetic."

"It's what?"

"Epigenetic. We had people working on it, but they all died before they could get anywhere. The aliens basically weaponized the upper atmosphere with self-replicating retroviruses. That's the light show you see at night. It filters down continuously, probably world-wide. We're breathing them all the time, but the rain brings the mother lode. Enters through the pores, not just breathing. The retro-viruses attach to a variety of genes. Genes that cover sexual arousal, for instance. But a lot of different ones, wrecks us pretty good, and it will go on until there's not a single human being left alive, I guess. Bastards know a lot more about our genome than we do. Anyway, the viruses trigger the mutated genes, which produce all sort of weird proteins, and, *bingo*, we're sick as dogs and nobody gets out alive. Kid, some of these genetic changes don't get going till you're well past puberty."

"I'm eighteen," Kylie said.

"Where you come from, were there any others like you – young, I mean?"

"Some, but they all got sick right away."

"You're not immune, Kylie. Nobody is. You're just a late bloomer."

Kylie wanted him to stop talking. She pulled the bag from his arms, and Wolcott swayed back, as if it had been counter-balancing him. "I'm sleeping up here, and I don't care if it rains. If I'm going to die tomorrow, I want to be able to breathe tonight"

Wolcott didn't look happy.

"You know I can't fly this plane, right?" Kylie said.

"Sure, I know. Kid, we just want to see it go. Like fireworks – you want to light 'em off, because that's what you do with them, right?"

"You guys are crazy."

"Yes, ma'am."

IT DID NOT rain. Kylie woke on the hard rubberized surface of the deck. In the morning light the green glow was gone. A thick blanket of clouds shrouded the dawn. The air felt damp and expectant. She wanted to get away from the Big Boat before any of the others woke (if they *did* wake) and expected her to light off the last firework. She rolled up her bedding and stuffed it back into the duffel bag and left it slumped against the nose wheel of the jet.

SHE RODE THE Goldwing back into the ruined city. With Billy gone and the Big Boat nothing but a floating death house there was no point in hanging around. *Gown*. She couldn't return to Oakdale – not unless she wanted Father Jim to cut her. She would try south. Maybe there were more survivors, or at least better weather, in Oregon or California. It didn't really matter. She wasn't immune. In her heart she had known that, but a piece of her had gone on believing she would live, that she was special – maybe even chosen. It was so completely stupid. She was no different than anybody else. Her hair would fall out, her teeth go rotten – everything she'd seen happen to others was going to happen to her, too.

She idled the bike in the middle of the street, taking a last look at Bremerton. Now she would ride south, until her gas ran out, and then whatever happened, happened. Thunder growled out of the clouds. A raindrop appeared on the wing mirror. She looked up, and the sky unloaded. She opened her mouth and closed her eyes. It was a suicide rain and it didn't matter. Then someone called her name.

A man in a baggy white full-body suit peddled a wobbly bicycle toward her. He was wearing rubber gloves. His head was covered by a hood. The face behind a clear plastic plate was Wolcott's. His voice muffled by the hood, he panted, "You have to get out of the rain."

She shook her head. "It's okay. You said I'm going to get sick anyway."

Wolcott dumped the bike and staggered to her. "Listen." His face was agonized behind the foggy, rain-beaded plate. "I like you, kid. You remind me of the good old days, right?" Kylie felt bad for him – the effort it must have taken, in his condition, to catch up with her.

"I'm not flying your jet," she said. "I can't. I'd just crash it, like Vina says."

"Fuck the jet. But you have to get out of the rain, okay?"

"Okay." She turned back the key, climbed off the bike and walked with him to the one intact building. It was dark inside the Red White and Blue Diner. Wolcott removed his hood and stepped behind the dusty counter. Sugar dispensers and salt and pepper shakers stood neatly upon it, waiting for customers to sit on the red vinyl swivel stools. Pictures of aircraft carriers and other Navy ships hung on the walls. Kylie turned away, feeling sad, and racked the blinds up on one of the big windows. The rain was really coming down.

"Hey," Wolcott said, and when she turned he tossed her a bar towel. "Dry off."

She caught the towel, patted her face, and dropped

the towel on the floor. It really just did not matter. Rain rattled on the roof like a shower of marbles. The Goldwing looked beaten down, obscured by blowing curtains. Kylie crawled into the booth and got close to the window. She had never seen such rain. It dumped out of the sky in a thundering flood.

"You've got a nice ass," Wolcott said.

Kylie scooted off the bench and faced him.

"Not that I care," Wolcott said. He sat on a counter stool, swiveling listlessly back and forth. "It's merely an observation. Man, I wish you *could* fly the *Penetrator*."

"Well, I can't."

"Maybe you–"

"I'm tired of *talking*," Kylie said.

"Right. Okay, listen, I want to give you something. Then I'll stop talking. Promise."

Wolcott slid off the stool and crossed to Kylie. He unzipped his bio suit, reached inside, and tried to hand Kylie a thing like an over-sized TV remote with a digital display grid. She made no move to take it.

"What is it?"

"Electromagnetic field detector," he said. "I fooled around with it, so it keys to the Dome's weird signature pulse."

"What do I need it for?"

"Nothing, since you aren't going inside the Dome. But if you were – I mean, if you changed your mind, or some miracle happened – you could maybe use it as a locator, track down the machine that maintains the Dome."

Kylie stared at him

"Get close enough and the reading will spike. That's the theory. There's never any shortage of theories, is there? Did you know all *kinds* of things produce

207

electromagnetic fields? Cell phones, the sun, microwave ovens. Human brains. There's even a theory that consciousness exists in the brain's EM field. Maybe that thing's a giant brain, huh?"

"Yeah, sure. Can we stop talking now?"

"All right. Hey, what's going on out there?"

Two men stood by Kylie's Goldwing. One of the men wore a long coat and a broad-brimmed black hat. "*Shit*," Kylie said.

"What?" Wolcott slid off the stool and joined her at the window.

"I know those guys. That's Father Jim with the hat. My boyfriend shot him in the head and he didn't die. He told people back in my hometown that it meant he was a messenger of God, and everybody believed in him. The other one's Ray Preston. He's an asshole."

Jim opened the storage compartments. A flask stuck out of Ray Preston's hip pocket. He reached for something on the control console and the Honda's engine started.

"Damn," Kylie said, "I forgot the key."

"Here comes the welcoming committee," Wolcott said.

SABs shuffled and lurched out of the blasted buildings, drawn to the noise of the motorcycle engine. There were even more than when Kylie arrived. Ray Preston, with his scarecrow body and scraggly Crypt Keeper hair streaming wet to his shoulders, could have been one of the skin-and-bone people himself.

"They want to hurt me," Kylie said. "Father Jim and Ray."

"Why?"

"They think I'm different. They don't know I'm going to get sick like everybody else. Even *I* didn't know that.

Father Jim thinks if he cuts my clit off like they do in the *National Geographic*, God will let everybody go to Heaven."

"*What?*"

Out in the street Ray had grabbed Billy's rifle out of its scabbard. He may have looked like one of them, but the SABs crowding around the motorcycle were definitely not his brethren. Father Jim tried to wrest the rifle out of Preston's hands. Preston jerked it away. The butt came up, clouting Jim in the jaw and sending him down. The weapon discharged. A bullet crashed through the window of the Red White and Blue Diner and ripped open Wolcott's throat. Wolcott spun away from the window, bright arterial blood spraying his white bio suit. Kylie caught her scream before it could escape.

With the window blown out the rain was deafening. Gunfire came in undramatic pops. Kylie dropped to the floor, below the line of sight and fire. She bit down on her knuckles to keep the next scream inside. Wolcott thrashed, making gurgling sounds, blood spouting from his torn carotid. He kicked a wooden diner chair over, tried to sit up, fell back and was still. A blood bubble grew out of the wound and burst at the same time that Wolcott's limbs stopped jerking and twitching.

Kylie cautiously raised her head above the window sill. Father Jim was on his knees, praying or stunned. Ray had Billy's big-ass revolver in his fist, the rifle cast aside, either empty or jammed. SAB bodies with ruined heads lay in the street. The other SABs appeared confused. Some stumped away, some loitered in their usual empty-chicken-head fashion. Ray removed the flask from his hip pocket, spun the cap off, threw his head back and finished the whiskey or whatever was in it.

Kylie reached into her boot, where her good-for-a-girl gun should have been, but it wasn't there. She had slept with the gun and must have rolled it up with the bedding and left it in the duffel. She yanked the boot off and shook it, unable to believe she had done something so stupid. But she had.

Ray Preston pushed the barrel of the Magnum into the face of a cowering SAB in a ragged business suit and pulled the trigger. The back of the SAB's head blew out. Nearby skin-and-bone people scattered in their halting, ineffective way. Ray chased after one, holding his gun out with both hands. Licks of yellow flame appeared at the muzzle, and the SAB pitched over. Ray leaped past the body on his bandy legs and chased down another target.

Kylie pulled her boot back on and crawled away from the window. Her hands skidded in Wolcott's blood. She crawled all the way to the dry storage room in the back of the kitchen. There was a ladder leading to a trapdoor in the ceiling. She climbed the ladder, her blood-slippery hands sliding on the rungs. At the top she shoved the trap open – the hinges stiff and complaining – and got a face full of rain. She climbed onto the roof, dropped the trap closed. A gunshot popped in the alley behind the diner. The slug pinged off something metallic. Kylie squat-walked to the edge of the roof and cautiously peered over.

A female SAB pressed face and hands against the brick wall of the diner, trapped between the wall and a big green trash dumpster. Ray Preston blocked her in, clumsily reloading Billy's revolver. He dropped a couple of bullets and dug more out of his filthy jeans. The SAB looked up the side of the building, saw Kylie. It was Linda, the SAB that had told Kylie to "gown". Kylie pulled back from the edge and looked around. Four cinderblocks pinned down the corners of a tarp. She picked up one of the cinderblocks with both hands and the wind blew the loose corner of the tarp up, flapping it like a pennant and revealing a few roofing tools, a broom with bristles glued stiff with old tar, a five-gallon drum. She lugged the block to the edge of the roof. Ray had finished reloading and was bringing the gun up. Kylie dropped the cinder block. On impact, Ray's head burst like a watermelon.

Linda looked up at her again. Kylie didn't smile, or wave, or give a thumbs up. She turned away and vomited. Ray deserved it, and he was going to die pretty soon, anyway. But Kylie had just killed him to save a thing that wasn't even human.

In the distance, the wind-up siren commenced its urgent wail. The P.O. calling them back to the *Carl Vinson*. Kylie lifted the trap-door and climbed back down to the diner.

Linda had found her way inside.

"I like it here," the SAB mumbled. Ray Preston's blood splattered her grimy waitress's uniform. Wads of brain matter snagged in her wet straw hair. Linda's head was a talking skull stretched over with drum-tight skin, a pair of big wet eyes slipping around in deep sockets. Kylie had murdered a man for this thing?

"I want to work here," Linda said

"Knock yourself out," Kylie said. She found another bar towel behind the counter and used it to dry her face and hair. Linda shuffled around the diner, bumping into tables and chairs, muttering. Kylie knew she should go to the alley and retrieve the gun from Ray's dead fist but she couldn't bring herself to do it. She dropped the towel and looked at her hands. Wolcott's blood smeared them. Sobs rose in her throat and she swallowed them back down and kept them there.

In the ladies' room, Kylie squirted liquid soap into paper towels and scrubbed at her bloody hands. She could hear Linda blundering around. Kylie pulled the restroom door shut and locked it. She sat on the floor in the dark and prayed Jim wouldn't find her. She had slept poorly the previous night. It was quiet in the rest room. She drifted.

She came awake in the dark and was frightened. Groping for the exit, she found a counter and sink basin. "*Fuck*." Ass to the sink, she put her arms out and walked straight to the door and out. Linda was gone. Kylie stepped around Wolcott's body.

The Goldwing idled in the street, gray clouds condensing from its tailpipes. A number of SAB bodies, heads blown and limbs twisted, lay around it. The rain had slacked off, though the sky remained turbulent. Father Jim was nowhere in sight. It had been hours and the Honda had idled away a good deal of fuel. Kylie mounted the bike and looked west, where Kitsap Way eventually connected to Highway 3, then she looked east, which would take her back to the *Carl Vinson*.

Soon Kylie would fall ill, like all the others. Sooner than that, something else would probably get her, alone on the road to California. She hadn't wanted to die crashing the *Penetrator*. But what if she didn't have to? What if there was a chance, a *real* chance, that she could fly into a world that at least appeared the way it used to be, before The Judgment? Father Jim was an experienced jet pilot. With him at the controls it was possible. He would have gone to the wail of the siren, gone to the *Carl Vinson*. By now the P.O. and Vina would have filled him in.

Of course, he might attack her on sight. Try to cut her. But it was worth the chance. Anything was worth the chance.

She swung off the Goldwing and ran back inside the Red White and Blue Diner. Wolcott's locator – the EM field detector – lay under a table near his body. She grabbed it and stuffed it in a deep pocket of her leather jacket. Like a good luck totem.

THE P.O. SAID, "We got us a *real* pilot."

"I know," Kylie said. "It's like a miracle, huh? Where's Vina?"

"Croaked last night. That's why I wound up the siren. You and Wolcott both gone, wanted to know if I was the last one standing. Instead of you guys, up walks this priest. Where's Wolcott, anyway?"

"Same as Vina."

"Fuck me," the P.O. said

The *Penetrator's* canopy was open and somebody was sitting in the pilot's seat. The wind blew his wild gray hair around like the scraggly strands of an old mop. He went still when Kylie and the P.O. approached, then turned his head slowly. Kylie winced. It looked like a little volcano was growing out of the priest's forehead. The bullet hole he kept gouging to keep it looking fresh was yellow and green, erupting with pus. "There's my little co-pilot," Father Jim said.

Kylie folded her arms, relieved and terrified. "Yep."

*   *   *

THE P.O. HELPED strap Kylie into her seat behind Father Jim in the narrow cockpit. He cinched the harness tight, almost too tight for her to breathe. Kylie grunted. "Sorry," the P.O. said. "Between the catapult and the thrust, you go from zero to a hundred seventy knots in two seconds. See this?" He pointed at a red handle between Kylie's legs. "That ejects you, seat and all. Keep your hand off it unless the plane's crashing. It probably will, so you better know what to do." He delivered a brief lecture on parachuting from a high performance jet aircraft.

"It sounds scary."

"Roger that." The P.O. patted the top of Kylie's helmet. "So long, kid." Like he was already talking to a corpse.

"Bye." Kylie had to pee.

"Good luck to you, Father." The P.O. shook Jim's hand. "You're going to need it."

"Ye of little faith," Father Jim said.

"Faith's got nothing to do with it."

"I'm ready," Kylie said. "Let's go before I chicken out."

After the P.O. closed the canopy, Jim said, "Just like old times."

"Are we going to crash?"

"If the Lord so wills it."

"Jim? It's not about God or anything. That guy Wolcott told me everybody gets sick. I will, too, if the plane doesn't crash. It's just because I'm young. But I'll get it, like everybody else."

"I have to concentrate now, Kylie."

"What I'm saying, it's not God's Judgment and it's not me holding anybody back. You can see that, right?"

With the canopy closed Kylie could smell Father's Jim's infection. It made her want to gag.

"Your cleansing is only postponed, either in this world or the next. God put me in this place to fly one last mission. I knew it as soon as the P.O. laid out the situation. There are no coincidences. We blow the Dome, end that abomination. But afterwards you and I have business. Verily, and He called His lambs home. No more talking now."

Jim reached forward, knuckled over a toggle and thumbed a button. The engine ignited with a primal roar. The airplane shuddered. A Heads-Up display winked on in front of the priest. Kylie stared through the top of the canopy at the sky. Lightning flickered inside purple-gray mountains of cloud. She was going to die. Kylie put her hand over the red handle between her legs.

The engine ran up to a piercing scream. The *Penetrator* vibrated and strained. Jim moved the ailerons up and down, swung the rudder, testing control surfaces just as he had taught Kylie to do in the Cessna 150 trainer.

"Hang on," he said.

Kylie tensed her body. There was nothing to hang on *to*. Jim throttled up. Kylie couldn't believe they weren't moving yet. Steam vented from the catapult below the deck and blew past the canopy. Suddenly they blasted forward, the force of acceleration pinning Kylie like a piston slammed into her chest. The deck fell away and the *Penetrator* yawed dangerously. The starboard wing dipped, inches from cartwheeling them into a fireball. Jim corrected the slip. The *Penetrator* angled away over black shallows, lost altitude, then nosed up, gained stability and sped into the wild sky.

The blasted lands dropped beneath them. The *Penetrator* roared through cloud canyons aflicker with electrical bursts.

The great Dome over Seattle dominated the horizon. It reached thousands of feet into the sky and appeared to be made of green glass – if glass could be in constant, seething motion. The city skyline wavered like a heat mirage. Despite her fear, Kylie gaped, awestruck.

Jim pulled the *Penetrator* into a steep bank. The wings leveled and they gained distance from the Dome, getting a run at it. The *Carl Vinson* passed beneath them like a great gray tombstone tumbled in black water. A brilliant shimmer occurred above them, different than the lightning. A blinding pinwheel swept out of the muscular cloud mass. Jim banked the jet again, shrieking into a turn so steep and tight Kylie thought the wings would rip away. Again they leveled off. Afterburners mule-kicked them straight at the green Dome. The plane shuddered with unbridled acceleration.

Pinwheel light strobed into the cockpit, played over Kylie's hands and thighs. She squirmed and gritted her teeth, as if someone were touching her. The pinwheel light retreated when the interior of the cockpit turned green. Kylie looked up in time to see the wall an instant before they struck it.

PART TWO

"To remember and to wake up are absolutely interchangeable."

THE EXEGESIS OF PHILIP K. DICK

CHAPTER TWENTY-ONE

THEY TUNNELED THROUGH a green syrup world that muffled all sound. Kylie tried to say something to Father Jim but didn't seem to have sufficient air in her lungs to produce words. Outside the *Penetrator's* canopy, embedded like insects in amber, planes, cars, buses, boats, animals and people tumbled past into the jet's wake. None of this had been visible from outside the Dome. Kylie craned her neck, trying to see it all. They passed alongside a ferry half the length of a football field, the name *Elwha* plainly visible on her bow. The boat heeled over – and appeared to *shrink*. Kylie rubbed her eyes in disbelief. As they left the ferry behind, it was no larger than her thumb.

The syrupy green gloom was growing lighter.

Something drew up alongside the jet, something moving against the tide – something tunneling. It was the pinwheel light that had chased after them outside the Dome. Its shape was clearly discernible now: a ball maybe twenty-five feet in diameter, with other, much smaller, balls orbiting this nucleolus in sharp geometrically precise patterns. It reminded Kylie of Discovery Channel animations of atoms.

The atom ship drew in closer. A node appeared on the side of the sphere, elongated, aiming straight at them. *They're going to shoot,* Kylie thought. *They're going to shoot us.*

The world grew lighter and lighter until the *Penetrator* punched through into a cloud-blown sky. The sudden shift in light dazzled Kylie. The jet shot forward with greater acceleration even than the catapult launch off the deck of the *Carl Vinson*. It crushed Kylie into her seat. The engine scream ripped into her eardrums.

FATHER JIM STRUGGLED to control the aircraft, afraid they would overshoot the city and plunge back into the Dome. Airspeed pegged at three hundred knots. He cut the thrust, dropped flaps, fought the stick. Something struck the aft section. A tremendous jolt rocked the plane. Buzzers and alarms sounded. The jet began to veer. Jim pushed on rudder pedals that offered no resistance – the linkages severed. The artificial horizon rocked wildly and the compass rolled like a roulette wheel. He craned his head around. The whole tail section was engulfed in a burning red glow that moved rapidly toward the cockpit, devouring metal.

IAN STARED AT his coffee – his third refill, this one gone cold. Espresso machines hissed like steam engines through the babble of conversation around him, while memories separated through the sieve of his compromised consciousness.

The roar of a jet engine jarred him out of himself. It sounded dangerously low and... *off*, like there was something wrong with it.

Ian followed about half the Seattle's Best customers into Post Alley and caught a glimpse of a military jet, wings rocking erratically, the tail section glowing bright red and trailing smoke as the jet hurtled east.

It's from outside, Ian thought, briefly grasping the significance, before the whole idea of outside and inside slipped down a memory drain, along with everything else he had been fighting to recover. Now fear eclipsed the struggle. He felt alien among all these *people* milling around him – these imposters. Ian started walking fast, and then he was running for his bike, fleeing toward the only safe place he could think of.

THE JET ENGINE roar backed off and the flaps dropped. The sudden drag threw Kylie against her restraints. Then something struck the *Penetrator* from behind. The airframe shuddered violently. Jim craned his head around, and she saw fear on his face. She turned to see what he was seeing. The tail was *melting*. The *Penetrator* nosed up steeply, gained a little altitude, then seemed to hang suspended. The stall alarm trumped all the other alarms already going off.

Kylie yanked the red ejection handle.

Explosive bolts blew the hatch. Wind roared into her face. She launched out of the cockpit at tremendous acceleration. It was so loud Kylie couldn't even hear herself scream. The P.O. had explained this part to her, but she was too rattled and everything was happening too fast. The little rocket motor attached to her chair cut out almost immediately, and the chair dropped away with her stomach, even as the drogue chute deployed. Her teeth snapped together when the harness, too big for her little body, jerked painfully into her armpits, and she swung helplessly up.

The *Penetrator*, more than half engulfed in the melting red glow, and with Father Jim still strapped in the pilot's seat, stalled, rolled over, and plunged through scudding clouds, By the time it hit Lake Washington it was a streaking meteor, not even recognizable as an airplane. On impact it made a big white splash and was gone. Steam rose from the water and boats began to converge on the spot.

Kylie drifted beneath a desert-camo nylon umbrella. It was suddenly quiet, almost serene. She looked around for the atom ship, thought she saw a flicker of pinwheel light on the periphery of her vision, but as much as she turned her head she couldn't quite catch up to it. Like the atom ship was *there* and *not* there at the same time, racing away at tremendous speed.

She didn't know how to control the parachute. The air currents carried her back towards Elliott Bay. Gradually, the ground came up. She would hit the jagged tumble of rocks bordering a waterfront park and the bay. Kylie tugged at the shroud lines, trying to steer away from the rocks. It worked. She sailed back, a hundred feet above the park. Women pushed strollers along a winding, paved pathway. Three guys spun a Frisbee back and forth while a yellow dog bounded tirelessly between them, trying to catch the thing. A guy jogging in a blue workout suit stopped and pointed.

The wind pulled Kylie toward a wooded hillside. Trees swung beneath her. She drew her legs up, trying to protect herself moments before she crashed through the branches. Bristly swags roughed her up, slapped her face. There was a thick pine scent. The chute snagged in the branch tangle and Kylie came up short, dangling ten feet off the ground like a broken marionette.

She groped for the quick release that the P.O. had shown her, couldn't remember what it looked like, started yanking and pawing at every buckle and hook. She needed to get *down*. To her left a well-maintained nature trail wound out to the park.

Voices approached, people climbing the trail to find her.

Kylie twisted a latch, expecting nothing, and fell clear of the shroud lines, hit the sloping ground at an angle, and pitched face-first into the bushes.

She hurt, but nothing was broken. Her face stung where the pine swags had slapped her. She unstrapped her helmet, pulled it off.

A woman said, "Are you all right?"

Kylie didn't move.

Somebody else, a man, said, "Call 911." Already a siren was rising in the distance. Was it for her, or the crashed jet, or a more usual emergency?

Before anybody else arrived, before anybody touched her, before she had to answer questions – Kylie dropped her helmet, bolted to her feet and ran like hell.

IAN LOCKED HIMSELF in his apartment. He checked the windows to make sure they were securely latched.

He turned off his phone.

His fear didn't seem to be *attached* to anything. He was used to living in a private bubble of formless anxieties. But this was far worse. Unrecovered memories, like shadowy beasts, humped back and forth behind his mind.

The apartment smelled stale, his dirty socks and underwear mixed up with the last of his clean stuff, scattered on the floor. Mundane chores, like going to the basement to wash clothes – Ian hated them, hated the necessary routines, the dullness. He avoided them as long as he could. The garbage needed to go out, too. He had cooked a Gino's pepperoni pizza a couple of nights ago and left the crusts on the kitchen counter. That stale pizza smell lingered.

He gathered his set of Marks-A-Lot pens out of his backpack and sat on the floor, his back to the wall. He held the pens loose in his open hands. Green, red, blue, purple. Black. It was a cheap set. He dropped the four colored ones and pulled the cap off the black one.

The ink mixed with whatever chemical they used to saturate the tips – it smelled like home. The only home Ian ever trusted. That home, like all his others, had ultimately failed him. But maybe there was some magic left, something to ward off the Bad Stuff now stalking him, from either inside or outside his head.

Voices spoke in the next apartment, muffled by the thick plaster walls. They didn't even sound human. What if they *weren't* human? He pictured Body Snatcher pod people, blank-faced, discussing the big takeover. He pictured animals, upright bears with vaguely human light in their red eyes. Worse: he pictured his dad's ancient turntable, the one on which he used to play Beatle records when he got loaded and fucked around with the basket-case Indian. The turntable and old-school amp in a blank room, two speakers attached and aimed at the common wall between the empty apartment and Ian's living room – faking human occupation for Ian's benefit. Trying to trick him into believing he wasn't alone, the last man alive. That shit wasn't going to work.

He held the pen close to his face, touched the tip of his tongue to the stiff fiber point, then twisted around and pressed the marker to the wall, pressed hard, making a tight scribble. The mark looked like a bullet hole, the way a comic book artist would ink it. He rolled onto his knees to continue – to make something out of the comic book bullet hole – but hesitated.

They weren't going to come through the fucking *wall*. Whatever 'they' were. Whatever crazy shit was taking over his mind now.

But really, start at the door.

He crawled across the room, knelt in front of the door. Someone walked by in the corridor outside his apartment, heavy footsteps, no voice. Ian held his breath. After the footsteps passed, he began. The marker squeaked against the door frame. He made rudimentary block letters, vertically climbing the frame:

W
H
O

He made more, and more – shaping letters between the letters, interlinking them, covering the door frame in a voodoo chain. But that seemed inadequate, so he filled in the door's three panels, as well, working close up, fingers crabbed around the thick barrel of the pen, inhaling the drug-home-scent of marker ink. By the time he finished the door, the pen was dead, dried up, the tip mashed to pulp. He tossed it and grabbed the rest of the set off the floor. There was also a half-empty Sabotaz can of primary red. Together, was it enough for the whole apartment? He doubted it. But he could do the windows then retreat to the bathroom. That would work.

Hours later, Ian slumped in the empty bathtub, surrounded by WHO tags in a variety of marker colors. He had used the spray can on the shower enclosure itself, and the letters ran like blood down damp blue tiles, channeled into the mildewed grout lines.

The stink of paint and ink was overpowering. His head throbbed. But he remained in the tub, behind the locked door and magic tags, stayed there while the hours ran out.

KYLIE FLED. BEHIND her, a man shouted, "Hey, hey!" She ran harder. No one tried to stop her. She sprinted out of the park, pounded along the waterfront of tourist bars, import shops, long piers pointing into the bay. Everything was so *normal*; a world wholly intact, even if it was some kind of illusion. Emotion kept swelling her throat. The restored world clobbered her senses.

A policeman mounted on a brown horse looked in her direction. She slowed to a jog that tapered into a normal walk, like she was just trying to get somewhere and was tired of running – not like she was running *from* something. She crammed her hands in her jean pockets and kept her head down, half expecting the cop to say something. He didn't.

Kylie walked for a while then stopped and looked into the sky of broken clouds, clouds that weren't full of poison, hanging over a world that at least *appeared* unchanged since before The Judgment. She wiped her eyes, swallowed down her emotions. The end of the world wasn't a Judgment of God, which was what everyone back in Oakdale believed. It wasn't 'The Judgment' at all; it was *the Invasion*.

Footsteps clocked on the pavement behind her. Kylie glanced over her shoulder. Two giants strode toward her. They wore rust-colored coats, like ribbed cones slipped over their bodies. Kylie stumbled on the curb, found her footing, turned again. Somehow, the giants had reduced to the size of men. Their heads were still bald and pink as baby skin, though. And the air above their heads and shoulders wavered slightly, like a heat mirage on a desert road. And like a mirage, the rising heat appeared to veil a secret image: the giants Kylie had first glimpsed. Even in the seconds she watched, the heat waver smoothed out, became invisible.

A trick.

Kylie didn't question the reality of what she saw. She simply reacted to it, jogging ahead of the bald men, into a more populated stretch of waterfront. When she looked back, they were gone.

The sky was rapidly clearing. Dazzling sunlight shone over everything, souvenir shops, fish restaurants with sidewalk access, tourist vendors selling balloons, hotdogs, ice cream. Big white seagulls sailed with the wind or hovered against it. Multitudes of healthy people, young and old, even children, even the very old, thronged the sidewalks And there were animals, dogs on leashes, horses harnessed to open carriages. Motorized vehicles, cars and buses and motorcycles. A blizzard of life and motion (if it *was* life), crashing Kylie's hungry senses. She was really here, in the *Sleepless* city, the *Say Anything* city. She closed her eyes a moment.

The World continued to invade her other senses. The salty smell of Elliott Bay, instead of the sour brackish stink of black water outside the Dome. Birds screeched, human voices gabbled, engines revved. The touch of moving air against her face. A ferry's horn sounded a great, shuddering blast, as the boat pulled away from the dock. Kylie remembered the *Elwha* in the soupy green space between the outside and the inside of the Dome.

She opened her eyes. It had only been a couple of seconds. But one of the bald men was standing right in front of her. In his palm was some device, like a joke shop joy buzzer with a red laser-bright dot winking in the center. And he was dressed differently, his long rust-colored cone-coat gone, replaced by a short-sleeved shirt, jeans and tennis shoes – his whole body wavering slightly in another heat-mirage trick, automatically blending in with the crowd. The only thing he got wrong was his arms, which appeared too long.

Kylie threw herself back, and another pair of apishly long arms wrapped around her, and a baby-pink head pressed over her shoulder, as if she were in a lover's embrace. At the same time she sensed the *other*, the secret giant looming over her, enfolding her against its alien body.

The laser-dot joy buzzer came toward her forehead.

Kylie made herself skinny. It was a trick she'd learned early on with Father Jim, before he had gone too far but still farther than they both knew he should have been going. *How's my little co-pilot,* he said one day, when she arrived at the airstrip and he had been nowhere in sight but had suddenly come up behind her, pulling her against him with his big arms. Kylie was little. She brought her arms in tight, bending her shoulders, narrowing her already narrow body, then going dead-weight and dropping, not caring about falling down and looking stupid, just needing to get *out* of Jim's arms, at least that first time.

It worked now, too.

She slipped through the bald man's long arms. Her ass hit the sidewalk between a forest of limbs. The joy buzzer came towards her face. She twisted away, scrambled to her feet, and bolted at a dead run into traffic. Horns blared. Kylie put her arm out as a yellow cab screamed to a halt on its front tires. And then she was across the road, leaping over a set of trolley rails, running full-out under the immense shadow of an elevated highway, massive gray columns of concrete and the rhythmic thud-thud of traffic hitting the spacers directly over her head.

She stole a backward look. The aliens weren't following. Or they might have been, only further disguised.

Kylie poured on a final burst of speed, pumping her legs up the hill to First Avenue. She swung right, tried to blend in with other pedestrians, then slipped into the lobby of the Alexis Hotel. A man in a sport coat and red tie looked up from a computer screen at the front desk. Kylie avoided his eyes and acted like she was waiting for someone. There were chairs and upholstered benches, and the lobby opened into a bar on one side and some kind of gift shop on the other. Kylie sat on one of the benches. Plenty of people circulated through the lobby, and no one took any particular notice of her.

But Kylie noticed them.

What if these *weren't* people? What if they were like Wolcott had said, some kind of biological robots – well fed and functional SABs, no different, fundamentally, than the skin-and-bone horrors she had seen out in the real world? But Wolcott could have been wrong. These could be real people, the real population of Seattle, trapped under an alien Dome without even knowing it, with the aliens acting as zoo keepers. Either way, how could Kylie tell? They all appeared so real and normal. She wanted to believe they *were* real.

She slipped her hand into the deep pocket of her leather coat. Wolcott's EMF detector was there, and a square of stiff paper. She withdrew the paper. It was the picture of her grandparents, the one she had taken from her mother's photo album the night she and Billy escaped from Oakdale. Kylie had forgotten all about it. Looking at the picture, the whole 'biological robot' idea retreated a little.

She replaced the photograph and took out the locator. It wouldn't hurt to see if the device worked. She held it in her lap. It was like an over-sized TV remote with a two-inch LED screen at the top. She thumbed the ON button. A grid came up. The screen glowed cold blue. She waited. Nothing else happened. She looked over at the front desk. The red tie man appeared busy talking to a fat guy with about ten bags piled around him. Kylie held the locator up and moved it around, trying to catch a signal. Nothing. The screen glowed blue and the grid remained empty. She got up and walked with it. Maybe outside...

As she approached the lobby door, a man pushed through it. He looked perfectly normal, kind of like a tourist, in tan pants and a loud yellow shirt, but the door's glass panel reflected a stooping giant.

Kylie ran into the gift shop, cut through it and out a side door. She halted on the sidewalk. Now what? She turned the EMF detector off and dropped it back in her pocket. What she needed was a safe place with plenty of people around. The library might work, and it was just a few blocks away, if she remembered correctly from the last time she was in Seattle – the real Seattle. Kevin, the boy-who-wasn't-a-boyfriend, had pointed out the weird glass and aluminum building that time they came for the Shins concert.

She grabbed a random book and installed herself at one end of a blond wood study table on the library's main floor. She shared the table with an intense guy in rimless glasses and a mop of curly black hair. He hunched over a book of poems, a couple more near at hand, waiting to be cracked. Kylie read the spines. Rimbaud. There had been a Rimbaud book at Billy's house, but Kylie had never gotten around to it. Thinking of Billy made her sad, so she stopped.

She wandered through the library, trying not to spend too much time in one spot. Periodically, she stepped outside, walked around the block, then came back in by a different door. She was hungry but had no money. She was also very tired. The library felt safe. She was afraid of another encounter with the aliens. What she really needed was a full night's sleep, for a change. She decided to get it in the library.

It was a matter of playing hide-and-seek, for a while, with security and staff. Only *they* didn't realize the game was on. Before closing time at six o'clock she ducked into a janitor closet on the second floor. After a while, someone approached the door, keys jingling, and she knew she'd made a mistake. Kylie stood in the floor sink, where they dumped old mop water, and pressed herself against the wall. The door opened, and she stopped breathing. The janitor switched the light on but did not come in. He went key-jingling to the restrooms on either side of the closet. First the men's. She heard the door bang against the wall. "Library's closed. Anybody in here?" Then at the women's room. The key man rapped his knuckles and spoke loudly, "Hello, anybody in there? Library's closing." The jingling keys sounded different when he entered the women's room. Kylie quickly slipped out of the closet and ran lightly into the periodical section, where she managed to stay out of sight until security completed its final sweep.

Eventually the library emptied even of janitorial staff, and Kylie came out of hiding. On the fourth floor she dragged a padded bench into the stacks and stretched out on it. She closed her eyes and tried to sleep. The tension in her body gradually unwound, and she lapsed into a dreamy doze. Some time later, when she opened her eyes, it was dark.

She sat up, groggy, rubbing her eyes. Not exactly a full night's sleep, but a decent nap. Her stomach grumbled and her mouth tasted bad. She found a water fountain, rinsed her mouth, and then she found an employee break room and raided the refrigerator. The big hand on an institutional-looking wall clock twitched within a couple of minutes of midnight.

Beyond the windows back in the reading room, the night city was lit up. Rain fell but not hard. Droplets beaded the tall windows, trembling with captured street light. Kylie didn't get too close, not wanting to risk being seen by someone outside.

She sat on the edge of a study table, gnawing on somebody's leftover deli chicken. A strange sensation came over her, unwinding in her stomach. She stopped chewing. Was the meat bad? Her head began to throb. She scooted off the table, an intense feeling of dislocation overcoming her. She dropped the chicken leg, stumbled forward on weak legs. Her vision grew hazy, and shadows began to spin out of the windows. She squinted, frightened and not understanding. Black, windless tornados spun out of every corner of the reading room, devouring space. She sank to her knees, head throbbing like a migraine, then tipped onto her side, whimpering. She pressed her hands over her eyes, pressed hard. The pain grew intense.

Then stopped.

Abruptly, the sick, twirly sensation in her stomach ceased. Pink light seeped between her fingers.

She brought her hands down slowly.

Morning.

That didn't begin to make sense. Only seconds ago it was the middle of the night. She stood up, barely breathing, and turned in a slow circle. Rosy morning light threw long shadows over the carpet. No fucking way was this really happening. She jerked when the elevator started, and she couldn't remember if she was on the third or fourth floor. For a moment she froze, facing the elevator doors, then ran for the stairs.

IAN PALMER FLOATED over his own dead body. It was like seeing it through crystalline water, as if he were a snorkeler noticing an interesting artifact sunk below him. He could flipper off, exploring, or he could drift down and have a closer look at the human wreckage. For a moment it really was a choice – one he failed to make. At which point the gravity of indecision drew him down. And the closer he approached the body, the muddier his thoughts became, until they were silted black and he felt the immense heaviness of his inert being.

He opened gummy eyelids, worked his mouth, almost tasting the stale air of his apartment. *Welcome to the Advent of a new day*. Whatever that was, some stupid commercial tag line for laundry detergent. He turned his head on the pillow. The red numerals on the digital clock said: 7:05AM.

Sleeping pill bottles crowded around the clock.

He sat up, suddenly frightened. Had he taken those? Vaguely, he recalled feeling depressed last night... desperately wanting to sleep...

Ian closed his eyes, held himself still, taking inventory of his body. He felt sleepy, but that was reasonable at seven am. If he had taken the powerful sleeping pills he wouldn't be sitting up in bed right now asking himself if he'd taken the powerful sleeping pills. One or two out of any of those bottles would have knocked him cold till noon.

He opened his eyes and the pill bottles were gone. He looked around the bed, on the floor. They were *gone*. Had he imagined seeing them? He stumped into the bathroom and looked in the medicine cabinet. All the bottles were there. His escape kit. He closed the mirrored door. His face mugged back at him, haggard and pale, chin peppered with two days' beard.

He peed, returned to bed, and pulled the sheet over his head. He had awakened out of a pleasant, floating dream, the details of which totally eluded him. But it would be nice to go back.

The phone went off before he got the chance. Startled, he flung himself over and fumbled the thing into his hand. ZACH, the little window said. Jesus Christ. Ian muted the phone and tried to go back to sleep. After a couple of hours of fitful tossing on the borderland, he gave it up.

The day stretched before him. He had every other Saturday off, so he didn't have to worry about work. A vague sense of gotta-be-somewhere niggled at him, but failing to retrieve the 'somewhere' from his sluggish brain, he dismissed it. Dirty dishes overflowed the sink. A Gino's pizza box lay on the floor. A fly trundled up the smudgy cabinet door over the microwave. Ian's stomach grumbled. He picked up the last banana. The skin was black, and what was inside felt like pulp. He dropped the banana in the trash and got dressed.

The inside of the apartment door was covered with graffiti. What the fuck? Between blinks, the tangle of WHOs vanished. Ian traced his fingertips over the wood, got up close, his nose practically touching the door. Nothing. Like the pill bottles, the graffiti was a memory so strong he could see it with his eyes, at least for a moment. But how did he even have the memory in the first place?

Seriously freaked, he got out of there, rode the Chief down to the waterfront, hoping to blow the ghosts out of his head.

HE PARKED HIS bike under the viaduct and started walking, the day loose about him like a shirt three sizes too large. He felt lonely, but no more so than usual. Certainly he wasn't lonely enough to return Zach's call. But that might change as the day progressed.

It was warm for October, almost summer-warm. There was even a vendor selling ice cream cones. Ian bought one, a late breakfast, and walked with it along the waterfront. People thronged the sidewalk, touristy types, a lot of them. A few horse-drawn carriages were parked at the curbside, waiting for suckers.

Ian stopped outside the Seattle Aquarium, something catching his eye. A jellyfish drifted in a silent world behind thick glass – a teaser to entice passersby to part with eight bucks. As a teaser, the jellyfish fell short. Ian stood watching it, while strawberry ice cream dripped on his shoe.

The jellyfish bothered him.

He watched it from a safe distance for a while, then asked himself, *Safe from what?* and approached the glass. Ian always felt vaguely afraid, or vaguely estranged, or vaguely lonely. But while The Great And Powerful Vague mostly ruled the day, a part of him rebelled and wanted to push back, to challenge his anxieties.

And, anyway, it was easy to challenge a jellyfish trapped in a tank.

As Ian started to step closer, an old guy in a blue 'Gilligan' hat walked in front of him. Ian pictured how the hat would look if somebody stuck it on a giant jellyfish. Okay, that was a weird thing to picture.

Ian moved closer to the tank.

The jellyfish drifted serenely through Ian's reflection. A ripple of irrational fear passed through him. Of *course* it was irrational. Ian had a touch of arachnophobia, yeah, but was there even a word to describe 'fear of jellyfish'? Probably. There was a word to describe almost every neurotic quirk he or anybody else could come up with. Ian knew that much from his on-and-off-again therapy and all the psychology books he'd read. Not to mention an intense biography of Phillip K. Dick.

He pressed his fingertips against the cool glass of the tank.

The jellyfish drifted.

A girl walked behind Ian on the sidewalk. He saw her reflection and turned. A teenager, twenty at *most*, wearing black jeans and a leather coat too heavy for the weather. Something like a clunky inventory scanner or giant TV remote stuck out of the pocket of her jacket. Kind of a biker girl with a bad haircut and a geek fetish. A really bad haircut. It looked like somebody had hacked at it with dull garden shears.

Ian recognized her.

Okay, that wasn't true; he didn't recognize her in the sense that he knew who she was. It was more like one tribe member in a strange land recognizing another member of the same tribe. Not that Ian *had* a tribe. But it used to be he could spot a fellow tagger or artist, even if he'd never seen them before. For a while, Ian's tribe had been the loose underground affiliation of graffiti artists. Not that this girl with the chopped hair was a bomber. But she was *something* to him. They were alike, the truth of it communicated instantly to him, like a pheromonal cannon blast. Almost before he knew what he was doing, he had ditched his ice cream cone and started walking after her.

CHAPTER TWENTY-TWO

KYLIE WAS ALONE. Oh, the city was jammed with people, or at least with things that looked and acted like people. But that just made her feeling of isolation worse. She was alone and she was hungry and scared.

She had been wandering the streets for hours, ever since the unexpected dawn forced her out of the library. With one eye open for alien tourists, she drank in the reality of the city. Everything about it was perfect – a perfect imitation of Seattle. Yesterday (if that word meant anything) this had thrilled her, like a dream of coming home to the restored world. But the illusion shattered when the day suddenly started over, like a DVD on replay. Would that happen every night, forever? It was a nightmare, not a dream. And now she was trapped in it with a bunch of dead doll-people.

Yeah, she was trapped – unless *she* did something about it.

She stopped walking and leaned on a rail, facing the bay. Twenty feet down, oil-sheened water slopped against the pilings. Beyond the waterfront a big green and white ferry churned toward a far shore – Winslow, or maybe even Bremerton. She thought of the real Bremerton, blasted and poisoned, a handful of people dying in the stifling lower decks of a crippled aircraft carrier, while skin-and-bone zombies shuffled around the ruins. Her anger began to rise. Anger at whoever *did* that to the world.

"Are you all right?"

Kylie started. A lean young man in a black hoodie and baseball cap loomed over her. Kylie's heart began beating faster. Her anger dropped away immediately. This wasn't another fake person or an alien; he was different. She sensed it immediately. He was different – like her. He was a real human being with fair skin, eyebrows like charcoal sketch marks, a small white scar on the bridge of his nose, and a trace of strawberry ice cream smeared on the corner of his mouth. She was tempted to wipe it away.

WHEN IAN NOTICED he was following the girl he almost made himself stop. Almost. After another block *she* paused, leaned on a rail, and stared into the distance. He pretended to be interested in the crap displayed in the window of a souvenir shop, but he kept looking over at the girl with the bad haircut. He could almost feel her unhappiness – unless he was imagining it, which he might have been. Soon she would resume walking. He couldn't just follow her around all day. Maybe he'd go over and lean on the rail, too. Maybe they could talk.

He never got to the casual-leaning-on-the-rail part, though. Instead he walked up awkwardly behind her and blurted, "Are you all right?"

It startled her. She turned on him – not unhappy but angry. The anger quickly dropped away, and a range of emotions passed over her face like the shadows of clouds. While this went on, Ian absorbed the fact that she was a stone fox, her skin pale, almost translucent, her eyes big and vivid, purplish blue in the sun.

"What?" she said. "Why did you ask that?"

"I… no reason. I don't know. You looked. I don't know. My name's Ian."

She stared at him, started to reply, but didn't. There was some kind of intense chemistry going on between them. Ian groped for words to describe the experiment, or at least to prolong the moment, but his mind was suddenly blank. If only he could touch her, that would be enough. He urgently *wanted* to touch her.

Maybe she picked up on that, because all of a sudden she was backing off, saying, "Look, uh, Ian? I have to go." And she walked away. He didn't think he could stand it, but since there was no alternative, he did stand it.

Still walking, she looked back at him, and for a moment he thought she was going to stop. But she didn't, and soon she was lost in the crowd.

"What the fuck was that all about," Ian mumbled. He felt a sense of being badly let down. The light seemed to dim, and loneliness enclosed him like a black wing. More than ever he felt estranged from the people around him. All he wanted to do was retreat, ride the Chief back to his crappy apartment and lock himself away.

*　　*　　*

KYLIE COULDN'T ALLOW herself to trust the guy in the hoodie. She was alone here and she had to trust *herself*. Not anybody else. Not this Ian guy who acted so weird. What if he was another disguised alien? Or a fake person? He had to be one or the other, not a real live man. Even as she walked away from him, though, she experienced the pain of separation. Because what if he *wasn't* a fake person or an alien? What if he was real – the only other real person under the Dome with her?

Yeah, what if.

She glanced back but kept walking. Maybe she just wanted him to be real because she couldn't bear to be alone in this place. But wanting him to be real didn't make it true. It wasn't like a fake person couldn't fake being nice and ask her if she was all right. She walked faster, losing herself in the crowd. Then all at once she didn't want to be lost. She stopped, and people jostled her, going around. Kylie's stomach actually hurt. She bent over a little, fighting back useless tears.

She looked up, then, and saw one of the disguised alien tourists.

At least she thought it was one, this guy in a bright yellow shirt walking straight at her, his right hand slightly cupped against his hip – concealing his laser-joy-buzzer. Kylie braced herself to run.

Except it wasn't a laser-joy-buzzer. It was just a cell phone, and the yellow shirt guy brought it up and started texting. Absorbed, he stepped around Kylie without looking at her.

More tears came. Kylie bit down on her tongue, to give herself something else to think about. Only she bit too hard. Tasting blood, she pushed through the people-who-weren't people, just wanting to get away from them and be alone.

Mixed in the traffic noise a very cranky-sounding engine approached. She looked around. It was the hoodie guy! Ian. He was wearing one of those Nazi-looking half-helmets and driving a gorgeous old motorcycle, like none Kylie had ever before seen. It rode low to the road and had big flaring fenders and a leather fringe around the seat.

Kylie started waving. He saw her and ran the bike over to her, jumping the front wheel over the curb. "I'm alone," she shouted above the blat and roar of the engine. "And I don't have any money."

"Get on."

She did. But when he jerked the bike around, her locator fell out of her pocket. "Shit!"

"What's wrong?"

"I dropped my – something."

He shifted into neutral and now the engine sounded like a dryer with a penny clicking and sliding in the drum. Walking the heavy motorcycle back, Ian misjudged what he was doing, and rolled the rear tire over Kylie's locator. She heard the case crack, a sharp snapping sound.

"Damn it," he said. "I'm an idiot."

"No you're not. It already wasn't working."

She tried to pick the locator up but her arm wouldn't reach that low while she was straddling the bike. Ian stretched down and grabbed it for her.

"Thanks."

"You want some coffee?"

She wanted lots of stuff, coffee not being first on the list. But she said, "Yeah."

Ian cranked the throttle. The beautiful low-slung bike stuttered and roared unevenly then leapt forward, the frame vibrating between Kylie's legs. She held on as he wove them skillfully through traffic. She had the most wonderful feeling that she was exactly where she needed to be. It just came over her. The *rightness* of it. She rested her head against Ian's back. He was real. She didn't know how, but he was.

IAN PARKED IN front of Dregs, which was kind of the anti-Starbucks, a few blocks from his apartment. The girl, Kylie, was still holding onto him. He removed his helmet and looked over his shoulder at the top of her raggedy head. "This is where we're going," he said.

"'K."

"You wanna go in?"

"Yeah."

"You'll have to let go of me first," he said, not really wanting her to let go.

She slipped her arms from around his waist and they went into the coffee shop. Incomprehensible rap/metal fusion pounded from box speakers bracketed to the ceiling. Violent slashes of color, paintings by some local artist, hung like open wounds on the walls. The tables were roughly the size of poker chips.

"God, this is the best coffee ever," Kylie said after slurping the top foam off a heavily sugared double latte. "My mom had this jar of crystals? She let me have like one cup a week."

"Vulgar's Instant," Ian said. "That ain't coffee. What was your Mom, a Mormon or something?"

"Huh?"

"Like it's against the rules to drink more than one cup of crappy coffee a week, is what I mean."

"She's Catholic. We had to ration the coffee."

"Why?"

"I'll tell you later."

"Can I see that thing I broke?"

Kylie handed him the giant TV-remote-looking thing. It was surprisingly heavy. Two things about it were particularly interesting: the letters EMF on the front and the Property Of US Navy sticker on the back.

"I don't think it was working anyway," she said.

"I'm good at fixing stuff like this."

Kylie laughed. "You don't even know what it is."

"I don't have to know."

"Can I have another coffee? And a muffin? I'm really hungry."

"Ah, sure," Ian handed her a five dollar bill and she practically ran to the counter. He sucked on his double shot until she returned. There was barely room for two cups on the poker-chip pedestal table.

"So, this is like some kind of electromagnetic field detector, right?" he said, holding up the device.

"Yeah, that's what this guy Wolcott said. But it's supposed to be like a locator."

"What's it locate?"

"A generator, I think. A power source. Some machine."

"Some machine."

"Yeah." Suddenly Kylie leaned across the table and kissed Ian on the mouth. She had a little brownish white foam on her lips. He tasted the foam, and Kylie's darting tongue, and a copper tinge of *blood*. His cock sprang instantly to life. Kylie sat back quickly and picked up her mug.

"I wish you didn't do that," she said.

"*Me?*"

"I don't know if I'm ready for this."

"Ready for what?"

She ducked her head down and slurped her espresso, her eyes rolled up to watch him. Ian shifted uncomfortably on his chair. His pants were suddenly too tight. And, of course, the chair was intentionally uncomfortable to begin with. Then there were the girl's possessive eyes.

"Where I come from," Kylie said, "all the men are impotent."

"Yeah? Where do you come from, the east side?"

"Eastside of Hell."

"Sounds like it."

"What time is it?" Kylie asked, with more urgency than the question might ordinarily warrant.

Ian consulted his phone. "Noonish."

"Let's do something else now."

"Like what?"

Kylie smiled. Ten minutes later they were standing on the steps outside Ian's apartment building, Ian thinking, *I am way out of my fucking mind*, while he fumbled with his keys. Behind him, Zach said:

"Hey, man."

Ian turned away from the door and stepped forward. "Hey."

"I need to talk to you," Zach said.

"Um. I'm kind of busy right now."

"I see that. Who is she?"

Kylie had retreated under the arch that formed an alcove around the building's entry door. There used to be a light in there but it had burned out and maintenance had never bothered to replace the bulb. Even in daylight the little alcove was thick with shadows. The amateur tags some punk kid had thrown up seemed to absorb what light there was.

"She's a girl I met."

"What are you talking about, a girl you met? You never meet anybody."

"I'm Kylie." She stepped out of the alcove, slipped her arm through Ian's, and stared a challenge at Zach.

Zach appraised her with such obvious suspicion that it pissed Ian off.

"Dude," Zach said, "we have to talk."

"Why, what's going on?"

"A lot."

"I'll call you later."

"We need to talk *now*." Zach didn't look good. Well, Zach never looked 'good', exactly. But at the moment he appeared particularly haggard and... stretched? "It's important."

Ian slipped his arm out of Kylie's and said to her, "Gimme just a minute."

Kylie didn't say anything, and Ian felt their bond slip off the one-way track it had been riding, which *really* pissed him off. He walked with Zach halfway down the block.

"Who's *she*?" Zach said.

"Kylie. What's wrong with you?"

"What about Sarah? You were gone so long I was sure you'd tried for Pullman again."

"What the fuck are you talking about?"

"Don't you remember *anything*? The Boogeyman, the time loop, me killing myself, any of that?"

"Killing yourself. Not funny," Ian said. "Not funny at all."

"Look–"

"I'll call you."

Something went out of Zach, and he slumped on his feet.

"Yeah," he said. "Whatever. I'll see you on the next round."

Kylie looked pensive and unhappy. The mood had collapsed; the big chemistry experiment had lost its reactionary force. "Who was that?"

"My best friend."

"You seemed mad at him."

"Yeah, well."

"But you talked to him anyway, like he mattered."

"Sure I did. He's my *friend*. I can be mad at him and still care about him."

Kylie thought about that, then said, "Will you take me someplace?"

"Where?"

"My grandparents' house. They live on Queen Anne Hill. Here's a picture. The address is on the back."

"What for?"

"Will you take me?"

"Yeah, okay."

IT WAS A big yellow frame house on a road lined with live oaks. Kylie recognized it immediately. She tapped Ian's shoulder and pointed, but he was already tucking the Indian into the curb. The motor quit before he could shut it off. Kylie dismounted and took the picture out of her pocket. She held it up. The house matched the photo perfectly, except there was no one standing on the porch.

"Haven't you ever been here?" Ian said.

"When I was little." Impulsively, she kissed him again; that feeling, buzzing chemical electricity, the *rightness* of it – was still there. They were the real people, the only ones. She had been thinking, if you could even call it thinking, that she might be able to stay here under the Dome with Ian. If they destroyed the Dome, which was what she had been thinking before, neither one of them would survive long out in the poisoned world. But even with Ian, she didn't think she could tolerate living in a world of phony people. Seeing Ian with his friend made her wonder if everyone else really *was* a fake. Maybe it was just some of them. Or maybe it was like when you were a kid and had a stuffed toy you loved. The bear became real because you wanted it to be real, because you *loved* it. Would life under the Dome with one real person be okay if she could trick herself into loving some of the fake people into life? For now she put aside the idea that her already-poisoned body would eventually became sick, whether she was under the Dome or not. Maybe Wolcott hadn't known what he was talking about. Maybe.

Even though her mom was estranged from Kylie's grandparents on her father's side and never took her to see them since she was little, Kylie still thought she would be able to tell if they were real or not. But that wasn't the point. The point was to find out whether she could *believe* they were real and be happy about it.

"Come with me?" she said to Ian.

"Yeah."

He swung off the bike.

Kylie said, "Only don't say anything weird, okay?"

"You're the one who's always saying weird stuff."

They crossed the lawn. A big flame-colored oak leaf

detached from an overhanging limb and see-sawed down in front of Kylie. She caught it, experiencing a little thrill of delight, and stuffed the leaf carefully in her pocket. The leaf wasn't real, but it was easy to believe in it.

There was a brass knocker on the front door. Kylie used her knuckles. Ian hung back a little. She liked knowing he was there.

The door opened.

"Yes?"

A woman in her early sixties with vivid lavender eyes, her face pressed with comfortable laugh lines. Like the house, she was a picture come to life. And a memory. Kylie's father's face lurked behind the sags and wrinkles of age.

"Hi," Kylie said.

"Can I help you?" the live photograph said. She glanced at Ian.

"No," Kylie said. "I mean, I wanted to ask you something."

The waiting expression on her face so familiar (her father watching her patiently while she built something out of colored blocks of wood). Kylie said, "I just wanted to know, are you having a good day, I mean a really good day?"

The woman turned her head a fraction of an inch, lips pursed uncertainly, ready to believe this was a harmless question from a harmless person.

"It's like a survey," Kylie said. "For school?"

A man of about the same age as the woman, wearing a baggy wool sweater and glasses came to the door. Kylie had to hold back her tears again, because he was like an aging duplicate of her dad. Until this moment she hadn't really remembered what her father looked like. She had recognized the waiting expression on the woman's face, but that was different. Suddenly the father she hadn't seen since she was five years old was standing before her. A fake person in a fake house in a phony city, making her cry real tears (if she would only let them out, which she wouldn't). Except he wasn't a fake person. He was her stuffed bear, and she could no more help believing in him than a little kid could help believing in Winnie the Pooh.

"What's all this?" said the stuffed bear that looked like her father.

"A happiness survey," Kylie's grandmother said, and laughed.

"Happiness survey, huh?" He casually put his arm around his wife and pulled her gently against him. He looked directly at Ian, but not in a challenging or unfriendly way.

"I'm just the ride," Ian said.

"So," Kylie's grandfather said. "What's this survey?"

"About happiness," Kylie said. "For school."

"Well, I'm happy as a clam," he said.

"I'm a clam, too," Kylie's grandmother said. "A happy one."

"Thank you," Kylie said.

"You're very welcome. That wasn't much of a survey. Gosh but you look familiar."

"So do you. Goodbye."

Kylie's grandfather called after Ian: "Nice Indian you've got there, kid. But it needs a tune-up. Heard you a mile away."

"We're leaving?" Ian said under his breath to Kylie.

"Yes."

*   *   *

BACK IN HIS apartment with a bag of Thai take-out, Ian hastily kicked the laundry, dirty and clean, into the closet and shut the door. He couldn't do anything about the overall dinginess, though. He never thought about it before, and only considered it now because he was seeing it through Kylie's eyes. At least the take-out noodles were displacing the usual stale odor of old laundry and unwashed dishes.

He switched on a couple of lamps. It was always dark and gloomy once the sun moved past two pm and no longer penetrated into the narrow alley his windows looked out on. With plastic forks they ate noodles, ginger chicken, steamed vegetables and rice straight out of the little white buckets, trading and mixing. Ian sat in the wicker chair he'd bought at Value Village. It crackled like a pile of straw. Kylie sat on the bed.

"Do you live around here?" Ian asked.

Kylie shook her head, a brown noodle dangling wormishly from the corner of her mouth. She slurped it up, finished chewing then said:

"I grew up in Oakdale." She nodded at the Nihiljizum poster on the wall next to the bed. Badass in a black hoodie, facing away with head down, a rusty scythe in one hand, Stratocaster in the other. "Is that a good band?"

"I doubt it.

"Can I use your bathroom?"

"Uh huh. It's that door."

To give her privacy, Ian turned the radio on, KPLX, alternative noise. Kylie was in the bathroom a long time. He finished eating and took his half-empty carton into the kitchen, threw his plastic fork in the trash and snagged a bottle of Fat Tire out of the refrigerator. Kylie

251

came around the corner and said, "You have a lot of pills in your bathroom."

"What?"

"Pills. How come you have so many?"

"I don't know," Ian said, instantly cranky.

"I wasn't snooping. I wanted toothpaste and there wasn't any out. This dentist in Oakdale? He used to tell everyone that a smile is your first hello. Isn't that dumb?"

"Yeah."

"Anyway, are you sick or something?"

"In a way, sometimes."

"Aren't you the big mystery man." Kylie grinned.

"No mystery," Ian said. "I have trouble sleeping sometimes, so I bought sleeping pills. I never take them, though. The others are anti-depressants and anti-anxiety drugs. I don't take *them*, either. I guess I'm just a pill collector. It's kind of comforting to have them. I don't know. My secret stash." He almost said 'escape kit'. He shrugged, and laughed self-consciously, wishing she hadn't noticed the pills. Wishing she hadn't made him think about them when for once he was feeling good.

After a moment, Kylie said, "You're weirder than I am."

"Not by a mile."

"Ian? Why do you have so many different *kinds* of sleeping pills? Some of those, I've never even heard of."

"I don't know. I don't really keep track of them." Ian put his beer back on the rack and started to close the refrigerator.

"Don't you want that?"

"Not really."

"Have it. I want you to."

"Why?"

"It reminds me of someone."

"Who?"

"I'll tell you later, I think."

"There's a lot of shit you're planning to tell me 'later'." He retrieved his beer and started to go back into the living room, expecting Kylie to either do the same or step aside so he could pass her in the narrow kitchen. But she didn't budge, and he found himself practically knocking her over. She pointed her chin at his chest, looking up at him.

"Don't be mad at me," she said.

"I'm not."

"You are, a little."

"I just don't like talking about the stupid pills."

"I don't care about them. Let's get back to where we were, okay?"

"Where's that?"

"We were at the part where I wanted to kiss you again."

Ian couldn't think of a verbal reply, so he leaned down and kissed Kylie.

"Hmmmm," she said.

In the living room he started turning off lamps.

"Leave one on," Kylie said. "That little one on the desk. So I can see you."

He left on the green-shaded library-style lamp. When he turned, she had shucked her leather jacket for the first time since he met her. Under it she wore an olive green t-shirt, her nipples poking the cotton up like little army tents. This was diverting, until he noticed the ragged scar around her right wrist. She saw him looking at it and held her arm out, the inside of the scarred wrist turned toward him. "It's not what you think."

"What am I thinking?"

"That I did it to myself, on purpose."

"It doesn't look like that kind of scar," he said.

"It's not."

"And you'll tell me about it... 'later'."

"If you're good. Come and sit beside me now."

She patted the mattress next to her. He approached the bed, intending to sit beside her. Instead, he found himself on his knees. He unlaced her left sneaker and pulled it off her foot, slipped her sock away, kissed her bare foot tenderly.

"I'm so dirty," Kylie said.

He stopped. "What do you mean?"

"Not *that* kind of dirty. I mean dirty. I haven't had a real shower in ages."

"I don't care."

Ian removed her other shoe and sock. He felt uninhibited, which was not the way he usually felt with girls. Always he was painfully shy, self-conscious, passive. Even when his body's desire finally impelled him over the brink, a significant piece of him hovered above his desire, watching his body thrash desperately for release.

With Kylie, he was *present*. Everything was now.

When she started to strip her undershirt off, he said, "Wait."

"All right, Ian."

He undid the snap of her jeans, dragged the zipper down, revealing lavender panties. They didn't quite match her eyes but almost. He looked up at her, and she caressed his cheek. "Ian, what if we were the only real people in the world?"

"We are." He tugged her jeans and panties off, kissed her smooth inner thighs, held his mouth above her sex, his heartbeat drumming away his mind. Kylie lay back on the bed cover. Ian let his tongue emerge to touch upon her in the most delicate way. Kylie moaned.

Much later, in an unwinding timeless place, Ian rocked into her body, drawing back and plunging, Kylie holding herself just so for him, and he felt his old resistance rising, his fear of surrender, but he was too far gone, and when he came it was with his whole being, and he cried out like someone in pain, and then he simply cried, and holding her and being held by her, he fell into exhausted sleep.

KYLIE LAY ENTANGLED with him, breathing the mingled scent of their love-making, feeling the life-breath of his body rise and subside. And she couldn't help it: she fell asleep, too.

MUCH LATER, IAN opened his eyes. For a moment he seemed to be looking back at himself. It wasn't a *good* moment. He closed his eyes, felt dizzy, then slowly opened them again. This time he was looking at the ceiling. He listened to the rain falling in the alley outside his window. One by one he gathered into himself the important physical inputs. The cornered light from his desk lamp, the whispering rain, the sheets airy on his naked body, Kylie beside him, the heat that radiated from her, the scents of her secret body. Each sensation braided with the others and tied him more firmly to the present moment.

He moved the sheet aside and touched the perfect slope of Kylie's hip. The irresistible sexual encounter had occurred. Now he was supposed to retreat as rapidly as possible to the sanctuary of guarded autonomy. If it were her apartment instead of his, he would have gotten up without waking her and left. Except this time, this one time, he didn't feel like doing that.

His hand glided over her hip and waist, hovering, barely touching the perfect skin.

"Beautiful," he whispered.

"Thanks," Kylie said.

"Hey–"

"You're beautiful, too, Ian."

"I prefer to think of myself as a macho he-man."

"Oh, you *are*. You rescued me like Indiana Jones."

"Indiana Jones is a punk."

She snuggled her head against his chest. "Ian, what time is it?"

He twisted around to see the clock. "Almost eleven-thirty. Why?"

"It's a countdown." She sounded nervous.

"Something going to blast off?"

"Us, I hope."

"We already did that, didn't we?"

"Hmm."

Ian felt himself growing hard again. Kylie must have felt it, too. She adjusted her body a little.

"Is the second time as good as the first?" she asked.

"That was your first time?"

"First with you."

"Sometimes the first is a total disaster."

"Mine wasn't. Mine was perfect."

"I meant your first time with anybody."

"Was your first time ever with anybody a total disaster?"

"Yeah."

"It's okay, Ian. Before you, it wasn't so great for me, either. You have no idea how un-great it can be. But it's you and me now, and we *are* great."

Ian began stroking her back, trailing his fingers down to the rising separation of her buttocks, urging himself over her.

"Ian?"

He kissed her throat.

"Ian?"

"What?" he said to the little hollow place at the base of her neck.

"I want to wait a bit, is that okay?"

He stopped kissing her, which required a certain amount of willpower.

"Sure," he said. "I'm sorry. I mean, I don't know what I mean."

"Just a couple of minutes."

"No problem."

"I *want* to do it now," Kylie said.

"I know," he said, and, surprisingly, believed he *did* know. She was resisting her body's urgency as much as he was resisting his own.

"Will you get me a drink of water?"

"Yeah."

He removed himself from the bed and went into the kitchen, feeling her gaze upon him. When he came back with the water she never stopped looking. He held the clear bottle in front of his erect cock.

"No peeking," he said.

Kylie giggled.

"What's funny?"

"It looks like you're holding a bottle with a really big penis in it."

Ian blushed, but said, "Maybe if you rub the bottle a genie will come out." A fading, cynical piece of himself thought: *what an asshole thing to say*. But he ignored the cynic and, shamed, it didn't speak again.

"I hope so," Kylie said, about the genie.

He slipped back in bed, pulled the sheet up to his waist, and handed her the cold bottle. She took a couple of swallows. He watched her and wanted to touch her again. She passed the bottle back to him and wiped her chin.

"Warm me up, but not too much yet."

Ian stroked the backs of his fingers over her belly. He caressed her thigh, letting his thumb brush her pubic hair. Kylie opened her legs a little. "Are you religious?" she asked.

"What? Not really."

"You have that cross on your back."

"Yeah. I don't know. I like the *idea* of Jesus. I don't even know why I got that tattoo."

"And you can't see it unless you use mirrors."

"That's how God is, probably."

"What if there isn't a God?"

"What if there is?" His thumb parted the moistened folds of her vagina. She moved against him.

"I guess we'll see."

She stretched over him, her breast brushing his cheek, picked up the clock and set it down again. When she lay back she was smiling. She took his engorged cock in her hand, and he felt the urgent throb of his blood.

"You're beautiful," she said. "Would you rather be a God or a genie?"

"I don't care."

She cupped his balls in her cool hand and squeezed gently. "Ah," Ian said. She closed her fingers around the shaft of his cock and stroked slowly up to the swollen head.

"Gimme my wish, genie."

"You're sure we're good on the countdown and everything?"

"Positive. Now gimme."

HE WAS PLUNGING, lost and found, immediate. Then his body began to tingle in a way unassociated with the sexual act. The room darkened. He was staring into Kylie's face, and shadows began to spin before his eyes. He couldn't *see* her. Shorted, flickering memories sparked in his mind. Kylie pulled his face down to hers, fingernails digging into his scalp. She held him, her strong legs locked around his rocking horse hips.

Stay, stay, stay...

A dramatic light shift dispelled the darkness. At the same moment, Ian shuddered and cried out with his ejaculation.

She held him on top of her, stroking the back of his neck, petting him, their bodies heaving, fragrant with sex and sweat and revelation.

Ian remembered everything.

CHAPTER TWENTY-THREE

CHARLES NOBLE SAT with his new friend, Curtis Sarmir, in a Pioneer Square nightclub called the Contour.

"The whole sexual preference notion is absurd, of course," Curtis said. "No one insists straight people *prefer* hetero sex. As if it's all a matter of taste, good and bad. The implication is derogatory. Don't you agree?"

"I'm hardly an expert in sexual matters," Charles said, then giggled, then stopped abruptly.

They had been drinking Cosmopolitans.

"Good God," Curtis said. "No one's an *expert*, precisely."

"Well... perhaps especially not me." It was funny, really. When Charles had been Travis Dugan in that little jerkwater town of Chewelah, he had longed to be himself. To that end he eventually *declared* himself. And he never again pretended to be attracted to girls. But neither had he ever found a companion of his own sexual persuasion. So here he was, a thirty-three-year-old virgin. Yes, he was himself, with a new name, but the same unfulfilled longings. Alone. Except it wasn't only Travis and Charles sitting across from Curtis Sarmir in the Contour – it was also the Curator. In fact, it was mostly the Curator's presence subsuming what had been Travis-Charles.

Self-consciously, he adjusted his Kangol cap.

"You and your hats," Curtis said. "In someone else I might consider it affected. But hats suit you."

"I like hats," Charles admitted.

Curtis tilted his stem glass back, finishing his third Cosmo. He set the glass down very precisely. Fingertips lightly touching the stem, he raised his eyes and said:

"Why you – *especially?*"

"Excuse me?"

"Especially *not* an expert on sex."

"Oh. Well. I've never actually had real sex."

"I understand."

"You do?"

"Of course. It's hardly unique, a lifetime of pretending to be what everyone expects you to be. Do you know you're wearing that cap backwards?"

"I am?" Charles removed the cap and looked at it. "But the little kangaroo is in the front. That's right, isn't it?"

It was how the original Charles Noble wore his cap.

Curtis *tsked* and took the cap away from him and turned it around, placing it back on Charles's head with both hands, fitting it with care, as if it were a crown.

"Frontwards suits you better, cap-wise. There. You look very hip now."

Charles gave him a cosmopolitan smile.

"Poor man," Curtis said. "Locked in the closet all by yourself for *how* many years?"

*   *   *

A COUPLE OF hours later Charles left Curtis's bed and shut himself in the bathroom. A tea light burned in a pewter dish, which was sufficient. He didn't turn on the overhead bulbs. A handsome, somewhat plump man with thinning brown hair and distant eyes regarded him from the mirror over the sink. The Curator swam to the surface of those eyes and saw more than the mirror captured. Before his star-dwelling soma, before jellyfish evolution and before absorption into the Cloud, he had been a bipedal creature not dissimilar to the one now looking back at him. Inhabiting the human simulacrum – becoming it – had triggered this memory.

"I am Charles Noble," the face in the mirror said. A speaking head, mobile lips, hinged jaw, and slippery, muscled tongue – a borrowed android puppet. Charles Noble: who was already a fabrication in the mind of Travis Dugan, and before Travis the name, the *character*, a fabrication in the mind of a forgotten novelist.

The Curator concentrated to erase and create himself. Name was function, and *Curator* had no function here

"I am Charles Noble."

Because that was preferable to the alternative, which was: *I am nobody.*

Looking down, he cupped his genitals in his hand, exuding unfamiliar tenderness towards his new body and the new things it had shown him it could do. Tender and lonely and a little sad, he ran warm water in the sink and used a soapy cloth to wash his penis. When he was done he dried himself and deposited the wet cloth and hand towel in the hamper.

Charles started back to bed, where loneliness and confusion might be dispelled. He wasn't sure he belonged there, but he didn't seem to have anyplace else to go or anyone else to be.

His clothes were folded neatly on the black leather ottoman, where Curtis had thoughtfully placed them, the Kangol cap on top. Charles paused.

Back in the bathroom he stood before the mirror, this time with his cap on. Finally he recognized himself. Almost. He turned the cap around, putting the little kangaroo in back. The face in the mirror smiled and it was him.

"Hello, Charles."

IAN TRIED TO push himself off Kylie's body, but she held him tight.

"Stay like this," she said. "Just a little longer."

"We have to do stuff."

"Not yet. Please."

"Okay. But there isn't much time."

"There's a day, the over-and-over day."

"Who are you?" he said. "I mean really."

"Just a girl from Oakdale."

"How did you get here?"

"I flew through the Dome in a jet. If you hit it fast enough you can tunnel through from the outside."

"It's all true, then. Nothing in the city is real."

"No," she said. "We are. We're real." She loosened her embrace, and Ian pushed himself up, hands planted flat on the mattress, their sticky bodies coming apart. His face directly above hers, he said, "God, you're beautiful."

"So are you."

He rolled away from her and stood up. The apartment was filled with pale morning light. He shuffled into the kitchen on weak legs, obeying some physical memory, somatic reflex. Like he was *supposed* to be making a cup of coffee at this moment. Lying in bed with Kylie wasn't part of the script. He watched his hands take down a cup from the cabinet, scoop dark roast into a Melitta filter, pick up the kettle and fill it with tap water. Watched himself, but not in the free-floating dissociative manner he sometimes experienced it, as if he were separate from his body; this was more like his body *owned* him, as if he were a passenger existing in the electrical impulses between brain and muscle. After a couple of minutes, he consciously asserted himself. "Stop it," he said out loud, to his body, to the hand grasping the kettle. And the hand set the kettle down on a cold burner, and Ian stood back from the stove. Kylie was right behind him and he bumped into her.

"That was scary," he said.

"What was?"

"It was like my body wanted to do its own thing."

She put her arms around him and squeezed him hard. "I like this body. Ian, how did you get here, into the Dome? Did you fly like me?"

"No, I was always here."

"But you're real. If you weren't real you wouldn't have stayed with me when the day started over."

"The Advent," Ian said.

"The what?"

"Advent. It's what the days are called in here. The guy who runs it all told me."

"What guy who runs it all?"

"He called himself the Curator."

264

"Is he one of the aliens in the bright, spinny ships?"

"No. Listen–" His cell phone started ringing. "Oh, fuck. That's Zach." Kylie released him and he grabbed the phone off the bedside table, slipped it open, said, "Hi."

Cautious silence on the line, then Zach said, "Good morning?"

"What do you think?"

"I'm coming over."

"No. I mean, I'll call you back."

"Damn it, don–"

Ian closed his phone and tossed it on the bed. "This is so nuts. I'm supposed to ride to Pullman today. I'm supposed to see Sarah."

"I don't know who that is," Kylie said. "But she isn't there, Ian."

"How do we really *know* that?"

"She isn't there because Pullman isn't there. The world isn't there, not the world the way you probably remember it."

Ian closed his eyes. "I've felt this coming for a long time. But I guess nobody really knows what it's like to lose your mind until it actually happens."

"You haven't lost your mind and you know it."

"Yeah, I guess. But crazy people never believe they're crazy."

"So... what, you want to believe you're crazy because that would mean you *aren't* crazy, since crazy people never believe they're crazy?"

"Something like that."

"I knew a crazy guy. He was the real thing. He wanted to cut me so I couldn't have orgasms. *He* didn't think he was crazy. It was like God's work to him."

"Cut you?"

"You know, like in the *National Geographic?*"

"I have to get out of here." Ian pulled on pants and shoes and a sweatshirt, grabbed his keys.

"Not out of the city," Kylie said. "You can't."

"I know. I just have to clear my head."

A couple of minutes later he was straddling the Indian, jabbing his key in the ignition. Kylie came around the end of the alley and stood blocking it. "If you try to leave the city, you know what will happen?"

"Yeah, some weird shit. Whatever."

"I kept you with me in bed. I did it on purpose. I had a *feeling* about you. I knew you were real, like me. I knew we were real together, Ian. Please don't go."

While she talked, Ian went through his cold start routine. Cold starting the Chief was usually a bitch. So he was surprised when he stood on the kicker and the bike came alive on the first try, the engine farting and shuddering. Ian rolled unsteadily to the end of the alley. Kylie still blocked the way. She had pulled on jeans and the flimsy olive drab t-shirt but nothing else. Her skin looked almost translucently pale. The sight of her little bare feet on the grimy concrete tugged at something in his chest.

"I have to *go*," he said. "I'll come back, but I need to go first."

"Just tell me one thing, okay?"

"What?"

"Why are you different, why are you like me? If you didn't come from outside, then how does that work?"

"I'm a ghost," Ian said.

"If you don't want to tell me then don't tell me." She stepped aside.

He dug the spare apartment key out of his pants and tossed it to her. "You're gonna freeze your toes out here."

"If you come back, I'll be here."

He throttled into the street, glanced at her in the jiggly mirror before leaning into the first turn, saw her white, white feet picking gingerly up the steps to his building. He felt a pang of separation, and it was much sharper than the guilt stabbing at his heart with little hesitant thrusts. Guilt about Sarah. Subtract all the bizarre shit from the situation, and what you had left was a guy cheating on his girlfriend. Ian tried to get behind the idea. It should have been easy. He was so used to bashing himself over the head with his own failures. But. But... Kylie was so *right* for him. She made everything and everyone who came before her look like a mistake.

Just before he hit the ramp that would carry him to the floating bridge, he throttled back and tucked the Chief into the curb, letting traffic rumble past him. Trying to ride to Pullman was stupid. He knew that. There *was* no Pullman, and there was no Sarah Darbro, not anymore. Crossing the bridge meant exactly one thing: Ian wussing out again. Bashing himself over the head, yeah, but mostly it was running away. His specialty. He would hit the bubble and maybe that would erase his mind, the way the Curator had wanted it to be. Then he would just be his usual clueless self in the forever repeating clueless world. Way easier than manning up.

Fuck that.

KYLIE WAS IN the shower, scrubbing at her body with a soapy face cloth, luxuriating in her first real honest-to-God hot shower in over two years. She heard the apartment door open, and stopped scrubbing. She turned the shower off and stood dripping in the tub, listening. Then Ian said, "I'm back."

Ian!

"I'll be right out!" She rinsed the soap off her body, dried herself with one of Ian's cheap, threadbare blue towels, then quickly pulled on a black t-shirt and a pair of cargo pants she'd found in the closet. They were girl's clothes, way too small for Ian, but too big for Kylie. She rolled the pant legs to her ankles. Using a corner of the towel she wiped the fog off the mirror and checked herself out. Her hair was the only really bad thing.

The smell of good, strong coffee hit her as soon as she stepped out of the steamy bathroom. Ian was sitting at his Salvation Army desk holding two disposable cups, the word Vivace's printed in red letters on the sides. He handed her one.

"Thanks," she said. "You came back. I love it that you came back. What's wrong?"

"Those are Sarah's clothes."

"Oh. I'm sorry. I wondered–"

"It's okay."

"She was your girlfriend?"

"Yeah. Only I guess it's more complicated than that."

"It always is."

"We broke up. Kind of. Only she didn't know it, and I wasn't positive myself."

"Been there."

"It's like I wanted her to be far away. I didn't want to not have her, but I didn't want to owe her anything. Does that make sense?"

"Not really. But I've been there, too, only on the wrong side of it. What are you thinking now, that you want her again? Instead of me? I mean, if you could."

"No."

"The truth?"

"Yeah. Besides, she's not even out there anymore, right?"

"Don't say it like it's *your* fault."

He shrugged, his face expressionless, like he was hating himself for wanting Kylie's sympathy.

She put her cup down and sat in his lap facing him, her legs straddling his thighs. The office chair creaked back on loose springs. She brought her nose right up to his, so close his eyes seemed to come together. "Ian, we have to deal with what's real, right now. Not mistakes or regrets or maybes."

"I know."

"You and I have something really, really special going on here. Don't you feel it, too?"

"Yeah, I do."

She drew back a little. "You hesitated."

"No, I didn't."

She kissed his mouth then stood up. "So it's the first day of the rest of our lives. Now tell me really how you got here. I know you're not a fake person, like everybody else. You're as real as it gets."

"I already told you. I'm a ghost, or I guess not a ghost exactly but–"

"Whoa. I think I'm going to want to lie down for this. Come on."

She pulled him out of the chair, and they lay next to each other on the bed. Ian started touching her, pushing her t-shirt up, caressing her bare belly. She tugged her shirt down and took his hand in hers. "Talk first." She gave his hand a reassuring squeeze, to let him know she wasn't *against* having sex again, just not at this exact moment.

Ian almost audibly shifted gears. Staring at the ceiling, he said, "Okay. That guy I told you about? The Curator?"

"Yeah.

"He's an alien, but not like the ones in the bright spinning ships. Those ones are called Hunters and they're pretty badass. The Curator, he works for something called the Cloud. This Cloud goes around screwing with races on other planets so they evolve in a certain way."

"What way?"

"The way the Cloud evolved, I guess. So they don't need bodies anymore?"

"Why's *that* good?"

"Fuck, I don't know. Who said it was good? I'm just telling you what he told me."

"So humans are one of the races that got screwed with."

"Right. Only, the Hunters don't go for it. *They* zip around looking for races that the Cloud is working on, and wipe them out."

"*Why?*"

"They don't like the Cloud messing with natural evolution. You know, everybody's got to be pure and all that shit. So they found Earth and they–"

"Wiped us out. They sound like Nazis. When I flew in here with Father Jim, one of their ships chased us and shot us down. I bailed just in time."

"Who's Father Jim?"

"This old guy. I'll tell you later. Keep going. All that stuff about the Cloud and Hunters is interesting, but it doesn't explain why you think you're a ghost."

"I said not a ghost, not really. The Curator said I was

some kind of rare freak. Okay, not a *freak* – but rare. Like an early version of what they were trying to turn the whole human race into? So when my body died, I kept hanging around and like started haunting *this* body, which isn't really my body. It's one of those things, like everybody else in the city, except you. An android."

"You're not a thing."

"The androids are perfect imitations of real bodies. You can't tell the difference. And check this out. They act like the originals act because they're *connected* to the originals. Like the tech that keeps this whole thing going can reach back in time and tap the minds of the original people the templates are based on, and it uses that to make the android people act real. It gets the mind stuff while the people are sleeping."

"The real people asleep in the past?"

"Right. Only there isn't any past or future or anything, not if you're the Cloud. It's all one big picture."

Kylie absorbed this for a while then said, "So you died but instead of really dying you just went out of your body and then started taking over this one you're in now."

"I know it sounds weird."

"Weird? No, what's weird about it?"

He turned his head and looked at her. They both laughed. Then Ian's face went all serious and he started to get off the bed. "This is too fucked up," he said. Kylie pulled him back down.

"No," she said. "Don't go clear your head again. Stay with me, okay?"

"Okay, okay."

"Do you know why this place even exists, this Dome city?"

"It's some kind of museum. The Cloud wanted to preserve what we were like, to show other evolving races. The Dome's even called a Preservation. I guess there's a bunch of them."

They were quiet a moment. Kylie held on tight to Ian's hand. She took a breath then risked asking the question that was burning her up to ask. "Ian? Tell me how you died."

He stared at the ceiling as if he hadn't heard her. With his free hand he tapped his first two fingers pensively on his lower lip, a thing she noticed he did sometimes when something was bothering him or he didn't want to talk – when he wanted to check out without actually leaving.

"Ian?"

"I don't know. Probably I killed myself."

She pushed his fingers away from his mouth. "*Probably* you killed yourself?"

"I killed myself, okay? Happy?"

He jerked his hand out of her grip and swung off the bed, and this time she couldn't stop him. He stood in the middle of the room, looking like he wanted to get away, looking cornered.

"You push too much," he said, half mumbling it, not looking at her.

She hated how he said things and didn't say them at the same time, like he wanted to have it both ways. She kept her mouth shut and waited.

"Never mind," he said, still not looking at her.

"I'm sorry," Kylie said.

"It's not important."

"Killing yourself. It's not important?" *Just shut up,* Kylie told herself. *Just shut your stupid mouth for once.*

Finally, he looked at her. "You know what?"

"What?"

"The Curator, he messed with my brain. So I'd forget everything and just be a good little android. I thought I was fighting it, like it's no fucking way I'm going to forget. But I don't think I was fighting all that hard. There's a lot of stuff I really *want* to forget, like taking all those pills, or hurting Sarah so bad, or what a fucking loser I am. You know? It's worth forgetting stuff like that."

"Ian–"

"Let me finish. You remember Zach?"

"Your friend, the one you talked to before we went to see my grandparents."

"Right. He called a little while ago. He calls every day. Every *Advent*. He always remembers stuff about being on the Preservation. Even when I forget totally, he remembers. He remembers and he's not even a *real person*. I woke him up when all this first started and I was so scared and alone. But you know what? The Curator hardly even had to erase my memory, because I was already doing that by myself. It was Zach who kept jerking me out of it, because Zach *wants* to be alive. Me? I just want to hide. I'm nothing but a–"

Kylie threw herself off the bed and slapped him. It wasn't much of a slap. She'd pulled back, shocked at herself. So it was almost like one of those Italian slaps in a Godfather movie, like a *love* slap. Except not really, because even though she pulled back, there was still some real heat, some real anger, behind it.

Ian stared at her, touching his cheek as if he could feel the fading red mark. "Why'd you do that?"

"Because you were pissing me off."

"How? I wasn't even talking about you."

"Look, I'm sorry. But I just hate that shit when you put yourself down. You're not a loser. You're special. You're probably one of the most special people who ever lived. You're – what? One in a billion, like the Curator called you. You can live outside your freaking body."

"If you call that living."

"Don't try to be funny when I'm being serious. You can't be all the time putting yourself down, not even in your own head. I did that. I did it a lot. My dad checked out when I was a kid and I always thought he left because of me, like I did something wrong, like I was too much trouble. I never said any of that out loud, but it's what I thought, so that's even worse. That's how I got hooked up with Father Jim. I hated myself, and that kind of hate leaves the door wide open for an asshole like Jim to walk through. Ian, I really *loved* my dad and he left anyway." Her voice snagged on a sharp emotion, and finally she stopped talking.

"I loved my dad, too," Ian said, and Kylie heard a whole world of pain behind the simple words. She hugged him as hard as she could and he hugged her back like he was trying to break her in half.

After a while, her face buried in his chest, she said, "You want to hear something? Jim and I had a mission when we flew in here."

"What mission?"

"Blow up the Dome. That's what that locator thing was for, to help us find the machines that make the Dome work. People outside think this place is some kind of zoo, or like you said, a museum. Everybody's dying out there and they never got a chance to fight back – to fight the Hunters. So this was the last chance."

"The Hunters didn't even make the Dome. Besides, if we blow up the Preservation everybody dies."

"Nobody's real anyway."

"You are."

"So are you."

"My body's not real."

"It sure *acts* real."

"Yeah."

"Ian, I don't want to blow up the Preservation."

"Okay."

"Maybe we can just, I don't know, live here?"

"You mean pretend it's all normal."

"For a little while, why not? Outside the Preservation the Hunters flattened almost everything then they poisoned the sky. The survivors, and there aren't very many, are all getting sick. Nobody will live much longer. Even if we could blow up the Dome or escape from here, we'd end up dead because of the poison. I might die anyway. Shit, I absorbed enough poison. But in here maybe we could live. Maybe I wouldn't ever get sick. I don't know. Probably I would. But maybe not."

"I doubt we could blow up the Preservation even if we tried," Ian said.

"Yeah, probably not."

Ian's phone started ringing. They both looked at it. The phone blinked and trilled and vibrated on the bedside table like a little creature trying desperately to get their attention.

"It's Zach," Ian said. "He never gives up."

"That's because he doesn't know he's a fake person."

"Maybe he *isn't* a fake person."

"They're all fake people. That's what you said. Androids. Ian, you should see them when they get bounced out of here. They turn into zombies after a while, like big dumb windup dolls that can't stop going. Like that stupid Energizer Bunny from the commercials."

"A little while ago you said something about your grandparents. You didn't say your fake android grandparents."

"It's a stupid trick is all," Kylie said. "Like really good special effects. They seemed real – you know, like those blue people in *Avatar* – but they weren't real."

The phone stopped ringing.

Ian said, "But what if they thought they were real? I mean Zach and your grandparents and whoever else. My sister, maybe."

"But they're *not* real."

Ian tapped his lip with his fingertips. "Maybe a fake android person who believes he's real is just as good as a real person who knows he's real. I mean, in this place, what's the difference?"

COMMUNION

CHARLES SAT IN a pew next to Curtis Sarmir. Fewer than a hundred people occupied the vast space within St. James Cathedral. Curtis described himself as an occasional Catholic who happened to adore St. James. They were at that point, the Curator and the android, where the android wanted to share things it adored. The Curator, who now thought of himself mostly as Charles Noble, found he was always interested to hear what Curtis had to say.

"Of course," Curtis whispered close to Charles's ear, "it's all hocus-pocus. Beautiful hocus-pocus."

"Of course," Charles whispered back.

They held hands and observed the ceremony of transubstantiation. The priest lifted a golden chalice, made the sign of the cross, and drank. "This is the blood of Christ." *Because he believes it is,* Charles thought. October sun lit up stained glass depictions of suffering and redemption. Curtis squeezed Charles's hand and leaned over again.

"I'm really glad you came with me today."

Charles smiled. "It's lovely."

He considered the possibility that the Cloud was a manifestation of hocus-pocus. Once, the Cloud had been a sort of Trinity. Three planets and their billions of inhabitants, united into transphysical singularity. The Ascension – those billions becoming the Cloud. And within the comforting light of the Cloud, the Curator's individuality had effectively been obliterated in the peace of an everlasting dream, and sent forth only occasionally to manage Preservation museums.

But now, abandoned while the Cloud retreated further into remote time and space, *Charles* began to forget the dream... and remember what he had been before singularity.

"You know," he whispered to Curtis, "hocus-pocus is beguiling, but I have always loved more practical and useful art forms."

"Then it's good you own a gallery."

"Yes. It's what I used to do. It's why I'm doing it now."

A blue-haired matron two pews in front of them turned and held a finger to her wrinkled, pink-painted lips. Charles and Curtis smiled at her, and she smiled back.

CHAPTER TWENTY-FOUR

"ICKY," VANESSA SAID, "I think I can't believe you."

They huddled in a Starbucks: Ian, Kylie, Zach and Vanessa. Ian retold the whole story to his sister, leaving out the part about everyone but Kylie being regenerating android constructs. That was also the part he left out when he brought Kylie over to Zach's an hour ago. One thing at a time.

Kylie drank espresso and contributed nothing much to the conversation. Ian wished she were more onboard with his idea of waking up android people. Maybe she would be, eventually. The thing was, in pre-Preservation life Ian had a crappy-to-nonexistent relationship with his sister. What had developed between them here, on the Preservation, was more real than what they'd had in the so-called real world – even if he did have to restart the familial relationship every Advent. Ian would never see his real sister again, but he had the android-memory-matrix version. Only he didn't want to *pretend* the fake Vanessa was real, because then he'd just be having a brother-sister relationship with himself, like a little kid pretending his stuffed toy was a real bear. If he could convince Vanessa to believe she was a real bear, then she *would* be one.

"But she already believes she's real," Kylie had argued on the way over to Zach's.

Yeah. But that didn't count, because Ness didn't know she was supposed to be *unreal*. First he had to sell her the idea of the regenerating day. Then Ian could tell her about androids. Her and Zach, too. It all made sense in Ian's head, but it was hard to get it out and explain it to Kylie. "I don't really get the point," Kylie had said.

"Yeah, I was afraid of that," Ian said to his sister when she declared her disbelief in alien Preservation Domes. "But there's a quick way to prove it to you. One of us could leave town. For instance, if Zach strolled past the point of no return or whatever you want to call it, and he *didn't* return, then you'd know he got absorbed in the bubble thing over the city."

"I wouldn't know it necessarily," Vanessa said. "Maybe Zach would just deliberately not come back."

"Oh, I wouldn't do that," Zach said.

"But I don't know you wouldn't."

"That's true," Kylie said

"Come on, you guys," Ian said. "Help me out here."

"Icky, reality simply can't be what you're saying it is."

"Maybe we're all on an un-reality show," Zach said.

Vanessa and Kylie laughed.

"Come *on*, you guys," Ian said.

Vanessa touched Ian's hand and said, "It makes more sense if I walk over the margin, don't you think?"

"No. Then you'd just be gone again. You wouldn't remember anything, and we'd have to start all over. Look, I promise you Zach won't fake it."

"I promise, too," Zach said.

"What do you say, Ness?"

"I suppose it can't hurt anything."

Ian stood up. "Great. Let's go."

"Sit down a minute," Vanessa said, then excused herself to the bathroom. She was gone ten minutes, and when she returned she appeared composed and serious.

"Okay," she said. "Let's go ahead then."

THEY PILED INTO Zach's VW, picked up Aurora Avenue North. "Stop on the Queen Anne side of the bridge," Ian said.

"I know, I know." Zach pulled out of the traffic stream, parked on a residential street a little ways up the east slope of Queen Anne Hill. They got out and walked back down to the bridge. Traffic thundered by. It was windy on the pedestrian walkway. Vanessa hung close to Ian, her arm looped through his. Normally he would have rejected this prolonged physical contact. But he was getting over that, he was becoming more human about it. Yet another reason – maybe the main reason – for waking up Vanessa and Zach. You can't have human contact without a few humans to contact *with* – even if they were only androids who believed they were human. Kylie was real, but was one person enough?

"Icky, if this doesn't happen, if there's no bubble, I want you to be calm about it."

"I'm calm," he said. "And I'm not crazy. The bubble's

there. The only thing I'm worried about is that you won't believe it when Zach doesn't come back."

"All right, Icky, let's get this over with."

A big moving van rumbled past them. The walkway vibrated. They crossed about three quarters of the bridge's twenty-nine-hundred-foot-length then Ian made everybody stop. "Not any farther. We're not sure where it starts."

"Right," Zach said.

Kylie leaned on the rail, looking at the view east. Boats moved along the ship canal a hundred and seventy feet below. Industrial gray paint was flaking off the rail like dead skin off a zombie. A sign bolted on just below the rail advised suicidal types to take advantage of a 24hr hotline. Blue and white emergency phone boxes were stationed at intervals along the bridge. Was Ian the only one who even noticed them?

"I was talking to you on the phone when you hit the bridge," he said to Vanessa. "Couple of seconds later there was this little static sound, and you were gone."

"Icky, I'm not gone."

"You know what I mean."

Vanessa looked at him worriedly, and Ian almost stopped believing himself. Like he had to fight to keep the insane truth alive in his head, even with Kylie to help him.

"Okay, I'm going," Zach said. "Ready?"

"Maybe I should go instead," Ian said.

"No!" Kylie grabbed his other arm and held on tight. "You're *not* wiping your memory."

"Okay, okay. But I was thinking... how do I really know for sure I'm not crazy?"

"Don't go there. We've already talked about that."

Vanessa, who had been watching them both very closely, said, "Icky, you're scaring me." A tractor trailer rig blasted by, the slipstream gust buffeting them, shaking the bridge. "I think maybe we should all go back to my office and talk about this."

Ian hated the way she was looking at him. He supposed it was the same look he used to give *her*. A mixture of pain, pity and fear. Poor, poor Ness on the psych ward. Poor Icky on the suicide bridge with a head full of aliens. "Damn it," he said, "that would just waste time."

"All right, already," Zach said. "You three keep fighting. I'm going to take the long walk."

Zach started off, his gait overly nonchalant, one hand in his jeans pocket, the other swinging widely. He paused just before the end of the bridge. "I'm still me!" he shouted back at them over the traffic noise.

Ian waved him on. "Keep going."

Zach waved, turned away from them, put his head down and *ran* for the end of the bridge.

"You know," Vanessa said, "this won't prove anything. Your friend is really putting his heart into it, though."

Well beyond the bridge, Zach was still running, elbows pumping away.

"It's not him anymore," Ian said.

"It certainly looks like him."

"It's not."

Zach ran until he passed out of sight.

"For goodness sake," Vanessa said, and she started walking toward the end of the bridge, the wind belling her overcoat out behind her.

"Ness, wait." He caught up with her. "Don't do it."

"Listen, why don't you call him and tell him to come back."

"That won't work."

"Why not?"

"It's like I told you about the Eliza conversations. Remember?"

"Text him."

"Come on, Ness. Oh, fuck it." He produced his phone and thumbed: *Get your ass back here.*

The return text was a smiley face emoticon. He showed it to Vanessa. "Zach's *gone*," he said. "He's back in the bubble. We won't see him again until the next Advent."

"That's bad for one very good reason," Vanessa said.

"What reason?"

"He's got the car keys."

She smiled but he stared at her and shook his head, feeling bleak. Waking up Ness or anybody else was hopeless. Zach was just some kind of special case. An android with a corrupted memory matrix, like the Curator had said. After a moment Vanessa reached out and squeezed Ian's hand. "Walk with me, Icky. I don't know what's going on with you and your friends, but I think it will be good if we walk together. Nothing will happen. Do it with me. Prove to yourself that everything's okay. Then if Zach doesn't come back, we'll catch a cab downtown and get my car."

"Ness, you don't understand."

"Icky. It's all right. Nothing's going to happen."

"It's not all right."

She pulled gently at his hand.

"Come, walk with me."

"No."

Kylie grabbed his other hand. "That's right. No."

Vanessa sighed. "Watch me, then."

"Don't do it, Ness."

"There's no Dome, Icky. Let me show you now. I'll walk past the end of the bridge and turn around. I promise." He let go of her hand. "Be right back," she said, smiling.

"Sure," Ian said.

Vanessa stepped briskly away. She paused near the end of the bridge, shrugged and waved, then continued on. After that she didn't wave anymore or look back. The traffic roared by. Ian put his arm around Kylie.

"Fuck it," she said.

THEY CAUGHT A bus back to Capitol Hill. It passed Dick's Drive-In on Broadway, the parking-lot wall still wearing Ian's WHO CARES. It would wear it forever, since there would never be a 'next day' to sandblast it away or paint it over. Kind of like having a piece on permanent display in a museum. Ian shook his head; he'd hit the mainstream.

The bus stopped, and they stepped down to the sidewalk. Kylie's face lit up. She pointed at a storefront across the street. *Salon Mimi* in pink neon script shone over a glass door. "Do you have any money left?"

"Some."

"I really, really want to get my hair done."

"What's wrong with your hair?"

She gave him a look, and Ian reached for his wallet to see what he had. Two twenties turned out to be enough for a shampoo and basic cut. He slouched in a chair yawning over an idiotic fashion magazine while a very young Latin chick 'did' Kylie's hair. It took forever but it didn't matter because the day was forever. Women occupied all four chairs in the little salon. Crappy fusion music played above the sound of sinks and blow dryers and babble. All normal. As long as Ian didn't think about it. Boring but normal, like real life. But when his mind started tracking off in the direction of android people he felt his depression rising. Only he and Kylie were real – and he wasn't so sure about himself. He pictured the other people in Salon Mimi as soulless automatons, utterly clueless, the Latin girl pawing and combing and cutting at Kylie's head, and it was all so weird and creepy he just wanted to get away and forget he knew the truth. But then Kylie stood up, and her smile was like a sun igniting through his gloom.

"How do I look?" she said.

THEY MADE LAZY love. Ian's erection would not sustain. Kylie didn't seem to mind. She took his hand and showed him where and how to touch her, what she liked, and he became absorbed in the lesson until she reached orgasm. But when she reached for him, he said, "I don't think I can."

"It's okay. You're tired. We don't get our sleep time because the day stops at midnight."

"Yeah."

She snuggled against his chest. "Sleep now," she said in a little-kid voice.

Ian closed his eyes but couldn't sleep. After a while he opened them again. Kylie was already out, her mouth open a little bit. Traffic noise filtered up from the street. He stared at the ceiling, remembered floating toward it, disembodied, after taking all the pills. He wasn't blocking it anymore – that had really happened, he told himself.

He slid carefully away from Kylie and stood naked beside the bed. Something thumped against the wall in the next apartment. Ian started. His heart thudded, and he pressed his hand flat to his chest. Jeans, t-shirts, wadded-up socks, paperback books and sketchpads cluttered the floor. Ian bent down and picked up a sketchpad and black Sharpie, sat at his desk and started working out a possible piece. The parking-lot WHO CARES was the last thing he put up. Right after that, the Preservation started. WHO CARES would never go away. That didn't feel right. Graffiti wasn't museum art. It was *supposed* to vanish because it was supposed to piss people off and make them want to erase it. Beyond that, WHO CARES sucked as a piece; it was his suicide note. After painting something that bad there wasn't anything left to do *but* kill yourself.

On the sketchpad he tried: WHO ARE WE under a crooked city skyline, scribbled that out, shaded in a WHO ARE YOU (annoyed by the existence of Daltrey and Townshend, but maybe going with it anyway) and a line of blank silhouette people, maybe do one with a face, or just big wide Miyazaki eyes, or one filled in red, some such cute shit. Maybe too cute. It would probably require a stencil, if he wanted to pull it off on a mass scale – which is what he was thinking.

Ian scribbled over his new sketch and tossed the pad on to a pile of dirty laundry. What he really needed to scribble out was the parking-lot WHO CARES. Still restless, he pulled Kylie's locator over. The plastic case was cracked. Rolling it under an eight-hundred-pound motorcycle will do that. He thumbed the ON button. Nothing happened. He unscrewed the back and pried the cover off. Circuit board, diodes, two lithium batteries like shiny slugs the diameter of nickels. One of the batteries was loose. He pushed firmly down on it, making sure the little spring clips engaged. Using a jeweler's tool, he checked the solder points, probing around randomly. Everything looked good. He flipped the device, grid face-up. This time when he thumbed the ON button the grid lit up, pale blue. It was supposed to locate the Preservation machinery, but if the whole city was a generated construct, the EM field or whatever equally distributed, there might not be any central point *to* locate. So the whole grid lights up, instead of a single point.

Ian wondered if it would read any different if he took it to XXX GIRLZ.

He put the thing face down, poked around in the back some more, then pushed it away. Not happening. He needed to *do* something, get out of the apartment. Kylie slept like a dead person. Ian grabbed his hoodie and keys.

"CAN I TALK to the manager?" Ian said.

The guy in the blue Dick's Drive-In shirt was about fifty, heavyset, with iron gray hair. He tapped the nameplate pinned to his chest. The plate said: Tom Masterjohn. And under that: MANAGER. "That's me," he said.

"Somebody did your wall. That graffiti?"

"So I noticed."

"I was wondering, are you going to fix it?"

"Why?"

Ian shrugged. "It's kind of lousy."

"It's an *eyesore*," Tom said. "And you bet I'm going to fix it. I have to, according to city ordinance. Tomorrow I got a guy coming out."

"I'll do it today, right now. For free."

Tom squinted. "Why would you do that?"

"Look, I used to do graffiti but I don't anymore. I mean, I was like addicted to it? But I got busted a few years ago. Now I hit these meetings, like NA, you know? It helps me, if I go around cleaning up bad graffiti. It's part of my twelve step. Making amends?"

"I didn't know they had twelve step for that."

"They do."

"I can't pay you."

"I don't care. It's one of my steps."

IAN HUNKERED IN the parking lot and poured paint from a gallon can into a metal tray. *Beige* paint. It rippled thickly. He set the can down and picked up the dry roller, gave it a spin with his fingers, then pushed it into the paint, rolling it forward and back, slopping some paint over the low end of the pan. He stood and pulled the dripping roller down the wall, making a wide, slash through WHO. After a moment, he repositioned the roller and pushed it up at an opposite, intersecting angle, creating a big beige X through the green WHO. Ex-ing out his suicide. The new paint was supposed to match the wall, but it was brighter and gleaming wet. Ian smirked. He was doing his civic duty. Maybe the mayor would give him a medal. He pictured Ned Beatty or some other asshole actor handing him the Key To The City, flashbulbs popping off, applause. Tonight he would hit the streets with his spray cans, do the whole fucking city. Why not? He was jazzed for it, and he didn't have to worry much about getting caught. It would all be erased with the next Advent. Basically, Seattle was his Etch-A-Sketch. His forever wall.

He slapped some more beige on the Dick's Drive-In wall and rolled it out like a house painter.

An hour later he ambled back to the apartment, feeling pretty good. It was almost a shame to wake Kylie up. Ian felt like he had his mojo back, like he didn't *need* somebody else. The not-needing was a familiar feeling, like coming home to an empty house. It was a *safe* feeling. He glanced at the sky, which was a pure, blameless blue – the kind of blue he occasionally used in pieces. Something flickered in the periphery of his vision. He turned his head sharply, but it was gone, if it had been there in the first place – a weird flickery light, like a clear glass ball spinning in the sun, hovering right over Ian's building.

He started walking faster.

Anxiety buzzed through him, killing the safe feeling. His mojo checked out. He didn't really want an empty house. It felt like he'd been coming home to an empty house since he was twelve years old, and he was sick of it.

He started running.

He let himself into the building and ran up the stairs. In the hall outside his apartment, everything felt wrong. He keyed back the dead-bolt and pushed through the door.

Kylie was gone.

He stared at the empty bed, glanced into the empty bathroom, stepped quickly to the kitchen. "Kylie–?"

She wasn't in the kitchen.

A dreadful weight settled in his stomach. He searched the apartment again, which was stupid. But maybe she had left a note.

There was no note.

But there were other things. Sarah's cargo pants, which Kylie had been wearing before stripping for bed. And her Converse high-top sneakers and socks, the socks balled up and stuffed in the sneakers at the foot of the bed. *She must have found something different to wear*, Ian told himself.

Yeah, like what?

Her own clothes. She probably dug them out of the laundry. Hadn't Ian bitched at her for wearing Sarah's clothes? That didn't explain the shoes, but maybe she had sandals or something in her leather coat. Which didn't explain why the *coat* was still draped over the wicker chair, except it was warm out and she didn't need it. But Kylie wore that coat constantly, whenever they went out. She wouldn't leave it in the apartment. Oh, fuck, what did he know about what she would do or not do? He'd just *met* her.

Ian grabbed up his keys again and headed out the door.

THE CITY WAS full of automatons, androids – fake people. Blanks. Thousands of them. And one real girl. Ian had no idea where to even begin looking. The Chief started reluctantly, coughing and grinding in protest. He babied the throttle for a while, until the engine smoothed out as much as it ever did, then popped the clutch and accelerated out of the alley. He cruised the streets around his building, steadily broadening the circuit, watching the sidewalks, trying to catch sight of a girl he feared was gone for good.

More than once he rumbled by Zach's condo. On every pass he looked at the third floor bay window. Zach was gone, too, over the margin, along with Vanessa. Fake people thronged the sidewalks, and he felt like one himself. Ian Palmer, at home in the empty house.

He retreated to the apartment and locked the door. His stomach knotted with hunger and loneliness. He couldn't even think about food. Evening arrived. The usual sounds of occupation occurred in adjacent apartments. Ian flopped on the bed, toed his shoes off, tried to sleep away the rest of the Advent, hoping Kylie would return with the fresh day, somehow. Maybe she would parachute out of the sky, or he would open his eyes and she would simply be there next to him – the magic girlfriend, the one who got through the bubble and all his walls.

He couldn't sleep. Listening to the thumpings, muffled voices and footsteps in the other apartments was like being surrounded by alien forces.

He flung himself off the bed and punched on the MP3. Nine Inch Nails raked up the stale air. Ian grabbed the sketchpad he'd tossed earlier. WHO ARE WE, scribbled over. He flipped to a clean page, hovered his pen over it, made a couple of decisive slashes. His pen felt constricted by the margins of the paper. He dropped both of them and went for his markers.

Fuck it, then.

He yanked the bed away from the wall. Dust bunnies ghosted for cover. He ripped down the Nihiljizum poster, popping thumbtacks. That cleared the space, gave him a canvas seven feet tall by maybe fifteen long. He smoothed his hand over the uneven surface of old plaster, the off-white coat sterile as two weeks in rehab.

He started small. Lying on his stomach, working with colored markers at baseboard level, he put up miniature variations of WHO ARE YOU until he landed on one he liked: *know WHO you are* – the lowercase letters broken-bone sharp, the WHO a trippy riff on his usual signature, not flabby old-school crap like what he'd done on the parking lot. These were preliminary sketches. In his mind he began to see the big picture.

The apartment was hot. He peeled off his t-shirt, jeans and socks, grabbed beer and spray cans. He took a deep pull on the Alaskan Amber, considered the wall, then triggered the Sabotaz blue, like spraying free sky into a W. After an hour, even with the windows open, the fumes hung like sweet poison. Blowback speckled his abs. His trigger finger wore a black and blue hoodie, and his head swam with the noxious vapors. He put his tools down, rummaged in the closet for the surplus respirator, a thing he rarely utilized, and went back to work. Now he was sucking air through micro filters, which was better than fainting.

This wall wasn't like his street stuff. Was and wasn't. He never took so much time on one piece. Linger this long on a city overpass, a parking-lot wall, whatever, his ass would be grass. But he wanted to get this first one perfect, like it was some kind of master template. He saturated his attention with details, turning the piece into a fucking mural. A dark city took shape. A city of soulless automatons, intermittently spark-lit with the awakened. In his absorption, Ian barely registered the ticking of rain at the windows. He was lost in a corner of the wall, smudging a human silhouette with his thumb, sweating under his mask, when shadows began to spin out of the paint. He hunkered back, blinked sweat and incomprehension out of his eyes.

The Advent was upon him.

He moved to the middle of the room, tore his mask off and tensed every muscle, staring hard straight into the Wall World. Queasiness wormed through his stomach, then light burst over him with shocking abruptness. Instantly the apartment was back in its usual configuration, bed shoved against the wall. It took him a moment to realize the difference of this Advent.

His mural was still there.

The Nihiljizum poster was restored, thumbtacked back in place, covering part of the cityscape mural – but his piece remained. Ian held up his empty hands. He had been gripping a spray can in one but the can was gone. So was the respirator. But his fingers were still paint-stained, his abs speckled with blowback.

"Holy shit. Kylie, Kylie!" He jumped up, checked every room, all empty.

Back in the living room, his wall was fading out. The sharpness dimmed away gradually, details vanishing. But it didn't dim out altogether. When the rapid fading halted, he could still see the piece, but it was very faint, as though it had been covered over with a cheap coat of latex. Ian got up close, moved his fingertips lightly over the wall. He had made something that stayed, like his last WHO CARES. But this was different. He didn't make this in the real world but during a Preservation Advent. That was significant.

But Kylie was still gone.

CHAPTER TWENTY-FIVE

IAN DIDN'T WAIT. When his cell rang he was standing under Zach's bay window.

"Man," Zach said, "are you–"

"I'm right here. Look out your window."

Zach appeared at the window, phone pressed to the side of his grinning face. He waved then disappeared. A minute later he banged out the back door of the building.

"I remember all kinds of shit," he said. "What happened after I went into the bubble?"

"Ness still didn't believe us, so she went in after you. Then Kylie and I bussed it home. She fell asleep and I went out, when I got back she was gone."

"Gone where?"

"I don't know."

"So what's the plan?"

"I want us to look for Kylie while we're waiting for my sister to come through."

"Look *where?*"

"I got an idea. Her grandparents' house on Queen Anne. It's the only place I can think of where she might turn up."

ON THE WAY, Zach hit a drive-through Tully's and bought double lattes and scones ("for the stake-out"), neither of which Ian wanted. He drank the coffee, though, out of automatic force of habit. They parked across the street from the yellow frame house with the live oaks in the front yard. Zach slurped at his coffee through the little hole in the spill-proof lid, bit into his frosted scone. Frosted crumbs rained onto his lap and he brushed them off.

"If this Preservation shit was a game it would suck. We never get anywhere. It's like there's no place *to* get. And the game keeps restarting. We can't even beat the first fucking level."

"We're getting somewhere," Ian said.

"Yeah?"

"If my sister re-gens and remembers like you do, then it means we woke her up. Which means we can maybe wake up other people, too."

"Okay, but then what?"

"How do I know? But it's not first level."

Ian picked up his coffee, held it a moment, then replaced it in the cup holder.

"One cool thing is we're immortal," Zach said.

Ian looked at him. "No, we're not."

"Hell yeah, we are. Look, we're stuck in this one day and we're in a zoo or whatever it is. But it could go on forever, right? And every Advent we start out the same age. So, in a way, we're immortal. I can get behind that."

"You're not immortal," Ian said. He needed the bathroom.

"I don't mean like *immortal* immortal. Just in the re-gen sense."

"You can only be immortal if you're alive in the first place."

"What's that supposed to mean?"

"Nothing."

Zach started to bite into his scone then put it down. "Wait a minute. What are you talking about?"

"Nothing. Forget it."

"Tell me."

"You won't like it," Ian said, wishing he'd kept his mouth shut. He had this idea of waking up as many androids as he could, but he wasn't so sure that would mean they were really *alive*. It was like a two-step process. Step one: clue the phony person into the fact that he *is* a phony person. Step two: convince the 'awake' phony person that he counts, anyway. Maybe he could make androids stay like the faded painting on the wall of his apartment. Only, Ian didn't feel like doing step one right at the moment. All he wanted to do was find Kylie – the only real girl in Seattle.

"So I won't like it," Zach said. "Tell me anyway."

Ian sighed. "Okay. You aren't what you think you are."

"What do I think I am?"

"You think you're Zach."

"I am Zach."

Ian stared at him.

"Okay," Zach said, "then who am I supposed be?"

"Not who, what. You're a regenerating android created by the Preservation. Like a robot, kind of."

"A robot?"

"Not really a robot."

"What, then?"

"An android, a perfect copy of the real you."

"I don't get it. How'd you come up with that bullshit?"

"The Curator said it."

"Said *what*, exactly?"

"There's a real you but he lives like a year in the past, before the Hunters blew everything up. The android draws from the real you but it isn't the real you, it *uses* the real you to *seem* real. This is some kind of fucked up museum. Get it? It's a human museum. You're part of it, but you aren't you."

"Oh, sure, yeah. Thanks for explaining. Are you out of your fucking *mind?*"

"Maybe."

"Because that shit you're saying doesn't make sense."

"You're right. Never mind."

"I'm *me*," Zach said.

"*Okay.*"

"Don't say 'okay' like that. Fuck you."

"Okay – I mean all right, I won't. Look. I don't know what I'm talking about."

"Damn straight."

"I'm sorry."

Zach finished his scone like he had a grudge against it, following it down with the last of his now-cold coffee. "Wait a minute," he said. "If I'm an android thing then so are you, right? So what are you so high and fucking mighty getting on my case about?"

"I'm not getting on your case."

"And I don't get what the big difference is. Even if what you say is true, we might as well be us, since–"

"I'm not an android."

"You're not."

Ian looked away. "I mean, I am and I'm not. According to the Curator I died right when they made the Preservation. Now I'm haunting my re-gen body, like it's a house or something. Like I'm a ghost?"

"That's messed up," Zach said. "You aren't a fucking ghost."

"Ghost or whatever. Not a ghost. That part's too complicated."

"I'm not as dumb as I look."

"I didn't mean–"

Zach nodded slowly, staring at him.

"Okay, okay," Ian said. "The Curator said I was like a genetic marker. The Cloud was messing with human evolution, trying to get us to evolve out of our bodies eventually, and–"

"Why?"

"I don't know. So it could absorb us or something."

"So you're a marker. Whatever that is."

"Right. And I'm way ahead of the evolution. So when I died I didn't actually die, I just went out of my body and then dove back into the android. Look, I'm just telling you what the Curator told me."

Zach looked out the window for a long while, thinking. Finally he appeared to come to some important conclusion. "Are you going to eat your scone?"

"No."

"Can I have it?"

"Help yourself."

He did.

They waited into the early afternoon, but Kylie never showed. When Zach returned after his second trip down to the greenbelt to pee, he said, "We can't just sit around here all day pissing in the bushes. Besides, some old lady with one of those shits-you dogs saw me zipping up this time."

Ian looked at his watch. "Ness will be coming through pretty soon. Let's see if we can catch her right when she hits the highway."

"Cool." Zach started the car. "Hey, I was thinking something, and it all came together while I was taking a piss. It doesn't make any difference, what you were saying about androids and ghosts and all that."

"*Yeah* it makes a difference."

"No, it doesn't. I'm me and you're you. We remember stuff. We think and feel the same as always. We're us, no matter what. Even if there's another us someplace else."

"I don't think you really get it," Ian said.

"I don't think *you* really get it," Zach said.

Ian thought: *Step two?*

Zach pulled the VW away from the curb and swung around. Ten minutes later they stood on the sidewalk watching traffic coming off the south end of the Aurora Bridge.

"All these people coming into the city get cheated out of a good chunk of the day," Zach said.

"Yeah, but they don't know it. And besides, they aren't people."

"Don't go there."

"Look, I think that's her."

A silver Jetta bore down on them. Ian and Zach started waving frantically. The Jetta immediately began to swerve. Traffic adjusted around it, horns blaring. The

Jetta, trying for the side street nearest Ian and Zach, jolted over the curb, screeched to a halt.

They ran to the car. Vanessa threw open the door and bolted out. "*Wow*, Icky."

She hugged him hard.

"I guess you remember," he said.

"Everything."

Ian was so relieved he didn't even mind the hug. In fact, it felt good.

"Dude," Zach said, "you're like fucking Keanu Reeves. You wake people *up*."

"Well," Vanessa said, "it probably helped that I gave myself a post-auto-hypnotic suggestion before I even walked across the bridge."

"When did you do that?" Ian said. "I didn't see you do anything."

"When I went to the bathroom back at the coffee shop."

"Why didn't you tell us?"

"I didn't want to encourage you. But I wanted to cover my bases, just in case."

"Hey," Zach said. "If you woke up that easily, other people will, too. Right?"

"We could certainly try," Vanessa said.

"That's my idea," Ian said, excited. "When androids wake up – become aware of what's going on – maybe they become something *more* than androids."

"I DON'T LIKE that, Icky."

They were in Vanessa's Bell Town office. Zach stretched out on the couch with his hands laced behind his head. Ian slouched in the chair and Vanessa sat on the corner of her desk, swinging her legs, looking troubled. Ian had just told her about androids.

"He's all hung up on us not being real people," Zach said. "Get used to it."

"I didn't say you weren't real. Just not original."

"Whatever."

Vanessa said, "That's so disturbing, Icky."

"Look, you guys, it doesn't matter. You feel, think and act like yourselves. So what's the difference?"

"That's what *I* was saying," Zach said.

Ian ignored him. "What about your idea, Ness, about hypnotizing everybody?"

"Not everybody. We were talking about waking people up, but there's so many. One at a time would take forever, even if it worked. But I woke up simply by giving myself a post-auto-hypnotic suggestion, right? So maybe it isn't necessary to go through a long convincing process with each individual. I can plant suggestions in my clients."

"But that's still not very many people," Ian said.

"No. That's where my idea comes into play. Have you ever heard of Rupert Sheldrake?"

Zach snapped his fingers. "Isn't he that magician who can make an elephant disappear?"

"Shut up," Ian said.

"No," Vanessa said. "He was a scientist. Sheldrake noticed that white rats were able to pass on their laboratory training to their offspring. The babies weren't trained – they were born already knowing. Do you follow me, Icky?"

"Sure."

"Well, here's the even stranger part. Sheldrake discovered that other rats in the lab, the control group that hadn't taken part in the training, *also* picked up the learned behaviors. So Sheldrake came up with what he called 'morphogenetic fields' – some kind of telepathic induction. Icky, what if we view the Preservation as one giant control group?"

"And we – you, me, Zach and Kylie and anybody else you can implant with the hypnosis thing – are the self-trained white rats?"

"Something like that, yes. Anyway, the more people we train by waking up with post-hypnotic suggestions, the more likely the morphogenetic field theory will kick in. This might be especially true if what you say about androids is accurate. We're all part of the Preservation field, then, just like our originals all shared a collective unconscious. In other words, we're already connected, under the surface. Maybe the idea of being real will spread even faster."

"Sounds good. Who's your first victim?"

"My... Oh, my first client is Matt Chadwick. He's a retired cop and he has nightmares about a bad shooting when he was young. I'll put him under and suggest the shooting maybe isn't his main problem. We'll see. Icky?"

"What?"

"I'm scared about tonight. About what happens at midnight. I don't want to disappear again, even if I do come back. What if this time I don't remember?"

"I don't know, Ness. Why wouldn't you remember, if you did this time? Anyway, we'll all meet back here, so we're together when midnight hits."

"I want to stay," Vanessa said, "the way you do."

"That could happen," Ian said, having no idea whether it could or not.

"All right. You two better leave now. My client will be here soon. Give me a hug, Icky."

During the hug Ian said, "It's going to be cool, Ness."

"Well, thanks for saying so, Icky."

Ian broke the embrace, even though he could sense she wanted to keep holding on. Then he thought something bad. He couldn't help it. She wasn't his sister, just a thing that looked and acted like her. Waking her up just meant he was hugging a thing that knew it was a thing.

Zach said, "I ain't hugging you, man. Don't even ask."

"Don't worry."

Back in the car Zach slotted the ignition key and said, "Where to? What's the plan?"

"Back to my apartment. I still have to find Kylie."

THE APARTMENT WAS empty. Big surprise.

"How'd you do that?" Zach said. He was looking at the faded mural. "How'd you get it all dim, like that?"

Ian, standing by his desk, said, "It wasn't dim when I painted it. I did it during the last Advent."

"But–"

"I know. Everything's supposed to re-gen, so why's my wall still up, even if it is faded?"

"Yeah. Why?"

"I have no fucking idea." Ian picked up the locator, which had been lying face down on the desk. The screen glowed pale blue; he had never switched it off after messing with it in the morning.

"What's that thing?"

"It's Kylie's. Some kind of electromagnetic field detector. She was trying to use it as a locator. It's supposed to zero in on the Preservation generator or whatever makes the Dome. She was on a mission to blow the thing up. Only the locator never worked, because–"

"What's wrong?"

Ian looked up from the device. "What if it did work?"

"Huh? I'm not following you, man."

"It's from outside. Outside the Preservation. It's the only technology under the Dome that creates a non-Preservation energy signature. Kylie told me... Kylie told me the Hunters were after her when she first landed. They chased her plane into the Preservation and shot it down. Then they came after her on the ground. Only they weren't so great at finding her. Except when this thing was turned on."

"She told you that?"

"Not exactly. What she told me, she said stuff like, 'I turned on the locator and the aliens started chasing me.' She wasn't making the connection. I wasn't either, until now. *Fuck*. I had to fix the stupid fucking thing. I couldn't leave it alone."

"Hey, man. You're just guessing. You don't know."

"It's what happened. I even saw one of their ships, on my way back to the apartment. Like it was hovering over the building, not really there. I didn't think I saw anything, but I did."

MATT CHADWICK SAT on Vanessa's sofa. If you stretched an Oz Munchkin to five feet nine or so and plucked out most of his candy-cane-red hair, that would be Chadwick.

"I'm hinky about going under," he said.

"It isn't like anesthetic, Matt. You'll be aware of

everything around you, but you will feel very, very relaxed and receptive."

"I guess it can't hurt. I mean, that's why I'm here. Real shrinks just want me to talk. I tell them I can't sleep, they give me pills. No offense meant about the 'real shrink' thing."

"None taken. Shall we begin?"

"Yeah, let's do it."

Vanessa held up a pencil and told him to concentrate on the little eraser end, and then she began to instruct his body to relax. Chadwick had Samsonite-sized bags under his bloodshot eyes. She could almost feel his exhaustion radiating like heat waves. She took him down, far deeper than she had told him she would, down to where only her voice filled his world. His eyelids became droopy. He swayed slightly on the sofa. Like a secret gardener, Vanessa planted her seed of self-reality. And she wondered, Who am I talking to? Where does this suggestion go? Does an android possess an unconscious, or does the seed lie in some alien matrix, waiting for the next Advent of re-creation to occur? What *was* this thing on the sofa?

And *what* am I?

IAN SAT IN the wicker chair with a sketchpad, trying to draw his anxiety away. He filled page after page with hasty slash-and-shade iterations of *know WHO you are*. Because he couldn't think of anything else to do but wait for Kylie to come back – which she wasn't going to do. He nailed his total concentration on the sketchpad. When Zach patted his shoulder he started; Ian had been so absorbed he'd almost forgotten Zach was there.

"I'm heading out. Take it easy, man."

Ian squirmed his shoulder, and Zach lifted his hand away. "Heading out where?"

"Back to my place. I'm not really here, anyway, right?"

"Sorry. I just want Kylie to come back."

"Yeah, I get that."

Ian looked around sharply, but Zach was sincere. Still, he really wanted him to go away. That's what people did, right? You open the door a little and they barge in and start to make you feel safe. Then when your guard is down they check out. So maybe quit opening the door. It wouldn't be so hard to close it on this Zach-thing, who wasn't a real person anyway.

"We're meeting your sister at eleven, right?"

"Yeah."

"I'll be back at ten-thirty to pick you up, then."

"Cool." Ian's head was down again, concentrating on the sketchpad.

"Ian?"

"What?" Why didn't he just go?

"Forget it."

Ian grunted. He barely registered the sound of the door closing. His full, laser-focused attention was on the sketchpad.

THE RAIN HAD begun. Ian pulled his hood up. The sketchpad was dry under his sweatshirt. He and Zach stood on the sidewalk outside Vanessa's office, waiting for her to open the door. A group of loud drunks spilled out of the Lava Lounge, laughing and playfully shoving each other.

"Maybe we need a drink," Zach said.

"I doubt it."

Vanessa opened the door. She looked nervous and sick. Ian said, "What's wrong with you?"

"I'm scared to death, Icky. What if I get rejected out of the Preservation this time?"

"You won't."

"I could. You know I could. Why not? I have a corrupted memory matrix and I'm trying to corrupt the memory matrices of other androids. The Curator has every reason to reject me."

"We don't know how it works," Ian said.

"But you *said* that's how it works."

"That's right, man," Zach said. "You're the one who talked to the Boogeyman."

Ian shot him an annoyed look. "Let's try not to lose it, okay?"

"I'm *not* losing it." Zach shucked his coat and dropped onto the couch. "I'm just sayin'."

Ian hiked his sweatshirt up and brought out his sketchpad.

"What's that for, Icky?"

"It's an experiment."

"What kind of experiment?"

"If it works, I'll tell you."

"The mystery man," Zach said.

Vanessa pulled open the top file cabinet drawer and lifted out a bottle. "I bought this today. There's half an hour to go. We're going to relax."

"Holy shit," Zach said. "Your sister's a fucking genius."

She poured paper cups full of the ruby port and handed them around. Zach drank his immediately and practically spat it back out. "What kind of wine is *that?*"

"It's port."

"Christ, it's really good. Not." He held his cup out for a refill anyway.

Ian watched them, his old detachment rising. He didn't fight it much. A bad feeling possessed him. A very bad feeling. "How did it go with the cop?"

"Fine. I planted the idea that at midnight he would stay wherever he was at that moment, that he would remember."

"Do you think it took?"

"Icky, how could I possibly know?"

"It's almost time," Zach said.

"Give me your hands, you two," Vanessa said.

"Why?"

"Because I'm scared, Icky. I told you. And maybe it will help."

Ian set his full cup down and Zach his empty one. The clock on the wall behind the couch was a tick or two away from straight-up midnight. Ian stuffed the sketchpad under the waist of his jeans again and reluctantly took Vanessa's hand.

"I love you, brother," she said.

Emotion grabbed at Ian's heart and he fought it off. Zach gripped his other hand.

"Everybody concentrate, concentrate on staying."

They both squeezed down hard on Ian's hands, these almost-people. *Fuck it*, Ian thought. *Fuck everything.* All he really wanted to be was alone, the way things used to be. It was easier that way.

Shadows, like blowing laces of coal dust, spun out of the faces of his sister and friend. Ian closed his eyes tight, bearing down with the full force of his concentration, rooting himself to the floor.

Suddenly his hands were empty.

CHAPTER TWENTY-SIX

MORNING LIGHT PENETRATED the tilted slats of the window blind. Ian stood alone in the office. The port bottle was gone. So were the paper cups. Ian opened the top file cabinet drawer. No bottle. He opened the other drawers. Files but no bottle. Ness said she bought the bottle yesterday, so she would have it when he and Zach arrived. She bought it while in an awakened state. But the office re-gened the way it probably always did, as if yesterday had never happened.

Ian reached around his back and yanked the sketchpad from the waist of his jeans. If objects always restored themselves to their original place and condition with every Advent, then why did the sketchpad stay with him?

Maybe the same reason the mural remained on the wall of his apartment – faded but *there*.

Ian flipped through the sketchpad. On a sheet in the

middle he'd penned: THIS WILL NOT DISAPPEAR. 8:15 PM.

The letters and numbers were sharp, ink rich and black.

"Okay, genius," Ian said. "What's it mean?"

He had no idea.

He looked around the empty office. Despite the morning light, it felt gloomy, the furniture dead, inert matter. The clock stared at him. Suddenly he wanted to talk to someone, even an android. Shouldn't Zach be calling about now? He called *every* morning. Ian fished the phone out of his pocket and waited. He hadn't really expected Ness and Zach to remain with him, to become unstuck. They weren't like Kylie or him. They were strictly Preservation constructs. The truth was, Ian hadn't really *wanted* them to stay.

What the fuck, of course he had wanted them to stay.

Except, maybe not. Maybe they were becoming too real, too close inside his own personal bubble.

Ian slid his phone open and thumbed Zach's number. It went straight to voicemail. He tried again and attained the same result. Suddenly he was more afraid than at any other time since the first Advent.

MATTHEW CHADWICK RECLINED in his Naugahyde lounger with a bottle of Bud in front of the plasma TV. It was almost midnight, and drinking a beer right now meant he'd be up dribbling in the toilet before the night was over, no matter how much he peed before bed. Or maybe not. Matt was afraid to go to sleep at all. It wasn't the nightmare, his bullet gone astray, that kid taking it in the neck, dying right there on the sidewalk while Matt knelt over him, helplessly. He *hated* that nightmare, that memory. Hated the stale residue of guilt he woke with almost every morning. But tonight what he was most afraid of was the failure of the hypno-therapy, what did she call it, the *suggestion* that would give him peace at last. What a word. Suggestion. Like, I *suggest* you don't feel like shit.

But maybe. Just maybe. It would work.

His wife had gone to bed two hours ago. These days he and Connie slept in separate rooms. A few weeks ago, during a night of violent thrashing dreams, he'd elbowed her in the eye. Sleeping with him had become *dangerous*. This situation above everything else was what had driven Matt to the hypno-therapist. Every other approach had failed to help him. His marriage was collapsing around his ears.

Matt held the Bud in his left hand and the television remote in his right. He flipped between three stations: A *MythBusters* rerun, ESPN, and a subtitled French movie on the Canadian station. He liked the look of the actress in the movie – she reminded him of Audrey Hepburn – but he didn't bother reading the subtitles. Because it was a foreign movie he was hoping that the actress would sooner or later find herself topless.

Matt felt something, then, and narrowed his eyes, listening to his body. Strokes had killed both his parents. Matt, now forty-seven years old, was always more or less waiting for his.

The inset clock of the on-screen cable menu flipped to 12:00AM.

A peculiar, shadowy web spun across his vision. A sudden light shift occurred, and the night was *gone*. The television was off, so was the lamp. Pigeons cooed outside the apartment window.

Matt didn't move. Except his eyes. His eyes slipped left and right, taking in the room. He lifted his empty hands and stared at them. In the bedroom Connie stirred. He turned his head. She came shuffling out in her robe and flip-flop slippers, yawning. She was wide awake and bright-eyed first thing in the morning, as always.

"Matt, what's wrong? Did you stay up all night again?"

He stared at her.

"Matthew?"

"I don't know," he said. "I don't *know*."

IAN STOOD OUTSIDE the lobby of Zach's building and thumbed the buzzer, waited, thumbed it again. He checked his watch. Eight-thirty. He dug out his key and let himself in. He climbed the stairs slowly, remembering the last time he'd been here, the time Zach shot himself in the head. *We should start our own suicide club,* Ian thought. *What would the t-shirt say?*

He knocked on the door. It was an old building, fully renovated. The walls and doors were thick, the hallway carpeted. Silent. The door seemed to absorb his knock. He hovered his finger over the buzzer but hesitated, afraid. Instead, Ian used the spare key. The condo smelled like a pineapple pizza. The fish tank burbled placidly. Ian moved down the entry hall, like a nervous burglar. He looked in the bedroom. It was empty, the bed unmade. He continued to the living room. The blinds were tilted closed. The lighted fish tank looked like a TV tuned to a vividly dull station.

Zach was asleep on the sofa. A gaming magazine lay open to a picture of Lara Croft busting out of skin-tight leathers. Next to the magazine was an empty wine bottle, a roach clip, and a tube of Lubriderm. Ian grimaced, then leaned over and tapped Zach on the head.

Like tapping a land mine.

"Guh!" Zach flung himself off the couch, tangled in the blanket. The wine bottle rolled across the floor.

"It's me!" Ian said.

"What the *fuck*, man?"

"Sorry. You didn't answer your phone or the door, so I got worried."

Zach fumbled his glasses on, squinted at the minimalist clock on the wall, two wire-thin hands that glowed neon blue, no numbers or hash marks. "It's practically *dawn*. What's going on, did somebody die?"

"No. I was just worried."

"Worried about *what*?"

"I don't know."

Zach stood up, scratching his head. He nudged the Lubriderm under the couch with his foot.

"Okay," he said. "Coffee."

In the kitchen Zach pushed a button on the coffee machine and a red light winked on. Soon black coffee began trickling into the pot.

"So what's going on?" he said. "For real. I know nothing except the Apocalypse is going to haul your dead ass out of bed before noon."

Ian cleared his throat. "Don't you remember anything weird?"

Zach removed his glasses, wiped them on his t-shirt, which was white with big black letters spelling BEER, and replaced them. "Weird? You mean besides a minute ago when you tried to give me a fucking heart attack? Uh, no."

"You don't have a feeling like stuff's been going on?"

"Stuff," Zach said.

"If I say 'Preservation' what do you think?"

"Strawberry jam?"

"Not *preserves*. Preservation. I'm serious, man."

"I know. But I can't tell what you're serious *about*."

"Just think for a minute. You know that deja vu feeling? Are you getting that at all?"

Zach poured coffee into a Mindwerks mug and handed it Ian. "No, man. What I've got is a 'What the fuck are you talking about' feeling.'"

"You really don't remember anything, do you."

"Anything about *what*?"

"Never mind."

A FEW HOURS later Ian stood by the side of Aurora Avenue North. Traffic out of the bubble roared by him. He waited until he saw Vanessa's car, then started waving frantically. She blasted by, tapped her brakes but never pulled over. Ian ran to the Chief, parked on a side street, and followed her downtown.

She was unlocking her office when he tucked into the curb. At the sound of the engine racket, she turned. Her face opened up in surprise and happiness at the sight of him. Mostly surprise. Ian killed the engine and removed his helmet.

"Icky!"

"Hi, Ness."

"*Your* hi Ness to you, buster. I'm so happy to see you. It's been almost a year, you know."

"I know."

"Icky, what's wrong?"

"Nothing, I guess. I wanted to talk to you."

"I have a client in half an hour. Can we do lunch right after?"

Ian felt sick to his stomach. They were both gone, really gone. Waking Vanessa or Zach up again would require starting from scratch. And even then, he wondered if it would work. Ness had feared being rejected out of the Preservation, and that's exactly what had happened. This was a brand new android; he sensed it, knew it. Ian was the only aware person in the city.

A squat, angry man with a few remnants of red hair came running at them.

"Hey, hey–" He was out of breath when he reached them. "What did you *do* to me?" he said.

"Mr. Chadwick, what's wrong?"

"*Everything's* wrong. My God, I think I'm losing my mind."

Ian interrupted, "She hypnotized you. You're that cop."

Chadwick glared at Ian. "What do you know about it, kid?

"I... nothing, really."

"I want to know what's happening to me."

Vanessa touched his shoulder reassuringly. "Let's go inside, Mr. Chadwick. We'll talk about it."

"Sure, okay."

She gave Ian a questioning look. He just shrugged and watched them go into the building.

HE RETREATED TO his apartment to await the next Advent. It occurred while he was lying on his back reading a battered paperback copy of *Notes from the*

Underground. It was one of those books he thought he'd get around to eventually but eventually never seemed to arrive. Now 'eventually' was a steady state. He picked up this particular copy of Dostoyevsky's novel from Twice Sold Tales that very afternoon. At midnight the print started to wriggle on the page, lacy shadows spinning out of the paper. Worms moved queasily in his stomach. Ian looked up from the book.

There was a sudden light shift, and the book was gone.

He stared at the ceiling, waiting for Zach to call. The phone remained silent. His eyes grew heavy and he slept a few hours. When he got up, groggy, his head aching, he thought about beginning the process of waking his friend again. There didn't seem to be any point. As soon as Zach become self-consciously aware of the situation, the Preservation would get a clue and reject him. Ian and Zach's big plan of waking up everyone on the Preservation was dead. Really, it died as soon as Kylie disappeared. How many Advents would it be before he began to doubt she had ever existed?

He thought of his sister and her morphogenetic bullshit, and he wondered about that cop. Was he still awake? What did Vanessa think about his story? How many times would the cop *tell* her his story? Maybe not that many before he got rejected himself.

Thinking about Vanessa depressed Ian, so he put her in a locked compartment of his mind, the one right next to the locked compartment that held Zach, and another – a bank vault, really, that held Kylie. Then he went out to re-buy *Notes from the Underground*.

* * *

THIS TIME WHEN the Advent came he anticipated it. He knew the book was going to disappear, and it pissed him off. *Stay, stay, stay.* In his mind he heard Kylie saying those words the first time he came unstuck from the endless cycle of Advents. And remembering her, the emotion of that moment overtook him. His chest tightened with grief and loneliness. He gripped the book like a vise. *Stay, motherfucker.*

The queasy feeling began.

Shadows spun forth, and in the sudden light shift... the book remained in his hand.

He held it up, turning it before his gaze as if it were some incomprehensible artifact. He could fix things permanently to the Advent by an act of desperate concentration – like when he tried to push the despair out of his head when he made WHO CARES.

He didn't read anymore that Advent; he painted. His apartment became Goya's Spanish house, only sloppier. Ian covered the walls with his own 'Black Paintings'. He was totally alone in the city and would be forever. Even death wouldn't release him but merely expel him from this jacked body. By late that night the walls reflected his reality. Buildings loomed like doom-shadowed giants over avenues thronged with soulless androids. Ian revised the faded mural he had put up a few Advents past, first by spraying over *know WHO you are*. Ian knew who he was, all right. More importantly, he knew *what* he was: Fucked.

He was trying to figure out how to do the ceiling, when the rain started. Just before midnight, he ripped off his respirator and stood naked in the middle of the room, his pale body streaked with sweat and paint. It was like removing his mask inside a paint shed; the fumes infiltrated his brain.

"Stay!" he shouted. "Stay, stay, stay!"

The sudden light shift briefly animated the paintings, but it didn't obliterate them. Ian breathed out, slowly turning, taking in his work. He could make this one room real, his Fortress of Solitude.

His head swam in the paint fumes, though.

He pulled on a pair of blue jeans, jammed his bare feet into sneakers, not bothering to tie the laces. He shrugged into his black hoodie in the hall. At the Rite-Aid on Broadway he bought a couple of fans, a box of Ritz crackers and a six-pack of Diet Coke. The parking-lot wall of Dick's Drive-In once again wore his lame WHO CARES. Ian tried not to look at it.

He lugged the fans and Coke back to the apartment. The fumes were still bad, but he hated wearing the respirator. He positioned the fans in opposite corners of the main room, pointed at the open windows, turned them on full-blast, and headed out to the park to get some sleep.

A COUPLE OF hours later he woke on a bench across the street from his building, his head throbbing. He blinked at the blue sky. A figure moved close, blocking the sun. Ian turned his head. A tall, lean man wearing a Hawaiian shirt and dark glasses stood over him. Ian's skin prickled. He sat up, headache stabbing like a spike.

"What–?"

The stranger turned and walked away. Just another zombie android, Ian thought. But it didn't feel that way. Ian got up and started following the man. The stranger passed by the fountain in the middle of the park. Mist from the geysering water drifted over him like sun-sparkled smoke. In the misty drift the shadow reflection of a much taller figure appeared, like an optical illusion.

Ian stopped dead, staring.

The illusion lasted only seconds. But that was enough. It was one of *them*. The Hunters. The ones who had taken Kylie.

Ian ran after the thing, shouting, "Hey, hey stop!"

The Hunter moved out of sight around the fountain. Ian pounded after him, but when he cleared the fountain the stranger was gone.

IAN SPENT THE rest of the day painting himself into a safe box, which was how he now regarded the apartment. The drugstore fans proved insufficient, so he reluctantly donned the respirator again. He drew hard at the saturated filters, sucking hot, oily-tasting air. The ceiling was the hardest part. He needed a scaffold. What he had was a bed, his futon. Standing on it he could reach the ceiling, but it was hard on his back.

First he conjured a black sun out of a nearly depleted Sabotaz can. Using markers, mashing their tips into the uneven plaster surface, dropping dead pens like expended cartridges, he sketched outward from this sun, discovering a doomed and dizzy perspective. He filled it all in using cheap brushes and True Value paint, ripping the alien sky out of his head like a paranoid dream. A wave of yellow pox stars bisected the ceiling. Muscled clouds bunched and crowded in from every corner. He had to take frequent breaks, his neck, back and arm aching.

He worked through the morning and afternoon, and by evening he was as done as he could get. Collapsed on the bed, exhausted, he stripped the respirator off his face and dropped it on the floor. He rubbed his eyes. Images of paranoia and isolation crowded him from the walls and ceiling – even the door to the hallway.

His safe box. Like retreating into his own head and armor-plating the inside of his skull.

He laughed, his sandpaper throat translating it into a gallows rasp. He could *taste* the fumes, like an oily film on his tongue and lips.

He sat up. The room was a shambles. He had dragged everything into the center of the floor, clearing wall space. His clothes and books and crap were everywhere. Kylie's Judas locator device lay in a tangle of underwear. She had brought it in from the outside, so it didn't re-gen. Her big mission to blow up the Dome.

Wait a minute.

Maybe blowing the Dome wasn't such a bad idea.

He rolled off the bed and crawled to the locator, thumbed it on. The grid lit up. Okay, he could do this.

"I can *do it*," Ian said, wrecked on paint fumes and exhaustion.

He stumbled into his jeans and sneakers, grabbed his sweatshirt and keys and banged out the door, slamming it behind him. The latch didn't catch. The door bounced off the frame and swung back inward. He fumbled after the knob, missed it, snarled, "Fuck you," and kicked the door hard enough to drive the inside knob through the wall.

He didn't need no stinking safe box.

"I'm *out* of here."

SATURDAY EVENING TRAFFIC jammed him up on the way to Pioneer Square. He left the bike in a red zone on Second

Avenue and walked the rest of the way. The fresh air cleared his head. He almost turned around, back to the apartment. Only his awareness of the utter futility of his existence prevented that retreat.

Triple Ex Girlz hunkered like a dilapidated bunker at the intersection of two empty streets. Phony graffiti looped and slashed across the plywood-boarded windows. Trash collected in the recessed doorway, but Ian knew the trash – like the graffiti – was camouflage. No bum ever slouched in *that* doorway.

He walked toward the building, bracing himself for the repelling field. *You can't stop me, you can't* even *stop me*. And it didn't. Ian never felt the repelling force. At the door, he stood a moment, all his senses wide open. Nothing. No repelling force. Was the Curator luring him in? Fuck him, if he was.

Ian placed his hand flat against the door and pushed. It cracked away from the jamb and swung smoothly inward. A close, stale smell comprised of ancient piss and beer and sweat wafted out of the dark.

Ian experienced a moment of doubt.

He stood on the threshold of either a vacant and abandoned strip club, or the secret core of a vast alien power.

After a few moments, Ian spoke into the dark: "You can't trick me, you bastard." He drew Kylie's EM detector out of his sweatshirt pocket and thumbed the power button. As a locator for the Preservation machine, the thing was useless. But Ian was certain the Hunters had used it to zero in on Kylie. Maybe they were still monitoring for non-Preservation-generated signals. Maybe they would get curious and drop into XXX GIRLZ. According to the Curator, they were hot to find this place. And Ian had a feeling the camouflage wouldn't fool them, once they got up close. Let the Hunters blow the Dome and end it all. Even if it meant Ian had to spend eternity floating around without a body. That would be better than the way he felt now. It had to be.

He entered the club.

What little light filtered in from the open door revealed scattered tables with chairs upended on them, a bar backed by empty shelves. On a low stage two stripper poles gleamed dully. Ian's doubts surfaced again and he pushed them down, strode between the tables, placed the EM detector on the stage, and retreated. He paused a moment before leaving the club, looked back at the gloomy interior. The pale blue grid glowed on the stage like a lost star.

A couple of blocks from XXX GIRLZ, in a slightly classier borderland of Pioneer Square, two shops side-by-side presented a pleasant invitation. One was a bookstore. *Biblio: Books New & Rare*. Tall, densely packed bookshelves stood in lamplight behind plate glass windows.

Ian angled toward the shop, hands balled in the pockets of his hoodie. But before he could even cross the street the bookshop's interior lights winked out. A man in a blue button-down shirt exited the shop, pulled the door shut after him, turned with a set of keys and locked it.

The other shop wasn't a shop at all but an art gallery. The big sign over the entry read: The Noble Gallery. Beyond the big window, soothing white space was interrupted by individually lit paintings, the details of which were indiscernible from Ian's position across the street.

The bookstore man walked a few steps and entered the Noble Gallery.

Ian crossed the street. Modern mainstream art didn't interest him with its self-conscious conceits and phony intellectualism. But bookstores always exerted an irresistible fascination, and he'd never heard of Biblio: Books New & Rare. He was glad the owner had left, though. Ian never wanted to talk to another android, never wanted to be faked out again.

He stood on the sidewalk a moment, peering through the window at the shelves. It was a small shop. In the real world he would have enjoyed browsing it, maybe buying a couple of books he'd never finish reading. But this wasn't the real world. He pulled his hood up and stuffed his hands back in his pockets.

As he passed in front of the Noble Gallery he glanced over – and stopped. Each painting was like a window into an obscurely meaningful world. The scenes ranged from mundane depictions of toys and furniture to disturbing acts of violence. The paintings exerted something like magnetic attraction. Ian felt it even on the sidewalk. He leaned closer. It wasn't the usual bullshit one-man show, or one-theme show. Every canvas presented startlingly different content from the others. What did an old-fashioned snow sled with red metal runners have to do with a blood-spattered shirt draped over the back of a kitchen chair?

He touched the glass with his fingertips, obscurely sensing there was something *in* there for him. But the two fake humans chatting by the wine bar dissuaded him from entering. One was the Biblio man. The other, half turned away from Ian, wore a white jacket and a fawn-colored Kangol cap and was pouring white wine into a stem glass. There was something familiar about him. He handed the Biblio guy the wine, and Biblio guy noticed Ian staring at them.

Ian turned and walked away, fast.

Instead of returning to his bike, he cut through an alley and came out on the next block across from XXX GIRLZ. Immediately he could tell something was different. The building *looked* exactly as it had a few minutes ago, but...

A steel clamp seized Ian by the back of the neck and hoisted him off his feet. He kicked at whatever held him. The pressure on his neck increased until he stopped kicking. The pain spiked when the clamp swung him around. Now he was looking into the face of a giant. Bald, skin curd-pale, eyes black and without pupils, too big even for the too-big face. Ruby light gathered in the giant's left eye and speared into Ian's *right* eye. The giant held him perfectly still. The ruby spear penetrated like a hot needle. Ian screamed.

The steel clamp fingers opened and dropped him to the pavement. The giant strode away.

Ian pushed the heel of his hand into his eye. His head ached like murder. With his other hand he rubbed the back of his neck, which felt like it had been squeezed by steel vise grips. He stumbled upright, his legs shaky.

As if a vacuum opened in the sky, there was a sudden windy up-rush. Ian gasped after his breath. Yellow newspaper sheets, fast food wrappers and cups and assorted trash swept into the air. Above XXX GIRLZ something like a spinning sheet of glass manifested. The spin rate increased and the glass became a bright pinwheel light as big as a truck and blinding bright. Ian shuffled back, still covering his eye.

An energy beam stomped through the roof of triple XXX GIRLZ. The walls bulged. Ian turned to run, but the explosion caught him, lifting and hurling him into the alley across the street. Vivid green and red flames unrolled like a wave. Intense heat baking him, Ian crawled behind a garbage dumpster. He drew his arms and legs in and tucked his face down. The dumpster shuddered like something alive.

The fire retreated. Ian unfolded himself and peered around the dumpster. Where XXX GIRLZ had stood moments ago, there was now a glowing crater. But no spinning ship and no giants.

Ian got to his feet slowly, cringing, watching the mild evening sky, as if expecting it to crack apart at any second. When it didn't, and he knew the Preservation machines hadn't been destroyed, Ian fled to the far end of the alley and the street beyond. But he couldn't outrun a nasty, burnt smell. His shoulder stung. He stopped, stripped his hoodie off. It was burned through, crisp and smoking. He dropped the hoodie and ran, shirtless.

The lights were off in the Noble Gallery.

Sirens began to wail from multiple directions. A news chopper hovered in, spotlight sweeping the crater.

Ian grabbed his bike, begged the engine to start. It did. He rode hard. Strange lights flashed out of the night sky. Buildings exploded, fires rolled up like flaming fists. In minutes chaos overtook the city. All he could think of was his room, his safe box, as if his brain was *telling* him to get there, even though it made zero sense. Ian dumped his bike in the alley behind his building. He made it to the third floor hallway. His door was still open, the way he'd left it, with the knob punched into the entry wall. He started for it and then the building shook violently. The lights went out – except for one in his apartment. The building shook again. Dust sifted through the rectangle of light that was his apartment doorway. Someone screamed. More doors opened, a flashlight swung frantically over the floor and walls, other tenants stumbling into the hall. Ian threw himself into his apartment, slammed the door and shot the bolt. His 'safe box' was a virtual gas chamber; even with the window open the paint and marker stink was miasmatic.

The green library lamp burned serenely on his desk. Cries and screams, the bedlam skirl of sirens entered through the open windows. Ian covered his ears with his hands but could still hear it. He stalked to the kitchen and slammed the window down. In the living room he hesitated briefly before the only other window. Except for the fires, every building within his range of vision was dark. He looked back at his lamp, which hadn't even flickered.

"What is this?"

He pushed the window sash down. The lurid light of a fire played over his bare torso. He started to drop the shade, and the window burst, coughing glass into his skin and across the floor, fragments scattering like diamonds. He staggered back. From outside: screams and sirens and explosions.

Ian brushed nuggets of glass off his body, blood streaking from a dozen tiny puncture wounds. He stepped forward, sneakers crunching glass, grinding fragments into the hardwood floor. The closer he got to the window the louder the chaos. He picked up a spray can – Sabotaz 'Signal Red'. It felt light as air but maybe he could get something out of it. A bizarre white light stuttered into the alley. Ian dropped the shade clattering in front of the open window. He triggered the spray can, coated the slats solid, grabbed a second can and looped out a random glyph. Did the same with the kitchen window.

The apartment assumed a deathly quiet.

He stood in the middle of the room, bleeding, breathing hard, completely surrounded by pieces of his paranoid mind. Only it wasn't paranoia. His city was burning.

But not his safe box.

In here it felt like XXX GIRLZ: that same eerie, muffled silence. *Bound in camouflage*, the Curator had said. The fat man had the power.

Maybe Ian did, too.

CHAPTER TWENTY-SEVEN

MIDNIGHT IN THE Fortress of Goya.

Shadows spun out of every surface left unpainted by Ian's spray cans and markers, out of the desk and bed and random debris of Ian's life. Worms twisted in his stomach. He kept his eyes open through the light shift, standing solid in the center of the room.

Advent.

His 'Black' paintings remained – unfaded.

"Check this shit out," he said to no one, looking around at the walls, as if it were work somebody else had put up. He remembered the weirdly compelling pictures in the Noble Gallery, the magnetic alienness and familiarity of them.

In the bathroom he picked a tiny fragment of window glass out of the skin below his right nipple, dampened a corner of threadbare bath towel and started to blot the blood off his chest and stomach. Contorting himself before the mirror, he craned his head to get a look at his back. There was a red burn the size and shape of a fried egg just below his right shoulder blade. The Hunters had reduced XXX GIRLZ to a smoking crater and all Ian got was this lousy burn.

In the living room he racked up the blinds on the routine morning. The window was restored. He pushed it up. Fresh, cool air breezed in. His Chief stood wheel-cocked in the alley. Situation normal. Just another Advent.

When the Hunters blew up the strip club that should have been *it*. Whatever machines were maintaining the Preservation should have blown up, too. Instead, everything went on. And the Hunters burned the whole city down. Again. Except for Ian's safe box apartment.

Bound in camouflage.

That fat alien had called him something. What was it? Ian grinned. "I'm a fucking *Lens*."

He was kicking around the clothes on the living room floor, looking for a minimally rancid t-shirt, when a second realization hit him like a hammer: the other guy in the in The Noble Gallery, the one whose back had been to Ian – that guy had *been* the alien. The *Curator*.

So he moved operations. That's why destroying the strip club didn't destroy the Preservation machines.

Got it.

He yanked the big closet open. Standing on tip toes, he reached way back on the high shelf. His fingers touched the shoe box, teasing it out until he could get a grip on it. He had made sure when he put it there in the first place that it wouldn't be easy to reach. The box was heavy. He flipped the lid off, lifted out the oily towel-wrapped object, unrolled it on the bed.

His father's .38 Police Special. Suicide toy. Only this wasn't about suicide. This was about *life*.

XXX GIRLZ STOOD tawdry but intact. Ian slowed the Chief as he rolled by. At the next block he goosed the throttle and leaned into the turn. He parked a couple of streets over, out of sight of the Noble Gallery, and walked the rest of the way.

It was still very early. Both the gallery and Biblio were closed. Ian slipped behind the gallery. He was not one hundred per cent certain. But it didn't matter. If it was just another fake guy in there, another android, Ian would know it immediately. And even if the guy called the police on him, so what? Worst scenario: Ian gets locked up for a few hours.

A featureless metal door confronted him. He couldn't tell if it was rigged with an alarm. In any case, there was no way to force it open, even with a pry bar – which Ian didn't have, anyway. He would have to wait until the place opened.

He started to turn away, and something went thud on the other side of the door. The bastard *was* in there. Ian withdrew the revolver from the waist of his jeans, planted himself square in front of the door. He held the gun behind his back and knocked, waited, knocked again, with more force. Was this really the right way to confront an alien from another planet? Knock first?

After a moment the dead-bolt snapped aside and the door opened.

A pudgy man in khakis, navy blue pullover and black baseball cap stood before Ian, holding a mug of steaming hot tea.

It was him.

Ian pointed the gun. "I know you. You're the Curator. No bullshit."

"I was the Curator," the man said, unperturbed. "But not any more. Now I am simply Charles Noble."

Ian pushed the barrel against his chest. It left a little oily ring on the cashmere. "Back inside, 'Charlie'." He followed him and kicked the door shut. They were in a small living space. Sink, microwave oven, little gate leg table with two chairs, Persian carpet and three shut doors. Ian's right eye started to throb, like the beginning of a drilling headache.

He said to the Curator, "They blew up the strip club on the last Advent. How come nothing changed?"

"What would change?"

"The Dome, the Preservation – why didn't it disappear? Did you move the generator or whatever it is over to this building?"

"There is no generator."

"Then what makes everything go?"

"Mr. Palmer, I already told you what makes everything 'go' on the Preservation. *You* do. Here, come with me. I wish to show you something." Not intimidated in the least by Ian's deadly weapon and the position of power it inferred, Noble turned and walked through the nearest door. Ian followed, irritated that he wasn't in charge.

They entered the gallery proper. Canvases covered most of the wall space. Ian glanced around but kept his attention on Noble. The paintings represented everything from a mundane pair of red sneakers to a vicious, snarling mongrel dog trapped in a giant soap bubble. A few pieces of sculpted art squatted on display pedestals. One, fashioned in molded acrylic, resembled an anthropomorphic jellyfish wearing a John Steed bowler: Drifter / Not For Sale.

Noble swept his arm grandly, "Do you see anything you like?"

Ian pressed the heel of his hand to his right eye. The pressure did nothing to relieve the throbbing pain. "Listen. I know what you are. You *told* me, for Christ's sake. So cut it out. I want to know how this thing works and then I want you to make it stop working. That's all. You have no right to *fuck* with me."

"If the Preservation stops, so will all of us who dwell here stop. I have a counter proposal. Together, we might effectively shield the entire city from future Hunter attacks. I can't do it alone, but with two Lenses it might be possible."

"I thought you weren't going to fuck with me."

"Not my intention, I assure you." Noble cleared his throat. "Are you certain you don't see anything you like? It might... relax you."

"Corporate art is shit," Ian said, stating one of his cherished knee-jerk opinions, though he knew that what surrounded him in the Noble Gallery was anything but corporate.

"Are you quite certain?"

Noble had one of those big open faces that invite generosity. A face full of good will and interest in people and life. Despite himself, Ian didn't want to disappoint a face like that. It was the Curator's face but the lingering element of alien coldness was gone. Ian sighed, lowered the gun. "I don't even know what's going on anymore."

Noble poured a glass of white wine and handed it to him. "I know it's early, but I think you could use this."

Ian brought the glass to his lips. The wine slipped cold and crisp over his tongue. He didn't really want it, but it was so good he took a second taste, this time holding the wine in his mouth a moment before swallowing.

"Acceptable?" Charles said.

"Whatever."

"Very good." Noble smiled and nodded at him, encouragingly. "You're quite right, you know. At one point, you might say, I was in charge of a somewhat larger establishment than this – the Seattle Preservation. At any rate, I *thought* I was in charge. And every time a real customer manifested, I would immediately reject him. I believe I was *afraid* of the real customers."

Ian drank his wine. He felt light-headed. The throbbing ache behind his eye subsided, minutely, with the introduction of alcohol. "Who did all these pictures?"

"I fill my gallery with the borrowed inspiration of those with whom I share the city. Their memory matrices are rich with personally significant images. I retrieve the image, alter it with therapeutic intent, and manifest it in my gallery. My walls are never bare and works change from Advent to Advent. No one can resist a work of their own imagination, especially if they are unaware of its origin."

"You steal art from people's brains then sell it back to the victim?"

Noble chuckled. "The truth is, everyone is more than delighted with the arrangement. Not that they know what the situation is. I'll tell you what, though. I've had a splendid week, so I'd like to make you a gift."

"I don't want any of this shit."

"Of course you do. Here, have a look." Noble gestured

with his open hand and Ian followed the gesture. On a small rectangular canvas there was rendered an old-fashioned claw-foot bathtub. It stood in an obscurely shadowed room subdued by dun and oxblood brush strokes. The tub itself was almost translucently blue-white – a tub made of bone china. It brimmed with cerulean water afloat with rose petals.

"You approve?"

Ian approached the thing, impelled by soothing currents that seemed to flow between him and the canvas.

"It's yours," Noble said.

"I said I don't–"

"Yours in the purest sense."

Ian forced himself to look away. He raised the gun. "Don't even *try* to mess with me. My girl is gone, you threw my best friend and my sister out of here on the last Advent, and you'd do the same to me, if you could."

"But I can't. And you're wrong about the others. I didn't reject them. You did."

"That's *bullshit*."

"It's the simple truth. Your Lensing ability has always been stronger than mine, and this Preservation belongs to you, not me."

"You're crazy."

Noble shrugged.

A man with black wavy hair and olive skin, barefoot, wearing slacks but no shirt appeared in the doorway to the living quarters. "Charles!"

Ian swung the revolver at him. "Who are you?"

The man's eyes widened. "My God, who are *you?*"

"It's all right, Curtis," Charles said. "Come here."

Curtis went to Charles and the men held hands, a united front. Ian experienced a ripple of irrational

336

jealousy: These two guys, neither one a human being, standing there like they *meant* something to each other. Maybe they did.

"There isn't any money, no safe, if that's what you're after," Curtis said.

Noble smiled sweetly at his companion. "He doesn't want money, Curtis."

"What *does* he want, then? And why does he have that *gun?*"

Ian lowered the revolver. "Take it easy. I'm not going to shoot it or anything. I just... I want. I don't know what I want anymore."

Noble said, "More wine, perhaps?"

"No–" Ian's eye began to ache massively. He brought his hand up to cover it – and stopped. A red light shone on his palm. "What–?" He dropped the hand and the light rayed out, painting a sickle on Charles Noble's chest.

"They've come," Noble said. "They used you to find me."

The building began to shudder. Ian's bathtub painting slipped from its hook and hit the floor, the frame cracking apart. 'Drifter' teetered on its pedestal. The lights flickered.

"Earthquake," Curtis said. "We have to get *under* something."

Ian looked at the ceiling. "No. It's the Hunters, isn't it? They're going to destroy the Preservation machines."

"There are no machines," Noble said. "Only a focusing Lens. You."

Ian dropped his gun and made for the front door. It was locked. He fumbled at the latch, flung the door open and ran into the street.

A brilliant light flashed and spun directly over the Noble Gallery. Ian threw his hand up to shield his eyes. A hot whirlwind tore at his clothes, threatened to sweep him into the air. The gallery exploded, then, and Ian's body rode the expanding fire bubble for an instant before the heat disintegrated him.

Bodiless, Ian found himself hovering above the city. The great Dome turned white and then imploded, a collapsing shell. Ian felt the collapse as if it were himself collapsing. Concentric shockwaves rolled over the surrounding landscape, obliterating everything they encountered.

PART THREE

"When two people dream the same dream,
it ceases to be an illusion."

PHILIP K. DICK, *THE UNTELEPORTED MAN*

CHAPTER TWENTY-EIGHT

OCTOBER 2011: IAN PALMER

IAN THRASHED AWAKE, his bed a drowning pool. The sheets tangled around his arms and legs, holding him under. He kicked free, sat up, and discovered a monster headache. The pain was so intense it blurred his vision. He sat on the edge of the bed, elbows planted on knees, head cradled in his hands, and waited. Eventually the headache subsided sufficiently to allow him to stand. Stepping delicately, as if his head were a brimming tea cup, he made his way to the bathroom. From the medicine cabinet he took down an economy-sized bottle of aspirin, twisted and pried at the child-proof cap until it popped free, shook four of the little white tablets into his palm and washed them down with tap water.

He remembered everything. He remembered the future.

The events on the Preservation appeared in sharp focus, like the memory of a super-dream (or psychotic episode), each detail rendered in hyper clarity, the ultimate piece, put up on the wall inside his own head by alien forces. Were Zach and Vanessa remembering, too?

Ian found his phone and slid it open. The tiny date/time in the corner display read: 5-Oct-11.

He felt more *there* – in the 2012 Preservation – than *here*, in the mundane Seattle apartment he woke up in every day. But he had no doubt of where – and *when* – this was. The Curator had told him the Preservation androids drew their illusion of life from connections across a space-time rift to the sleeping minds of the real Seattle population. When the Preservation Dome collapsed, so did the connection.

And Ian woke up. Remembering.

"This is too weird."

He looked around the room, which was the usual disaster. Notably absent: the smell of markers and paint; his Goya murals were gone, erased by the reality shift, the walls and ceiling restored to blank plaster. No, not erased. In the real apartment they had never existed in the first place.

His old backpack slumped in a corner of the closet like a dead dog. He'd flung it there when he quit *getting up*, quit bombing the city, quit the midnight world of spray cans and outrunning the police. Since then, life hadn't been so good. Not that it had been exactly *good* before. But at least graffiti used to shatter the recurring tedium and low-grade depression. Now he was in full-on drone mode most of the time, unless he was high.

Except that wasn't true anymore. Now was then. And Ian had brought something back across the Preservation dream warp or whatever you called it.

A purpose.

He swung the backpack out by the straps and unzipped it on the bed. *This is a test of the National Reality-Check Network.* A few cans, a random palette of markers. He grabbed the black marker and uncapped it. The tip was pristine. It would be, though, even if he were still living on the Preservation. But his walls presented dingy, blank faces, except for the Nihiljizum poster. The nightmare 'stay' murals were gone. That more than anything else proved he was where he was.

Kneeling on the bed, he applied the black marker to the wall next to his pillow and wrote: *know WHO you are*. Immediately, his good feeling began to ascend. He jumped up on the mattress, jazzed and excited, and wrote the same words on the ceiling. A reminder. He proceeded to letter the same reminder onto the wall over his desk, the kitchen cabinet where he kept his coffee mugs, the apartment door (changing markers by now, the black one gone dry) – even the bathroom mirror, the fresh green marker squeaking on the glass.

When he finished, there wasn't a direction he could look or a room he could retreat to without seeing at least one *know WHO you are*.

That was good. Because Ian *did* know who he was, knew that if he wasn't careful he would start doubting the whole thing. And as soon as he doubted it, the reality of the Preservation would begin to slip away from him. Which would be bad, considering Ian and Ian alone knew the exact day on which the world would end.

But he didn't really believe he would lose track of that knowledge. Because he had something beautiful and perfect in his head that was more effective than all the reminders he'd just put up.

Kylie was alive. Here, in this now, Kylie was alive.

* * *

"HOW'S IT GOING?" he said to Zach on the phone.

"How's it going?"

"Yeah."

"Great. How's it going with you?"

"Fantastic. Man, when you woke up today, did you remember a dream?"

"Ah, no."

"Did you have a really bad headache?"

"What are you smoking?"

"I'm just asking you a question."

"No, I didn't have a headache," Zach said.

"And you really don't remember anything?"

"Anything like *what*?"

"Nothing. Never mind. I'll talk to you later."

"Dude, whatever."

Square one.

HE SAT IN a Starbucks on Second Avenue with his sister, who was sipping green tea. Ian slurped at a double latte. It tasted burned. Well, it was Starbucks.

"Icky, how *are* you?"

"Fine, good. Really good."

"You look tired."

"I'm a little tired." Why did she always have to do the big sister thing, like she was filling in for their mother? And how easy it was to slip right back into their accustomed relationship. Understandable on Vanessa's side; she knew nothing of the future Preservation or the evolved relationship her android would share with him.

"Well. It's good to finally see you again," she said. "It's been so long. I'm glad you called."

"Yeah. Listen, Ness. Do you remember anything... strange?"

Her eyes narrowed slightly. "Strange how?"

"Just strange. What I'm talking about is a dream. Or you might think it was a dream. It's hard to explain."

She gave him a long, measuring look. "Icky, what is it?"

Like Zach, she remembered nothing. Ian began to lose his high feeling; he couldn't help it. On the Preservation it had been relatively easy to 'wake up' an android. But here in the real world how would he ever convince real people that the world was going to end in a year and he, the ultimate loser, was humanity's only chance? He couldn't begin to say it. Vanessa would think he was crazy. "It's nothing. Never mind."

"Okay, Icky. By the way, I found something you might want to see."

"What?"

"Let me show you."

She rummaged in her handbag and took out a little green book with a tied binding. It looked old. She handed it to Ian. On the front was the word JOURNAL.

"What's this?"

"Mom's diary, from when she was a teenager."

"You're kidding. Where'd you get it?"

"That box of personal stuff Dad left. I've had it in a storage locker for years. I never wanted to look at it. To be honest, I didn't want to be reminded of the past. My life is good now, Icky. Good enough, anyway. But when you called I thought about the box and decided to go through it, so we could divide it up or whatever you wanted to do. There were a lot of pictures, birth certificates, that kind of stuff. The diary was in the bottom of the box."

Ian opened the little green book. The paper had a faint, musty smell. He read the first page. It was written in blue ink, an eccentric flowing script, cursive mixed with slanted block printing. Exactly the way Ian wrote longhand. The date at the top of the page was June 2, 1965. His mother had written, exuberantly: *Last day of school, yah!*

Ian looked up from the page. Vanessa was grinning. "Isn't it wonderful?"

"It's like a different person wrote it."

"Not a different person, Icky. The same person, but one we never knew. Although I think I saw her a little bit when I was a kid. When things were more all right. Before she started to slip away?"

"I guess I just got the slipping away part."

Ian turned a few pages over. The girl his mother had been was so alive and *excited* about everything. Not the withdrawn, brooding mother he knew, the woman who cried for no reason, who cut herself, who cared too much then didn't care at all, about anything. The woman who swallowed a whole lot of pills, then took a bath.

Vanessa touched his arm. "Why don't you come out to my place this weekend and we'll go through the box together?"

Instinctively, he wanted to pull his arm away from her touch. He fought the instinct. Waking up here was like waking up in a room he'd carefully arranged and was loath by habit and fear to change. Part of the arrangement consisted of booby-traps designed to keep him safe and alone. He turned a page over in his mother's diary. Some boy kissed her at the movies.

What did it even mean, that his mother could have been the girl in this diary? Was anybody one complete person through their life?

"Icky, what about coming over Saturday? There's a great Thai place right around the–

"I'll see what's happening and give you a call."

"Please come, Icky."

"I will. I'm just saying I'll give you a call first is all. I don't really leave the city that much."

"I live in *Wallingford*. That's not leaving the city."

North of the suicide bridge, Ian thought. "I'll call," he said.

"All right, Icky. You keep the diary, okay? I've already looked through it."

"Thanks."

His phone rang.

"But I'll be disappointed, if you don't come," Vanessa said. "I mean it."

"I have to get this." He opened his phone. It was Juan, a guy he worked with at Charlie's.

"Ian, man, are you coming in or what?"

"I don't know. I have the day off, I thought."

"Since when?"

Since a year from now, when I bump shifts so I can ride the Chief to Pullman and see my girlfriend. Oh yeah, the girlfriend who isn't even my girlfriend anymore.

"Since never, I guess. Sorry, man. I'm on my way."

SURREAL. FRYING UP orders, scraping bubbling grease off the hot top, the usual riot of clanging pans and dishes, the stifling heat. Ian re-enacted the moves he'd made hundreds of times before: building sandwiches, omelets, frying meat and onions. His body could have performed this function by itself. In fact, it was, as he checked out mentally, watching his hands doing their tasks. This wasn't the out-of-body weirdness he'd experienced repeatedly on the Preservation but rather a return to his usual estrangement. The faces of waitresses appeared at the order window like a series of animated masks. Juan sweated, joked, rocked and swayed, his hands flying over the hot-top, like some fantastic wind-up thing. For Ian, the real world wasn't that different from the world of android fakes; he could almost x-ray-vision see the biological mechanics of meat and bone through Juan's skin.

One year until the end of the world.

Ian put his spatula down. "Gotta take a break."

"You can't take no break now, Cholo!"

The order wheel sprouted new slips as fast as they plucked the old ones off. "Got to. Sorry."

Ian walked out of the kitchen. On the loading dock he removed his apron and stared at the sky. It was a typical October gray. He had this idea he was going to throw the apron in the dumpster and go do something important, because the world was soon ending and he was the only one who knew it. Of course, he didn't know *what* important thing he was going to do, but it had to be more important than frying another Monte Cristo sandwich.

Behind him, the door squeaked open on its rusty spring hinge and Carla, the head waitress, said, "Juan says if you're out here to please come back because otherwise he's gonna have a stroke."

Ian's mind grasped at future disaster, but for a year he would still have to pay the rent and eat. "Yeah, okay."

He slowly put his apron back on.

*   *   *

SIX HOURS LATER he was back at the apartment, standing in a hot shower. He planted his hands on the wall and let scalding hot water pound the back of his neck. The sharp reality of the Preservation had softened and dimmed and now dwelt in his mind like an ordinarily vivid dream. By tomorrow what would it be? Gone, like any other dream? A few drifty pieces?

He cranked the shower off.

Standing in front of the sink with his toothbrush, he wiped a film of steam off the mirror – and the heel of his hand came away green.

know WHO you are

HE STRETCHED OUT on the bed and cracked his mother's diary. Most entries were short, less than a page, sometimes only a line or two. He read the entire diary, looking for any reference to depression, any hint of seriously bad mental states – looking for the dark turn in the road. But it wasn't there. The closest it came was stuff like: *Sad. Margaret's brother has cancer. I made her a card, but I can't do anything to cheer her up. I wish I could. Now I need somebody to cheer me up, too.*

How was this the same person he knew as 'mother'?

Know who you are. Did he? Would a night's sleep dull the picture of himself he now held in his mind? Would the Preservation and all that happened there be 'just a dream' like in some bullshit story? Because he did know himself, Ian could see the future, all right. This morning, realizing Kylie was out there, alive, he had

349

been filled with excitement and something like joy. Of course, she wouldn't know him. She would be just like Ness and Zach. There was no real point in approaching her. So he would, what, just pick up his life where he left it last night when he fell asleep? And Kylie could be the ultimate 'safe' girl for him – conveniently distant. The ultimate safe girl, since in this timeframe he hadn't even met her, had never shared even one intimate hour with her. In 2011, Kylie was no more to him than a longing dream. Had at least some of that first joy been based on the perfectly balanced estrangement of the situation? Kylie would never dump him, never require a mutual declaration of love – would never require *anything*, since she didn't even know he existed.

And it could get worse.

By tomorrow, he would begin to doubt she even existed beyond the idea he held of her inside his own head. Things were already becoming slippery. Was Kylie just a girl he had a dream about and thought the dream was real? He could sleep-walk through the next year. And this time when the Hunters burned down the world and the Preservation sprang up, Ian might not return to haunt his android. It was his *suicide* that made him reach back to life. This time there would be no Sarah-situation. Knowing it was coming, he would make sure it never occurred.

So in the end, there would be no one to wake up the androids. Christ, there might not even be a Preservation. According to the Curator, Ian himself had 'Lensed' it into existence.

He needed to remember what was going on. He needed to stay *on top* of it. Otherwise, slippage. And when the world ended, so would he. There would be no Preservation, no android people to wake up, and nobody to wake them up if there were.

The end.

HE NEVER KNEW Kylie's last name. But Google 'Kylie Oakdale Facebook', and you get a headshot of an achingly familiar face – not a mask but a memory toggle activating a flood of emotion. Maybe one of the memory toggle's favorite things turns out to be Friday night movies at the little town's Olympic Regal Cinema.

TWO MINUTES TO midnight. Zero hour. He straddled the idling Chief in the breakdown lane about fifty yards south of the Aurora Bridge deck. His heart was beating like something desperately afraid, hiding within the cavity of his chest with its eyes closed. The Chief's engine sounded like a blender full of gravel. Cars blasted by him at forty miles an hour, red taillights fleeing down the highway like lost-soul eyes down a well. Ian babied the throttle, keeping the Indian alive.

Now at the moment of action, he asked himself: *What if I'm still on the Preservation?*

Really. It could be a trick. What made *him* such an expert? Maybe all the Curator had to do was perform a couple of adjustments and the Advents got longer. Maybe an Advent could last a whole year. Ian would never know it. He would just ride into the bubble, thinking he was on his way to Oakdale and Kylie. Instead, he would be stuck, and re-gen with a blank mind. The trick added up. His fearful estrangement from the supposedly 'normal' people around him, even his own sister – was it the old feeling he always experienced, or was it an accurate perception of a non-human world that he had been fooled into believing was gone – another Preservation mind-fuck? The Curator had rejected Ian's android sister and friend (forget what he said about *Ian* doing the rejecting). But Ian was different. To get rid of *him* the Curator had to trick Ian into rejecting *himself*.

So don't fall for it; go home.

Barricade yourself in the apartment and paint juju pictures and magic words all over the walls to keep the big bad fake world out.

Ian considered it, seriously. He crept the bike forward, rolling along the breakdown lane to a side street that dropped off the highway just ahead of the bridge. If he crossed the margin, *if* he made it all the way to Oakdale on his father's piece-of-shit Indian, *if* he found Kylie – *if* all those ifs happened, it would prove the world was a real place. Because Kylie was not a regenerating android fake; she was the only real person he'd ever known. The only person he'd allowed to be that way.

He checked the clock on his phone. Midnight was happening.

He waited for a break in the traffic then cranked the throttle and roared onto the bridge and through his fear.

CHAPTER TWENTY-NINE

THE OLYMPIC REGAL never met a first run movie. Two years after the rest of the world sold out every show, *Star Trek* meandered into Oakdale. Kylie scrunched down in the back row with a sixteen ounce Pepsi and a small popcorn. She sipped on the Pepsi once in a while but didn't have an appetite for the popcorn. Slouched so low in her seat, she enjoyed a better view of the silhouetted heads occupying the row in front of her than she did of the movie. Which was fine. She came here to turn her brain off for a couple of hours; the movie was irrelevant.

She liked the guy playing Captain Kirk, though.

He was supposed to be some kind of bad boy in the first part of the movie, and Kylie liked bad boys. She liked them but she didn't believe in them, not in real life. She *used* to believe a bad boy would rescue her from the smothering tedium of Oakdale. But the real life bad boys she had screwed around with were nothing like James Kirk, let alone James Dean. Mostly they were pathetic jerk offs – with one or two minor exceptions.

Now she had herself a bad *man*. And that was a whole other thing. Last Saturday, at three thousand feet over Dyes Inlet, bouncing along in Father Jim's little red and white Cessna, the father figure in her life had pushed his big knuckly old man hand between her legs and left it there. Fortunately she was wearing jeans. Neither she nor Jim mentioned the hand. He kneaded her thigh, caressed her in a rough, proprietary fashion. Scared, Kylie wanted to lock her thighs together, but she couldn't do that and work the Cessna's rudder pedals. Jim went right on conducting the weekly flying lesson, his voice instructing her through the headset.

"Make a shallow left turn then level out and head for that peninsula, where you see the blue water tower."

Kylie started the turn. The nose dipped and the airspeed came up. She was flustered, shaking.

Sternly, Father Jim said, "Ease the yoke back. Make a level turn. Eyes on the *ball*, Kylie."

The 'ball' was a little black ball that kind of floated in and out of a box on an instrument. As long as you kept the black ball perfectly centered in the box the plane remained in a clean level turn. It wasn't *hard* to do – except maybe when the flight instructor had his hand jammed between your legs.

He never moved his hand further up her thigh, never touched her *there*. Never said anything about it. Never changed the script. They were having their flying lesson. Situation normal. Kylie had known Father Jim since she was six years old. She trusted him. He had filled a big gap in her life. A big gap left by her real father.

Jim was strong, understanding, helpful. Like the best uncle. Everything he did seemed to be important, non-frivolous. She trusted him. If he told her to do something it must be the right thing to do.

When he left his hand between her legs and didn't speak of it or try to otherwise fondle her, there must have been *something* right about it. Thinking about it later, she actually wondered if it was really some part of the flying lesson. Like he was using his hand to steady her leg? Her mind so much wanted it to be that way that it presented her with false but supportive details and self-doubts. How bad a person *was Kylie* that she could think for one second Father Jim would touch her sexually? What kind of dirty mind did she have, anyway?

That was a week ago.

Tomorrow, Saturday, was another flying lesson. And slouching in the back of the Olympic Regal, Kylie asked herself: would she be there? She was on the verge of the most important decision of her life, and there were no bad boys to rescue her from it.

AFTER THE MOVIE, she dumped her popcorn and Pepsi in one of the big red trash cans in the lobby. The concession lights were already off, the popcorn machine emptied and clean, and a nine-year-old girl was pushing a little carpet sweeper around the blue rug even as a hundred or so people strolled through on their way out. The Olympic was a one man operation. One man and one daughter. Sandy helped her father every Friday and Saturday night. Sandy's mother was dead, and Ralph DeVris seemed brittle these days. Sandy was a *good* daughter, but Kylie sometimes wondered how many more Fridays and Saturdays she would be willing to surrender, as she got older, became a teenager. At least Sandy *had* a father. Most of the town pitied her and Ralph, but Kylie felt envy.

Kylie ducked into the bathroom, and when she came out she was the last person in the theater besides Sandy and Ralph.

"Goodnight, Kylie," he said. After his wife died he had lost a ton of weight, but in the last year he had resumed packing it on. His belly sagged over the waist of his khakis like dough sagging over the edge of a pie pan.

"Goodnight," she said, and pushed through the glass door and stepped out onto the sidewalk. A few people lingered, talking about the movie. She knew a couple of the girls, Sandra and Tiffany.

"Hey!" Sandra said. "We didn't even know you were *in* there."

"I was kind of in the back."

Sandra was tall, with a body that boys loved to sniff around but a horsy face that kept real relationships at bay – at least in the inbred little jerkwater town of Oakdale. Tiffany was her opposite number, a movie star face on a squat little hobbit body. Kylie liked them both because they were smart and unaffected and social outsiders. But at the moment, she wanted to be alone.

Across the street, sitting on the coolest motorcycle Kylie had ever seen, a boy was watching them. He wore a leather jacket over a black hoodie. His silver half-helmet dangled by the chin strap from the handlebar. He had long black hair, which normally was a turn-off for Kylie. But not this time.

Sandra said, "Do you know that guy?"

"No."

"He's looking right at you," Tiffany said.

"He's looking at all of us."

"No he isn't."

"Whatever."

"Come on with us to the diner," Sandra said.

"That guy is really *looking* at you," Tiffany said.

"I think you're right," Kylie said. "Hey," she called across the street. "What do you think you're staring at?"

"*Don't,*" Tiffany said. "Geeze."

He didn't appear dangerous. Did and didn't. He wasn't serial killer dangerous, but there was definitely an edge, something *up* with him. He smiled, which even from across the street looked forced and unnatural, then dismounted the bike and walked over, hands stuffed in his tight jeans, like a self-conscious way to show he was safe or something.

"Oh, God," Sandra said. "Here he comes."

Kylie wasn't afraid, but she was also aware that Mr. DeVris was in the lobby right behind her and there were still plenty of people strolling around the streets. It wasn't like Oakdale was New York City, where some crazy guy could probably cut her up like a side of beef in the middle of Times Square without anybody bothering him.

When he got closer he didn't look quite so young. He wasn't *old*, but he wasn't a schoolboy, either. The first words out of his mouth were so unexpected that she laughed.

"Is your name Kylie?" His second words were, "What's funny?"

"Nothing. How'd you know my name?"

"I guessed?"

"I don't think so."

Tiffany and Sandra gaped at them.

"You're right. I didn't guess. We sort of know each other, but it's in a weird way."

"Do tell," Kylie said, because she thought it made her sound sophisticated.

"Yeah, do tell," Tiffany said.

Kylie shot her a look. "Weren't you guys going to the diner?"

"Yeah, *with you.*" Sandra made big are-you-crazy eyes at her.

Kylie ignored her. She felt totally reckless. The movie hadn't taken her mind off tomorrow's flying lesson. The whole week had only intensified her anxiety; and she was farther than ever from making a decision But now, for the first time, talking to this stranger, she felt *clear*. And she wasn't going to let that clear feeling go, not yet.

"So what's your name, since you already know mine?"

"Ian."

Behind him, Tiffany mouthed the word *fake*.

"And what's this weird way we supposedly know each other?"

He glanced back at Tiffany and Sandra. "Uh, can we walk? I mean just around here. I'll try to explain it."

"I guess so."

Sandra wagged her hands. "Kylie–"

"I'll meet you guys at the diner in a few minutes. Okay?"

"You better," Tiffany said.

THEY WALKED. IAN kept his hands in his pockets. All the way from Seattle he had pictured this moment and tried to imagine what he would say that wouldn't make him sound like a lunatic. Last night he rented a room at the Motel 6 a few miles down the highway. He hadn't been able to sleep, and no matter how hard he tried to think of the right words there simply weren't any to cover this situation. He had finally given up, hoping vaguely that if he found Kylie she would somehow recognize him, even though he hadn't known her as an android, and only androids had the dream connection to their originals in 2011."Look," he finally said, "what if we were the only real people in the world?"

"That's dumb. We're not."

"But what if we were?"

"Are you going to tell me how you knew my name or not?"

He took a deep breath and sighed, "We used to know each other in the future."

Kylie laughed. "That's original."

"It's true."

"You're a time traveler from the future, is that it? Come on, we're walking back this way now."

They had reached the end of the street, the edge of Oakdale's business district. Kylie turned back the way they had come – back to all the lights and people. Was she afraid of him? Ian stood with his hands in his pockets, feeling frustrated and a little hopeless.

Kylie waved him forward. "Well, come on, future-man."

He shook his head. "What I said? It's true. But not exactly the way it sounds like."

"You didn't say *anything* except we knew each other in the future. That's *obviously* not true."

He walked with her again, back towards the Regal. "It doesn't matter," he said. "But look, all I'm saying is you should think seriously about moving to Seattle before next October fifth."

"Why?"

"If I told you, you'd laugh at me again."

"I wasn't laughing at you. I was laughing at something you *said*. There's a difference."

"Yeah, whatever. Look, I want to give you something." From his back pocket he withdrew a folded piece of paper. Last night in the motel room he had carefully printed his name, phone number and address on the paper. He handed it to Kylie and she unfolded it, frowned, looked puzzled, almost irritated.

"Why are you giving me this? Who are you? Just tell me."

He ached to tell her. But the more detail he presented her with the less she would believe him. Kylie was real – which meant this world was real – but she didn't know him and he couldn't explain anything to her. She wouldn't accept his story, not a word of it, no matter how sincere he was. He had known this yesterday, had known it when he sat across the street on his bike, waiting for her to come out of the theater. And he knew it more than ever right at this painful moment. Emotion tightened his throat, choking off his next words. He swallowed hard. This was the thing he always feared, wasn't it? You let someone in, you *love* someone, and they leave you. It was so freaking simple and the pain was so easy to avoid: Don't love. It wasn't Kylie's fault. She didn't even know she had left him, since she had never met him in the first place.

He fought off the emotion that was closing his throat and said, "You look beautiful. Your hair is really nice."

"My hair is nice?"

"Yeah. The thing about your hair is when I knew you in a couple of years it was like the haircut from hell. You were always complaining about it."

She laughed again. "Are you for real?"

"I don't *know*." Ian looked across the street to his motorcycle. He imagined himself riding back down the 101, tunneling the dark with his dim yellow headlamp and the wind cold in his face. He wanted to be doing that. On the other hand, it was the loneliest thing he could imagine.

"So in the future you're like some kind of barber?"

"What?"

"It's a joke."

"Oh, yeah. That's funny."

"No, it wasn't."

"I know."

They both laughed, Ian wondering if he was laughing because she was laughing or if he really felt it. He leaned toward real. Kylie always did that for him.

HE WASN'T DANGEROUS, she felt positive about that. Of course, that's probably what all victims thought right before the serial killer lured them into their vans and cut their heads off. One thing Kylie noticed, she hadn't thought about the flying lesson since she first saw Ian sitting on his bike across the street. He was such a weird combination of goofy innocence and intensity. She liked him, instinctively. There was *chemistry*.

"What kind of motorcycle is that?"

"It's an Indian, a Chief."

"Seriously? I never heard of that."

They're pretty old. Kind of the classic American bike. This one was built in 1947."

"Wow. I mean, sincerely. But I thought Harleys were the classic American bike."

"Indians came before Harleys. My dad refurbed this one. It's not all the original bike, exactly. Most of it is, but he bought it as a basket case."

They wandered over to the Indian. The chrome was dull, pitted with rust. Oil streaked around the engine seals. The leather seat was dried out and cracked. But the bike was still beautiful.

"What's that mean, 'basket case'?"

"It means my dad bought the Indian basically as a frame and a box of parts then built it from the ground up. He had to improvise a lot."

"At least it's not a mini-van."

"Uh, yeah. It's not a mini-van."

"Did you help your dad?"

"I watched and fetched the beer."

"One of those father and son things, huh?"

"No, not a chance. My dad, it didn't matter if I was there or not. He was checked out, after my mom died."

"My dad checked out for real, when I was six."

"Yeah, I know. You told me about it next year."

He said it so matter-of-factly she almost believed him. "Ian, where do you come from, I mean do you live anywhere around here? I know you aren't from Oakdale. Do you have, like, a relative or somebody in town?

"No, I came to see you, just like I said. I live in Seattle."

"But *why* me?"

He tapped his lower lip with two fingers and looked shyly past her. "I wanted to know if you were real. I *had* to know."

"Okay, that's a little scary." Her phone blooped and she glanced at it. A text from her mother, followed by another bloop and a text from Tiffany. Reluctantly, she said, "I think I have to go."

"Look, will you have lunch with me tomorrow?"

"I don't know—"

"Come on. You want to know how we meet in the future, don't you?"

He stared right into her eyes with sudden, focused intensity. She felt the same way she had the first time Father Jim took her up; a sense of magic possibility and fear. "The Lucky Diner is two blocks that way," she said. "Lunch tomorrow."

"What time?"

"Like one o'clock? There's a guy, he's giving me free flying lessons. So I got that going on first."

"Right, that ex-marine pilot."

Her mouth opened. She shut it then opened it again and said, "How did—"

"I'm future man, remember?"

It took him three attempts to start the bike, and when the engine finally kicked in it sounded like the mother of all broken lawn mowers. He put his silver half-helmet on, not bothering with the chin strap, and roared off down Main Street, rattling windows. his long hair blowing around. At the end of the street he raised his left hand in a backward wave, then leaned into the turn and was gone to the highway.

CHAPTER THIRTY

IAN LAY ON the Motel Six bed, fully clothed except for his shoes, watching the ancient tube television. A ghost scent of cigarette smoke clung to the room.

On TV Bruce Willis was *kicking ass*, because he was such a tough bastard. It wasn't so bad, with the sound turned off. Besides, the guy renting the room behind Ian's head was watching the same movie with the sound turned way up. All the explosions came through the wall but the dialogue was muffled and wooden. Pretty much the perfect way to watch a Bruce Willis movie.

Lunch tomorrow with Kylie. He had decided to lay it all out for her – the whole truth, as he remembered it, and no matter how whacked it sounded. Other options included somehow convincing her or tricking her into moving to Seattle before the Hunter event. But like most lame ideas this one sank like a brick. He couldn't trick Kylie, or anyone else, into moving to Seattle.

He was stuck with the truth.

One thing he would leave out, was the idea that after the Preservation started neither he nor Kylie would be real human beings anymore. There was no point in freaking her out any more than he had to at this stage. But eventually he would tell her, after he had already made her real.

Fingers laced behind his head, Ian looked past the television, past the cheap motel room – past everything, to the future. In this vision, Kylie *did* move to Seattle. In fact, she moved in with Ian. They would be the only ones who knew the truth after the Hunter attack. And knowing the truth would set them free. In time, Ian would *own* the Preservation, just as the Curator had said. He would make new people out of the android fakes. He would set them free by telling them what they were and what they could be. And he would fortify the Dome against the Hunters, just as he had fortified his apartment with the Goya walls – that part was sketchy, but he would figure it out. He and everyone on the Preservation would be a new race of immortals, and eventually they would emerge from the Dome and reclaim the planet.

Ian chuckled. What total bullshit, like one of Zach's game scenarios. But Ian liked to think about it, play with the idea. Maybe because it kept his mind off lunch tomorrow and the foregone failure of convincing Kylie of anything.

He was starting to drift off when something startled him wide awake.

Flying lessons.

His life on the Preservation dimmed in and out like an electric dream. Sometimes fear provided extra power. And just as he was sliding toward a more usual dreamland, a piece of the Preservation life lit up bright and hot.

Kylie flew in with this priest who used to be a Marine Corps pilot. And the priest was crazy. He had wanted to *cut* her.

KYLIE PEDALED HER bike to the grass airstrip a half-mile northeast of Oakdale on the old Fairview Road. Many times she had come this way, her heart bursting with anticipation.

This time it was like pedaling toward a bad dream, like driving her wheels through mud or wet cement.

All week she had been carried toward this morning on a river of helpless inevitability. Jim's hand between her legs was only the first gesture toward something she had been prepared to accept since she was a little kid. Something *Father Jim* had prepared her to accept. Only now, she didn't think she *would* accept it. Before last night, talking to Ian, she had been willfully blind. Why talking to future-guy should make any difference, she had no idea. Except he wasn't from her tight-ass little world of Oakdale and he wasn't the usual bad boy. And when she was near him, no matter what the bullshit factor or how sketchy her friends thought him, she felt *good* – like, here was someone she could be alive with, and no work required.

A white arrow sign with the word AIRPORT pointed down a dirt road. Kylie seriously considered skipping it, making a wide turn and pedaling back to town. Instinct compelled her to do just that. But years of obeying a counter-instinct to make Father Jim happy, to be a good girl for him, to court his approval no matter what, directed her to turn onto the road.

In summertime the airport road was pleasant with sun and shade and sweet, growing smells – like traveling down a secret tunnel, her rubber wheels bouncing in the deep ruts left by cars and pickups. This October morning the tunnel was cold and oppressive with damp shadows, and again her instinct to retreat rose up, and again she did not obey it.

She jolted into the clear. The airport consisted of a three-thousand-foot grass strip, a battered hangar that looked like a rusty overturned galvanized tub with a pair of faded red wings painted on its face, and an above-ground fuel tank. A dozen or so small planes, most of them Cessnas like Father Jim's, were tied down at one end of the strip. The windsock, old and tattered and paled from its original bright orange to a light shade of pink, stirred in the breeze.

Father Jim's burgundy Crown Vic was parked next to the hangar. It was the only car present. Jim was sitting behind the wheel, barely visible through the smoked glass windshield. The church music he liked so much, the Gregorian chants, were cranked loud – Jim working himself up to something.

She coasted to a stop and stood in front of the car, straddling the bike frame. The chanting cut off. The driver's door opened and Father Jim unfolded out of the Crown Vic, floppy-brimmed black hat first.

"How's my little co-pilot," he said.

And just like that, she knew it was over. She would never again tuck herself into the jaunty red and white Cessna with Father Jim. In fact, after today she doubted she would ever be alone with him anywhere.

"I'm okay," she said. "Only I think I'm going to skip the lesson today."

His expression, his usual stony neutrality, didn't change. His expression almost *never* changed, whether he was delivering a sermon or feeling up a teenage girl – as though his face were a mask that concealed his true thoughts and feelings.

He stepped forward, though, and gripped the handlebar of her bike in his big, knuckly fist.

"Why, what's wrong, Kylie?"

"I don't know. I guess I don't feel good."

"Felt good enough to ride all the way out here, but not good enough to fly?"

"Yeah, I guess not."

Jim nodded, his expression stone-neutral. He held the bike rigidly immobile, as if his hand were welded to it. "You can tell me what's wrong, child."

"There's nothing wrong. I just don't feel like it today."

He nodded again.

"Anyway, I guess I better go back home."

"I think we're getting a little off track," Jim said.

"Off track?"

Jim tilted his head back, evaluating the sky. There was a moist little razor nick on the underside of his jaw. "That's a low deck. It's going to rain, anyway. So you're right, it's a bad day to fly."

"It's not the–"

"But that doesn't mean we can't talk, does it?"

"Talk about what?"

"About what we're doing here."

"We're not doing anything."

He lowered his head and stared straight into her eyes, which she could only tolerate a few seconds before looking away. That stare made her feel like she was six years old again.

The rain started, a few cold drops landing on Kylie's neck.

"Come with me," Jim said. "We'll get out of the weather."

"I think I can beat it home."

"You're being foolish. Come with me, now."

She climbed off the bike, which she could not have moved anyway. He let it go and took her hand in one movement. The bike fell over. He started walking with her, pulling her along. She thought they were going to the car, but instead he veered toward the hangar. That's when the alarm bells starting going off in her head. She walked with him but pulled back on her hand at the same time. Jim merely bore down harder, and she stopped resisting. It wasn't exactly a struggle – not yet; but she didn't want to go in that hangar.

Dr. Lee's Beechcraft Bonanza with its distinctive V-shaped tail that served both as vertical and horizontal stabilizers was the only aircraft under cover. Jim referred to the Beech as "the Cadillac of private aviation," like there was an ad from Flying Magazine in his mouth. After the first couple of flying lessons, Jim had shown her the Beech, helping her up on the wing so she could get a good look in the cockpit. Jim's Cessna 150 was like an old beater Volkswagen by comparison. The instrument panel looked like something on the flight deck of a 747 and the seats were milk chocolate leather. This was a good memory, Jim pointing and explaining things to her, his other hand steady on her shoulder, protective. Kylie had loved looking at that airplane, but now the good memory was getting spoiled.

The rain started in earnest, bursting down on them as if someone had fired buckshot into a vinyl cloud and released a torrent.

Jim yanked her into the hangar, before they got soaked. Rain rattled on the metal roof. It was dim inside the hangar. Besides Dr. Lee's Beechcraft, the floor was clear, just an air hose on a basket wheel, a couple of padlocked storage cabinets and a Sears Craftsman tool chest, a big one with ten drawers and a flat work surface. The Craftsman was chained and padlocked to an iron support rib, part of the hangar's back wall. There was also a square glass-enclosed office.

Jim removed his hat and shook the rain from the floppy brim. His gray comb-over was messed up, his white scalp showing through the long, thinning strands.

"Well, we got ourselves out of that just in time, didn't we?" He smiled, but there was something mechanical about it – as if Father Jim were thinking, *Okay, it's time to smile now, show some friendly teeth.*

He still hadn't let go of her hand.

"Yeah," she said. "Maybe you could drive me home? I mean, we could put my bike in the trunk, or even leave it here, that's okay, too."

"After a while, we will do that."

He started walking toward the glass office. He produced a key and unlocked the door. Inside was a small metal desk, a file cabinet, an office chair, and a cot. The cot was made up with fresh-looking sheets and a wool blanket. There were two pillows, although the cot was narrow, meant for one person.

It didn't feel like Jim was holding her hand very tight anymore. Kylie pulled on it more aggressively than she had outside, but it wouldn't come loose. Jim did not bear down harder, or say anything. He simply walked her into the office, swung the door shut with his foot, and drew her down beside him on the cot.

"Sometimes," he said, after a silence that lasted more than a minute, "God puts two people in the way of each other." Father Jim set his hat on the desk. The office was so small he could do this without rising from the cot.

Kylie lowered her head. He released her hand and rested his hand firmly on her thigh. He began to caress her in a bluntly mechanical fashion. Kylie closed her eyes. A strange thing was happening in her mind. She seemed to be floating apart from herself, disassociated from her own presence. She wanted him to stop touching her. The word 'stop' occurred to her floating-apart-self but couldn't quite make the transition to the mouth of the girl sitting on the cot next to Jim.

Outside the hangar, a revving engine ripped through the drumming rain. Jim's hand stopped moving but remained on her thigh. The engine noise racketed up like something running hot and broken then dropped suddenly and quit.

Jim stood and went out of the office, pausing in the doorway to say, "Stay here."

Kylie said, "Okay." She could utter the word because suddenly she wasn't apart from herself anymore. As soon as Jim left the hangar she stood up and followed him out.

Ian Palmer was sitting on his antique motorcycle in the thundering rain. He had his helmet off and his sweatshirt hood up, which was doing him absolutely no good. The rain pounded down hard and loud.

Kylie ran past Father Jim. She yelled to Ian: "Give me a ride back to town?"

He nodded, adjusted something on the engine, stood on the kick-starter and came down hard. The bike failed to start. He tried again, and Father Jim grabbed her arm.

"Don't be foolish," he said. "I'll drive you."

The motorcycle kicked in, racketing up louder than the rain. Kylie jerked her arm free. Jim wasn't holding on very tight this time. Ian scooted forward on the bike, and she straddled the seat behind him. In moments they were jolting down the rutted airport road. She looked back once. Father Jim was picking up her abandoned bicycle.

The Lucky Diner was crowded, but after a twenty minute wait they managed to score a booth. Kylie took the time to go into the bathroom and clean up, or at least try to. Her jeans were muddy and soaked, her hair plastered to her head. She looked like something dragged out of a wet hole in the ground. She dried her head with paper towels and tried to do something with her hair. It was hopeless. The weird thing was, the girl in the mirror wasn't the same girl who had been sitting in the hangar office with Father Jim.

At the table, she looked straight into Ian's blue eyes and asked, "Why did you come to the airport? Why didn't you just meet me here, like we said?"

"I knew something was going to happen that you probably didn't want to happen, so I decided to ride out there."

"*How* did you know?"

"I remembered it last night at the motel."

"You—"

"I'm Future Man, remember? You told me about it next year. Only, some of what happens is vague, like pieces of a dream? But all of a sudden I remembered about that priest." He shrugged.

The waitress set brimming coffee cups before them. Kylie sat back, thinking. "Okay," she said, finally, "tell me everything."

Ian dumped some of his coffee onto the saucer and added a gallon or so of creamer. He picked the thick white mug up with both hands and slurped at it, put the mug down, tapped his lip with two fingers, thinking, then said, "In about a year, on October fifth, aliens are going to destroy the world."

Kylie laughed, then stopped. "Shut up. That's ridiculous."

"Yeah, and it's not even the weirdest part."

HE TOLD HER everything – even the part about becoming an android – and she didn't believe him. Of *course* she didn't. But by saying it out loud, *he* believed it even more. The future memories cohered, became clear, sharper than dreams. He felt sure of himself, committed to the truth of what would happen.

But Kylie didn't believe him.

"Listen," he said, leaning forward. "Promise me you will be in Seattle on October fifth next year."

"I can't promise that."

"If you aren't there you won't become an android. That's the only sure way of surviving, even if it isn't you surviving. I mean, it is and it isn't. Anyway, nothing says things will happen the same way this time. I think I changed that by showing up and taking you away from that guy at the airport. You can't count on flying a jet into the Dome."

He was talking too fast, too earnestly. Kylie's face began to close him off. He stopped abruptly, slouched back in his chair. "I know," he said, "I sound like an idiot."

"No. But I... Ian, it's impossible."

He nodded, not looking at her. "It sounds that way, yeah."

"Don't be mad at me, geeze."

"I'm not mad."

"If I told *you* that story you wouldn't believe me, either. I mean, if you didn't already believe it and everything."

"Right."

"Ian? I really like you."

He looked up, smiled. "I like you, too. What if we went out, would you do that?"

"Like dating, you mean?"

"Yeah."

"Maybe. But you don't even live here."

"It's not that far. I'll come back next weekend. We can even go to the movies, if you want. Something normal." *And I better borrow some money from Zach and get the Chief up to speed.*

She thought about it, sipping her coffee. "Okay. But not the movies. Meet me right here, at the diner."

"I usually work Saturday nights, so how about like a late breakfast thing?"

"That works."

The waitress brought the bill. Ian picked it up and reached for his wallet. He drove Kylie home in the rain, following her shouted directions. She pointed at a yellow split-level tract house, and he rolled into the driveway. The engine racket brought Kylie's mother to the window. Kylie waved at her, swung off the bike, stood awkwardly a moment, then offered Ian her hand. He shook it, wanting to take all of her, wanting it to be like it had been on the Preservation, the two of them almost like one person in the bed.

"What are you going to do now?" Kylie asked.

"Go home and get ready."

"For what, our date next week?" She laughed.

He laughed, too, though it felt a little forced. "No, the end of the world. It's only a year away."

CHAPTER THIRTY-ONE

AT HIS DESK in Seattle, Ian hunched over a two-foot-long sheet of poster board, working on it with an X-Acto blade. In pencil he had carefully lettered the words: 'know WHO you are'. He drew the razor-sharp tip of the blade along the pencil lines, cutting out the letters. When it was done, he held the poster board up to the ceiling light, looking for rough edges. It was a clean cut. He stood, grabbed a can of blue spray paint, pressed the stencil to the blank wall next to his desk, triggered the can, sweeping smoothly back and forth, lifted the stencil away, leaving the painted words just as clean and sharp as the razor cuts. Not bad. But the wrong color. He switched to red, experimenting with different shades, finally settling on something that looked like ruby neon light – an urgent, emergency red. Something that seized attention and didn't let go. Later on he'd include the web addy.

* * *

"I NEED HELP," he said to Zach. They were sitting in the Deluxe Bar & Grill on Broadway, drinking beer. Ian waited until Zach was deep into Fat Tire number two before bringing up the help thing.

"Yeah, I know, but the men in white coats get Sundays off."

"I want to set up a webpage. Something text heavy, nothing fancy. A direct address, also a Facebook page with the same text, and I want to get it on as many local list servers as possible."

"That's simple. What do you need me for?"

"It has to be that no one can trace it back to the point of origin, like if they were looking for me. It has to be secret. You can set that up, or you probably know guys who can. Do a proxy server or something. Mostly I don't want the site killed. I want to get the word out about something, and I've got a pretty aggressive idea about how to point people in the right direction. I'm talking about Seattle people, very local. You know, a couple of big ads in the local weeklies wouldn't be a bad idea, either, only I don't have any money."

Zach drank his beer, set it down, drummed his fingers on the tabletop. "Get the word out. You planning a revolution or what?"

"Man, it's an *evolution*."

"Give it to me, then we'll talk about the secret server shit."

Ian ordered two more beers then he told Zach everything. Zach listened, not interrupting, then said, "Why don't you want to tell me what it's really about?"

"I just did tell you what it's really about."

"Aliens are going to destroy Earth and then we're all going to turn into androids?"

"Kind of like that, yeah."

"And you want to be like some kind of Messiah and clue everybody in."

"I didn't say Messiah."

Zach rolled his eyes. "What's this website?"

"Like I said, it's a text block. Same thing I just told you. I'm going to stencil the city red. I'm going to be everyfuckingwhere. People will go to the site. Maybe they'll think it's a movie gimmick or video game teaser. Doesn't matter. The idea is to go local viral, get it *out* there, plant it in as many minds as I can before the Hunters attack and the Preservation starts. My sister had this idea – I mean her android did – of hypnotizing so many Seattle droids that something called, ah – called morphogenetic resonance, would happen."

"What the hell is that?"

"Well, with mice it means if you teach *some* mice something important, other mice will just sort of... know it without being taught. On the Preservation, Ness and I came up with this thing where if you could convince a certain number of androids that they weren't who they thought they were but were real anyway, that the idea would spread through the population. That's what I want. Get it into as many heads as possible before the end of the world, so the android people remember it, like it's not a totally bullshit concept, so when Ness starts morphing everybody it will have a better chance of *working*. Get it?"

"You are seriously fucked up in the head."

"Will you help?"

"You don't want it traceable because you're going to graffiti every wall in the city, that it? Because it will get locals to look at the site? Something real-world, guy seriously hanging it out there. So it must be important, at least to him."

"Yeah. I want to start something."

"I'll get back to you on the proxy server. Who's buying the beer tonight?"

"Oh, you are."

It was hardest telling Vanessa, but he wanted the idea firmly planted on the first Advent. He would need his sister to make the evolution work. He began to cultivate their neglected relationship, meeting her once in a while for lunch or drinks at The Pink Door. Eventually he accepted her invitation to dinner at her apartment, where she cooked spicy stir-fry and they killed a couple of bottles of Riesling before dragging out their father's box of family stuff. Ness cracked a third bottle. They laughed, and cried a little over the old memory-junk, the pictures, the family Bible, their mother's jewelry. When they finished sorting through it all, Ness stretched out on the sofa with a water glass half full of white wine. Ian took a deep mental breath, put his glass down and sat forward on his chair.

"I got something to tell you, and you aren't going to believe it."

She smiled. "Maybe I will, you never know."

"Yeah, well, I doubt it."

Holding the glass in the fingers of both hands, she brought the wine to her lips, sipped, lowered the glass. "It's all right, Icky. Speak, brother."

He cleared his throat. "On October fifth something really bad is going to happen."

She stopped smiling, watched him, her expression neutral.

"Ness – I swear to God this is true. The world is going to end."

"Icky, don't."

Don't *what*? he thought. Don't ruin the night by dragging her into Crazyland? Don't tell her what he was about to tell her? Just don't.

But he did.

She listened, didn't interrupt, didn't get mad. She lay on the sofa and drank her wine and listened and looked progressively sadder. When he finished, she said, "Okay, Icky," and sounded very tired.

"Okay? That's it?"

"What else do you want? I don't believe a word of it, of course. I can see you're serious. I can see you mean it. But that makes it worse."

"In a couple of months, when the Hunters attack, you'll know it's all true. Then you won't know again, because on Preservation Time the big attack won't have happened. But they–"

She threw both hands up, palms out, as if fending off an attack. "Icky, *stop*."

He stopped.

"I know all about the fucking Preservation. I *read* about it."

"Oh."

"You're the 'know WHO you are' guy, right?"

"Yeah."

"I can't believe you haven't been arrested yet. That message is everywhere. How do you even cover so much territory by yourself?"

"It's not only me. Some of my old posse is helping."

"Do *they* believe you?"

"Fuck no. But they like the anarchy aspect."

She shook her head, still looking sad.

"Vanessa, I'm not nuts."

"I know."

"But you don't believe me."

"I don't."

"That's okay. Nobody does... yet."

IT WAS KYLIE he needed. He knew he couldn't make the world real unless he had Kylie to make *him* real. He had to get her over the margin and into the bubble before there *was* a bubble.

He started out seeing her twice a month, riding the Chief two hours up to Oakdale every other Friday, taking her to lunch at the O.K. Diner. They talked about all kinds of stuff. They walked around town. Sometimes they held hands, and it was like an electric bond he could feel though his whole body. Ian never brought up the Preservation, never spoke of it unless Kylie did first. He didn't want to spook her; he was working up to bringing her back to Seattle, making sure she was over the margin on October fifth. The eve of destruction. At midnight the attack would begin. That was the point of regeneration, the reason the Preservation Day always ended at midnight. If Kylie weren't in Seattle October fifth, her android would never be created.

A couple of times, the Chief crapped out on him, stranding him on the 410. This pissed him off so bad he borrowed a thousand dollars from Zach and had a classic bike shop work on it. The owner of Ye Olde Classic Bike Barn was a Harley guy, big-gutted, with one of those beards.

"Do it right," he said, "what this mother needs is a total engine re-build. Tear it down, clean it, replace the worn parts, build it up again. Even then, I don't know. Gotta tell you, dude. You ain't loved this bike the way she needs it."

"I know. How much?"

It was substantially more than a grand. Ian went back to Zach-the-bank. The loan was not a big deal, since aliens were going to burn down the world before much longer. In the meantime he could shine Zach on – not that he felt great about doing that, even if it did serve the greater good. Harley Dude offered to "add some amenities" such as a fuel gauge and switching the throttle to the right side. But that was more money and Ian skipped it.

IN JULY, A few days past her eighteenth birthday, KYLIE came to Seattle for the first time and stayed overnight at his apartment. They had kissed, mostly in the back of the Regal Cinema, but until now that was as far as they'd gone. For her mother's benefit, Kylie made up a plausible excuse for the trip: a Green Day concert and a sleep-over with an older girlfriend (and co-conspirator), Katie, who had moved to Seattle the previous fall to attend the UW.

At first sight of Ian's apartment Kylie said, "Wow, it's really organized."

"Yeah, I picked up for you."

She laughed. "I was joking?"

"Oh. Right, yeah. Look, it's weird but I'm kind of nervous."

"That's not weird; it's sweet. I'm nervous, too."

They were standing very close, next to the bed.

"Aren't you going to kiss me?" she said.

He put his hand on her hip and leaned down to her face. Their lips touched, and he stopped thinking much at all for the next two hours.

LATER, IN BED, with the light dimming through the blinds, Kylie said, "What's that mean?"

She was pointing at his early stencil experiments, the blue and the bright red 'know WHO you are' sprayed at tilted angles on the tan wall next to his desk.

"Just something I've been messing around with." The new stencils had the web addy razored out in smaller letters, an underscore.

It was warm in the apartment and they had kicked the sheets off. Their bodies were damp with sweat and sex. Ian brushed the backs of his fingers lightly over her belly.

"Hmm. You know, I read your manifesto, or whatever you call it," she said.

"You did?"

"Katie sent me the url. It's a hot topic on campus. They think you're like some kind of crazy Zorro or something."

"Why didn't you say something? I mean after you first read it."

"I don't know." She was staring at the ceiling. "I guess it makes me uncomfortable."

"I wish it didn't."

"It does."

"Kylie, do you ever think like you might want to move here?"

"To Seattle? Or do you mean in with you?"

"Either way."

"I'll think about it."

"What about if we're in love?"

"*Are* we?"

"Yeah. I mean, aren't you?"

"Maybe."

"Oh."

"Hey, I'm not ready to *say* it, is all. It's not something I go around saying a lot."

"Me neither."

"Getting out of Oakdale is probably a good idea, though. For certain reasons."

"What reasons?"

"Father Jim."

Ian propped himself up on his elbows. "What about him?"

"He's getting creepier."

"What's he doing?"

"Okay, I haven't talked about it because I don't want it to be part of our thing. But it's like since that day at the airport, you know when you showed up and we left together? It's like since then he's really been *focused* on me. I totally avoid him. But he watches me. And when he looks at me it's like he's hungry."

"What do you mean he watches you?"

"Maybe I'm not positive, but I keep noticing him at places I go to. He's always turning up. The real creepy part is, I think he watches the house, too. I was changing clothes one time to go out, and I had this feeling. The curtains were open, which was dumb, I know. But I looked out the window, just wearing my bra and everything, and there he was right across the street under one of those oak trees. At least, I think it was him. It was dark."

"Did you tell your mom?"

"Uh-uh. She doesn't need the grief, you know?"

"Promise me something. Promise me you'll be in Seattle on October fifth."

"Okay."

"Why'd you say it so quick? Don't you mean it?"

"Sure I mean it."

They stopped talking, and after a while they made love again. And the next day Kylie took the bus back to Oakdale. It was July twenty-sixth – nine weeks from the end of the world.

"DAD–?"

"Ian! It's so late, son."

Later than you think, Pop. "I know. I wanted to ask you something."

"Go ahead."

Can you come to Seattle, be here on the fifth of October?"

"Oh, that's a bad day. Carrie and I are going to New York. We've had the tickets for months."

"Dad, it's really important."

"Well, we have these tickets and… Ian, what's it about?"

"Vanessa and I want to see you is all. We're doing a party, like for our birthdays, and we really want you there. You and Carrie, I mean. Dad, I really, really want you to come. It's important."

"But your birthday isn't until the end of the month. I could come *on* your birthday. Why are you doing it so soon?"

"We're combining, me and Ness."

"But your sister's birthday is in November. You aren't making sense, Ian. Hey, are you crying?"

"I don't know."

"Son, if it's that important I'll see what I can do."

"Great, that would be really great."

"Okay, take it easy. I'm going to be there. You said it's okay to bring Carrie?"

"Sure."

"Keep your chin up. We'll talk again before the day. Fourth of October, right?"

"Fifth."

"Yeah, okay. Got it. Wrote it down."

HE CALLED SARAH Darbro. She would be out of the city on October fifth, unless he convinced her not to be. It was a hard call. She didn't really know him this time around, since he had never made the moves necessary to establish their relationship. She was just some girl he dated briefly, and in some ways she was less real to him than a talking jellyfish. But Ian knew he had to save her, if he could.

"Sarah?"

"Yes, who is this?"

She had deleted him out of her phone.

"It's Ian. Ian Palmer?"

"Oh. Oh, hi."

And his mind went blank.

"So what are you calling about?" Sarah said, sounding ticked. After he woke from the Preservation dream he had avoided her calls, had avoided *her*. Eventually she gave up. The relationship had been in the beginning stages and maybe it wasn't so hard for her to give up. But nobody likes to be rejected.

"Listen, can you come here, can you be here in Seattle on the fifth of October? It's important."

"It's important? Gee. Well, then guess what? Drop dead."

She hung up.

Yeah, people really *hated* getting rejected.

A MONTH LATER his father called and left an awkward message, the gist of which was he and Carrie would not be arriving on the fifth of October. The New York tickets were non-refundable, etc. He sounded like he was fighting to keep the edge of irritation out of his voice, only he wasn't fighting it all that hard, like he wanted Ian to know he didn't appreciate being put on the spot.

Ian did not return the call.

CHAPTER THIRTY-TWO

IAN WOKE EARLY on October fifth. Lying alone in bed, he whispered, "Tonight." But did he believe it? After a year his future memories were a fluid composition of memory, imagination, and the dreams that haunted his sleep. He got up and made coffee, remembering the endless Advents he'd done the same thing.

Kylie was supposed to arrive at the Greyhound station at five o'clock in the afternoon.

"That's cutting it too close," Ian had said on the phone yesterday.

"It's plenty of time. You said we have till midnight."

"Sure, but why take a chance?"

"Ian, I don't like you so worked up about it."

"Well, Jesus—"

"Look, I'm going to hang up now. I'll see you soon."

*   *   *

HE WAS MEETING Zach for lunch at the Deluxe but had a few hours to kill. Churning with nervous energy, he walked. People gave him funny looks, and Ian noticed he was crying. He wiped his eyes and nose roughly and kept walking.

Then he stopped.

A red, white and blue barber pole rotated in front of a barber shop. He had been thinking about doing something to mark the first Advent. On impulse, he pushed through the door and told the guy to shave his head. He sat stiffly in the barber chair, the electric clippers nibbling up from the back of his neck. On the sidewalk people strolled by the REBRAB window. Across the street a whole cluster of 'know WHO you are' glowed neon red across the stone face of a nightclub.

"DUDE," ZACH SAID at the restaurant, "what the fuck happened to your head?"

"I got it shaved, obviously."

"Uh, looks really great. A little bumpy, but great."

"I wanted to mark the first Advent."

Zach nodded. "Yeah, right. The first Advent. You want to tell me again how that's going to work?"

"You'll see at midnight, when the Hunters burn down the city. Then you'll forget it happened when you're reborn as an android and it's always the day before the attack, I mean it's always *today*. But your *android* will remember all these conversations and 'know WHO you are' and all that, and eventually I'll wake you up."

"So you shaved your head, because getting killed by aliens and then turned into an android isn't enough to 'mark the day'."

389

"Something like that."

"Wait a minute. If the Day-That-Never-Ends is going to be today, then how do we know it hasn't already started? I mean, ended."

"It hasn't."

"But how would we *know* that?"

"*I'd remember the attack*, all right? So I'd know the Preservation had started."

"Dude, are you crying?"

"Just eat your fucking cheeseburger, okay?"

"Sure, okay."

HE WAS WAITING at the Greyhound station an hour early. Kylie hadn't answered her cell all day, and she didn't answer it now, as he paced around the bus station, punching redial so hard it was like he wanted to stab his thumb through the keypad. The number kept going to voicemail. He thumbed a couple of texts, waited. Nothing.

The security guard was watching him. Ian wiped his eyes, crying again. He retreated to the men's room and splashed cold water on his face. God, he was losing his mind. It was the stress, that's all. Not just the stress about Kylie, either. According to Charlie Noble, Ian was going to be responsible for starting the Preservation. Last time he did it accidentally, trying to take back his suicide. This time he would have to *mean* it. And if he failed it would all be gone, the whole world, and he would be, what? Some bodiless nothing?

He looked up, his hands braced on the sink. The face in the mirror belonged to a stranger. His freshly shaved scalp was almost zombie-white, his eyes red from all the stupid crying. Christ, he looked like that lunatic in *Taxi Driver*, except without the mohawk. No wonder everybody kept staring at him. He pulled his hood up and went back out to the waiting area.

The bus pulled in. A couple of dozen people stepped off, none of them Kylie. Ian began to panic.

AFTER SEVERAL FAILURES to reach her by voice or text, he dragged his salvaged Dell laptop to Vivace's, which had free wi-fi. On Facebook Kylie's icon appeared active. He sent her an instant message:

"What are you doing, why weren't you on the bus?"

After a long hesitation, during which Ian began to doubt she was there, Kylie typed:

"My ticket's for tomorrow. I guess I made a mistake on the date."

He stared at the screen in disbelief. It was almost seven o'clock.

"ARE YOU OUT OF YOUR FUCKING MIND?" he typed.

"No. And don't yell at me."

"But you have to be here today. You have to."

"I'll see you tomorrow, Ian. It's going to be okay."

"It's NOT going to be okay. Look I understand if you don't believe me about the end of the world. I get that. But don't do this, don't fuck around with this. This is our only chance."

"Calm down."

Ian pounded his fist on the table, making the sugar spoon jump. Heads turned toward him. He was out of his mind with fear and frustration.

"Anyway, there's nothing to do about it now," Kylie

typed. "No more buses tonight. I know this is hard for you, Ian. But you'll feel better tomorrow. We'll talk all about it."

"There IS no tomorrow. Stay at your house. I'm coming to get you."

He slapped the computer shut without waiting for her reply, left it on the table and bolted from the coffee shop.

IAN LEFT THE Chief idling in Kylie's driveway. It sounded sweet, a steady thrumming, no skips, farts or coughs. Thank God he'd had Ye Olde Classic Bike Barn tear the engine down. He felt confident striding to the front door of Kylie's house. There was still time to get back to Seattle before the attack. And even though they were cutting it insanely close, his anxiety level would be twice as high if he had to worry about the Chief quitting on him. He should have checked the gas, though. He really should have.

Ian pounded on Kylie's front door. Her mother answered it, then almost slammed it in his face. Ian pulled his hood over his vampire head.

"I have to see Kylie," he said.

"Who are you?"

"I'm a friend of Kylie's." There was no *time*. Kylie appeared on the stairs behind her mother. Ian waved frantically.

"Come on, I have to talk to you right now."

Kylie's mother blocked the door with her foot. "Honey, do you know this man?"

"Yeah, I know him. It's okay, Mom."

"Well, why don't I know him?"

"It's complicated, Mom."

Kylie's mother reluctantly stepped aside and Kylie slipped onto the porch, shrugging into her jacket.

"Be back in a while, Mom."

"Be *safe*."

"Mom."

"I'm just saying be safe."

The door shut and Ian said, "We should get her to Seattle. Could you talk her into driving you there tonight, right away?"

"*No*."

Kylie grabbed his hand and started walking with him away from the house. Ian tried to calm down. In his head a big clock was ticking toward midnight. Of course, if he was the guy who made the Preservation then why couldn't he make it right here in Oakdale? Because fucking *Oakdale* doesn't get nailed in the first attack. And besides, he wanted everything to be as close as it could to the way it had been first time. That meant the city and Zach and Ness, all of it. He wouldn't be killing himself this time, he wouldn't be driven back by that regret, driven to recreate the world he'd abandoned. This time he would have to *Lens* it all deliberately. *We are so fucked,* he thought.

"Kylie, your mom will be way out here when the Hunters attack," he said. "You'll never see her again."

Kylie let go of his hand, stopped walking and faced him. "God, will you *shut up* about that."

"Kylie–"

"Shut. Up."

He closed his mouth.

"Your stupid space aliens are going to wreck everything."

"I *know*, that's what–"

"Ian. They are not real. They can't be. Do you get that?"

"I get that you don't think they're real."

"They're *not* real. You know, I really like you. I might *love* you. That's big for me, Ian. But I can't accept crazy. I've had plenty of crazy in my life and I don't want any more. Even if I have to give you up, I don't want any more. You see that car that was parked right around the corner from my house. No, don't look now."

"If I don't look, how can I see it?"

"You don't have to see it That's Father Jim's car. He watches me. He's got something in his head about us that's not real. He's... Hey." She pushed Ian's hood back and her eyes got big. "What did you do?"

"It's nothing, a haircut."

"A *haircut*."

"I was nervous all day and wanted to do something for the... for the event."

"Okay, I'm going home. Don't give me that look. I'm not dumping you, but this is all I want for tonight." She started walking back.

"Wait. Please, wait."

She stopped, faced him at a safe distance, hands in her pockets.

"You're right," he said. "The aliens are impossible. I know that. Look, I've had plenty of crazy in my life, too. Shit happens around you when you're a kid, it screws with your head. But I'm *not* crazy. What it is, I think I grab onto an idea and get compulsive about it. I know I go overboard and cross the line, sometimes. I know it."

"Wait. You're saying you *don't* believe in the aliens?"

"I believe in the *event*, but it's my event. I made it. All the 'know WHO you are' shit, the website, the whole fucking city stenciled with my words, a lot of people thinking, maybe there's something going on for real. I made all that happen with my art. So, yeah, I believe, but maybe it's because I *have* to. You know?"

"You're saying it isn't going on for real?"

"What do you think?" He put on a smile and hoped it looked real. The truth is, he didn't know *what* he was saying. It even occurred to him that there might *not* be any aliens. What he just told Kylie about creating an event with his art, that sounded pretty good.

"Well, what the fuck, Ian? You just picked me out randomly for your 'event' thing?"

"No, it's more complicated than that. Can we go someplace and talk?"

"Aren't you going to die or something if you aren't back in Seattle before midnight?"

"Kylie, come on."

She gave him a long, evaluating look. "I don't believe you."

"About which?"

"I don't believe you that you changed your mind or that you never believed what you've been saying about the aliens."

"Why not? I'm a pretty good liar."

She laughed, and he joined her, hoping it sounded genuine. He wasn't sure whether it was or not. All he wanted to do was get on the fucking bike and *go*. She shook her hands fiercely, like she was trying to get something off them. "God," she said. "You drive me crazy.

"Good or bad crazy?"

"Jesus Christ. Okay, we'll talk. I guess it's a good sign. Let me tell my Mom we're going to the Lucky Diner."

*   *   *

THEY ROLLED PAST the diner on the Indian and kept going.

"You better stop this thing," she shouted into his ear.

"Don't worry," he shouted back.

At the town limit he cranked the throttle.

ROARING DOWN A desolate stretch of the 410 at seventy miles an hour and the Chief started coughing. *Oh my fucking God,* Ian thought. *What now?* The engine revved, skipped a few strokes, caught briefly, then died. Ian played with the throttle, reached down and thumbed the primer. Nothing.

Out of gas.

Ian couldn't believe it. He coasted onto the berm, braked, kicked the foot-stand down. "Fuck! I didn't gas up. I fixed the God damn engine. I was *worried* about it. And then I left Seattle so scared I forget to gas up. Stupid fucking piece of ancient shit doesn't even have a gauge. Fuck you, Dad! Fuck you for giving me this piece of shit!" He tore his helmet off and flung it into the night.

Kylie swung off the bike and stood by the side of the road with her arms tightly folded. "It's not your dad's fault. You're the one who didn't look in the tank. This is really wonderful, by the way. I mean, who do you think you *are?* You can't just kidnap me, you know."

"Take it easy."

"You take it easy." She dug in her pocket for her cell. "I'm calling my mom to pick us up – and she's going to drive us back to Oakdale. You don't want to come, you can *walk* to Seattle."

"*No.*" With a panic reflex he slapped the phone out of her hand and it disappeared into the bushes.

Kylie's mouth opened and she took a step back.

"I didn't mean to do that. I'm sorry. It's just that there's no–"

"Don't say it."

Ian was reaching for his own cell phone, thinking maybe he could call a cab or something, when a pair of headlights appeared on the highway, traveling from the direction of Oakdale. Ian closed his phone. No cab was going to drive all the way out here to get them. The headlights got closer. A large dark-colored sedan slowed, passed them, and pulled onto the shoulder, brake lights flashing. It sat there a while, engine idling, exhaust pooling red in the tail-light glare . Leaving the engine running and the door open, the driver climbed out and started toward them. He was a big man wearing a black overcoat and a floppy-brimmed hat. Gregorian chants and the door-ajar warning buzzer issued from the Crown Vic like a weird post-modern theme-music-mix for the guy.

"Having some trouble?" Father Jim said, looking straight at Kylie.

"Ran out of gas." Ian tried to look goofy-hapless but he probably just looked insane.

Not even glancing at him, Jim said, "Get in, Kylie. I'll drive you home."

Kylie threw her hands up. "No thanks." She tramped into the brush, looking for her phone.

"Actually, we need a lift to Seattle," Ian said.

Jim ignored him.

"Kylie, will you tell your friend we need a ride to Seattle like right now?"

She shot him a look then went back to looking for her phone, hunched over, stepping carefully, as if she were stalking a mouse.

Ian tapped Jim's arm, like tapping a two-by-four in a sleeve. "Mister, it's really important we get to Seattle as fast as–"

"I'm not going to Seattle. Kylie, come with me."

"I'm looking for my *phone*."

"Come with me. Now." He tramped into the bushes and grabbed her arm and started pulling her toward the Crown Vic.

"Hey." Ian grabbed the arm that was holding Kylie.

Jim looked at him, like he was looking at a dog that just pissed on his shoe. "You can wait here. Somebody will come along."

"Let me *go*," Kylie said, twisting down on her arm.

"In the car," Jim said, and dragged her toward the passenger door.

Kylie's face bunched into a vivid expression of pain, and it broke Ian's control. "*Hey*. Let her go, man." He seized a double handful of Jim's coat sleeve and wrenched on it, half spinning the larger man around. Jim let go of Kylie and turned the rest of the way, his stone face re-chiseled to fury. He stepped into Ian and shoved him hard with both hands, striking Ian's chest like a pair of steel pistons, knocking Ian off his feet. He hit the road, the back of his head bouncing on the pavement, stunning him.

He sat up, tried to shake it off. For a few moments it was hard to draw a breath. Outside himself with fury and frustration, Ian rolled onto his feet and charged Jim, ramming his head into the priest's belly. Jim grunted and staggered back. Ian came up, swinging his fists wildly. Jim blocked most of the blows then threw one of his own, his big fist slamming into the side of Ian's head, knocking him dizzy. Ian lurched around, vision doubled.

Jim hit him again.

Like a brick landing on Ian's jaw, sending him to his knees. Ian spat blood, raised his hands to fend off the next blow, and Kylie screamed.

"Stop! Stop hitting him. I'm getting in the car. Jim, see, I'm getting in the car."

Everything stopped. Ian on his knees, his mouth bloody and hands up defensively before Father Jim, as if waiting for some terrible sacrament. The priest standing over him, a giant, the knuckles of his clenched fist skinned raw. Kylie half in the passenger side of the Crown Vic, one foot on the berm, leaning out to watch what happened next. Ian swayed on his knees, taking it all in – especially the tremendous fury of the priest. Like one of those rodeo bulls boxed in, waiting to explode. If Jim threw one more punch he would be out of the fucking box. Probably he'd pound Ian until there wasn't anything left breathing *to* pound.

"We can go some place and *talk*," Kylie said, pleading, almost sobbing. "You're always saying you want to talk to me alone. We can do that. Alone. Tonight, right now. Just please don't hit him anymore."

Ian braced himself. The priest dropped his fist, turned toward the car and started to walk away. Ian spat another gob of blood, gave the man one step and then dove forward, grabbed his ankle and hauled up on it, dumping Jim face down on the road. Ian lurched around him like a drunk and made for the car. Jim was up and after him instantly. Ian threw himself behind the wheel, popped the emergency brake. Jim clawed at his arm. Ian jerked the clutch into DRIVE, grabbed hold of Kylie's jacket (she was still half out of the car), and jumped the gas. The big car roared forward, rear wheels churning gravel. Jim lost his grip and spun away. In the mirror he was a red-glare tail-light devil and then he was nothing, lost in the dark. The Crown Vic fishtailed and screeched until Ian got it under control.

Kylie slammed her door and buckled up. "God, will you slow *down*."

Ian pounded the dash with his fist, stood on the gas. "We're not going to fucking *make it*."

POST HUMAN POSTSCRIPT

BUT THEY DID.

Ian drove like a lunatic most of the way, hunched over the wheel, intense, focused on the road, wailing about missing the first Advent. Basically out of his mind. Kylie cinched her seatbelt tight across her lap and white-knuckled the ride. She didn't try to talk to him – reason with him. He was driving so fast, any break in his concentration and she feared they would careen off the road. But when they hit the I-5 corridor between Tacoma and Seattle the traffic thickened and he *had* to slow down. Some of the tension drained out of Kylie. Soon they passed the big green neon T that had replaced the R when Tulley's bought the old Rainer Brewery on the south side of Seattle. Kylie said, "So, we're here, right?"

"Right."

She pointed at the clock on the car's CD player. "Seventeen minutes to spare. That should make you happy."

He nodded. "Yeah."

Rain speckled the windshield

There was something wrong. Hesitantly, Kylie reached up and thumbed the Dome light on. Hesitant because she had a weird feeling, like that wasn't Ian in the driver's seat anymore. But it was him, of course it was. He looked over when she turned the light on. He had a black eye. His lip was swollen and shiny with blood, like a smear of high-gloss lipstick. It was Ian, fresh from a beatdown by Father Jim. It was Ian, but... it wasn't Ian. She turned the Dome light off.

A dim, localized flicker occurred in the clouds over the city. Then several more, in different places, like someone was popping off camera flashes.

"What is that?" Kylie said. "Is that lightning?" She knew it wasn't.

"Hunter attack."

"Yeah, right. You should get your story straight. You've been saying the attack happens after midnight."

"The main attack did, yeah."

"Did?"

Ian exited onto James street, accelerated up the hill. "Kylie, it's over. We made it in time. Seventeen minutes later, the Hunters burned everything down and I managed to Lens up the Preservation Dome."

"What are you talking about?"

"To you it feels like we just got here. But listen: that was a long, long time ago. We're on the Preservation now."

"Oh, come on. I don't believe it."

"You always say that."

Another muted flash occurred, almost directly overhead. Immediately it dimmed away, leaving clouds and rain. Ian turned the windshield wipers on. Suddenly Kylie felt cold.

"They're persistent," Ian said. "But they'll never crack through. Charles and I fortified the Dome. We're going to wait them out, wait for the Earth to restore herself. There's nothing but time, Kylie."

"Why are you *talking* like that? You don't sound like yourself. Can you turn the heat on?"

"We're here."

He braked the Crown Vic next to the park across from his building. The park was full of people, hundreds of people, everybody standing quietly, like they were waiting for something to happen.

"What are all those people doing there?"

"Waiting for us. Come on."

"No."

"There's nothing to be afraid of."

"Whatever." Kylie *was* afraid. She felt it through her body, an absolute dread. "I'm not getting out of this car."

"We've got about eight minutes before the next Advent. You'll go away but I'll stay right here. Seventeen minutes before midnight, we'll be in the car again, crossing into the city. See, this is the problem. We have forever to live, but only seventeen minutes to convince you that it's true."

"I told you I don't believe it. Take me home."

"You always say that."

"Fuck you, Ian. *Fuck* you. Take me home. I want to see my mother."

"You can't see her anymore. I'm sorry."

"Don't say that."

Two men and a woman stepped out of the crowd and approached the car. One man was chubby, wearing a tan overcoat and a Kangol cap. The other was tall and thin, with a hawk nose and shaved head. The woman was short and delicate-looking and her features, in the street lamp light, were similar to Ian's.

"Who are they?" Kylie scrunched down in her seat.

"My sister Vanessa, and my friends, Zach and Charles. The rest of the people are the Awakened. Some of them, anyway. They're all here to welcome you."

Vanessa, Zach and Charles stopped in front of the car, smiled and waved.

"They're trying to look friendly," Ian said.

"Jesus Christ."

"Kylie, look at that crowd. Do you think I even *knew* so many people in the old world? I barely had one friend."

Kylie wiped her eyes. "I want my mother."

"I'm really sorry."

"You don't have any right to fuck around with my head."

"I know. And I wouldn't do that."

He scooted over on the bench seat and held her. Kylie's heart was racing.

"I'm unstuck, Kylie. I live outside the cycle of Advents. Almost everybody in the city does, now. We can't stop the Advents, because we need them to keep refreshing the android bodies. Even when you stay, your body gets rejuvenated. I'm unstuck, Kylie, but every night I surrender in time to completely re-gen in this car with you. I'll never give up. A long time ago – you have no idea how long ago – I figured out that you make me real. There's only a couple of minutes left. Will you get out of the car with me now? I want to show you something. You don't have to be afraid. I promise."

"Okay."

They climbed out of the car. Kylie scooted out the driver's door after him, never letting go of his hand. He led her to the back of the car.

"Look," he said.

On the broad rear deck of the Crown Victoria, in bright green spray paint, the words: *know who you love: Ian + Kylie.*

"I know, cheesy as hell," Ian said. "But I wanted to make a point. I did that on the last Advent, then I held my hand out like this and said: STAY. Like I've got the power, right? You *know* that wasn't on there before. You know it."

"Oh, God," Kylie said. "Oh, my God."

"It works with things. Stay works with things. But I can't make android people stay unless they want to and believe they can. Otherwise, I'd do this–" He placed his hand lightly on her chest, this Ian who was so different – confident, matured – and yet the same as the Ian she knew. "–and I would say, *stay*. Please stay."

Kylie breathed out, almost a sigh. She put her hand over his. All around them, lacy shadows began to spin forth out of the material world. *Know who you love* glowed steady in the seething dark.

"I'm going to miss my mother so much," Kylie said.

"I know. I miss mine, too."

He held her hand and she squeezed it as hard as she could while shadows devoured the world.

Then it was over, and the sudden light shift dazzled her.

THE END

ACKNOWLEDGEMENTS

I WANT TO thank my wife, Nancy Kress, for reading earlier versions of the manuscript and offering invaluable suggestions. I also want to thank Daryl Gregory and Ted Kosmatka, good friends and good writers, for doing the same. Patrick Swenson and Blunt Jackson, as always, provided moral support along the way. Finally, this book wouldn't exist without my sister, Sonja.

NOTE: Astute readers may have noticed some of the Capital Hill locations in this story more closely resemble a version existent before the massive light rail construction project began to radically alter the local environment in a not-so-good way. Such readers can rest assured that they are not mistaken.

Harmony

Keith Brooke

'A progressive and skilful writer.'
Peter F. Hamilton

UK ISBN: 978-1-78108-002-3 • US ISBN: 978-1-78108-001-6 • £7.99/$8.99

The aliens are here, all around us. They always have been. And now, one by one, they're destroying our cities.

Dodge Mercer deals in identities, which is fine until the day he deals the wrong identity and clan war breaks out. Hope Burren has no identity, and no past, struggling with a relentless choir of voices filling her head. In a world where nothing is as it seems, where humans are segregated and aliens can sing realities and tear worlds apart, Dodge and Hope lead a ragged band of survivors in a search for the rumoured sanctuary of Harmony, and what may be the only hope for humankind.

'Bears comparison with the best of Philip K Dick's paranoid, alternate-history fantasies. It's beautifully written and undeniably powerful.'
The Financial Times

LAVIE TIDHAR

OSAMA

A NOVEL

UK ISBN: 978-1-78108-076-4 • US ISBN: 978-1-78108-075-7 • £7.99/$8.99

In an alternate world without global terrorism, a private detective is hired by a mysterious woman to track down the obscure creator of the fictional vigilante, Osama Bin Laden...

Joe's identity slowly fragments as his quest takes him across the world, from the backwaters of Asia to the European capitals of Paris and London. He discovers the shadowy world of the Refugees, ghostly entities haunting the world in which he lives. Where do they come from? What do they want? Joe knows how the story should end, but is he ready for the truths he will uncover... or the choice he will have to make?

 WWW.SOLARISBOOKS.COM

Follow us on Twitter! www.twitter.com/solarisbooks

'A cliché it may be, but
there really is something
for everyone here... an ideal
bait to tempt those who only
read novels to climb over the
short fiction fence'

*Interzone on The Solaris Book
of New Science Fiction, vol. 2*

THE NEW SOLARIS BOOK
OF SCIENCE FICTION

SOLARIS RISING

EDITED BY
IAN WHATES

FEATURING
NEW WORK BY

Alastair Reynolds
Peter F. Hamilton
Stephen Baxter
Ian McDonald
Paul di Filippo
Ken Macleod
Adam Roberts
Pat Cadigan

AND MANY MORE

UK ISBN: 978-1-907992-08-7 • US ISBN: 978-1-907992-09-4 • £7.99/$7.99

Solaris Rising presents nineteen stories of the very highest calibre from some of
the most accomplished authors in the genre, proving just how varied and dynamic
science fiction can be. From strange goings on in the present to explorations of
bizarre futures, from drug-induced tragedy to time-hopping serial killers, from
crucial choices in deepest space to a ravaged Earth under alien thrall, from gritty
other worlds to surreal other realms, Solaris Rising delivers a broad spectrum of
experiences and excitements, showcasing the genre at its very best.

 WWW.SOLARISBOOKS.COM

Follow us on Twitter! www.twitter.com/solarisbooks

FEATURING ORIGINAL STORIES BY
James Lovegrove // Paul Cornell // Nancy Kress
Allen Steele // Adrian Tchaikovsky // Robert Reed
Norman Spinrad // Nick Harkaway // Kay Kenyon
AND MANY MORE

EDITED BY
IAN WHATES

SOLARIS
RISING 2

THE NEW SOLARIS BOOK OF
SCIENCE FICTION

'One of the best SF anthologies published this year...
there's almost nothing here that isn't good or outstanding.'
Gardner Dozois, *Locus* on *Solaris Rising*

UK ISBN: 978-1-78108-087-0 • US ISBN: 978-1-78108-088-7 • £7.99/$8.99

Solaris Rising 2 showcases the finest new science fiction from both celebrated authors and the most exciting of emerging writers. Following in the footsteps of the critically-acclaimed first volume, editor Ian Whates has once again gathered together a plethora of thrilling and daring talent. Within you will find unexplored frontiers as well as many of the central themes of the genre – alien worlds, time travel, artificial intelligence – made entirely new in the telling. The authors here prove once again why SF continues to be the most innovative, satisfying, and downright exciting genre of all.

 WWW.SOLARISBOOKS.COM

Follow us on Twitter! www.twitter.com/solarisbooks